MW01703531

In the year 1958, when
Texas governor Price Daniel strenuously objected. His reasoning was quite simple: He did not want there to be a state larger than Texas. President Dwight D. Eisenhower became so tired of Daniel's protests that he threatened him. He told Daniel that if he did not shut up, he would divide Alaska in half, and there would be two states larger than Texas.

Daniel refused to stop complaining, not taking Eisenhower seriously.

He should have done so.

Eisenhower did exactly that and on January 3, 1959, North Alaska and South Alaska were officially declared states of the Union.

They did not get on well. There was peace between them, but an uneasy peace, and it was certainly not helped by the fact that the majority of the populace wielded guns. A frontier mentality gripped the separated regions and it slowly devolved over time...

And then a new governor made it a lot worse, and it descended into war.

Special thanks to:
Evelyn Kriete
for services above and beyond

Production by
ComicMix Pro Services
http://www.comicmix.com/pro

Cover illustration and design by Glenn Hauman
Interior design by Glenn Hauman

ISBN 978-1-939888-37-2

First edition

ALTERED STATES OF THE UNION

Russ Colchamiro
Peter David
Keith R.A. DeCandido
Debra Doyle
Brendan DuBois
Malon Edwards
G.D. Falksen
Michael Jan Friedman
David Gerrold
Robert Greenberger
Alisa Kwitney
Gordon Linzner
Sarah McGill
James D. Macdonald
Meredith Peruzzi
Mackenzie Reide
Aaron Rosenberg
David Silverman
Hildy Silverman
Ian Randal Strock
Ramón Terrell
Anne Toole

Glenn Hauman, editor

CRAZY 8 PRESS

Dedication

To the republic
for which it stands

These, the people,

who pre-ordered to form a more perfect

ALTERED STATES OF THE UNION...

Lorraine Anderson
Ryan Anderson
Aslanscub
Daniel Barringer
Diane Bellomo
F.J. Bergmann
Lee Billings
Ken Board
Edmund Boys
Kevin T. Brown
Hollie L. Buchanan II
Michael A. Burstein
Patrick Curtin
Charlie Daniel
Keith DeCandido
John R. Donald
Dennis P Donohoe
Ricarda Dormeyer
Lawrence Dunmore
Jonathan Ezor
Andrew Foxx
Esther Friesner-Stutzman
Eric Gasior
Gilee
Martin Greening
Mateen Greenway
Jacqueline Greff
Christina L Gunning
Pamela Hauman
Shael Hawman
Mary Jane Hetzlein
Jeremy Hunter
Kevin Robert Jacobson
Carol Jones
Andrew Kaplan
Vaidah Katz
Alice Kessner
Jay Kilpatrick
Kevin Lauderdale
Blair Learn
William Leisner
Rachelle A. Lerner
Jeff Linder
Brian Lintz
Alice Loweecey
Stephanie Lucas
Margaret Lyman
James D. Macdonald
David Mason
Chuck May
Ashley Mcconnell
Michael J Medeiros
Jeff Metzner
Justin Mohareb
Matthew Nagler
Ralph "Sasquatch" Nelson
Christina Neno
Amanda Nixon
Doug O'Loughlin
Meredith Peruzzi
Sherry Peruzzi
Benjamin A. Philip
www.ericponvelle.com
Launi Purcell
James Quick
Zan Rosin
Jack Scheer
Rivka Seid
Rick Shaffer
Sally Smith
Sherwood Smith
Pam Splittstoesser
Larry St. Cyr
Corey Tacker
Sean Tadsen
Jeffrey Teitel
Andrea Alberto Terno
Pedro Timoteo
Tasha Turner Lennhoff
David Viale
Laura Watkins
Benjamin Wilbur
Chara Williams
Larry Yudelson

And for the support of this Document, they mutually pledged to us their Lives, a small part of their Fortunes, and their sacred Honor. We thank and salute you.

TABLE OF CONTENTS

To John
Best. Peter David

Thanks, John!
GHauman

GLENN HAUMAN, EDITOR

PREAMBLE

As I started to write this introduction, we were coming to the close of the 2016 New Hampshire primaries. Victory that night went to two people who were not even considered possible contenders this time last year— one a loudmouthed billionaire who's never been elected to any public office in his life, the other a democratic socialist who is the first non-Christian to ever win a Presidential primary.

And as I finish it, the United Kingdom has just voted in the Brexit referendum to leave the European Union, which is prompting Scotland and Ireland to split from the UK. Meanwhile, numerous Americans emboldened by their overseas counterparts are suggesting parts of *this* country break out on their own.

It started with a third of the residents of the Lone Star state, pushing for what they called Texit. Then other names were suggested. Oregone. Coloradios. Floridone. Ohiout. Tennesseeya. Disconnecticut. Nevadieu. Vermoved. Louisianschluss, combining French and German. Iowon't. Oklahellno. Washingtonrightoutofhishair. Even Montanananaheyheygoodbye. And we won't even mention the politicians who talk about the "spirit of sovereignty," insisting that the United States should not only get out of the UN and NATO, but also the EU.

Brace yourself.

America has been surprisingly static over the last half century, especially in contrast to everything else in the world that's kept the mapmakers busy. And yet, our people are as polarized as they've ever been, so much so that they've forgotten what a commonwealth is for.

And there's a strong hunger in the nation to toss everything up in the air and start over— as the national anthem says, "Everybody wants the thrill of paying anything to roll the dice just one more time."[1]

The truth is, we have never been fully united states. We have had numerous divisions over the years— rebels and royalists, slave states and free states, dry counties and wet counties, urban and rural and that new beast suburbia, gold versus silver versus paper, cat people and dog people, Indians and Europeans, dirt farmers and robber barons, red states and blue states, gun nuts and gun grabbers, immigrants and nativists, Wall Street and Main Street, New England Patriots fans and everybody else. We argue. We fight. We've had insurrections, uprisings, and a civil war. And every time we speak of healing and unity and we come together, new divisions appear— it's like kickball at school, and after the last game, everybody gets to choose sides again. This time, we're going to settle whether to call it a hero or a sub; and we don't want to hear from you grinder and hoagie heretics.

We're a contentious and cantankerous bunch, we Americans.

And yet, we do agree on a lot.

We are Americans. And we, the people, have always lived on stories of hope. Whether those stories were spoken or sung, whether told around a campfire, in a cinema, or in a church, whether told by an immigrant, a native, a president or a King, they all spoke of a promised land.

For some, that land was the shore they landed on, a bountiful refuge. For others, it was the land they would make for themselves, claiming destiny. And for some, it was the way station on the path to glory, still unseen in their own eyes but alive in their children's.

There is an American dream for all of us— and even though that dream is different for every single one of us, the dream is what drives us. Our hopes are not common, nor are they common between us... but all of us in common, hope. Hope unites us.

And even though these stories may not be true, as our 44th President said, "In the unlikely story that is America, there has never been anything false about hope."

But it's only a story if no action is taken. Contrary to the belief of some, there's nothing inherently exceptional that makes America great, and there never was. We aren't automatically entitled to America, even if we're born here— we earn it and we build it, time and time again, through work and sweat and the

---

1 Okay, that's the anthem from yet another alternate America, the one where there actually *is* a South Detroit.

choices we make. And there are a lot of choices, past, present, and future, that can change what we think of as America.

That's what the diverse hands we've assembled here want to show you— how different choices make different unions, some more perfect, some less so, but always striving towards an idea of America, and how out of one idea we get many Americas[2]. Even though the stories here show you wildly different Americas than the ones we know, they are still American stories. And there is no destiny we can conceive that we could not endure.

Most of all for me, I don't want amatuers making up false visions of American history to promote their own political platforms and ideologies. If I'm going to have to get that, I want my histories made up by *professionals*.

As for you, if you prefer, these stories may console you— as weird as we've gotten, we haven't gotten *that* weird. Yet. (On the other hand, the official release date of this book is July 19, 2016, right in the middle of the Republican National Convention.)

Hang on tight, fellow citizens. As these stories show you, America does a lot of things well. . .but slowing down ain't one of them.

—July 4, 2016

---

2 A brief aside: James D. Macdonald, showing off his pre-Vatican II education, notes that the quote on the cover, "E Unum Pluribus," is not an accurate translation of "From One, Many." Latin (as I'm sure you're aware) is an inflected language, not a positional language (as is English). "E Pluribus Unum", "E Unum Pluribus", "Pluribus E Unum", "Pluribus Unum E", "Unum Pluribus E", and "Unum E Pluribus" are all exactly the same phrase with the same translation. If you want to say "From One, Many" in Latin, that's "Ex Uno Plures". While he is indeed correct, most people are going to understand the meaning much faster as written.

In other words: yes, we're contributing to killing a dead language and the dumbing down of America in the hope of making a few more book sales.

Ian Randal Strock

"SHALL NOT PERISH FROM THE EARTH"

From the *Encyclopedia Americana*:

The founders of the United States of America created a document that allowed disparate states to act together cohesively to form a greater union. Unlike the empires with which the founders were familiar, the Constitution granted the smaller portions a greater degree of control of the central government. To avoid the tyranny of the ruler, they set the capital to roaming about the country, moving from state to state each decade. To give all the constituent units a say in the government, they created a legislature comprised of two representatives from each state (the Senate). And to maintain a system of checks and balances, a Supreme Court....

In the middle of the 19th Century, the growing divide between the Northern and Southern states over the issue of slavery created increasing factionalism and strain on the union. Presidents Franklin Pierce and James Buchanan attempted appeasement from the capital in Concord, New Hampshire, as a strategy to keep the union together. Southern interests were agitated, but knew that the capital would be moving to Columbia, South Carolina, following the election of 1860....

—•—

In 1856, out of the remains of the now-defunct Whig party, the Republicans formed and ran their first candidate for President. John C. Frémont won one-third of the popular vote, and the votes of the eleven Northernmost states. He lost handily to Democrat James Buchanan, while former President Millard Fillmore—this time the standard-bearer for the American party—won the electoral votes of Maryland. It was not an inspiring showing for the Republicans, but it was something to build on.

Abraham Lincoln came to national prominence with his abolitionist speeches during his own failed political campaign: Stephen Douglas defeated him in 1858 in their campaign for a seat in the Senate representing Illinois. But Lincoln impressed enough people that he was invited to New York to give a speech before a powerful group of Republicans at Cooper Union. That speech catapulted him to the forefront of the race for the Republican nomination in the home state of two of his chief rivals: William Seward and Salmon Chase (both of whom would wind up serving in Lincoln's Presidential Cabinet).

In May of 1860, the Republicans nominated Lincoln for President, with Senator Hannibal Hamlin from Maine as his Vice Presidential running mate.

The Democrats, meanwhile, were suffering from party factionalism mimicking that of the country. The Northern branch of the party nominated Lincoln's old nemesis and fellow Illinoisan, Stephen Douglas, for President. The Southerners, however, threw their support behind Vice President John C. Breckinridge.

The stage was set for a landmark election. The Republicans, having formed as the anti-slavery party, were nearly by definition the anti-Southern party. Curiously, Lincoln himself took almost no part in the election of 1860. Instead, he stayed home and monitored the proceedings, while his party faithful advertised, wrote, campaigned, and spoke, spreading the word.

If nothing else, the results showed that the United States of America was a starkly divided nation. Lincoln took all the Northern states, Breckinridge the Southern. Douglas—who was himself a fence-sitter on the issue of slavery, not favoring it but not urging its abolition—won only the state of Missouri, itself a fence-sitter, being Northern but permitting slavery.

When the results were made known, Southerners seethed their disapproval. Slavery was an institution, a way of life; and its abolition, they assumed, would bring financial ruin and Northern domination to their home states.

Radical elements in the South urged dissolution of the union, breaking away from the North before Lincoln could be inaugurated and set his plans in motion. But cooler heads prevailed. The national capital, after all, would be spending the next decade in Columbia, South Carolina, seat of the South. With the capital in their pocket, Lincoln's promises could be thwarted, he could be made to see reason, or, as a last resort…

—•—

Following his election, Lincoln planned a whistle-stop train tour to take him east from his home in Illinois, through several Northern states, and then South to inaugurate the decade in Columbia and begin his own term as President. He chose to bypass the New England states. The capital was at that time leaving Nashua, New Hampshire, but New England was out of Lincoln's way, and Vice President-elect Hannibal Hamlin—a native of Maine—was delegated to stand-in for Lincoln at the farewell ceremonies.

Early in February, as Lincoln was beginning his journey, security officer Allan Pinkerton warned him of an assassination plot, and urged him to bypass Baltimore.

Lincoln's long-time friend, Ward Hill Lamon, who also took on the self-appointed role of Lincoln's bodyguard, dismissed Pinkerton's warning as fantasy. He feared that sneaking into the new capital would make Lincoln look weak at a time when he needed to show strength.

In the end, Lincoln chose caution. He hurried through Baltimore late at night, avoiding the crowds and the potential danger, and driving a wedge between Lamon and Pinkerton. No one knew of the deception until Mary Lincoln and their children arrived on the regularly scheduled train the following afternoon. They were greeted by crowds, but those crowds—including any lurking assassins—were disappointed at missing the President-elect.

Lincoln arrived safely in Columbia at the end of February, and was greeted with the honors Presidents-elect had come to expect since George Washington's arrival in New York City. The new national capital building—which was scheduled to become the new capital of South Carolina in 1870, following the departure of the federal government to a Northern capital—was ready, and retiring President James Buchanan greeted Lincoln as a friend. Buchanan had arrived two days earlier, on a special train from Nashua, accompanied by incoming Vice President Hannibal Hamlin.

At the time, little notice was paid to the missing Senators, though they would loom large in history. Specifically, there were seven newly elected Senators from Northern states who had not yet arrived in Columbia. The 61 Senators who were present attended Abraham Lincoln's inauguration and inaugural speech. Later that afternoon, the Senators were sworn in by the new Vice President. The absence of the seven was noted in the minutes of the special session of Congress. Senator Nesmith, of Oregon, was assumed to have been delayed in his long journey. Some surprise was expressed at the absence of Senators Lane and Pomeroy—new state Kansas's first members in the legislative body. The other four, however, were merely assumed to be absent.

—•—

President Abraham Lincoln had come to office on the Republican platform of ending slavery, and after nominating his Cabinet, he set about writing legislation to bring about the abolition his party sought.

That was when he realized the import of those missing Senators. Even though his fellow Illinoisan Lyman Trumbull was available to introduce his legislation, and Vice President Hamlin was fulfilling his role of presiding over the body's deliberations, those seven vacant seats meant the Southerners had an effective majority in the Senate, and could dictate its actions, regardless of the President's desires.

Lincoln via Trumbull introduced several pieces of legislation—attempts to curtail or end slavery—during the three weeks the Senate was in town. All of them were voted down with a minimum of fuss.

Following long-standing tradition, the Senate adjourned at the end of March, and the Senators scattered.

—•—

There was an outbreak of smallpox in Columbia in December of 1860, and at that time, there was discussion of shifting the capital to Charleston for health reasons, but at such a late date, a move was deemed impossible. Instead, authorities in Columbia downplayed the extent of the smallpox outbreak, and Lincoln was never even advised of it.

Thus, after battling the Senate for three long weeks, Lincoln viewed the adjournment—without legislative action—with a certain degree of relief. He retired to his bed for nearly a month, and though the word was that he was exhausted, modern evidence suggests he was in fact suffering from a mild case of smallpox. It was never formally diagnosed, and the few resultant scars were most probably hidden by Lincoln's life-long poor complexion. And while smallpox does not become chronic, it is assumed that Lincoln's case damaged his respiratory system, leaving him more susceptible to later ailments.

—•—

After recovering from the depression of his first three wholly ineffective weeks dealing with the Senate (and possibly from smallpox), Lincoln spent the month of April setting up his government, receiving foreign ambassadors, touring the new capital city, and talking with the few reporters who'd bothered to stay in town. But he knew he wasn't accomplishing very much, and making no inroads toward his goal of abolishing slavery.

He tried to integrate himself with the local culture, but found himself repeatedly rebuffed as an outsider: respected as President, but viewed with suspicion and trepidation as a Northerner, especially one who loudly and publicly agitated for abolition.

He was a stranger in a strange land; an oddity on display, but little respected.

—•—

The problem with truly effective conspiracies is that they are secret. Even today, we may never know the full extent of the machinations against Lincoln, especially in the Spring of 1861. It is known that Senator Jefferson Davis—who had been Secretary of War during Franklin Pierce's administration, and who was a Southerner, from Mississippi—was involved, however reluctantly. In his personal writings, Davis expressed his misgivings of what was to come. But he viewed himself as a patriot: loyal to his native Mississippi. And Mississippi, as part of the South, was a slave state and opposed to Northern domination, so Davis did all he could to support the cause.

Also known was William Henry Gist—formerly the governor of South Carolina, he had refused to seek another term, rather than play the genial host to the federal government headed by Lincoln—who was definitely one of the underground leaders.

Beyond Davis and Gist, however, the cabal is still nameless and faceless. It surely included the household staff assigned to the President, as well as most of the city government who were hosting.

What is known of the cabal is its effectiveness. In an era not far removed from George Washington's invisible ink and letter-transposition codes, they managed to intercept nearly all communications to and from the office of the President.

Davis must have been involved in the near-continuous rewriting work that kept Lincoln supplied with the correct volume of cables, letters, and wires, while modifying their content and moving to isolate Lincoln...

—•—

A scrap of paper in Lincoln's hand, assumed to be a fragment of a now-lost diary:

> *What's happened to me? I came to Columbia full of excitement. We were going to change the world, fulfill the promise of the Declaration. We've been here two months, accomplished nothing, and I seem to have lost all the hopes I had after the election.*
>
> *Mary recommends that I "enjoy being the President for a while, rather than trying to force the issue."*
>
> *"Enjoy" seems horribly inappropriate, when so many live in bondage, but she keeps pushing me to "Get out. Travel around. Maybe take a trip home, feel some Northern adulation."*

—•—

In May, before the cabal had solidified its control over Lincoln, he tried to call the Senate into special session. He'd spent two months recovering from smallpox and fuming over his ineffectiveness, and finally, he had had enough. The cabal was unable to stop the call from going out, but they were able to piggyback onto it a notice to Southern Senators, and those thirty Southerners rejected the call (all but Mississippi's Jefferson Davis, who had remained in Columbia as part of the cabal, to keep up his campaign of Presidential miscommunication and misdirection). And thus, once again, the seven missing Senators changed the course of events. The thirty Southerners were a minority of the full-strength Senate, but the seven—who had not arrived before the Senate adjourned in March—were not counted in the Senate's membership, and would not be until the Senate, in session, swore them in and accepted them as members.

The Senate did not meet in the summer of 1861.

—•—

Lincoln's first summer as President saw a remarkable change in his personality. The formerly gregarious, outgoing lawyer became taciturn, almost non-communicative. Indeed, other than appearances at Independence Day celebrations, Lincoln was not seen in public until late October. And this long absence did not go unnoticed by the cabal.

The Senate finally returned in December, and the formerly missing Senators were present, each arriving with a harrowing tale of danger or threats that had kept him from entering the South. Though it was a federal crime to interfere with a Senator's attendance to a duly called session, none of the seven could identify their attackers. And once again, the pervasive Southern sentiment surrounding the government was sufficient to quash further investigations. "They are here now: we should look to the future, not the past," became a mantra, headlining editorials, and titling a popular song.

In the end, the Senate's investigation was cursory, inconclusive, and forgotten.

With a full Senate—nine months after Lincoln's inauguration—the President finally had hopes of pushing through his legislative agenda.

Those hopes were quickly dashed.

Lincoln's first proposal for a Constitutional amendment outlawing slavery died quietly in committee. As did his less sweeping proposals to limit its expansion. Meanwhile, competing proposals reaffirming states' rights clogged up the legislative agenda.

Despite his role as President of the Senate, Hannibal Hamlin knew there was almost nothing he could do, and there were times during the session of 1861-62 that he discussed with Lincoln the possibility of resigning.

—•—

From *The Autobiography of Hannibal Hamlin*:

> *"John Adams called it 'the most insignificant office that ever the invention of man contrived.' And as this session dragged on, I knew more and more what he meant. But beyond the uselessness of the Vice Presidency, I felt even more ineffective as President of the Senate. President Lincoln, however, convinced me to stay. 'We are an embassy of Northern rationality in this cesspool of slave-owners,' he told me in a private moment. 'If you were to leave, what support would I have? It would be ceding the whole government, the entirety of the United States of America, to the scourge of slavery.' And so I promised to soldier on with him. Indeed, seeing how passionate he was—how frustrated, but still so passionate—I returned to the Senate with renewed vigor, and a renewed determination to bring about the true freedom for which we both fought."*

—•—

Hamlin's new-found strength to push back against the Southern obstructionists was met with threats. Hamlin never did reveal who he spoke with, but soon he was reporting back to Lincoln of concrete threats of secession.

Lincoln, fearing the possibility of presiding over a government in enemy territory, told Hamlin to back down, and the session of December 1862, opened with amity amongst the Senators. No real business was accomplished, but neither did seething distrust break out into open rebellion.

—•—

In February of 1862, 11-year-old Willie Lincoln—the second of the President's three surviving children—contracted a severe case of typhoid, and died.

This loss affected Lincoln almost as much as Mary. The illness, it is also assumed, exasperated Lincoln's lingering respiratory problems from his bout of smallpox.

Whether it was only mourning, or mourning combined with his own sickness, Lincoln was not seen for several weeks, as he remained cloistered with Mary in their apartment.

Wrangling the government nearly single-handedly was a much larger job than Vice President Hamlin expected at that point, and the resultant overwhelm forced him to focus on the day-to-day operations of the government at the expense of the Republicans' planned legislative package. The Southern Senators took advantage of this feebleness, and nothing further happened during that session.

—•—

When the Senate adjourned in 1862—having accomplished nothing other than thwarting the President's legislative agenda at every turn—Lincoln joined the exodus, returning home for the first time since his departure a year and a half earlier. His immediate plans were to mourn the loss of Willie and to recuperate.

He had planned several whistle stops on his journey home, but the first few, in the Carolinas and Virginia, proved so disappointing that he told his staff to cancel the rest, and just run on through. Mary, however, urged him to continue with the original plans, if only to show that he was still the President and still in charge.

When the train reached Pennsylvania, the crowds that greeted him reminded Lincoln that he truly was President of a divided country. Indeed, the adulation and support he received at every stop north of the Mason-Dixon Line was like a revivifying tonic, and those traveling with him remarked on his changed appearance. He stood straighter, spoke with a stronger voice, and seemed to grow younger as the journey continued.

By the time the Presidential train reached Illinois, Lincoln seemed to be on the campaign trail, running hard, rather than simply greeting well-wishers. He accepted their condolences for the loss of Willie, but the burden of that loss seemed to have lifted along the railway.

At home, Lincoln rested, recovered from the strains of the office, and remembered what he was struggling for.

One notable event during the President's sojourn in Illinois was his meeting with Ulysses Grant. The former soldier was living in Galena, struggling through a series of failed business ventures. Upon Lincoln's election, Grant had sensed impending military action, and managed to get himself appointed a colonel to train up volunteers. And when Lincoln was home in 1862, they met. Grant left the meeting with a Presidential promotion to brigadier general, and a Presidential command to expeditiously increase the number of trained soldiers across the North.

In letters he exchanged with Hamlin over the summer, it was clear that the Vice President's experiences were similar to Lincoln's: the journey home was medicine for his soul. Lincoln asked Hamlin to join him in Illinois for the trip back to Columbia in November.

Optimists seeing the President and Vice President on their return to the seat of government saw a triumphal procession, supporting their champion on the way to battle. But pessimists feared it was a valedictory journey, and that they would not see Lincoln alive again.

The timbre of the crowds changed immediately as the train entered the South, but Lincoln carried the memory of his months at home with him, and used it as a cloak to fend off the condemnation of those few Southerners who turned out to see him.

—•—

By the time the Senate convened in December, 1862, the energized Lincoln and Hamlin had planned out a full legislative agenda: limiting slavery, strengthening the federal government, and funding the trans-continental railroad. They knew they faced an uphill battle: the recent elections promised to make the Senate an even-more polarized body, if that was possible. But those ten seat changes would not happen until March. There was still time, or so they thought.

The lame-duck session, however, proved even more skittish. Senators were completely unwilling to debate any issue more contentious than what to have for dinner. Legislation died in committee, and though the Senate was in session, it was a rare day that a quorum of Senators were present.

Which was not to say that Lincoln's time went unused. He had discussions and negotiations nearly constantly, and almost all of them seemed to designed to unsettle and upset him.

The cabal, at this point, began to make itself known. Not as a specific roster of people, but the existence of a movement to modify the United States in a manner that would make it unrecognizable. It was, it seemed, a movement to make the federal government subservient to those of the states, and specifically to those states of the South.

—•—

A fragment from Lincoln's diary:

Former Governor Gist requested a meeting with me, and for courtesy's sake, I granted it. Gist has been out of the government for several years, so I was unsure what he wanted.

Thus, I was surprised when he bustled into my office, sat down, and exuded the confidence of an ambassador negotiating a peace treaty.

I was shocked when the first words out of his mouth were a demand—demand—that amounted to full-scale surrender. Certainly, he couched his demand in diplomatic terms. "Several amendments to update the Constitution, bring it into the modern world," he said, handing me a sheaf of papers. "I think they'll make the government more effective, more efficient, more representative of what the people want."

I knew, even before I read his papers, that effectiveness and efficiency were not Mr. Gist's goal.

—•—

Those proposed amendments, as everyone now knows, would have been the emasculation of federal government in the United States, removing the last vestiges of central authority over the states. They resembled nothing so much as the original Articles of Confederation, but with a more explicit acceptance of slavery.

Needless to say, Lincoln did not approve.

In the first months of 1863—the last of the 37th Congress—the Southern Senators' former obstructionism turned to outright hostility. No longer were they content to merely stymie Lincoln's proposals, but now they began a campaign of active opposition to all Northern ideals. The Union's only salvation, at the time, was the presence of the seven previously missing Northern Senators, and the perfect attendance of every Northerner.

Gist continued to meet with Lincoln, but they both knew their sessions were futile, pro forma gatherings to give the appearance of ongoing negotiations.

At the same time, far from public view, Jefferson Davis was setting up his own shadow government, and preparing military options to compel Lincoln's acquiescence.

As the session sputtered to an end, the newly elected Senators were sworn in, but their presence merely served to exaggerate the dichotomy between Northerners and Southerners, and the first three weeks of the 38th Congress became unique for the legislature's inability to approve any legislation.

Lincoln's depression had returned, and with it, his physical infirmities. He looked forward to his trip home, yet he knew he'd be returning with his tail between his legs.

The Congress adjourned, and the Senators sped out of town.

Lincoln, however, was unable to join the exodus.

—•—

There is no record of the conversation that took place when Mr. Gist visited President Lincoln on March 15, 1863, the day after the Senate adjourned. John Hay—one of Lincoln's personal secretaries—reports what is known: that Gist left the meeting with a spring in his step, and ashen-faced Lincoln called in Ward Hill Lamon for another closed-door session.

After Lamon left, Lincoln called in Hay and John Nicolay. As Hay recorded, "The President told us to gather our belongings, pull our hats down low, and hurry back to Illinois as quickly and quietly as possible."

While neither of Lincoln's secretaries would ordinarily think of questioning him, in this they presented a united front to oppose the President. "We wouldn't think of abandoning you," said Hay.

"No, sir," echoed Nicolay. "Unless you're coming with us, there is no way we can leave the capital."

The argument continued, but eventually, Lincoln told them Gist had threatened his life if he attempted to leave Columbia. "He is granting Mary and Tad safe passage home if I give my parole." At this time, Tad was a month shy of his tenth birthday, while Robert—nineteen years old—was at Harvard.

"Parole? Then this is war?"

To that, Lincoln offered no response, except to say he needed to confer with the Vice President immediately.

—•—

From *The Autobiography of Hannibal Hamlin*:

On March 15, 1863—the day after the Senate adjourned—I was sitting in my office, glumly mulling over the events of the last several weeks. My Senatorial duties were ended, and wouldn't pick up again for nine months. Based on the last two years, I knew that the time between Senate sessions left me with almost nothing to fill my official time, and I was again considering a trip home, and how best to explain my ineffectiveness to my neighbors.

Lincoln's aide, Nicolay, barged in breathlessly. "The President needs to see you," he said without preamble.

I followed Nicolay upstairs to Lincoln's office, expecting... I'm not sure what I was expecting, but such a peremptory summons was completely out of character.

I found him sitting calmly at his desk, a brooding expression on his face. Mentioning that expression reminds me that it wasn't something I would have remarked on, at the time, after the two years we'd been in Columbia.

Nicolay withdrew silently, and the President came right to the point.

"I'm a prisoner here. Gist has agreed to grant Mary and Tad safe passage home if I give my parole. If I don't... I'd rather not think about that. So I need you to leave, Mr. Vice President. Go home to Maine as if it were a standard vacation. But don't come back."

"Mr. President?"

"I need you outside the capital. This is a city under siege. They're not letting me out, and I feel certain they'll be cutting off my communications very soon, if they haven't already begun censoring them."

"What good will it do if I'm home in Maine?"

"You're the Vice President of the United States, Hannibal. I feel I'm going to need you to imitate your namesake."

"Find a herd of elephants and come marching over the Appalachians?"

"Something like that. Go home to Maine. Make it a public trip: the Senate has adjourned, so you're taking a vacation. Tell the public you're tired, and need to rest at home. Don't see anybody, don't give any interviews: go quiet. And then take a much more quiet, much more important trip. Visit as many of the Northern capitals as you can, and convince the state legislatures, the governors, and as many of the senators as you can find, that the South is in rebellion. The Constitution says the capital is here in Columbia for this decade, but it doesn't say the government has to do its work here. Tell the senators to stay out of the South. And tell the governors it's time to train up their militias."

"It'll look like a coup. I have no authority to call the government together."

"You're the President of the Senate. But you're right: trying to move the government into Maine will seem like a power grab."

"Somewhere else, then."

"Springfield, Hannibal, set up a government in Springfield."

"Then it will seem like your power grab, sir. Trying to move the government to your home state."

"I fear I'll never see Illinois again, Hannibal. I'm ill, but even that, of late, has become more remote in my thinking."

"Are you setting yourself up as a martyr, Mr. President?"

"I'm not hoping to, but it's feeling more and more as if that's the only road left open to me."

"We're not dead yet."

"No, and this may just be the wild imaginings of a frustrated, fevered mind. Nevertheless, I need you free and in the North. Gather the government, catch as many of the Supreme Court justices as you can, and tell Grant the training program we set up has to move double-time."

"Grant? That drunk?"

"Drunk when he's a civilian. But when he's in uniform, it does something to him. Ulysses Grant is the most brilliant strategist since… well,

since that other Hannibal. I commissioned him last summer. You and [Secretary of War Edwin] Stanton will have to give him the full command, because we may have to attack the South to free the government."

"How will I know if it's time to cross that Rubicon? If they censor your communication…"

"It's coming to a head, Hannibal. If I don't send you a clear, unambiguous 'cease and desist' by the end of June, I'll have lost control of the situation. And if you don't hear anything from me, well, I'm probably dead, you're the President, and then it's all on your head."

—•—

From the diary of John Hay:

Sitting with the President as he watched Vice President Hamlin's entourage leave the capital today, I could feel the weight of the nation on his shoulders. He was stooped, morose, a man completely on his own.

Mrs. Lincoln and Tad left Columbia a few days ago, and Hamlin's departure was the last public event he had scheduled.

He is still urging John and me to leave, but we discussed the situation, and decided that we're staying with him. He needs friendly faces and sympathetic ears, and while Mr. Lamon is here for the President's personal security, we will continue to help him keep the government operational.

—•—

Following those departure ceremonies, Lincoln wasn't seen again in public. He continued to communicate via letters and wires, but no one outside his official "family" saw him. And many years later, Hay and Nicolay confirmed that the reports issued from the office of the President had indeed been tampered with, and were not Lincoln's own words, or, in many cases, even his own ideas.

Jefferson Davis later confirmed his own role in rewriting Lincoln's letters and wires. But he never admitted to holding Lincoln prisoner.

The assumption is that Gist, along with still unknown members of the cabal, handled that facet of the coup, for a coup it was, in deed if not in word.

Hay and Nicolay, too, were held in seclusion. They were allowed to see Lincoln, individually, infrequently, and never alone.

After two months of this house arrest, Lincoln eventually convinced Lamon that it was time to leave his side. Lamon never wrote of his experiences during this time, but it is known that Gist allowed him to leave Columbia. He made his way north, and eventually to Vice President Hamlin's government in exile in Springfield. Hamlin later wrote that Lamon's arrival, more than anything else, convinced him that the tipping point had arrived, and that it was time to act.

—•—

At the same time Lincoln was convincing Lamon to leave, Hamlin was continuing his errand. After his public journey home, he stayed in Bangor for less than a day, before privately setting out on the 80-mile journey to Augusta, Maine, to confer with the governor of his home state. Leaving Augusta, Hamlin made a sub-rosa tour of the Northern state capitals. Such a grand effort, however, could not long be kept secret, and by the time he reached Columbus, Ohio, Hamlin had attracted such a following that he decided to go public.

"President Lincoln has charged me with preserving and protecting the Union. He is currently being held by forces intent on destroying our United States of America. Their aim is to take power for themselves, to extend slavery to free territories, and to make the federal government subservient to their local interests. This cannot be allowed.

"Therefore, in accordance with the President's wishes, I am heading to Illinois, Springfield to be exact, to convene the government there, and to determine—within the bounds of the Constitution—what we can do to maintain the nation and to free the President."

Standing with him for the speech, to show it wasn't a one-man show, were the Secretaries of State, the Treasury, War, and the Navy, whom Hamlin had met with on his trip West. Hamlin hadn't yet reached Attorney General Bates—at home in Missouri—and Secretary of the Interior Usher (in Indiana). Postmaster General Blair, of Maryland, was assumed to have gone over to the South.

"I call on all Senators to join me in Springfield for an extraordinary session, to begin as soon as practicable.

"And I call on the Southern insurrectionists to reconsider their course of action, to free the President and accept the primacy of the Constitution. Join with us to heal the nation. Men of good conscience can disagree, but allowing that disagreement to rise to the level of a coup d'etat is wrong. I urge you to see the error of your ways, and reverse this course before any more damage is done."

As one might expect, Hamlin's speech was met with shocked silence and strong resolve… in the North.

In the South, he was called a traitor, and letters appeared, supposedly from the office of the President, firing the Cabinet and calling for the impeachment of Hamlin. Northern newspapers refused to print them.

—•—

Upon arriving in Springfield, and even before meeting with the Senate, Hamlin called for Grant, and they cloistered themselves in an office for several hours. As they later revealed, the sole purpose of that meeting was to plan the Northern attack on the South, with the twin aims of freeing the President and breaking the Southern will.

After making their plans, they met with the Cabinet and received unanimous approval. Then Lamon spoke up. As the last person to have seen Lincoln, who could most reliably report on the President's condition, Lamon was almost distraught in urging Hamlin and Grant to move up the schedule. "It is inconceivable that the President will live that long."

Unfortunately for Lincoln, Grant was a master strategist, and he knew there was no way the North could launch an attack in less than three months.

—•—

Grant went to organize the Army, and Hamlin sent for Allan Pinkerton, ordering him to plan a guerilla raid to free Lincoln.

The old animosity between Lamon and Pinkerton reappeared. Lamon demanded the right to rescue Lincoln, but Pinkerton rightly pointed out that he had access to a larger, well-trained organization, where Lamon was but one man. Hamlin made his point stick through sheer force of will.

Pinkerton was able to sneak into the South, into Columbia, and into the Presidential apartment, but even as he was breaking in—disguised and unnoticed—he knew there was no way he'd be able to bring the President back out.

Nevertheless, Pinkerton was stunned when he snuck into the President's bedroom, and saw how drawn and ashen he was. "Mr. President?" he tremulously woke the once-great man. "The Vice President sent me to get you out."

"You look like a man who knows he can't do something. Mr…?"

"Pinkerton, sir. Allan Pinkerton. We met on the trip to your inauguration." Was Lincoln's mind going, too?

"Ah, yes, Mr. Pinkerton. I think you realize there's no way I can sneak out of Columbia. I'm so weak that I doubt I could even ride, let alone walk, to the city limits. I shall not see Illinois again."

Lincoln's symptoms led Pinkerton to report, much later, that he assumed Lincoln was suffering a return bout of smallpox, or typhoid, or some sort of poisoning.

"No, sir, I don't think you will."

"What is Hamlin doing?"

"Following your orders, sir. Grant is in the field, but won't be ready for several months. That's why I was sent."

"You were sent to take me out of here, but if I die in the escape, nothing will be solved."

"What are you thinking, Mr. President?"

"I'm thinking that I'm a husk of the man I once was. There's not much else I can offer the world, except, perhaps, my death."

"Your death, sir?"

"My death. As a lonely pilgrim dying on the road, I am nothing. But as the President of the United States, murdered by a Southerner in a Southern capital, I may—just may—be a symbol of the importance of the Presidency, and of the changes that must be wrought on the government."

"Murdered, sir?"

"Murdered, Mr. Pinkerton. It's not so horrible to contemplate. At most, it will hasten my end by a few days. But if I can serve by my death... Find someone to do it. Make it a public spectacle. Let it embarrass my soi-disant hosts. Let my death be the rallying cry Hamlin needs to wrest control of the government from the petty, squabbling states."

Horrible as the idea was, Lincoln quickly won Pinkerton over to his way of thinking. "It will have to be in public. Not something hidden in this room, sir."

"Public, yes, public. Independence Day. Davis was in yesterday. The day before? Whichever. He said there's to be an Independence Day celebration, at which I am expected to appear. But he warned me against saying anything. Then. At that celebration. That's the time to do it."

"Sir, do you understand what you're saying? What you're asking me to do?"

"What I'm ordering you to do, Mr. Pinkerton. I'm ordering you to find some Southern patsy to murder me, and to loudly claim he did it for disunion. Don't let it be traced back to you."

"But your family?"

"My family. Poor, dear Mary. This will cause her great grief, but even without this plan, I will not see her again. I must ask something else of you, Mr. Pinkerton. When you get back to the North, be sure to tell her that my last thoughts were of her and the children. That I love her still. That I'm sorry I cannot be with her."

"I will, Mr. President."

"Then off with you, Mr. Pinkerton. Set it all up, and then get out of Columbia, out of South Carolina, as fast as you can."

—•—

As everyone knows now, Lincoln's plan was a success. But at the time, and for many years after, all we knew was that a middling-successful actor—who apparently had no idea what was really happening among the upper echelons of the government—had joined a conspiracy to decapitate it.

Photos of Lincoln at the Independence Day celebrations show him looking pained and drawn, sitting uncomfortably and resting on a cane. And yet, he also seems to be at peace, as if he knows what is coming, and the good that will come of it.

Of the actual moment, we have eyewitness reports: actor John Wilkes Booth approached the President from the back, pulled a pistol, shouted "Iura Australi," and shot Lincoln in the back of the head.

Even though Lincoln was surrounded by people one would assume wanted him dead, including Davis and Gist, the shock they all displayed at Booth's grisly act seemed both genuine and horrified.

In the bedlam that followed the gun shot, Booth was able to escape, and he ran.

The police caught up with him hours later, while he was holed up in a barn. Through shouted negotiations, Booth blamed a conspiracy, and demanded to know if Vice President Hamlin and Secretary of State Seward were also dead. Apparently, he was unaware that they weren't even in the South.

Eventually, Booth walked out of the barn with his hands in the air and no evidence of a weapon. There was much shouting, and several gun shots, and Booth died.

Many years later, on his death bed, Allan Pinkerton finally admitting killing John Wilkes Booth, and his role in the assassination of a President.

The National Archives then confirmed that President Hannibal Hamlin had issued a full—and secret—pardon to Pinkerton. "He never could thank me, because it was my action that made him President. But we both recognized the necessity of my acts for the greater good, the survival of the nation."

—•—

From the *Encyclopedia Americana*:

Following Lincoln's assassination, Hannibal Hamlin assumed the Presidency and, with Ulysses Grant in command of the Army, the Union forces managed to smash the South's defensive blockade, and bring Lincoln's body home. They also captured Jefferson Davis, William Gist, and the other leaders of the Southern uprising, thus ending the Great Schism.

The Senate refused to meet again in Columbia, and, in concert with Hamlin and the Cabinet, demanded a new, neutral site for the government. A commission was appointed, which decided the best course would be to carve out a capital territory, a District of Lincoln, on the border between the North and South. A suitable location was found, an unoccupied parcel of land straddling the Ohio River bordering Northern state Illinois and Southern state Kentucky (centered at 37.5 degrees North, 88.1 degrees West). Both states donated the land for what would come to be known as the capital city, Washington, D.L.

President Hamlin was elected to his own term in 1864, with the Southern states not participating. By late 1865, the war was over, the Schism healed, and the South brought to heel.

The capitulating South agreed to the 13th and 14th Amendments, ending slavery and setting out a plan for a permanent, extraterritorial national capital in Washington, District of Lincoln.

President Hamlin spent the remainder of his term overseeing the construction of the capital city from temporary quarters in Springfield, and agitating for a stronger centralized government.

In the election of 1868, General Ulysses Grant was easily elected President.

Allan Pinkerton founded a security and investigation firm, but he wore a haunted expression for the rest of his days.

MALON EDWARDS

INTO THE BREACH

I'm off my bunk and into my jodhpurs, knee-high leather boots and flight jacket the moment the long range air attack klaxons seep into my nightly dream about Caracara.

Muscle memory and Secret Service training kick in; I'm on auto-pilot (no pun intended) and a good ways down the hall buttoning up both sides of my leather jacket to the shoulder a full thirty seconds before I'm awake.

And just so you know, the ever so slight tremble in my hands and fingers is not fear. It's adrenaline. I'm cranked and ready to put my foot all up in it.

A door to the right opens and Pierre-Alexandre falls in on my right flank, his steps brisk like mine. Our boots echo down the long hallway as we make our way from the underground bunker at Soldier Field to the bunker at Meigs Field.

"What you think we got?" he asks.

My reptile mind—that wonderful, hedonistic thing of mine—notices how lovely his make-me-jump-up-and-dance-like-I-just-caught-the-Holy-Ghost-in-church dark skin looks in the red emergency scramble lighting.

And yeah, I know. I'm going to hell for that.

A door to my left opens and René-Bastien, better known as Pretty Boy, falls in on my left flank and matches our stride.

"My guess is fifteen bogeys coming in hard and fast from the south," he says.

His flight jacket is only half buttoned and he's not wearing his T.I. issued white tee-shirt (that's Tuskegee Institute for those that don't know). I flicker a glance at his beautiful, honey-hued, well-muscled chest and frown.

I bet he just left some police academy recruit in his bunk. Good-N-Plenty is going to smack him upside his head for entertaining unauthorized personnel after lights out. Lax discipline gets people killed. We've had enough of that, lately.

"It don't matter what we got," I tell them, throwing open the double doors leading to the enormous underground hangar at Meigs Field, "as long as we finish what they start."

We hustle down the short flight of metal stairs and fan out to our respective bright-shirted handlers waiting for us at our outfit stations: me to Skittles, Pierre-Alexandre to Sour Patch, and Pretty Boy to Good-N-Plenty. Good-N-Plenty pops the back of Pretty Boy's neck with a comb before she hands it to him and buttons up his flight jacket.

Skittles catches my eye as I pull on thin leather gloves and stand shoulder-width apart on my platform, arms outstretched.

"You okay?" she asks as her fingers flow across her station console, manipulating my exo-suit into place from above.

I hesitate for a fraction of a second before I answer. "M byen. I'm cool."

Skittles tries to hold my gaze. She knows I'm still grieving hard. Instead, I look at the empty outfit stations scattered throughout the hangar. Once, there were thirty-six of us, including Caracara. I still can't bring myself to look at her station on my right.

Robotic arms lower the torso of my powered armor onto me and outfit my arms and legs with the rest of my sleek exo-suit. I feel all components lock into place, one by one.

"You're online," Skittles says, handing me my helmet.

"Systems check?" I ask her.

"All systems green, including weapons."

"What's the gouge?"

Skittles glances at a second console screen. "Thirty-one bandits, south by southwest. City-state airspace ETA five minutes."

Shit. This isn't just a show of force. The State of Illinois wants to crush us. Wipe us out. Smother us in the bed of our city-state infancy.

"Is the Sable safe?" I ask her.

She nods. Safe and protected in an undisclosed location with Marie-Therèse, Marie-Louise, Jean-François and the last CPD contingent.

(That's Chicago Police Department, for those that don't know.)

I smirk. "I told them they'd outlive us."

"We're not dead yet," Pretty Boy says, and his voice echoes as it carries to me from across the almost-empty bunker.

"We will be if you don't put down that damn comb," Pierre-Alexandre tells him.

I pat my tight and right Janelle Monáe before I wreck it with my helmet. "I'm taking the scissors to your hair when we get back," I say to Pretty Boy.

If we get back.

Pretty Boy shakes out his hair before he puts on his helmet. "Cut these beautiful curls," he says through our helmlink, "and you take away my power."

"Your power of bullshit," Pierre-Alexandre says.

I can't help but smile. Good thing they can't see it. They might think I'm getting soft.

"Scramble in thirty seconds," I tell them.

Skittles starts the countdown clock before she steps onto my platform and throws both arms around me. Kale je. Her voice is soft. Hesitant. I needed that hug. I don't tell her that, though.

"My eyes are always open," I say instead.

Except when Caracara died.

"It wasn't your fault," she says, putting on her headset and switching to our private commlink. Skittles is a good handler. She knows me better than I know myself.

"Tell that to my dreams," I whisper.

One hundred feet up, the roof of the bunker slides open, taking its sweet time. Skittles steps off my platform and goes back to her console. I watch the last ten seconds to lift-off flip down to zero on the huge digital clock affixed to the far wall.

"Anmize ou byen," Skittles says in my earcomm, her voice now normal-husky like far-off water over rocks. "Tandiske fè atansyon."

I laugh into our private commlink. "Both fun and careful are my middle names," I tell her before I touch my left thumb to base of my left pinkie.

The rocket pack molded into the powered armor Skittles designed and built for me roars to life. Not wanting to be left in my diesel exhaust—drawers down and ass-out embarrassed again— Pierre-Alexandre and Pretty Boy fire up their rockets, too.

I look over at them, and then up at the so small dark sky.

"Men m la pran m," I tell them.

Catch me if you can.

I didn't think that day would be our last together.

I didn't think that would be our last sortie.

I didn't think I would never see you again.

You gave me no reason to think that way.

You were fierce. You were bold.

You didn't take shit from nobody.

You never doubted yourself.

At least, that's what I thought.

You'd always said, If we doubt, we die.

I often wonder if you'd ever thought, I just may die today.

But then, I shake those thoughts away. And I put on estipid bravado along with my armor.

Like I did just now in the hangar with Skittles.

Yeah, I was frontin'.

Tankou si ou. Tankou granpè nou.

Just like you. Just like our grandfather.

We must have gotten it from him. And look where it got you.

I wonder if I'm going to die today.

I hope I don't die today.

I'm afraid of dying today.

But not if that means I get to see you again.

Not that I didn't believe Skittles, but I'm still surprised to see ten Maybach 62S exo-fighters escorting twenty-one Conquest Knight XV shit shells over the south suburbs, just miles short of city-state airspace.

Well, I did tell Skittles fun is my middle name.

And careful, too. But to hell with that.

Bèl Flè, grann mwen—my grandmother—used to say, kapon antere manman l. Cowards bury their mothers.

Or in my case, their sisters.

I don't want to be a coward today.

"Get your guns ready, boys," I tell Pierre-Alexandre and Pretty Boy as we tease out the sound barrier to play with us over Park Forest, Illinois.

"Ready to go hard and fast," Pierre-Alexandre answers.

"I hope you didn't tell her that last night," Pretty Boy lobs to him.

I can already see where this is going. Pierre-Alexandre has never been that bright. Strong and reliable, yes. But a neg sòt, too.

"Tell who?" he asks Pretty Boy.

"Palmetta."

There's a brief pause, and then Pierre-Alexandre says, "You just mad 'cause it's gon take you five hours to get your butters back done up after this."

Pretty Boy kisses his teeth, sadness in his voice. "You ain't said nothing but a word."

I clear my throat. "While you boys are mourning Pretty Boy's hair, I'll just go defend our Sovereign State and its freedom."

I touch the tips of my thumbs to the tips of my middle fingers, as if I'm about to meditate for enlightenment. Not quite.

Side-mounted Browning M2 .50 caliber machine guns unfold from a compartment in my exo-arms. One hundred and seventy-five rounds each. My radar shows me that Pierre-Alexandre and Pretty Boy are now armed and have done the same.

Our guns and ammo don't leave room for much else, but they do go well with our exo-suits: my Mercedes Benz S-Guard 600 powered armor, also known as Lark; Pierre-Alexandre's Audi Attack 8 powered armor, also known as War Eagle; and Pretty Boy's BMW 7 Series High Security powered armor, also known as Peacock.

Yeah. You heard right. Peacock.

Just know I didn't hand out code names when I first assembled this outfit.

"We doing the usual maneuvers?" Pierre-Alexandre asks me.

No. The usual got Caracara killed.

Out loud I say: "No. Fall back. Let them think we're buggin' out because we're surprised by their numbers."

I pull up and hover. Pierre-Alexandre and Pretty Boy flank me. White, wispy-thin clouds broker the distance between us and the Illinois National Guard's shit shells.

I am surprised by their numbers. And somewhat cowed.

But I lift my chin at our enemy, my voice flush with that estipid bravado I inherited from granpè mwen (Jean-Baptiste Point du Sable, for those that don't know). The same estipid bravado he had when he seceded Chicago from the State of Illinois, established the City-State of One Hundred Fists and named himself Lord Mayor.

The same estipid bravado that killed Caracara.

"When their shit shells open their hatches to let loose their turds," I tell my dwindled team, "move into position beneath and blow them straight to hell."

Before the air attack klaxons sounded, I'd been dreaming I was five years old again, sitting on my grandfather's knee. Michaëlle-Anicia was sitting next to me, on his other one.

"Tell us again where the gold is, Grandfather," I'd said to him.

"And the silver! And the diamonds!" Michaëlle-Anicia piped up.

Grandfather chuckled and kissed the loose, dark curls at the crown of our small heads. "The gold and the silver and the diamonds," he told us, "are in the same place when I first settled in Chicago many coffee harvests ago."

"San rekòt kafe?" Michaëlle-Anicia asked him.

Grandfather pulled us close and laughed again, so deep and so rich that his big belly shook both our backs. "Ti chouchou," he asked my twin sister, "do I look that old to you?"

"Wi, Granpè," she answered, and pushed on his big belly with her tiny fists. I giggled, both hands over my mouth.

"Non, non," Grandfather said, shaking his head, "I have seen nowhere near one hundred coffee harvests. Now, your grann, Bèl Flè mwen, she has seen many rekòt kafe. I bet she has seen more rekòt kafe than you can count."

"Nuh uh!" Michaëlle-Anicia flared, sitting up straighter with challenge.

"How many has Grann seen?" I asked.

"Can you count twa san rekòt kafe?" Grandfather asked us.

"Wi!" Michaëlle-Anicia answered, and she could. So could I.

"Grann is not that old," I said, my mouth pursed in disbelief.

"Oh, but she is! Grandfather assured us. Bèl Flè mwen, lanmou cheri mwen—your grandmother—she saw the bombs drop and scorch the land, many, many coffee harvests ago."

Our eyes widened with wonder and pride and fascination as Grandfather told us again the story of Chicago's history and our family, a story we could never get enough of.

"But remember, ti chouchou," Grandfather went on to say, "it was also grann ou who rebirthed Chicago. It was she who purified the soil and cleansed Lake Michigan again. It was she who put the gold and silver and diamonds—and the copper and the uranium, too—deep down in the earth, and called it the Gold Coast. All so we could rebuild and thrive and live."

"And the big bad State wants us to give it all to them!" Michaëlle-Anicia shouted, her fists clenched angry.

"Just like the big bad wolf!" I shouted with her.

"Ah, but ti fi cheri mwen yo," Grandfather said, "we should always share with those who are less fortunate."

"Why?" Michaëlle-Anicia asked, her fists still angry. "They take and take and take, and they never give anything back!"

" 'E vre!" I shouted, wanting to be louder than my twin sister. "They will take until we have nothing left!"

"No, they won't," Grandfather told us, his voice deep and calm. "We will only share until they have enough. Until they can rebuild and thrive and live. Just like us. And when they are finally able to do so, we shall share no more, and they will take no more."

"Non, Granpè!" Michaëlle-Anicia said. "Ou fè erè! They will always take and take because they are bigger and because they are bullies!"

"Ah, ti chouchou," Grandfather tutted, "but I am right. The State of Illinois will take no more than we give them because you and your sister will not let them."

Michaëlle-Anicia turned to face Grandfather and looked up at him, her eyes narrowed and her head cocked to one side, so I did the same.

"And if the day ever comes where they try," Grandfather continued, kissing the crown of our small heads again, "Senyè, lonje men ba yo."

It's as if the Illinois National Guard knows what we're doing. Their shit shells hold and hover as well. Standoff.

Not that this was ever meant to be a complex plan.

What now, bòs? Pierre-Alexandre asks me.

Kounye a, my grandfather is somewhere hiding in a deep, dark basement—afraid—waiting for the city he rebuilt from its ashes to fall on his head.

I never thought I'd see the day granpè mwen would cower. From the time I was ti fi, I always believed he feared nothing.

He is a gwo nèg. A bon nèg.

He is the rebèl who gave the Land of Lincoln the double middle finger. The politisyen who made Chicago a Sovereign State, and gave Kreyòl and English equal legal weight. The innovateur who manufactured the armor that seduced me and Caracara with its sleek, sexy power—a power manman nou, our mother, never forgave us for embracing.

Not even on her deathbed.

Caracara is supposed to be here. Caracara is supposed to be doing this.

I guess it's up to me now.

I look at Pierre-Alexandre and then Pretty Boy. "Back to the usual maneuvers," I tell them. "I'll take the point. Follow my lead."

She did always say: go big, or go home.

I never call her Caracara in my dreams. It's always Michaëlle-Anicia.

And she never calls me Michaëlle-Modeste. It's always Lark.

So when Caracara said to me, "Lark, love of my heart, if you die today, I will kick your ass," I knew my dream had changed and we were no longer five years old sitting on Grandfather's knee.

"Grandfather shouldn't have made me head of his Secret Service," I'd told Michaëlle-Anicia. "He should have chosen you."

Michaëlle-Anicia took both my hands in hers. We stood, facing one another. My mirror. Her mirror.

"He chose you," she said, "because he knew I would die. I am foolish. You are not."

"Non," I told her, shaking my head. "I never wanted this. But I put on my armor because you put on your armor first. I wanted to do everything you did. You were born for this. Not me."

"Non," Michaëlle-Anicia countered, shaking her head harder than my headshake so her loose, dark curls flew. "You were born for this, just as much as I was. Bèl Flè—grann nou—made you strong, just as she made me strong."

"I don't believe in Bèl Flè," I said, dropping her hands, my voice small. "We are no longer ti fi, I went on. We no longer have short curls and skinned knees. I don't believe Granpè's tall tales anymore."

Michaëlle-Anicia scowled at me. She looked disgusted. "Because you are afraid they are true."

"Non," I said, "because—"

But Michaëlle-Anicia shouted me down, challenging as always. "Because you are afraid to embrace Bèl Flè's legacy! Because you are afraid to lead! Because you are afraid everyone knows your flawed decisions killed me and almost every single one of your team members!"

Her shouts bounced all around us before they were swallowed by a white, loud silence that rang in my ears. Never before had my twin sister said anything like that to me. Not in my dreams. Not when she was alive.

I turned away from her, from my mirror, so she couldn't see me struggle not to cry. "Se pa vre," I whispered at the whiteness all around me, "that's not true at all."

But Michaëlle-Anicia didn't answer because the air attack klaxons sounded, shattering my dream, taking her away from me.

"You're stressing your armor," Skittles says in my earcomm, her voice calm and quiet, as it always is during battle. "A lot. Any faster, and Lark will break apart."

"Mwen pa bay yon mèd," I say, my voice just as soft, and I push even further past the sound barrier, toward the Illinois wedge of exo-fighters and bombers.

"Michaëlle-Modeste!" Skittles scolds, shocked by my language. That's the loudest I've ever heard her speak. And the most pained.

"Well, I don't care!" I scream at her, just as loud, and la pou la, I wish I could take those words back.

I check my heads-up display radar to make sure Pierre-Alexandre and Pretty Boy are still flanking me before I apologize. "Eskize'm," I tell her, my voice small and five years old again. "Really, I am."

"That armor is my life," she whispers.

"I know," I tell her.

"I've devoted more time to Lark than I have to manman mwen ak sè mwen," she says.

"I know," I say again.

"I love Lark as much as I love you."

"I know," I repeat a third time, because I don't know what else to say.

"Stop saying I know," she yells at me again, "and start respecting her! And while you're at it, she goes on, stop feeling sorry for yourself because your sister is dead, and go bust some Illinois ass!"

She doesn't have to tell me twice.

As I streak toward the Illinois wedge tankou moun fou—like a crazy person—I line up the ten Maybach 62S exo-fighters and twenty-one shit shell bombers in my sights, fists outstretched, Supergirl-style. My .50 caliber Brownings tear through five of the ten Maybachs. Jagged, black pieces of exo-suit go flying, end over end.

I'm not surprised. They're just fodder. The shit shell bombers are the ones with the heavy armor. They do all the damage.

The return fire is hot. I point my toes and roll onto my back, dodging most of it with my usual grace as I watch the five Maybachs spin away from their wedge and fall to the earth, limp and broken.

Just like Caracara fell.

But I'm not graceful enough. Blazing pain rips into my left shoulder and right hip.

"How bad is it?" Skittles asks, la pou la.

"Se pa mal," I lie, as my blood streams out to mix with the thin clouds. "Se pa anyen ditou."

"You never were a good liar," she chides, her voice softer than usual.

"Yell at me when I get back," I tell her, my voice just as soft, and then I say louder into my helmlink: "How are you doing out there, boys?"

"Eight bombers down," Pretty Boy answers, "but they're starting to shit all over the world."

"Well, we can't have that," I say, my voice wavering yon ti kras, "now can we?"

"You keep those Maybachs busy," Pierre Alexandre tells me, "and we can finish off these shit shells in about di minit. "

"Knowing you and Pretty Boy," I say, rolling onto my stomach, "I'll be done here in five and have to save your asses."

I'm channeling Caracara big time now, talking shit and everything. Wish I would have known wedge busting was this fun before she died.

"How's the armor holding up?" I ask Skittles, forcing strength into my voice.

She doesn't buy it. "Better question is," she says with all the gravity in the world (no pun intended), "how are you holding up?"

"M byen," I tell her, good enough to do this.

I put my arms tight to my sides for better aerodynamics and climb straight up to the dark edge of space, ak tout vitès. The Maybachs pursue, just as I expected. My teeth rattle as the g-forces try to tear me and my armor to pieces.

When I can't take it anymore, I bank left, hard. Two of the Maybachs go with me. The other three shake apart and tumble back to the earth.

My neck, my head, my lungs, my heart scream with pain as I try to circle behind the last two Maybachs. I'm too far up. The turn is too tight. I won't make it.

And then, the white-hot fire from their bullets rip my left side open.

I don't hear my crash avoidance alarms going off. I don't hear Skittles crying and screaming at me to right myself. I don't even hear the howl of the wind as I spin and fall. I push that all aside.

I just focus on the two Maybachs above, diving for me, arms at their sides.

And—after one revolution, two revolutions, three revolutions—I smile, let loose my guns, and blow both Maybachs straight to hell.

Michaëlle-Anicia had been our wedge-buster.

Lib-e-libè. Wild at heart. Our free spirit.

More than one hundred and fifty sorties. And hardly a scratch to Caracara.

She'd been badass that way.

Michaëlle-Anicia had also fiercely believed in Bèl Flè.

She believed Bèl Flè had been stricken with polio by Babalú-Ayé, the god of sickness and disease, who withered every last one of Bèl Flè's organs when she was ti fi.

She believed gwo grann, our great-grandmother, took Bèl Flè to a steam surgeon who specialized in metallurgy and glasswork, and told him to fix her daughter.

She believed the steam surgeon removed all of Bèl Flè's withered organs, gave her a steam clock heart and compost boiler, and then encased her torso with nigh-unbreakable glass.

She believed Bèl Flè's compost boiler, powered by the most high-quality coal dust, creates rich, dark, pristine topsoil every three weeks.

She believed Bèl Flè used that rich, dark, pristine topsoil to cover the scorched land and glowing ash left by the bombs and warheads.

She believed healthy and vibrant grass, plants and trees grew from Bèl Flè's rich, dark, pristine topsoil.

She believed the transpiration from the healthy and vibrant grass, plants and trees reversed the effects of nuclear winter, bringing fat, cleansing raindrops not seen for years on the North American continent.

And she believed, after the war, Bèl Flè placed gold, silver and diamonds, and uranium and copper, too, deep within the earth beneath Chicago, called that land the Gold Coast, and left it all for Granpè to govern as Lord Mayor.

Those were the beatitudes of Michaëlle-Anicia.

But now, as I streak toward the earth tankou yon boul dife—like a ball of fire—I recite her beatitudes and make them mine.

And they give me strength.

Robert Greenberger

THE REPUBLIC OF MADAWASKA

The New Brunswick jail was cold, the winter chill seeping through the stone construction and stealing whatever warmth came from the single stove that heated meals, coffee, and was to provide the prisoners some measure of comfort.

There was little activity within the small structure as a deputy dozed near the meager heat and the sole occupant sat on a thin mattress and huddled under his threadbare, woolen blanket. He ignored his hunger and steeled himself to prevent his teeth from chattering so as not to chip them. He craved companionship and conversation, both of which were in as short supply as the heat. The prospect that things would get colder in the coming weeks filled him with dread.

As a result, he was lost in thought and never heard the scrape and rattle of hinges protesting and the wooden door being forced open. It wasn't until the booted footsteps approached his cell that he finally realized someone else was now in the building. He presumed it another prisoner which heartened him with the prospect of a companion to while away the hours.

He looked up to see a smartly dressed man, wrapped in wool with leather gloves. He was a stranger to him, of average height, with wrinkles that peeked through the scarf and spoke of age although the hair was dark. The man openly stared at him in return, each taking the measure of the other.

"Mr. John Baker?"

"*Colonel* Baker," the prisoner said.

"I am Samuel Barrell, Special Diplomatic Agent," the man replied. "How do you earn the rank?"

"I earned it from the Maine Militia," Baker said. "Agent for who?"

"I am here at the behest of Henry Clay and President Jackson," Barrell said. His voice was deep and pleasant. A voice Baker would not tire of any time soon, but then again, he had spoken with few people since his arrest months earlier. That someone from Washington D.C. was here for his case caused his heart to beat faster, blood pumping through chilled veins, and the specter of hope appearing before his eyes.

"I would offer you a chair, Mr. Barrell, but I will have to be the poor host," Baker said.

"Not to worry, Colonel Baker, I have arranged for us to sit somewhere more comfortable and private where we can speak."

"And what shall we speak of?"

"The Republic of Madawaska."

Barrell was a man of his word, and within the next quarter hour, the awakened deputy arrived to escort Baker from his jail home to a nearby tavern where there was a space sufficient for their needs. Baker reveled in the warmth and familiar smells of beer and beef, both welcome compared with the stench of rotting straw and unclean buckets at the jail. Barrell said little until they were settled and he had ordered them both beer. The stranger then slowly unwrapped himself of his garments, revealing a woolen suit of modern fashion, with white shirt and colorful blue ascot. His hair was dark but beginning to thin on top and he had a paunch, the result of too little exercise. Baker was a woodsman, having built up a business with his brother Nathan and he retained strong muscles, even after months of too little use.

"You have stirred up quite a bit of trouble between America and the British crown," Barrell said once the beers were placed on the rough wooden table. Baker barely heard, taking a long pull of the beer. It was watery but far better than the fare served in jail. Not that his treatment was poor, but the length of it had worn off any novelty and the sameness of the meals turned them to fuel to keep him warm and little else. He hoped they'd talk long enough to force Barrell to have dinner brought them both. Right now, he'd settle for cheese if beef were not offered. His host seemed disinclined to even suggest food. Baker understood, since even watery beer had alcoholic content and without food, he'd find his tongue loosened. Of course, he'd drunk his fair share of men under the table so could go for some time before worrying about saying too much or the wrong thing. First, he needed to understand why Clay would send Barrell.

The Special Agent reached into a leather bag he had been carrying in a warm, gloved hand. He withdrew several sheafs of paper, studying them with squinted eyes and then appraised Baker once more.

"Did you really declare your spit of land a Republic?"

Baker smiled at that. "That I did," he said with pride.

"Tell me about it," Barrell prompted.

Well, that was easily done. After all, he rarely acted rashly but deliberately, it's how he and Nathan – god rest his soul – prospered. Hard to tell now that New Brunswick was squeezing him for three hundred pounds he did not possess in ready cash. It was why he languished in jail until a trial, the date for which seemed never to come close.

"Do you not have my tale written down already? I spoke at some length with Charles Daveis, who investigated on behalf of Governor Lincoln."

Burrell did not look down at his papers but nodded in affirmation. "I have read his findings and would now like to hear them from you in unadulterated form."

"You suspect Mr. Daveis of being a poor amanuensis?"

"Nothing of the sort, but given the grave importance of the matter, I wish to hear the story for myself."

"Grave import," mused Baker. His little uprising sounded positively operatic, not that he'd been to a performance, but had read enough to understand. Curious, he considered.

"I guess you could say it was an act of independence," Baker began. "Sophie and I were hosting a part on July 4, which just happens to be America's birthday."

Barrell smiled and nodded.

"In addition to our neighbors, Mrs. Baker and I decided to invite several of our French friends as guests. To celebrate the occasion, my wife had sewn a flag which we raised over the house."

"Your home, as I understand it, is located on British soil."

Baker paused to sup from the mug, actually savoring the weak liquid. "Well, now there's the rub of it, Mr. Barrell. To me, Madawaska is on American soil and we're loyal to Maine and the United States of America."

"But the region in question is largely a part of New Brunswick, adjacent to Maine. The Madawaska River flows into the Saint John River in this area. Most of the land, by most accounting, is British."

"Maybe, but enough is in Maine and the United States to keep the question alive, am I right?" Baker countered.

"All too true," Barrell sighed.

The Special Agent nodded then signaled the passing waitress for two more tankards. "In July it was American soil, as you say, but that changed to something else in August."

Baker laughed at that, recalling the looks on the people when he first made his declaration. "The thing of it is, Mr. Barrell, is that where Madawaska stands can be argued as both American and British soil. When we first arrived here in 1820, Nathan and I had been informed by the local population that both countries lay claim to the area thanks to some less than precise notations in various documents signed by both parties."

"The Treaty of Paris, you mean," Barrell asked, clearly seeking the very preciseness the document lacked.

"Yes, the one that allowed us to formally tell King George III to bugger off," Baker said, enjoying the surprised look from his guest. "It's been decades and neither side has backed off their claim."

"So you took it upon yourself to settle the matter," Barrell prompted, handing a coin to the girl who brought two fresh beers. Baker's eyes lingered off her youthful figure, missing his wife and their first child. Sophie had two with Nathan before he died and since they married five years earlier, it had taken more than enough time for them to produce one of their own.

"I am given to understand you did not fly an American flag," Barrell prompted.

"That's true," Baker agreed. "My Sophie improved on it a bit, adding an American eagle with a semicircle of stars. That got me to thinking."

"Feeling inspired?"

"That is certainly one way a learned man such as yourself might look at it. You see, Mr. Burrell, I love America. I love the idea that a group of men could conspire to take a continent away from a King then fight to retain it. There's as much benign neglect of New Brunswick as there was in the colonies. If Madawaska meant something to either government, the matter might have been settled by now. Instead, they continue to trade and sometimes trade shots with one another. I have a going concern here and one I would like to protect. So, yeah, I felt inspired."

Burrell seemed to soak in all the information, storing it away, but did not betray agreement or dismissal. Instead, he shuffled the papers as if he was getting ready to deal a hand of cards. Selecting one, he studied it and once more turned his attention to Baker.

"You seem to show your preferences on July 15 when you James Bacon, and Charles Studson attempt to get Pierre Marquis and Abraham Chamberland to sign a declaration that rejected British authority..."

"Peter Markee," Baker corrected.

"I beg your pardon?" Barrell said, clearly confused.

"Monsieur Marquis changed his French name to Peter Markee, his own way of showing his American predilection."

"I see," Burrell said and then took a draft of his drink to clearly stall and regroup his thoughts. Baker seized the opportunity to speak further.

"You know, Mr. Burrell, I find it passing strange that the Federal authorities would trouble themselves with this entire matter. We founded Madawaska with sixteen families and built a business out of trees and a river. Something must have changed to summon a man of your import."

"Assaulting a British representative might be considered a provocative action, one requiring our intervention. Do you agree?"

Baker paused to divine which act he was describing but then hit upon the exact one. "The postal carrier?"

"The very one," Burrell agreed. "On the Saint John's, no less."

"Aw, I meant Pierre Sélesse no personal harm. But, he was traveling the Saint John and Madawaska Rivers, which falls into disputed territory. I decided it was time to police the lands and waters that were, by rights, American territory."

"Lands that you yourself admit are actually in dispute."

Baker took a long pull of his beer and nodded. "Ah, that's the truth of it."

"One might conclude that for two weeks by then, your actions took on a deliberate color. A good lawyer might suggest you had planned these actions allowing you to make your startling claim."

Burrell paused, clearly hoping to read something in Baker's face. The lumber man, though, drove hard bargains and stared down more than few adversaries. He had long since learned to school his face, betray nothing and here that is exactly what he did. Burrell seemed to wait him out.

In time, Burrell seemed to give in and once more consulted his papers. Baker strained to try and glean information from the neat script writing, but it was upside down and too small to discern. He admired how much there was—so Burrell was prepared, and the questions all were ones he already knew the answers to. He was probing and the real matter had yet to be revealed.

Baker enjoyed the beer and the warmth and was not at interested in shortening the interview so would answer any and all questions directed his way.

"Much like a well-wound clock, you caused another incident precisely a week later. I understand from Justice of the Peace George Morehouse received a complaint that you and your followers were interfering with militia training."

Baker laughed at that and clapped his hands together. "Well, your facts are a bit askew. The complaint may have been written on the 25th, but that was a Wednesday and the incident itself was the previous Saturday. If what we were accused of was so distressing, perhaps he should have written Mr. Morehouse with greater haste."

"Mayhap," Burrell said, clearly unperturbed by the correction. "Be it Saturday or Wednesday, it prompted Attorney General Wetmore to order an investigation."

"Poor Morehouse had to come here and conduct the interviews himself," Baker allowed. "Never bothered to ask me a thing, just spoke with the King's citizens. Instead, he had the gall to show up at my door and insist Sophie's flag be taken down as it was an affront to the King."

"Is the record accurate that you refused, telling Morehouse, 'nothing but a superior force to ourselves shall take it down'?"

"That sounds right. A man defending his home and land," Baker said, instilling each word with pride and force.

"But you were not done, were you?"

Baker smiled. "I was wondering if you heard about that. Consider it a final act by despicable men, forcing me to act in Madawaska's best interest."

"On August 9. . ..it was August 9, I presume," Burrell said.

Baker grinned and nodded.

"An American, one Phineas Hofford, swore out a warrant against a John Bacon, prompting Constable Joseph Sansfaçon to attempt to carry out the legal order. However, you and eleven other men intervened. You even brandished a sword to prevent Bacon's arrest. You even dragged your son into the matter."

"We learn by doing," Baker said with perfect equanimity. "Clearly things were irritating us on all sides. We felt harassed, territorial boundaries a muddy mess, and clearly no peace was to be had."

"Which is when you declared your little community a sovereign Republic."

"To be precise, Mr. Burrell, it was the following day. A Friday if it helps your report."

Burrell smiled at that but said nothing further, but Baker read interest in the man's eyes. It was almost palpable so they were finally getting to the meat of the matter.

"I won't bore you with a recitation of the letters back and forth on all sides of the issue. Your actions were quite the irritant to His Majesty and your representatives in Washington. We know you wrote to Maine's governor begging protection while your notion of independence still lingered in the air. We also know Morehouse feared you would not back down and issued your arrest warrant."

"And here we are."

"Why are you rotting in jail rather than be with your family?"

"Do you mean to tell me your reports don't have that little detail? Why, Mr. Burrell, your representatives have not been very thorough. I could have posted a £100 surety bond but then Robert Sherar heard of my arrest and decided now was a good time to collect £230 he was owed."

Burrell's dark eyebrows shot up in surprise at this information. Baker laughed at catching the man unaware of some fact but then again, it was not primary information to the matter at hand.

"Sherar won the judgment against me in 1821 and wouldn't wait any longer for payment. I did not possess £330 so here I sit in Fredericton."

Burrell nodded and returned to reading from a different document. He began reading, skipping over sections, giving the oration a hesitating quality that bothered Baker, but he knew the words, having heard them more than once.

"It says here we you were 'endeavoring to persuade and procure divers of the inhabitants of Kent Parish, York County… to depart from the allegiance which they owe to His said Majesty… and for violently opposing the execution of the laws of the realm of England and of this province within the said parish and… conspiring together to subvert His majesty's authority and government in that part of this province'."

Burrell paused and let the words linger in the air then he signaled the waitress and finally ordered them both bowls of stew and bread. Baker adjusted his seating, sitting straighter and made certain he appeared appreciative.

"Colonel Baker, what if I told you there was a way out of your dilemma?"

"Whatever you propose, I can't pay for it, Mr. Burrell."

"My solution does not involve money you pay."

"Then I would be most appreciative of hearing you out," Baker said and broke into grin. Whatever came next, he knew it would be interesting, maybe even memorable.

"In the less than two decades since the Treaty of Ghent was signed, there has been little official trouble between England and America. We'd like to keep it that way and avoid further little distractions such as this mess. We all possess mapmakers and someone should have settled this matter further but it does not appear a priority to either government. Still, there are forces afoot that suggest we should expand north as well as west. Britain would vigorously defend this land and its riches so everyone with half a mind fears a new conflict.

"And truth to tell, Colonel Baker, there are greater issues festering across the land. The Indians dislike our settling on the land we purchased from Napoleon. We have southern states looking to avoid any discussion of slavery. Our economy needs to get stronger. So many greater issues."

Baker took it all in, never before considering the matters before the young country. He was not given to national politics, preferring to run his business and look after his family. The issues seemed mighty ones and beyond his imagining how to solve any one of them, let alone all of them.

"Colonel Baker," Burrell said as he reached into his leather bag for more papers. "The United States would be interested in recognizing the Republic of Madawaska in exchange for certain guarantees."

Of all the things Baker imagined, this was not on his mental list.

Christmas was fast approaching and Baker wished to be home with his family. He'd been in jail for three months total, his fine still unpaid but he knew engines were turning and matters were falling into place. He had expected Barrell to act with greater speed but then again, it was such a tremendous distance between the Fredericton jail that served as his home and Washington, D.C. The approaching winter also meant snow and frozen rivers, further slowing travel.

"You have a visitor," the gruff, pot-bellied deputy said from beneath his mustaches and opened the cell door.

Baker rose and worked out the kinks that ached in his arms and knees. The cold meant he couldn't get comfortable and he was feeling every bit his age. He ran a hand through his dirty hair, attempting to organize the mass, and then wiped away dust from his too-thin attire. He emerged into the main part of the building, fully expecting to see Burrell but instead saw a taller, thinner man, complete in powdered wig, despite that no longer being the fashion. He was easily fifty if not more, and the red, ruddy cheeks meant he had been out riding for some time. His cloak was dark blue and his black boots looked very expensive.

"Mr. Baker, I am Charles Richard Vaughan, Envoy for King George." He extended a hand, clutching the gloves in his left hand. Baker felt the warm, firm handshake and nodded his head.

"It's Colonel Baker, actually," he corrected.

"Is that a fact?" the man said, sounding utterly unconvinced.

"I have arranged for us to sit privately and discusses affairs of state if that would be sufficient," Vaughan said.

"Quite," Baker said, envisioning a return trip to the tavern. Instead, the two men were led to a boarding house and were shown up to Vaughan's room. It was no doubt the largest in the building, with a wide, thick bed and roaring fire place. A servant took their coats, made certain they had properly primped chairs by the fire and withdrew, leaving them alone.

"You've caused quite a bit of a stir around these parts," he said, his English accent heavier than Baker was accustomed to. "I have been traveling the United States for two years now and find the country quite different than England. There's so much more variety to the populace and quite a bit of industry. The manners also leave something to be desired. That said, I also saw the fierce independence that allowed the colonists to wage and win their war of freedom. Are you a revolutionary, Mr. Baker?"

"I run lumber," Baker said, refusing to divulge more than he needed to, herding his information into a corral, releasing only what he needed in order to keep the conversation moving.

"Quite right," Vaughan said. "But this past summer you also engaged in activities that one might construe as insurrection against His Royal Majesty."

"I mean the King no disrespect, but given that I have helped tame this land and have prospered from it, I object to feeling obligated to someone I will never see or meet. He has little interest in this land beyond whatever revenues he can derive. That, to me, is no leader I feel any obligation to."

"But you feel otherwise toward the Americans?"

"Were Madawaska be part of Maine, as I have previously submitted it should be, then I have a greater chance of knowing my Congressman, maybe even meeting Governor Lincoln. Were I to head down to Washington, I daresay, the President welcomes his citizens within his home. Would King George welcome me as such?"

Vaughan seemed to consider the question and steepled his hands. Baker chose to let the silence bring added pressure to the conversation.

"Your point is taken. But, that is an irrelevant point considering your own declarations. Do you truly believe your tiny stretch of land deserves the title of Republic?"

Baker smiled at that, and suspected that was why Vaughan was here. He had little doubt the British Envoy heard about the Special Agent's visit and possibly even the content of their conversation. No doubt it took time for word to read New Brunswick ears then to track down Vaughan, who needed time to do his own reconnaissance. And now they sat, ready to deal.

"Republics come in all shapes and sizes, I would think, Mr. Vaughan. Why couldn't Madawaska thrive as its own nation?"

"The small size of your borders would suggest it could not be sustained. You could not build any sort of thriving community and certainly your taxes would never be enough to cover the expenses of outfitting a militia."

"I would argue instead sir, that given our unique position, we would count America and Brittan as our friends, not adversaries. And our very size means we pose no threat to either side. Why would I need a militia?"

Vaughan considered the words and he frowned. The idea that a nation not need armed forces was an alien one to the Envoy. That much was clear. But given all his time in a jail cell, Baker had plenty of time to think about the meaning of being a nation. There were no Indians with which he need worry about nor were enemies liable to penetrate from the rivers that crossed his land. Beyond the copious lumber in the vicinity, there was no other desirable wealth to be obtained. Instead, he had envisioned Madawaska as the most peaceful place on Earth, a tranquil land where families could work and raise children, not worrying about wars, conscription, or sneak attack.

"Mr. Baker, I will be blunt..."

"About time we got down to the meat of it," Baker interrupted.

The Envoy did not look pleased at being interrupted but Baker needed to be assertive now that they were dealing man to man.

"Mr. Baker, we are given to understand that President Jackson is ready to recognize Madawaska as an independent Republic. What do you think King George's reaction would be to learning that land that can be argued belongs to the crown is being recognized as yet another winnowing of Britain's holdings? How long before he dispatches his troops to assert the crown's claim to the territory?"

"And risk another war with America," Baker shot back and gave a short laugh. "What you need is another option. War should never be the first reaction to a dispute."

Vaughan had no answer to that and appeared to be seeking other ideas, none of which were clearly coming to mind. Baker figured a man used as an Envoy would be filled with options and in that he was a touch disappointed with his companion. Worse, he had not even offered a drink, let alone a meal.

"Let me suggest, Mr. Vaughan, that you have several options. We're not so large a space that I am sure you could convince Lord Aberdeen to round up enough troops to surround us. It's been a long time since there was a siege and I suppose you could starve us out. An alternative would be to invade the space and force us from our homes, but I suspect that wouldn't look very good to your subjects or American neighbors. A variation on that would be to hire mercenaries to do the deed but then you have to worry about something admitting who paid for the work. That might smack of cowardice. I suppose you and America could finally sort out the borders once and for all and insist that those of us living on the disputed land rededicate our faith to either His Majesty King George IV or to President Andrew Jackson," Baker said, ticking off each option on upheld fingers. Vaughan sat immobile, listening to the suggestions without betraying any emotion. Still, Baker got the sense that none of the options were appealing in any way.

"Finally," Baker said and Vaughan lifted an eyebrow with some interest. "Let us be. I mean leave us alone. Let Madawaska exist on its own merits."

"Join America in recognizing your sovereignty?" The tone betrayed Vaughan's skepticism.

"What do you have to lose?"

"First, the land is British soil and you'd be a barrier to the rivers. We already gave away most of a continent. Should we give away more land, others may see as weak or easy prey."

Baker shook his head.

"Mr. Vaughan, I truly do not think the people of Europe will care on whit whether or not these few thousand square miles are British, American, or Madawaskan. Most of you are still dealing with the after-effects of Napoleon's campaigns. I know enough European history to know two of you will be at each other's throats before too much longer."

Vaughan actually nodded in agreement with that assessment. "And our neighbors to the south? What will they think?"

"Some will approve because independence is like a virus and the more the merrier. Some will disapprove because they have designs on the northernmost portions of the continent. And the rest will like the notion of a country acting as a buffer between America and England, to prevent further conflicts."

The British Envoy nodded slowly in silent agreement with some of Baker's statements, encouraging the man. Baker decided the time had come to press his point because it could very well mean he would be freed from imprisonment after too long.

"Recognize Madawaska as the Americans are poised to do and claim the credit. His Majesty recognizes the independent spirit of the people and looks forward to having a new trading partner. I will happily enter into negotiations with England regarding borders, treaties, and tariffs."

"Tariffs? Aren't you being presumptuous? Should we allow Madawaska its independence, who is to say the people of the new Republic will elect you their leader? And what sort of government are you suggesting rule the land, small as it is?"

Baker, having had plenty of time to daydream about these very issues was prepared and without hesitation launched into his explanation.

"I am enamored of the town council and town meeting setup used in New England. We can't grow in size thanks to the borders we will fix so everyone should manage to have a say. We can have a council and the council shall have its president. I submit we both know if such a structure were to exist, I, the spokesman for the people so far, would likely be its president so let's avoid the pretense.

"As for tariffs, clearly we will need to trade with our neighbors both north and south. You will want passage on the rivers plus our wood. I am ready to negotiate fair terms so you, in turn, will allow us to purchase goods and services without reaching too deep into our pockets."

There was a silence that grew heavy in the air and Baker hoped his direct talk would have a positive impact. As it was, his growing thirst and hunger were beginning to gnaw at his attention but given his current condition, he was not in a position to act the host.

"I find it utterly bizarre that I am apparently in negotiations with a prisoner of the British Empire," Vaughan admitted. "Yet another unique aspect of my time in the country.

"I would fully expect to be freed upon conclusion of our business and my fine forgiven," Baker said.

"What of the other money owed by court decree?"

"I would arrange terms with my creditor in order to maintain good relations with our new neighbor," Baker said affably.

"This is most peculiar," Vaughan admitted.

"Imagine how the Americans felt. They were quick to recognize my claim of freedom because it celebrated their own successes. President Jackson is even dispatching the Secretary of State to come visit once we are fully operational. And that brings us to where we sit right now. I would be ever so kind to have you order my release so I can return to Madawaskan soil and begin organizing the new government."

Vaughan laughed.

"You are a cheeky one, Mr. Baker. I possess no power to recognize your country. I would have to send word back to His Majesty and await his reply. At best we're talking four months at which time your trial should be well underway."

"You could offer a provisional recognition, enough to get me my freedom so I can be prepared. And since America sees us as a Republic, that could prompt an interesting international incident, the kind of unique experience I am sure you would rather avoid."

That caught Vaughan short and Baker pressed on. "Sir, in exchange for such consideration, I would happily enter into immediate negotiations with you for a special price on my timber. No one disputes the trees are mine to cut and sell. New Brunswick is growing and you need lumber for homes and business and churches. I can make a deal with you right now in exchange for considerations. Have you pen and ink so we may sign a deal? If not, return me to my cell because I will otherwise miss my supper."

Baker had previously bartered away certain fishing rights as part of the deal with the American and their funding of the new government, seed money as it were, was contingent on getting Britain to consider similar recognition.

Vaughan continued to consider in silence for some time until Baker, sensing he needed to prod the man, began to rise from the chair. The British Envoy gestured for him to remain in place.

"We are not used to working so quickly and there are more terms to work out. Let us say, for now, that I will arrange your release and put you up for at least a night or two as a guest of His Majesty's government. Then we may see if Madawaska and England can do business with one another. I would hate to leave without protecting our interests."

"I would hate to remain in a cold jail, knowing two reasonable men can accomplish far more than two governments."

"On that we agree," Vaughan said and extended a hand.

As he clasped the Envoy's hand, Baker silently memorized the moment—for it put him and the people he was pledged to on a course that would give them freedom from international politics. They wanted to do their business and be left alone. Baker wanted to assure that although as the hands remain clasped, he was already conjuring up the lengthy list of matters to attend to, starting with banking and currency, and who else they could trade with — the French maybe? — in order to assure Madawaska was not beholden to just these two countries.

So much to do… but John Baker couldn't help but grin because a silly lark of intemperate comment exploded into something unimagined.

The Republic of Madawaska. Long may she stand.

Sarah McGill

THE CITY OF OIL AND PAINT

"I feel that every time someone looks at me, all they see is oil – oil pouring out of me, turning my skin black as airplane smoke. When the war ended, my sister told me, 'They're signing a treaty and making Persia part of America.' I told her, 'If I wanted to live in America, I would live in America.' She said, 'You'll live in America soon.' So I left. Beat them to it, didn't I? Aren't I clever?" The woman laughed as though there were dust in her throat.

Josie looked at her and saw oil too, in the woman's yellow hijab and under her fingernails. She glanced at her own hands and saw paint – blue and red and yellow. All those straight lines like train tracks or bullet trails. All those blocks of color stamping the same patterns across the city street and the stretched victory banners and empty champagne bottles declaring the end of the Great War. Or at least, she'd once known how to draw white and red contours onto her cheeks and eyelids so her face looked like a magazine cover.

Josie hadn't meant to talk to the woman. She'd seen her walking on the street, face and clothes so obviously Persian, and meant to act just like everyone else – mildly horrified at the intruder in her country. But the woman called a greeting in Persian to someone else and Josie felt the Persian her parents had taught her turning in her mouth like a propeller. She hadn't spoken Persian since her parents moved to the other side of the country at the first rumors of war and Josie had to taste those words again. She'd only meant to speak a few words. But somehow she was still talking.

"But you got here first, didn't you?" the woman said. "Speak English, don't you? Not like me. You don't even wear anything on your head. Except that silly hat."

Josie clutched her red cloche hat, with the bow on the side, as though she could make it paint her back onto city streets that didn't care that she looked so Persian. But it didn't. It only sat on her head.

"Did you come here before the war then?" the woman asked. "I came ten months ago, as the war ended. Couldn't have told me two years ago I'd be living in America in 1919."

"No. No. I was born here. I'm not Persian. I don't know anything about Persia. I only speak it, that's all. My parents grew up in Persia, but they didn't tell me stories about what it was like."

"Not Persian?" The woman sighed and put her hands together. "I suppose neither am I, anymore." The woman offered Josie her hand and a short goodbye and then she was gone, into her city of diesel and greasy wheels.

Josie scratched her nails over her palm and watched the oil running under her shoes, dark purple rainbows catching the sunlight.

Josie went out that evening and sat at a cherry wood table, drinking red wines that smelled like oak and vinegar. She listened to jazz, the trumpets pounding their diamond-ringed fingers on the walls and the trombones swinging silk coattails.

Beside her, Patsy twisted her wedding ring in endless circles. Patsy watched the dancers a couple tables away and then the bar with blue glass bottles and then, flicking her finger under chin, looked up at Josie. "I was thinking, is it strange for you? All the Persians coming here?"

Josie looked down at her wine glass.

"Only I know your parents didn't talk about it much. Do you wish you'd known more about Persia?"

"I'm not Persian. I just speak the language."

"Well, that's a lot."

Josie kept from shaking her head.

"Have you tried to talk to the people who've come over?"

Well, she'd tried not to, hadn't she? If only her parents' language hadn't been so desperate to get out of her mouth. "Only a little. There's nothing I want to ask them."

Patsy frowned and pushed her chin into the side of her fist. Josie pressed her elbows together and tried not to feel offended. Patsy had never asked about those things before the war.

Josie looked at the band instead. The dancers kicked up narrow heels and shoe-polish black shoes. They rammed their chests together in whatever dance they liked – Charleston and Lindy Hop and Foxtrot all tangling up together and spitting out blue.

She looked at those dancers and saw paint – *Vogue* covers trailing gold feathers, blaring green backlights, extending silk-draped arms and glossy paper lips. They looked like they'd been drawn that way, just like that. Just one more red blush on her cheek, one more stroke in his coattails, and it'll be perfect. Ready to stamp on a thousand covers and ship to the world so everyone else can paint their own face that way.

People didn't ask Josie to dance anymore. They saw her colors and her angles and she could see them thinking it – *Persian*.

And she had to hold her fingers against her eyelids, afraid gasoline would came out.

There hadn't been much dancing during the war, at least not with the people she knew. They'd all giddily jumped into their Victory gardens, fluttered their rationing stamps like romance novels, knitted socks, and saved lint. Josie had started staying home, holding the blinds open with her fingers and scratching at the city that was slothing off her like paint in bleach. Her roommates bought window boxes and started two herb gardens. They didn't ask her to help and, depending on the day, she was either glad or offended.

Josie started marking days on her wall, like a factory would mark the number of days since the last accident. She was marking the days since someone had called her *dahati* and spat at her feet.

"That's a Persian word," she wanted to say. "You don't even know what it means." It got worse when Persia was annexed.

She'd danced before the war. It was easier then, when no one was thinking about Persia. She'd danced with her friends after midnight and too many sugar cakes. She'd danced with strangers sometimes and when she'd closed her eyes, she was the right angle of a window, the streamlined perfection of a skyscraper.

She was marble steps and ceramic floor titles the color of champagne. She was nameless and unnamed and everyone else was too. Names were just rouge and a new set of gloves. She always forgot them under her chair, or they would fall from her pocket on the way home. And the dancers would be all the steps and tiles across the city again, making squares and triangles out of their bodies. And then there was no thinking about her and them, because they were all painted just the same.

For a few days Josie thought, if she could avoid the black-slick towns where the Persians – Americans – were filling up the houses and thickening the air with the smell of roasted lamb, people wouldn't know when they looked at her. They wouldn't hear the residual Persian on her lips or see the oil in her footprints.

She walked through dance halls painted with blocks of blue and red and hoped it would smear off onto the back of her legs. Outside the Art Deco Expo, the streets were silver and polished, gutters running with paint like dancing shoes and golden cities. If only she didn't feel like an accidental smudge on the paintings of pink dancing ladies in furs. Why couldn't she press her face to their cool indifference and sink their arms to dance the waltz?

And then someone called out *dahati* and she had to erase the chalk mark tally with her arm.

She didn't mean it, but on Sunday she was standing at the edge of one of those towns, watching women in hijabs and men with dark hair. Josie walked the tight, labyrinth alleys and people watched her pass their windows. She rubbed her hands on her skirt and tried not to stare back.

Josie walked until she saw the woman she'd met before. The woman raised a hand.

"You came back, I see. Come into my house and eat a meal. We have rice, pumpkin, onions, and chicken. I miss our pomegranates. You don't have any here."

Josie held her arms over her chest. "I was just passing through."

"Of course. And every passing through deserves a meal. It's well past noon. You must be hungry. You don't look like you've eaten all day."

Josie protested inside her mouth, but she was already so many alleyways into this corner of town. It hardly seemed to matter if she went inside one of the houses.

"I live with three sisters who came here together. We like to sit together with a fire going hot. It keeps the flies away, and the men." The woman patted her hijab, orange today, and led Josie into a little door with cracks around the brass doorknob. "The women will like to see you. They'll like to hear you speak Persian, so they know someone who's not losing her teeth is still speaking it. Only a few months and they can't remember that their brother's children speak Persian back home. The younger ones here are eating up English as quick as they can."

The room was made of brick, mortar falling out and leaving mouse holes. A yellow rug, colored like burnt chemicals, was laid at the center of the floor and worn threadbare at the edges. Three women crouched beside a fireplace, spooning rice and stew into bowls.

"One more bowl," the woman said and another bowl appeared beside the others.

Josie wrinkled her purse under her arm and wished she had something to give them for the meal. Something so it would feel like an exchange of goods and not a familiar thing you did for a friend.

The woman told Josie the other women's names. Josie cringed under the pronouncement, unable to keep the unfamiliar words on her tongue or in her head. Her family hadn't lived with other Persians. She'd learned Samuel, Mary, Peter, and Beatrice. She didn't know these names and couldn't even hold them long enough to look at them before she dropped them. The only name she swallowed was of the woman who'd brought her here, Ava.

"Josephine was born here," Ava said.

The other women smiled, nodded. They sat along the edges of the rug, placing a bowl for Josie at one corner.

"Why did you come here?" Josie asked, hunched around her bowl, holding the broth on her tongue until it was almost cool.

One of the women shrugged. "It was like someone built a bridge and I wanted to know what was on the other side. I thought, on the other side the world won't be made of the same things or even the same color. I wanted to see it. It was so strange. They say, 'You're the same country now as another country. But that country is so far away. So many days of travel. Over there, they don't even speak your language.' What is all in the middle that isn't America?"

The second woman said, "Our country is leaking. Fuel, gas, oil. It all leaks over here. Even us." She smiled and laughed a little.

Ava nodded. "A whole city leaked out, drain pipes and gutters, wet pavement and spinning wheels, oil lamps and dusty glass. The city leaked through the ocean, under our feet, all the way to America. That's the city we're in now, with all of us in it."

Ava laid a hand on Josie's arm. "It wasn't just America that did it. Persia did it too. They both wanted the oil over here and it was cheaper for both of them. No tariffs, you see."

"Sometimes," the second woman said, "I think that they signed the treaty and all they were talking about was oil. Then at the end of it when people started moving, Americans suddenly remembered that Persia was made of people too and if you want to take over a country, you have to take its people too. I think they forgot that, really."

Ava said again, as she'd said to Josie several days before, "People look at us and they see oil. Then they forgot about the people underneath."

Josie scratched her nails over the bowl and was sorry the smell wasn't a familiar thing to her. She wanted a thrill to run through her stomach and her neck and she wanted to remember a little room where her parents had fed her rice, roast meat, and just the right spices. She wanted them to have told her, 'This is what we ate, when we were small like you. Maman used to make this for me and tell me to leave a little on my plate, to show I wasn't greedy.'

Josie looked at the four women. "What do you do during the day?"

"We take shifts at a factory. Two at a time," Ava said. "They don't recognize between us, so we switch – Monday, Wednesday, Friday and Tuesday, Thursday, Saturday. We take apart airplane engines. They're making car engines further down the line." Ava rubbed her fingers together, like they were still slick with the grease of her job.

"Do you like it?"

Ava shrugged.

"They're long hours," the second woman said. "I didn't work back home. I had a husband, but he died at war."

"At least there's enough that we can give you some rice and some stew," another woman said.

"Is it better?" Josie asked.

Ava clucked her tongue. "What is better? It is different."

The second woman raised her head. "I might go back. It's hard here, and in ways I don't like. People shout at us, even though they signed the treaty. We were so far away. They didn't have to. They could have left us – Ottoman, Persian, Arab. But they wanted to drink us down and fuel their cars and throw their planes higher into the sky. I didn't say no. Not even to my politicians who nodded and said they wanted to be part of this different country and sell oil without tariffs. The people here shouldn't get to say no back to me. I don't know if they even think before they start shouting."

Ava shook her head. "It was hard there too."

Another woman patted the second woman's hand and smiled in what seemed a silent, small disagreement with Ava.

"What do you do?" Ava asked.

"I'm a typist at an architecture firm," Josie said. "My parents moved away a few years ago, so I found an apartment with a few other girls and started working at the firm." She scraped up the rest of her rice, turning her knees towards the women. "I've tried really hard to understand everything I'm typing. I didn't study architecture and I don't know all the terms, but I've been learning and keeping up on my math and studying styles – the firm is influenced by a lot of French designs."

"Do you design anything?"

"I'd like to. I sketch things sometimes, although I'm no good at perfectly straight lines."

"Josie," one of the women said, "where is your Čahār Šanbé Sūrī?"

Josie cringed all over again, toes pressing down into the rug. "I beg your pardon...?"

Ava leaned over. "It's a spring festival. You must come here. It's not so long from now. Just next week. On Wednesday."

"Oh." Josie gathered up her bag in her arms. "I don't know. I'll have to look at my calendar."

"Yes." Ava and the other women stood with Josie.

"Thank you," Josie said. "It was good. Thank you."

She turned too quickly and left too quickly, her feet drawing scuffs on the ground. She walked with her head down, rubbing the hairs on her arms the wrong way.

Planes hummed through the clouds, black-spotted wings tilting as the sky around them filled with smoke and fuel. They traced the streets with dirty patterns, cutting through cafes and church steeples with their shadows. Josie imagined petroleum gathering like dewdrops on the air and falling onto her face, running down her cheeks.

Josie traced the lines of the buildings with her fingers. She decided not to go to the spring festival. She decided to go to a bar and listen to jazz and dance until the floor had pulled her insides out through her feet. She decided it would be easy.

Josie sat in her corner, at her cherry wood table, drinking wine. She curled her fingers against the table and pushed her back into her chair, afraid someone would look at her and mutter that word. The saxophone rubbed like corroded metal over her ear and scratched at her skin. Her friends danced and she lost them in the low lights.

Josie stared at a poster in dull washes of green and yellow that told people to welcome their new sisters and brothers. She couldn't focus on the faces drawn with jovial grey lines.

What was all in the middle that wasn't America? Were there people there building a sky bridge out of fighter jets or a sea bridge out of black smoke? Was it empty space with no people at all, just an invisible wall between America and itself? Josie wondered which side had reached out and wrapped their finger and thumb around the other country's border. She wished she could pull back a little and snap the bridge; watch it collapse like an airplane falling in juttering arcs towards trees and towns.

She drank more wine when she realized she was thinking about things she'd decided not to think about. When Patsy sat two seats away, waving her husband back onto the dance floor, Josie turned to her.

"How's the dancing?" Josie asked.

"Good." Patsy smiled, wiping sweat from her hair and brow with her pinkie. "You should dance more. You don't dance so much these days."

Josie shrugged.

"You know, I was thinking about what you said the other day and I just don't understand. I think it would be exciting that the Persians are coming here. It's something that you can own, when a lot of other people can't. You can say, these are my people."

"We're all American now." Josie's arms slid down the edge of the table until her wrists rested on the wood and her shoulders hunched by her ears.

Patsy pushed on her cheek with her thumb. "I don't think anyone thinks of it like that. It's a little strange, spending a couple years thinking really hard, I'm American. I have to plant carrots and tomatoes and buy war bonds and save nickels and eat corn instead of wheat. I have to tell my brother, yes, you got to go and be a soldier. Now it's, 'There are people who live really far away and they're America too.' I know they didn't fight against us in the war, but they weren't on our side either. They were a place where the two sides showed up and fought each other." Patsy scratched the table with a ring's stone. "It's so far away."

Josie nodded.

"But so many people are coming anyway." Patsy spread out her fingers. "Anyway, why not call yourself Persian, even if it isn't a country anymore?"

"There's nothing wrong with it." Josie picked up her glass and watched the wine leave red drops on the side of the glass. "I wasn't Persian growing up. I never thought about that. Now you look at me and call me Persian. But if I did say I was Persian, I wouldn't change because of it. I was still born here."

Josie tried again to focus on the poster, but it was too dark, too far away. The colors looked so dim. They were the wrong blocks of color, outlined in lines that were too smooth, fading into the green background.

"I was born here too, but I still tell people I'm Irish sometimes," Patsy said.

"Okay. But no one said you had to call yourself that."

Josie's hands weren't as solid as they'd once been. They weren't steeples and spires printed on magazine covers. They weren't the buildings she'd sketched onto napkins and journal pages. She wanted to just be those buildings, the designs of offices that would be built here, be distinctively part of this country.

It would have been alright too, she thought, if her hands had been something else; if they had a little grease under her nails from cooking rice and kababs. Or if they toured in circles her neighbors' houses for dinner, gathering once a week to pray on thick, red rugs. If they were the metal on the inside of a plane wing, left scraped across a wall in a city far, far away. But they weren't that.

Her hands were flaking, dripping, getting the table wet, and leaving smears of themselves behind her.

She looked up at a man and the look on his face was unfriendly, suggesting she'd done something to him. Simply by being there. She saw the word forming on his lips, about to spill out onto the table in front of her.

"That's our word," she said, standing. "*Dahati* is Persian."

The man squeezed his lips shut, pulling back a step.

Josie pushed her curled fingers up over her mouth. "I think I'll go home then." Josie fled and forgot to tell Patsy goodbye.

In the middle of the night she woke and her feet felt wet when she reached down to touch them. It was sweat, she was sure, since she'd been buried under layers of folded blankets, but in the darkness it felt slimy and black.

She sat with her elbows pushed between her knees, rubbing her fingers together, until the window glass began to turn light blue. She decided to go to the festival and decided not to. She decided it would be impolite not to go and assured herself she had plans. She shivered at the thought of someone seeing her walking into that part of town again and wanted to go just to spite that sort of person. She told herself she was Persian whether she liked it or not and told herself that was stupid since Persia wasn't a country anymore. She told herself what mattered was where she was born and what mattered was where her ancestors were from.

But, really, she couldn't pretend people didn't still think of Persia as their country. And she couldn't pretend there were people who were not Persian who thought of Persia as some people's country. And she did speak Persian. Her parents and all her family were Persian, even if she hadn't met most of them. It seemed the most she could do was call herself what she was rather than wait for other people to slather their own words on her.

When she got out of bed, she ran her fingers back and forth over her calendar, like she could rub off the numbers and boxes. There was nothing on

Wednesday and she couldn't come up with any possible reason not to go to the festival.

On Wednesday, Josie stood outside Ava's door, pushing the loose cloth of her bag into as many folds as her fingers were able. People passed behind her and it felt like they were looking. She pulled her hair over her shoulder, wishing she'd tied up under her hat, and knocked.

Ava appeared a moment later, brushing crumbs off her fingers. "Good evening," she said.

"Good evening."

"Come in, then. We have all kinds of good things." Ava turned and Josie followed her into the little room. There was a small group gathered at the edge of the fire. "Noodle soup, pistachios, almonds, hazelnuts, dried figs. We couldn't find apricots, but there's fried garlic and spearmint. Just like back home."

One of the women Josie had met before stood and came to place her hands on Josie's arms. "We weren't sure you'd come. We're so glad. The men are about to start a little fire."

"I told them we ought to light it in the street, but they're afraid to," Ava said. "That's how we did it back home, you see – out in the street. But they say people around here won't understand."

The other woman smiled and went to fetch a bowl of soup.

"Um." Josie reached into her bag. "I brought wine, if that's alright. It's a type I drink at a local place. There's dancing there. Anyway, here it is."

"Oh, you didn't have to," Ava said as she took the bottle, staring at the faint sketches on the label and then back at Josie.

"I know. It's a thank you, for inviting me. I appreciate it, really."

"Well, then. Thank you."

Ava turned and settled the bottle at the table where bowls were being filled. Josie watched several men roll away the rug, clearing the dust from the concrete floor so they could light a pile of tinder and broken twigs.

Ava returned to stand by Josie. "We make wishes tonight. If you're lucky, they come true."

"What do you wish for?" Josie asked.

Ava shrugged. "I have wished for better doors and better clothes. I've wished for my parents to get enough food and, well, I'm not happy about it, but I sometimes wished they would die and I wouldn't have to care for them anymore. Though that's a bad wish and I'm sorry I made it. During the war, I wished the Ottomans would leave the war and armies would stop fighting on our soil.

"I was happy and proud of my country, that they didn't take a side. I'm sorry France and Germany and Russia and America scrabbled over our dirt. I wished once that America wouldn't sign a treaty and make us their country. I was afraid if they did, I would not be one whole Persian. I would be Persian-American. And I don't know anything about being America, so I was sure I would not treat that part as well as I should.

"I'll tell you, I left in part because if I stayed in Persia, I felt that that part of me that must now be American would be ignored. I would be Persian, with something in the back of my head telling me I was lying.

"I don't like not being one whole Persian and it would have been better not to sign the treaty, but it's better now to admit that I'm also American, because, one way or another, it's true now."

"Maybe I should wish for the treaty to be taken back," Josie said.

Ava laughed. "I would like to wish for that sometimes. But you may make a wish for yourself. It's all right. And if you don't want to, you don't have to jump over the fire. That's all right too."

Josie nodded. "I'll think about it."

Josie stood with the other women while the men laughed and the fire began to burn. It was a little thing, choking out black soot on the floor, tossing out grey ashes and yellow embers that burned away quickly. There would be a stain on the floor afterwards, like oil rubbed deep into the cracks. A man took a few steps back and then leapt over the fire, shouting something as he did. The other men clapped and did the same, one after the other.

Josie leaned over to one of the women who lived with Ava. "Tell me your name again."

"Mohtaram," she said.

A woman stepped out around Josie and hopped over the fire, bundling her skirts against her legs. She laughed and joked about how small the fire was this year.

"I burned away all my hem two years ago. A lamb could cross this. Why you men must not have any skills at all."

The women laughed and drowned out the men's protests.

Josie set down her bag and held her arms. She looked at the women, all wearing dresses much longer than hers, and the men still clapping. The noodles smelled almost familiar and she wanted them to be more so. She took a few steps forward and could feel the fire on her bare ankles as she came closer, like warm metal against her skin. When dressing, she'd thought about taking out one of her long skirts that touched the ground. If she wore long dresses and a hijab, she could look like these women, as she couldn't quite look like the painted faces and shining skyscrapers anymore. But it had seemed too formal and too on purpose. She liked the blue cotton standing at a perpendicular angle to her thighs.

She looked at the women behind her who smiled, waiting for her to jump. She went onto her tip-toes and stepped over the fire. For a moment she stood over it, pushing her skirt against her leg, although it wasn't long enough to be in any real danger of burning.

She decided not to make a wish. She decided to think instead that she was all right being here. She thought she would be all right coming back another day too. And she would be all right listening to jazz and dancing with her friends when it got too dark outside to see the sky. Maybe she would just dance with her friends for a while, just with people she knew, so she could stare down at their shoulders and kicking heels when she saw ugly words on other people's tongues. Thinking about that word, she wanted to go back home again and not leave her room. But she'd come out tonight. She could probably come out again on another night.

She skipped across, almost into the arms of one of the women, her feet like a small swing-out in the Lindy Hop, drawing a straight line in the dust with her heel. Ava clapped, moving around the fire towards Josie.

"Do you dance at all?" Josie asked. "I know only a few dances, but if you'd like to learn..."

Ava handed her a cup of the wine. "I don't dance much. My knees have gotten very old. But if it's a slow dance, I can learn a little."

MICHAEL JAN FRIEDMAN

HOPE

As Buri stood in front of the fellow he believed was Cornelius Rosencrans, train wheels rumbling beneath their feet, he hoped he hadn't made a mistake.

The figure before him, folded into a generously upholstered, black-leather chair in the corner of the wood-paneled railcar, was all but buried in the pages of *The Wall Street Journal. And until I see his face,* Buri thought, *I can't be entirely certain, can I?*

There was still the chance, however minute, that it was it some other well-to-do fellow with a plastering of grey hair, a substantial paunch, and the thick, sweet smell of deodorant about him.

Then again, who else rode this car at this day and time? Who else kept the shades drawn on even this brightest of spring days, preferring the drabber light of the gas lamps on the wall? And—most tellingly—who else would have kept a glass of straight-up absinthe on the table beside him?

Rosencrans had a particular fondness for absinthe sans water. Buri had learned that in his study of the man. So more than likely, he had the right fellow after all. *Yes*, he decided, *it's Rosencrans. It has to be.*

He felt relieved. It would have been awkward beyond measure if he had pulled a pistol on someone *other* than Rosencrans.

Not that the man had taken any notice of the firearm. He was too busy with his newspaper.

After a while, Buri cleared his throat. But Rosencrans didn't so much as glance up at him. All he did was refold his newspaper and say, with some irritation, "Go away, damn you. I'll let you know when I'm ready for dinner."

The situation would have laughable were it not for the life-and-death nature of Buri's mission. Again, he cleared his throat.

This time the rich man muttered a curse, thrust aside his newspaper with undisguised pique, and shifted in his chair so as to glare at Buri through narrowed eyes. "I said—"

He stopped in mid-sentence, and his eyes narrowed even more, and his gaze fell—ultimately encompassing the pistol in the younger man's hand. After a moment or two, in which he seemed to digest the reality of the firearm, the grey-haired man looked up at Buri again.

"You're not my cook," he said, a tinge of irony in his voice.

But no fear. Not even surprise, really, now that he had moved past that first, frozen moment.

Like most men, Cornelius Rosencrans had changed over the years. True, he had the same thick moustache turned up at the corners, the same humorless eyes, the same lantern jaw. But the moustache was grey where once it had been a dark brown, and the eyes had distinct bags under them, and the jaw had softened to jowls.

But it was Rosencrans, all right. The same man whose newspaper picture Buri's mother had kept in her dresser drawer for the last fifteen years. The man she had cursed—bitterly, red faced, calling on every saint she could muster—every time her husband's name came up.

Rosencrans, who—for all his canniness when it came to business—had become a man of habits, and had allowed his habits to become too well known. The fact that he liked to travel between Boston and New York in a particular private rail car, for instance, heading south every Monday at nine-fifteen and back north every Friday at four-thirty.

Or that he liked a glass of absinthe, uncut with water, to accompany him in either direction.

"Astute of you to notice," Buri said, with the same tinge of irony. "In case you were wondering, your cook has taken the afternoon off, encouraged by an abiding dislike of you and the prospect of a sum sufficient for passage to Chicago, where he intends to pursue a lifelong dream on the stage—a sum he will, unfortunately for him, never receive."

Rosencrans's lip curled. "You're a Hummer."

"An impressive observation," Buri said. He indicated the glass of absinthe with the business end of his pistol. The liquor, as green as grass after a rainstorm, took up only half the glass. "I guess it's true what they say—you *can* hold your drink."

"Definitely a Hummer," said Rosencrans, his tone one of unabashed arrogance. "I can smell the milk on your breath."

Buri didn't take the bait. "We say Hummerlander," he replied evenly. "Hummer is impolite."

The rich man went on as if he hadn't heard the rebuke. "My bodyguard will be back in a minute."

Buri shook his head. "You don't have a bodyguard."

Rosencrans sat back in his chair. "Really? Then why don't I look the least bit worried?"

"Because not looking worried is an art, and you've mastered it."

"And what have *you* mastered, boy? The art of robbing your betters?"

"I haven't come to rob you," Buri said.

The older man laughed a short, ugly laugh. "I don't believe you. Hummers only come wandering down the seaboard for one reason—to steal money from real Americans. Are you an outlaw?"

"As a matter of fact," said Buri, "I am."

"There, you see? All of you, sneaking down here and rooting in people's pockets for greenbacks, so you can go home to your miserable farms and make good on your miserable debts and get your miserable lives back in form. Well, Hummer, I haven't got any money for you beyond the few ragged dollars in my pocket—and they won't get you far."

More than likely, Rosencrans was telling the truth about the contents of his pockets. And unlike most men of his station, he didn't wear jewelry. Not even a watch. But then, Buri had known all of that going in.

"How inconvenient," he said.

"For *you* it is." Rosencrans leaned forward and poked the air between them with a soft, ruddy finger that had never known the plow. "If I were you, boy, I'd jump off the train before I took another breath, just jump off and hope not to break a leg in the process. Because otherwise I'd find myself in shackles the moment I reached Pennsylvania Station."

"If you haven't noticed," Buri said, "you're in no position to give advice. Perhaps you can use some yourself."

Rosencrans snorted. "And what would that be?"

"When a man has a gun pointed at you, it's best not to call him *boy.*"

The grey-haired fellow chuckled and sat back in his chair. But he didn't offer anything resembling an apology.

"Why do you still make the trip to New York?" Buri asked. "You've got no business there anymore. Your divorce has gone through. You can make all your stock transactions from Boston. And the Lubec Mine Company is finally closed."

Rosencrans's forehead furrowed from his eyebrows to his hairline. After all, what would a common thief know about Lubec?

"Do I *know* you?" he demanded.

"You knew my father. He was an outlaw as well."

"What's your name?"

"Buri. Buri Jonsson."

Rosencrans scowled. "So your father's name was Jon. That's no help. I've known a great many Jons from Hummerland. What was his last name?"

"Gudmarsson."

Buri saw a glint of recognition in the older man's eyes. "Gudmarsson..." he repeated.

"You remember him."

Rosencrans tilted his head slightly, seeming to view his antagonist in a new light. "You don't look like him. Not in the least."

"I favor my mother's side of the family."

"Thank your stars you do. Your father, if I may say, was rather a weasel of a man."

Again, Buri exercised restraint. "You know why he came to you, don't you?"

The rich man shrugged. "The way all Hummers came to me. He ran up a debt to someone and couldn't pay it."

"A man named Styrrson," Buri said.

Rosencrans dismissed the detail with a flip of his hand. "Whatever you say. Your father fell short of his obligation, that's the point."

Buri continued. After all, he was the one holding the gun. "Styrsson owned the neighboring farm. Some say he hated my father for a wrong neither of them spoke of. If so, he wouldn't have been the first to lay a trap for a fellow by lending him money.

"My father was to pay Styrsson back with a healthy dollop of interest besides. The term was one year.

"Unfortunately, my father didn't come close to discharging his debt. In his heart, he must have known he was incapable of doing so, that he just didn't have a head for business. But the alternative had been to give up the farm without a fight, leaving us homeless, and he couldn't have done that either."

"And in Hummerland," said Rosencrans, picking up the thread, "a man who defaults on his debt is made an outlaw at your Allthing. Albeit a *lesser* outlaw." He reached for his absinthe, took a sip, and savored it—all without taking his eyes off Buri. "You people love your little laws, don't you?"

"As a matter of fact," said Buri, "we do." No hint of irony this time.

"I don't know why Washington allows them," said Rosencrans. "Hummerland and Louisiana, two heathen backwaters I'd as soon see cut loose from the Union. Were it up to me, I'd dump them in a heartbeat."

"And yet," said Buri, "we persist as states, and have done so for more than eighty years."

Rosencrans settled back into the cushions of his chair. "In any case, your father had three years to get up the money. Yes?"

Whatever discomfort he had experienced on seeing Buri was long gone. He looked now as if he were discussing the prospects of some racehorse rather than addressing a man who could kill him with a twitch of his finger.

"Yes," Buri said. "Three years."

"And if he failed, he would become a *full* outlaw. In that event, he would have no more rights in your state than a thieving wolf. He could be accosted, or maimed, or even killed—by anyone, anywhere, under any circumstances—nor would his assailant be held accountable."

"Yes again," Buri said.

Rosencrans shook his head. "The most outlandish legal system in all the world."

Buri shrugged. "The customs of our forbears."

"Of course, your Viking forbears. I know the story as well as anyone. But this is the nineteenth century, nearly the twentieth. Don't you think it's time to put away childish things?"

"You quote the Bible."

"Corinthians," Rosencrans said, and took another sip of his absinthe.

"I'm surprised you know it so well."

The older man sloshed the absinthe about in his glass. "I'm surprised *you* know it at *all*. I didn't think Hummers read, what with all the plowing and seeding and harvesting they have to do."

"We read more than you think, Mr. Rosencrans. Lately, I've become familiar with the work of a fellow named Dostoevsky. A Russian. You know him?"

"You've read Dostoevsky? Really. And what wisdom has the fellow imparted to you?"

"To live without Hope is to cease living. That is one bit of wisdom he imparted."

"Hope," Rosencrans repeated, as if it were the punch line of a sad, old joke. "He that lives upon hope will die fasting. You know who said *that*?"

"I don't," Buri confessed.

"Benjamin Franklin. One of the fathers of our country, you'll be interested to know. If you want to read, read *him*, not some God-forsaken Russian."

"We were speaking of my father," Buri said.

"Right. Now there was a man starving on hope."

Buri felt a pang, put it aside. He wouldn't give Rosencrans the pleasure of seeing his discomfort.

"The hope," Buri said, "that he—like so many others who had been outlawed at the Allthing—could in three years' time earn the money he needed, in your mine. After all, you were advertising a handsome wage in our newspapers. Never mind the danger—the fact that the mine flooded when the tide got too high, and that men perished that way from time to time. It would be worth it if it gave my father a chance to clear his name—a chance to return to his family and his farm."

"That's the other thing you love," said Rosencrans. "Your damned *farms*. Not a Hummer in my mine that didn't yearn for a clod of dirt in Hummerland."

"My father was an exception—not that you would have had occasion to know that. His farm was only a means to an end. It was his family he held in high esteem, his family he pined for while in your employ. Three years away from us, his wife and his sons. . .that was torture for him. But it was nothing compared to the penalty for failing a second time to discharge his debt. If that came to pass, he would forfeit his family's companionship forever."

"The standard deal," Rosencrans observed.

"Like the agreement you made with him when he came to you seeking work in your mine. The standard deal. Except in the end, you cheated him. You paid him half of what his contract called for. *Half*."

Buri's voice finally betrayed his anger, and Rosencrans's gaze drifted to the younger man's gun.

"And my father," Buri continued, "wasn't the only Hummerlander you cheated. You cheated others as well."

"*Cheated*," said Rosencrans, as if the word were a piece of meat left in the sun. His face reddened, betraying some emotion of his own. "I had my reasons for restructuring the payroll. Sound reasons. Business reasons. Not that someone like you would understand them."

"What I understand," said Buri, under control again, "is that you overestimated the value of the mine when you purchased it."

Rosencrans's eyes turned steely. "What in blazes would a Hummer know about the worth of a mine?"

"I know the veins there were never as big as you thought they would be. Around the mouth of the mine, in the side of the cliff, there were huge deposits of lead-rich galena ore--twenty or thirty tons' worth by some accounts, which is why the previous owner did rather well with his seaside operation. But once you got deeper into the mine, there was less. Much less."

"Rubbish," said Rosencrans, flushed now with anger. "There was plenty of ore. It was the accidents that ran us aground."

"Accidents?" Buri echoed. "Or calamities you could have avoided by evacuating the mine before the tide came in?"

"All the damned Hummers had to do was watch the time. Or the tide. A monkey could have survived."

"Was that the problem—their inability to watch the time? Did they not fear they would get less than their day's wages if they left the mine too early?"

Rosencrans harrumphed. "How do *I* know what they feared?"

"You know how they died, don't you? You saw the bodies as they were carted into town."

"Men die doing all sorts of things, not just mining lead."

"So you accepted their deaths as the cost of doing business. But your government didn't see the situation the way you did. They cited you for the danger in which your miners worked, day in and day out. Of course, you could have taken measures to mitigate that danger—"

"*Expensive* measures," Rosencrans snapped.

"No doubt. But time and again, you avoided doing so. Eventually, The Maine Mining Commission grew tired of your excuses and closed down your operation. You appealed, to no avail. This past September, you laid the Lubec Mining Corporation—if not the ghosts that haunt it—to its rest."

"The Mining Commission. A bunch of bleeding hearts. They didn't care that Hummers were working there of their own free will."

"Out of desperation."

"They needed the money, didn't they?"

"They needed what you offered, not what you paid."

Suddenly, Rosencrans was on his feet, his eyes popping. "I didn't create their problems, damn you. I offered them a goddamned *solution*." He stood there for a moment, fuming. Then he took a deep breath, let it out. "A solution," he said, and sat down again. "So what if they were paid a little less? It was still more than they would have gotten anywhere else."

"But not *enough*. At least, in my father's case. Not the amount you agreed on."

"So is that why you've come down here? Why you've invaded my rail car and pointed a gun at me? To get the other half of your father's wages?"

"At the time," Buri said, "I would have done *anything* to get those wages. But not now. You know what happened to my father, Mr. Rosencrans?"

"He went home, like they all did. At least, that was my understanding."

"Yes. He came home. And after three years, we couldn't have been happier to see him, or he us. I remember the way he hugged me, both loving and hating the way I had grown in his absence.

"But there were shadows under his eyes. My mother told me later that she knew something was wrong, even before he opened his mouth to speak—before he told her he had only half the money he owed. His employer, he said, had cheated him of the rest. A man named Rosencrans."

The older man looked down into his absinthe.

"Our Law," Buri said, "had been devised to protect those who had suffered at the hands of others. But it was up to the sufferer to carry out the sentence—if he could. Unfortunately for my father, Styrsson was more than capable of inflicting punishment.

"My father went to see him, hoping for leniency. It wasn't granted often, but it was worth a try. He begged Styrsson to understand. He had half the money—surely that counted for something. And he would get the rest as soon as he could, he swore it.

"Styrsson took the partial payment and thanked my father for his act of good faith. Then he shot him square in the forehead."

Rosencrans's eyes lifted from his drink, and they were angry. "And you think that's *my* fault? Not the fault of the bastard who trapped your father, as you say, and then pointed the gun and pulled the trigger? In your provincial little Hummer brain, you think the blame should be *mine*?"

Buri allowed a hint of his own anger to show. "What do *you* think, Mr. Rosencrans?"

His words hung in the unmoving air of the railcar. The rich man considered them for a moment. Then he said, "Let me tell you something about your father. You say he loved his family—that may be so. But he loved indolence more. His first six months here, he worked as hard as anyone. In the next six months, noticeably less so. And after that, hardly at all.

"My foreman spoke to him all the time, telling him he wasn't pulling his weight. For a day or two, he'd work a little harder, but there was no lasting effect. I myself spoke with him. Can you imagine? I let him sit across a desk from me, like a man.

"I told him that he would only be paid for the work he did. He said it was hard work, dangerous work. I told him that was the work he had contracted to do, and why he was being paid at the rate he was. If he wanted easier work, or safer, there were a hundred factories and two hundred farms that regularly hired men such as he.

"But of course, such employment would not yield the money he owed in a span as short as three years. So he remained with me—which is to say that I allowed him to do so. And in this, I tell you, I was benevolent. Probably too much so.

"Another mine operator would, without question, have cut him loose. After all, he was not merely an underachiever. He was also an anchor, dragging down morale. None of the other men liked him. They resented his laziness and his complaints. They were resolved to work off their debts, even if his prospects of doing so were dim.

"Maybe you don't believe me. Maybe you think I'm lying to save my skin. You know how to use a telephone? They've got those even in Hummerland, don't they? I'll give you a number. I'll give you a *dozen* numbers. I'll give you the money to make the calls. Talk to the men who worked with your father. Ask them what he was like down in the mine. See if I'm lying."

For the first time since he looked up and saw Buri standing there, Rosencrans sounded sincere. And for the first time as well, Buri believed him.

"You say my father was a ne'er-do-well," he said. "I have no trouble believing as much. It was his proclivity for daydreaming rather than doing his work that landed him in hot water to begin with. The farm he took over from my grandfather was a thriving one. In other hands, it would have remained so. In his, it ran up a hill of debt."

"Then. . .you know the truth?"

"I do."

Rosencrans looked puzzled. "And yet you're here, holding a gun on me."

"I'm not here for revenge. I have every right to it, but I'm not a vengeful man. It's not in my nature."

"Not vengeful, you say. And not after my money. Yet you've gone to a fair amount of trouble to confront me in my private railcar."

"Maybe I'm just curious," Buri said.

"To see what I would do if you pointed a pistol at me? Whether I'd puke my guts up in terror? Plead for my life?"

"I confess the question occurred to me."

Rosencrans didn't look ready to do either of those things. "And has your curiosity been satisfied?"

"It has."

The older man smiled to himself. "I knew it. If you were serious about killing me, you would have done it already. You just wanted to lord it over me, make me feel your family's misery."

"Something like that."

"Then let's dispense with any further drama, shall we? I'm going to make you an offer, and a generous one. Leave me and I'll forget any of this ever happened."

"You want me to trust you."

"Clearly. The question is…what do *you* want? Not to put a bullet in an old man. You need to go back to Hummerland and salvage what's left of your life."

"Maybe so." Buri lowered the gun.

"There you go," said Rosencrans, looking pleased. "You seem likeable enough—unlike your father. Maybe your creditors will find it in their hearts to cut a deal with you. Or, alternatively, you can remain in the civilized states and seek your fortune here."

"And never see my mother or my brother again."

Rosencrans held his hands out. "They can come here to see *you*."

"If they can afford the ticket. Most can't."

The older man made a sound of exasperation. "My God, man, must I solve *all* your problems? If that's all it will take to get you out of my hair, I'll pay for a couple of damned train tickets. Happy?"

"I appreciate the offer—but I can't see myself staying down here. There's too much distrust of Hummerlanders. Too many taunts. Too many whispers."

Rosencrans laughed. "What do you expect? You do things like *this*."

Buri didn't laugh in return. "You look at life differently from the way we do."

"Damned right we do. It's business. Nothing personal in it, no feuds, no grudges. Just business."

"I see the wisdom in that. In fact, it's business that brought me here."

Rosencrans looked at him askance. "You said you hadn't come for money."

"Not *your* money. But you see, you have value in Hummerland—value not only to my creditors, but to others as well. To everyone, in fact, who lost a loved one in your mine, or to a creditor because you cheated them out of the wages you promised them."

Rosencrans blanched and dropped his glass on the carpet. Some of the absinthe splashed his shoe.

Buri raised the gun again and took a step closer to his target. "I'm not very good at business, I concede that. And yet I stand to kill a man and make a profit from the killing. What do you think of that, Mr. Rosencrans?"

The older man didn't answer. Then a light appeared in his eyes. "You gave me hope," he said in a weak voice.

"Of course I did. Just as you gave hope to my father. It makes the end more painful, does it not—having seen a doorway and then having the door smashed in your face? So much more poignant. So much more satisfying."

Buri placed the nose of the gun against Rosencrans's forehead, and tightened his finger on the trigger.

"Not for you, of course. But," Buri said, "very much so for me."

The older man's eyes widened. "You bastard," he rasped.

Buri relaxed his finger on the trigger—and smiled—and pulled back the gun. "You thought you were a dead man. Admit it."

Rosencrans stared at him hollow-eyed, a bead of sweat tracing a path down the side of his face. "What...?"

"I needed to show you something—how vulnerable you are. You see, while your mine was open, no Hummerlander dared come after you. What you offered—the chance to clear a man's name—was too valuable.

"Now that your mine is closed, there's no longer a reason to spare your life. There will be more like me coming down from Hummerland, men seeking revenge for their fathers and their uncles who perished in your mine, or at the hands of their creditors. You will need protection from these men, Mr. Rosencrans, the kind of protection that only a Hummerlander—someone who knows them—can provide."

The older man took out a handkerchief and dabbed at his face. When he spoke, his voice shook with relief. "You--you want to be my..."

"Your *bodyguard*. At a substantial wage, of course. One that takes into account the fact that you've owed my family my father's money for some time, and that there should be interest paid on that sum."

Rosencrans drew a deep, trembling breath, and let his head fall into his hands. "Thank God," he moaned. "Thank God." And he began to weep—quietly at first, and then with great, wracking sobs. For all his bravado, it seemed, he had been fearful after all, and only now was that fear pouring out of him.

To be replaced by hope.

"Mr. Rosencrans," said Buri.

The older man looked up, his eyes red-rimmed. "Y-yes?"

"I was only joking, sir. " The Hummerlander raised his pistol again. "I *am* here to kill you."

And, counting on the rumbling of the train wheels to mask the report, he fired.

Keith R.A. DeCandido

WE SECEDED WHERE OTHERS FAILED

Good evening, folks! Welcome to President Tony's Saloon! Yeah, that's right, this is the place where Ernest Hemingway used to drink back in the day. See, this is the site of the original Sloppy Joe's, but the owners moved around the corner to that tourist trap on Duval. Tony Tarracino is the owner these days, even when he was President of the Conch Republic. All the most important Cabinet meetings were right here in this bar, matter of fact, back when he was President. Point of fact, he's talking about running against President Wardlow in '83. Not sure he's got much of a chance, though I guess we'll see next year, won't we?

Anyhow, enough of the tourist brochure. Where you two from? Chicago? Very nice. So what can I get you good folks?

Ooh, I'm sorry, no, I can't give you any alcohol. See, you're from the United States.

Yes, it's true, we originally seceded from the Union back in '25 because of Prohibition. Matter of fact, Hemingway was one of the people who pushed for it, especially after some Treasury Department goon decided to come down here and get all in our business. It was hurting the tourist trade, and they actually shut down the railroad! Most of the rumrunning was by boat, anyhow, but they had to go and cut off the train line, and that was that. All the Keys pulled out at that point and the Conch Republic of the Florida Keys was formed. Kept trying to get Hemingway to run for President of the Republic, but he wouldn't go for it.

You folks flew from Chicago and then took the train down from Miami, right? Yeah, that's the best way to do it. I mean, sure, you could get a connecting flight from Miami to the Mel Fisher Airport, but then you don't get the view.

Nothing in the world beats going across the Seven-Mile Bridge on the railroad, I'll tell you that for free.

Anyhow, since you came by train, you saw that checkpoint at the border up in Florida City? Yeah, I bet it delayed your train. It'll be worse on the way home. I guess I wouldn't blame you two if you flew home straight from Fisher. It's folks leaving that they're searching. Looking for refugees and drugs—drugs, mostly. I tell you, it hasn't been this bad here since all the nonsense with Kennedy and Cuba twenty years ago. I was a kid then, but I remember being scared to death that the U.S. would bomb us, just because we're allied with Cuba.

Or at least we were. That was back before Castro. You know that train line you came down on? It was trashed in a hurricane back in '35. Would've wiped the Republic out if Cuba hadn't paid to rebuild it. Rail was how they were getting their tobacco out anyhow, so they were motivated, and the U.S. wasn't about to help out an upstart bunch of islands that quit the Union.

What's that? Oh yeah, I heard some folks tell that story, that the U.S. offered to loan us money to build a road, but who'd want to drive through the Keys? Besides, I never bought that. U.S. don't give a tinker's damn about us. Which is just ungrateful. I mean, the Keys seceding was the big reason why Congress passed the Twenty-First Amendment back in '30.

Anyhow, you want to know why you can't have a drink. Well, to be fair, you can have a drink—but you'll have to renounce your American citizenship first. And then swear your loyalty to the Conch Republic.

See, there's a story behind this. We used to have a regular in here who was a conductor on the railroad. Artemio was on the first train that the U.S. border patrol detained at the Florida City stop back in April. Raised a big ruckus, especially once they started asking if he was a legal citizen of the Conch Republic. Artemio was born in Cuba, but his parents moved him to the Republic when Castro took over in '59. Those border patrol goons started accusing him of all kinds of things.

Now, Artemio didn't do a thing wrong. In fact, he's never done anything wrong. Hasn't done much right either, mind. Artemio's one of those fellas who dreams big, but doesn't really get to do much with it. He's always making noise about owning a boat and doing tours or scuba diving or fishing or some other thing, but he just kept working at the railroad and coming here to drink beer.

Oh yeah, he also played on the stage here a few times. And did a few acoustic sets, but he actually isn't that good. I think he finally sold his guitar, which we all counted as a kindness.

Anyhow, he gave the U.S. troops some static, as well he should've, if you ask me, and they arrested him. Didn't have any charges, just put him in cuffs and put him in a cell.

Well, President Wardlow didn't take too kindly to that. He flew up to Miami and had some words with the Border Patrol. Eventually, they let Artemio go, but it took a while.

Meantime, there were all kinds of protests. You probably heard about it. No? Well, I guess it isn't news up in Chicago, but it was a big deal here.

And the U.S. hasn't taken those guards away yet. Been months. Everyone has to go through the checkpoint like they're criminals or something. It's hurting the industry.

Well, the tourist industry, obviously. I mean, there hasn't been much tobacco coming up these days, but the Republic is still paradise as far as most folks are concerned. You know that President Harry Truman his own self retired here? He always said the saddest day in American history was when we seceded. Had a house over on Whitehead until he died back in '79.

Anyhow, we weren't about to turn people away, but we figured that the U.S. needed some kind of retaliation. So no alcohol for American citizens.

Oh yeah, you noticed that I said Artemio used to be a regular. You Chicagoans are observant folks.

See, the main thing that annoyed Artemio was that they were accusing him of running drugs on the side. In fact, part of why they set up the checkpoint, or so they said, was because of reports that a train conductor was running heroin. Artemio was the only Hispanic working on the train, so they went after him. That was a big reason why he got so mad, and also something that President Wardlow pointed out to them when he went to Miami.

Anyhow, Artemio came home with the president and he got a special party night here at the bar. It was huge—all the living presidents of the Republic were here. In fact, it was the first time Presidents Tarracino, Wardlow, Heyman, and Buffett were all in the same place at the same time.

Which made the next thing that happened really bad for poor Artemio. See, those folks on the checkpoint weren't total morons. There was a conductor who was dealing, it just wasn't Artemio.

See, one day there was a nasty rainstorm, and one of the conductors, a fella named Eugene, had his house all flooded. He never showed up to Flagler Station, busy as he was trying to save his house, so Artemio got a frantic call on his day off to come to work to conduct the middle cars of the 10:50 train back up to Miami.

He busted his butt and got himself over to Flagler and put on his uniform and got on the train when it pulled in at 10:30.

And then at 10:45, some little guy came on the train, put a package in the overhead rack, then left the train. Artemio went and checked it out, and it had Eugene's name on it.

There was a whole mess of heroin inside the package.

Now, Artemio, he had himself a decision to make. Eugene was his colleague. What's more than that, he was his friend. That time he got up on the stage here to play with his acoustic guitar? Eugene was the bass player in the band he sat in with.

It wasn't just that, though. See, Artemio really didn't like being arrested just because he was Cuban. How could he just rat out his friend to people who would do that?

But then, there was this package full of heroin. Was he just supposed to ignore it?

He decided to hide the package in his cubby on the train, and when the 10:50 went over the Seven-Mile Bridge, he tossed it out the window.

When his shift ended, he went straight to Eugene's house to ask him what the hell was happening.

He got there, and Eugene was screaming at somebody on the phone. Then when Artemio showed up, Eugene hung up and screamed at Artemio, asking him where the stuff was.

When Artemio told Eugene that he threw it into the Gulf of Mexico, Eugene kind of went nuts. Asked him how he could do that to him, he ruined his deal, his connection in Miami was going bonkers, and all kinds of other things.

No apology for putting Artemio in the jackpot like that. No gratitude for not turning him in.

The next day, Artemio turned Eugene in to the Conch Police. The day after that, he went to Flagler Station and resigned from his job as a conductor, and then came in here for a beer afterward. He raised a toast to Eugene, then left.

Nobody's seen him since.

But those guards are still up there. Still stopping trains, and still harassing Republic citizens and tourists alike. And there's less and less of those tourists because of it.

Eugene? Oh, he got arrested, and then we extradited him to the U.S. Last I heard, he was giving state's evidence to put that Miami connection of his away.

Anyhow, we lost two conductors, and that's just the beginning of it. Sure, Eugene was a jerk, but he was our jerk. And you know what? That checkpoint didn't stop him. Didn't even find him. It was one of ours who found it out, and one of ours who got him arrested. Meantime, people are cancelling their trips because of the checkpoints.

So that's the deal. The U.S. is screwing us, so we're screwing her people. If you want to have a beer or a margarita or alcohol of any kind, you'll have to renounce the United States of America and embrace the Conch Republic. The good news is, you'll be welcomed as citizens of the finest country in the world.

What?

Oh, no, of course not! No, you can keep your passport. We understand that you have families and friends back home, and we promise to keep your new-found citizenry in this fine Republic our little secret.

Promise.

Okay, hold up your right hands. Now repeat after me:

I, whatever your name is—doesn't have to be yours, just pick a name—do swear my fealty to the Conch Republic of the Florida Keys. As a newly sworn citizen of the Republic, I do also swear the following:

I swear to greet others with joy and conviviality.

I swear to forego the wearing of socks.

I swear to embrace the humidity.

I swear to consume as much fresh fish as I can possibly eat.

I swear to smoke only Cuban cigars, if I smoke at all.

I swear to imbibe the drink of my choice, whether alcoholic or not, at least once a day.

I swear to listen to as much live music as I can stand—preferably at President Tony's—you don't actually have to swear that part, we just prefer it here.

I swear to worship the sunset at the end of every day.

I swear to share this good fortune with others.

And I swear to live completely free of stress and worry for all the days I am in the Conch Republic.

Congratulations, Mr. and Mrs. Longno, you are now officially citizens of our fair land. Allow me to pour you each a beer.

Here you go. No, no charge. First one's on the house. After all, it's your first drink as a citizen of our fine nation, the least we can do is provide the first drink gratis.

A toast: to Artemio, wherever he may be!

Gordon Linzner

INDEPENDENCE DAY, HUZZAH!

"Ms. Parsons? Lucy Parsons?"

Aluki Parsons turned to face the earnest young man pushing through Pearson Airport's holiday crowds. The Amalgamated Press International intern looked barely old enough to legally drink, and obviously hadn't read the sign he was holding.

"Aluki," she corrected, looking up to meet his eyes.

"A-loo-kay," he responded awkwardly.

"Key." She waved her pedantry away. "Close enough."

"Jason Rathbone. Welcome to Toronto. I'll be your aide and liaison during your assignment. Can I collect your luggage?"

Parsons looked at his extended hand, shook it, then hitched her shoulders to indicate her backpack. "I've only got carry-on. I expect to be back in New York the day after. Few people take this Northern Secession movement seriously." Exactly the kind of story she would have turned down when she worked at United World Press, before that wire agency downsized. She'd been at API almost five years now, and still hadn't worked her way back to that level. Considering how many of her colleagues now worked as Uber drivers or short-order cooks, though, it could be worse.

A handful made passable livings doing their own news blogs, a route Parsons often considered. If she left API, though, she wanted go out on her own terms, with one last big memorable story to her byline. Not likely to happen anytime soon, given these lightweight holiday assignments.

"The bosses must think it's newsworthy," Rathbone said, defending his employers almost by rote, as he led her through the maze of Terminal One to the passenger pick-up gate. "Or they wouldn't have bothered flying you in from the New York office instead of using one of our freelancers."

Parsons' lips thinned. She had her suspicions about why she was given this assignment, despite being assured that one of the interviewees represented her ancestral home of Nunavic, and that her background was mere coincidence.

The heat outside the terminal was almost too thick to walk through. The sun sat low, to her right. She'd been due around noon, but high winds and heavy holiday traffic delayed her flight several hours. The air was calm now, oppressively so. She hoped for a breeze off of Lake Superior when they got downtown.

Tomorrow promised to be a brutally hot Fourth of July.

The driver of the Royal Limousine climbed out to open the back door. "Do you want to stop by the office," asked the intern, "or go directly to the hotel?"

"Is there anyone at the office I need to talk to right now, Jason?"

"I doubt it. For certain, Mr. Robineaux won't be there. We're doing the live podcast interview from your hotel. The equipment's already in your suite. Greg will get there about nine tomorrow to set it up and answer any technical questions. Greg Bingay. He's good."

Cool air engulfed the reporter as she settled into the smooth leather back seat, backpack on the floor between her feet. No point in opening the boot for one small bag. "I'm glad to hear it. Less for me to worry about. Any idea why we're doing it live when it'll go up on the website within an hour?"

"Independence Day. API is doing live podcasts all day, through the night's fireworks." Rathbone addressed the limo driver, then entered through the opposite door to join Parsons.

"How soon do we reach the Best Western?" she asked.

Jason started. "They didn't update you?"

"That's your job, to take the heat for delivering bad news." She offered a reassuring smile. "Don't tell me I've been downgraded to a B&B."

"The opposite. You're staying at, and broadcasting from, the Benedict Arnold suite at the Thorp International Hotel and Tower. The space was comped to API by Travis Thorp himself."

Parson grunted. "Mr. T looking for some media good will and free publicity, no doubt, after those bribery and sex scandals. Now I know why the last minute switch from Quebec. Are the protests still happening, demanding the hotel tower be renamed?"

"They've thinned out, but we still get a few every day, handing out flyers and gathering names on a petition. Not that it would be legally binding. The police are being fairly hands-off. They don't want a repeat of the G20 conference disaster."

"Glad I'm not covering that story." She offered the intern a thin smile. "You can call me Lucky, by the way. Most people do. But not, I'd suggest, when your bosses are around."

"Thank you, ah, Lucky. To answer your question, ten, maybe fifteen minutes to the hotel."

The limo started its circular route out of Pearson.

"Relax, Jason. I was once in your shoes. So, is that bulging panel behind the driver's seat a mini-bar, or is he just glad to see me?"

"I'll check." He fumbled with the latch, lowered a flap that became a table with glasses already in their holders, and fished out a long thin bottle. "Just this. Looks unopened." He held it out for her inspection.

"Sortilege Whiskey and Maple Syrup Liqueur," she read aloud. "Sounds like something to pour over ice cream. Or pancakes. Well, when up north..." She accepted a glass, watched the brass-colored liquid trickle out, held up a hand when it was one-third full. "Pour one for yourself, too, Jason. It's almost seven. You must be off the clock by now."

"Thank you, ah, Lucky. Can I get you anything else?"

She took a long, slow sip of the sweet liqueur. "A colleague told me I should try the peameal bacon sandwich while I'm here. Anywhere to stop on the way?"

Aluki Parsons sat cross-legged at the head of the king-size bed, rereading her notes, though she'd already memorized the talking points. On the wall across from her was a competent but unremarkable print of a painting of Benedict Arnold, hero of the Battle of Quebec City, taking the place of the late General Montgomery to accept General Carleton's surrender. In the adjoining room, Greg Bingay did a last minute check of the sound and video equipment. She'd greeted him when he first arrived; he seemed friendly, but wasn't much of a talker.

At least this wasn't being treated like a damned television show, with make-up and hair people interrupting her. TV was not the ideal medium for a short, stocky woman with narrow eyes and hair that would not stay in place using anything short of superglue.

There was a timid rap at the bedroom door. "Ms. Parsons?"

"Come in, Jason. I'm about as decent as I get."

The intern opened the door wide enough to slip in, then shut it behind him. He clutched a cell phone in one hand. His pained expression did not bode well. "Sorry to disturb you, Ms. Parsons..."

"Lucky," she corrected.

He shook his head, pointed to the phone. A higher-up was listening.

"Lucky, that is, that I've just finished going over my notes. Our three guests will be here in, what, half an hour?"

She guessed the answer from his uneasy stance. "There's a problem."

I knew it, she thought, heart sinking.

"I've already briefed the professor and the lawyer from the local Independence Party chapter in the bar downstairs. They'll be up in a few minutes so Greg can test their lapel mikes and do the final camera placements. I came up ahead of them to let you know the rep from the Inuits, Tuuq, wasn't at his pick-up point this morning. In fact, no one's seen him since dawn."

Parsons resisted the urge to roll her eyes. She'd been dreading this, the real reason she'd been given this weak-tea assignment. "Who's on the phone?"

"Derek Robineaux. He needs to talk to you."

Crap. Robineaux wasn't top man at the Toronto bureau, but he was high enough that she wouldn't have time to go over his head. "Put him on speaker."

Rathbone touched the screen and laid the phone on the bed between them.

"Mr. Robineaux. Aluki Parsons. Jason tells me there's an issue with one of our guests?"

"Turn off the speaker," Robineaux snapped. "This conversation is for you, not some lowly intern."

Parsons offered Rathbone a sympathetic look, then swiped the screen and held the phone to her ear. Robineaux could have called her room directly if he'd just wanted to talk to her privately. Of course, that wouldn't have given him a chance to put Rathbone in his place, as well as let the intern take the brunt of her initial disappointment.

"It's off."

"Good. Your man's name was Tuuq."

"Yes, Jason filled me in on all the details."

"He was supposed to be reliable but, frankly, those people have no sense of time. I was afraid this might happen."

Not as much as I was.

"But we're in luck. You're a perfect choice to represent the Eskimo slant."

Not exactly living up to my nickname. "The proper term is Inuit."

"Whatever. It makes API look good to give a minority a voice. So you'll take his place in the discussion. Double duty. I'm sure you're up to the task."

And there it was. "Respectfully, sir, for me to do so would be a violation of journalistic integrity."

"Ease up, Parsons. It's only a puff piece. Even when we put it up on our site and maybe offer transcripts for some in-print Sunday supplements, there won't be more than a few thousand in the audience."

"Mr. Robineaux, I don't know who told you I was qualified to talk for those people. My great-grandmother left the Inuit community as a teenager in the 1950s, during the High Arctic location. She had no interest in exploring her roots, and I've kept up the family tradition. Until I majored in journalism at Columbia, I'd never been north of Maryland. My knowledge of Inuit culture is minuscule, and I find throat singing really creepy."

"I've seen your photo, Parsons. You'll pass."

"Not well."

"This isn't a suggestion, Parsons, it's an order. You know what you were going to ask him, so you must have anticipated the answers. Don't forget to mention your location in your intro, and maybe a couple of times during the discussion. Make sure Jason gets lots of pictures of the view from your suite, for our website. Mr. Thorp is being quite generous, especially considering how booked the hotels here are this week. We owe him." The phone went dead.

Had the cellphone been hers, Parsons would have hurled it across the room; instead, she handed it limply back to the intern. Rathbone opened his mouth; she silenced him with a handwave. "I'll work around it. Not the first time I've dealt with this crap. Go to the window. He wants pictures."

"Good morning, America, and all our overseas friends. I'm Aluki Parsons, podcasting live from Thorp International Hotel and Tower in Toronto, 4th largest city in North America, on this beautiful 4th of July. Barges are already moving into place for tonight's fireworks on Lake Superior. Today is not only the anniversary of the Union of North America, but the date Ontario in 1867 officially became a separate state from Quebec. Considering that history, today we will discuss the current controversial proposal to separate the northern states from the rest of United North America."

Parsons knew she sounded bland, almost robotic, but couldn't help herself. Her love for print journalism had drawn to this career, finding the right angle for a story, doing due research. It was a calling that had been dying out even as she'd graduated Columbia.

"Our guests today," she continued, "are Marie Lavelle, prominent defense attorney and a leader in the Independent Northlands Movement, and Roger Kensington, professor of American History at the University of Michigan in Flint."

The talking heads sat equidistant on the opposite side of the coffee table, so the three formed a rough triangle. Lavelle was a head taller than Parsons, thin to the point of emaciation, and wore a grey pantsuit so severe it made Parsons' own look like a party dress. Kensington slumped in his seat, his jacket not quite closing, his tie just askew enough to be distracting.

"Ms Lavelle, let's start with you. Why do you feel secession is necessary, and why now?"

The woman turned away from Parsons to look directly into one of the cameras. She'd done this before.

"Frankly, Ms Parsons, many of the states south of the Great Lakes are an embarrassment. More than that, a threat to the future of the UNA. Enormous amounts of Federal tax dollars are being squandered by Congress trying to turn the clock back on social progress of the past century, sabotaging international relationships, or futilely attempting to protect low-lying areas such as Florida from the inevitable rise of sea levels."

Parsons turned to Kensington. "Professor, you're on record as being opposed to this movement. What is your reaction to these points?"

"I sympathize with both Ms Lavelle's priorities and sense of embarrassment," Kensington replied, "but this petition is an overreaction. Our ship of state has gone off course before, but has always managed to right itself. The process may take a few decades, but eventually it succeeds."

"The world is changing faster every day, Professor," LaVelle responded. "We can't spare those decades. The Northlands will be able to progress both scientifically and ethically much faster if not held back by ignorance and superstition."

"History says otherwise. A hundred and fifty years ago, eleven states petitioned for, and were granted, the right to form their own country. Before the century was over, each of them, one by one, asked to be reinstated. Between the weakening of their agricultural-based economy by the Industrial Revolution, frequent slave rebellions, and most notably increased aggression from Spain, they had no choice."

LaVelle jumped right in, which suited Parsons. The longer these two kept at each other, the less time she'd have to speak.

"The northern states, Quebec, Ontario, Minnesota, Manitoba, your own Michigan and the others, are in a far better position today than those states were, both politically and economically. The major driving force behind that secession was maintaining a regressive social structure. Our local governments are by and large much better equipped for a progressive agenda."

"Having political goals, no matter how well-defined, is not in itself enough, Ms Lavelle. There are practical considerations."

"You want practical? The northern states control the largest supply of fresh water in the world. We have ample ore and oil reserves, and are leaders in developing renewable energy, not just in the UNA, but the world. And as the Earth's climate continues to change, our arable land will increase, creating a more sustainable agricultural base."

"Which makes the territory increasingly desirable to outsiders. This new nation you propose will not develop in a vacuum. Russia, in particular, has for years been pushing to dominate the Arctic Circle. Don't you think a fledging government might be vulnerable? They could put economic, political, even military pressure on your new country. The Union of North America would almost certainly have to intercede, as it did in the Spanish-American War to protect – and eventually re-absorb – the Confederacy. Given modern weaponry, the results could be far more devastating."

A loud rap sounded at the door of the suite. Bingay looked up from his board in annoyance. Parsons signaled the guests to keep talking – the last thing she wanted to do was stop them. They could edit the rap out later.

Jason Rathbone moved to answer the knock.

"I doubt the Russians," LaVelle countered, "or any other interested party, would risk destroying the very assets they covet. They would be more open to a mutually beneficial partnership without the saber-rattlers from Washington undercutting every attempt at peace the UNA makes."

Rathbone caught Parsons' eye. It's Tuuq, he mouthed.

The reporter could barely keep the relief off her face. Bingay passed another wireless set to Rathbone, who took it out into the hallway to fit the newcomer.

In a brief pause in the discussion of the shifting magnetic north pole – API really should have booked a climatologist, as well – Parsons cut in. "There's a side issue I'd like you both to address, in the few minutes we have left. What do you think would be the impact, pro and con, on the natives living in our country's northernmost reaches? If their already meager resources are further squeezed from both sides, could this be the end of their culture?"

The lawyer shook her head. "Washington doesn't give a damn now about the few thousand Inuit living in the far north."

"I agree," Kensington added. "The federal government has done a poor job of fulfilling its obligations to all First Nations people, throughout the sixty states. Yet I doubt a new government could do any better in the midst of its growing pains. At least some structures are in place to address those issues now, even if they aren't yet very effective."

"Not very effective. That puts it mildly. Suicide rates among young Inuit are ten times the national average, due to poverty and lack of opportunity. What we're done to their communities, their children, is a national disgrace. A new, more focused government, closer to their home, could protect and respond to their needs more quickly. They would be better represented."

"Fortunately," Parsons said, "we have an additional panelist to give us the native perspective." She nodded to Rathbone, waiting at the doorway, who then admitted the Inuit and pointed him in the right direction.

"Mr. Tuuq, thank you for joining – us."

Parsons faked a cough, covering her face to conceal her dismay. Please tell me I'm not seeing this.

Tuuq entered the room wearing full traditional Inuit winter gear: fur-lined parka, watertight boots, and double-layered caribou-skin trousers. All he needed was a harpoon to look as if he'd stepped out of a vintage Eskimo Pie wrapper. The choice of outfit had to be deliberate, and ironic. Outside temperatures bordered on ninety degrees Fahrenheit, and Tuuq's weather-beaten face shone with sweat.

"Please join us," she repeated. "Glad you could make it."

A microphone wire dangled loosely from the clip at the side of his parka's hood, connecting to the unit stuffed clumsily in an outside pocket. Bingay used his remote to swerve the camera away from the two panelists to follow the newcomer's approach. Tuuq grunted, providing the first opportunity for a sound check.

Parsons stood up. "Mr. Tuuq? Should I fill you in on our discussion so far? Would you like a seat?" She knew better than to offer a handshake to an old-school Inuit, but was damned if she'd rub noses.

He peeled off his heavy gloves and waved away her offer. "I know what must be said," he muttered. He turned to face all five people in the room, and slowly opened his parka, at the same time removing a small device from his left hand pocket.

Strapped to his torso was a crude vest lined with plastic cylinders. Parsons recognized a faint tar odor; the explosives in the cylinders were real, and no doubt surrounded by steel balls, nails, and other deadly shrapnel. From her coverage of terrorist attacks in Boston and New York, she knew the device could demolish this suite, and the rooms on either side, with flying shrapnel impacting many more victims on Bay Street, twenty stories below.

Lavelle and Kensington immediately rose to back away. Tuuq pointed the detonator in his left hand at them like a pistol. "Sit. Everyone must hear."

Bignay's hand poised over his board, ready to kill both camera and sound. Parsons shook her head. Take away the audience, and Tuuq would have no reason not to push that button. They were live on the internet. Help would already be on the way.

Stall.

"We're listening, Mr. Tuuq," she said. The panelists shakily returned to their seats. Kensington's knuckles whitened as he gripped the arms of his chair; LaVelle crossed her legs and wrapped her arms across her chest.

Tuuq blinked at Parsons, as if confused by her calm, then began to speak in a low monotone. "For generations, our people have been all but forgotten – do not move!" Rathbone had been silently inching toward the suite's door. He froze.

"For generations," Tuuq began again, "our people have been forgotten: neglected, abused, and..."

"A moment," Parsons said.

"Do not interrupt! Please! Do not interrupt!" Half-angry, half-pleading. "I must finish!"

"Of course. Take all the time as you need. It's just that, since your message is so important, you might want to face the camera next to Mr. Bingay. Are you sure you don't want my seat?"

"No!"

She backed away from the chair slowly anyway, keeping her distance to assure him she was no threat, until she perched on the edge of the coffee table.

Tuuq blinked. "Yes. Thank you." He kept his gaze on the five of them as he warily lowered himself into the armchair. "For generations," he restarted, in the same overstudied, deliberate monotone, "our people..." He paused, swallowing hard.

"Jason, bring Mr. Tuuq some water. There are bottles in the fridge behind you."

"My people," Tuuq started again, voice pitching higher now, in a mixture of pain and anger. He was obviously an amateur, untrained, but that made him no less dangerous.

Parsons gradually leaned forward, as if to hang on his every word.

"You foreigners – invaded our land – took our children – this building embodies all that is wrong with your country – our country –" He laid his left hand palm up on the arm of his chair, thumb poised over the detonator button.

Rathbone approached slowly, brandishing the water bottle. Tuuq's right hand swung up to wave him away.

Parsons and the intern moved as one. She pinned the old man's left arm to the chair with one hand, grabbing the detonator with the other, as Rathbone dropped the plastic bottle and pinned Tuuq's right arm.

"Now I know why they call you Lucky," Rathbone whispered.

"Remind me to ask Robineaux to double your pay, Jason."

"Twice nothing is still nothing."

"Cheap bastard." She glanced at the engineer. "Feel free to leave that in, Greg. I assume the Emergency Task Force is on its way?"

"I've been monitoring them. They're just getting off the elevator now."

"Open the door, would you? Let them know we've got things under control."

"What about us?" asked LaVelle.

"Go outside, but don't leave the floor. I'm sure the police will want statements."

Tuuq began to sob, struggling feebly. "I failed. My family. I failed them."

She tried meet Tuuq's eyes. He turned away. For the first time in her life, Parsons felt she'd perhaps been too ready to dismiss the history of her ancestors.

"Bomb squad's coming, as well," Bingay added. "Would you like some of these?" He held up a handful of plastic cable zip ties.

"Oh yeah. I don't know about Jason, but my hand's already starting to cramp up."

Parsons had spent a long afternoon and night sitting in windowless rooms, first at the local police station and then at FBI headquarters. She hated being part of the story. Finally released from questioning, she went straight to the hotel bar and, when they stopped serving at 2am, raided the mini-bar in her suite. She'd skipped the fireworks, which had almost been cancelled due to heightened security.

Despite the heavy drinking and lack of sleep, Aluki Parsons felt deathly sober as a secretary led her into Derek Robineaux' office at ten the next morning.

Derek Robineaux leaned back in a high back leather chair, facing her across a desk the size of her king bed at Thorp Tower as he steepled his fingers. "I'm glad you asked for this meeting, Parsons. Wanted to congratulate you on a job well done. Hits on our web site are way up. Video's gone viral. Advertising tells me sales have quintupled. I've already sent a note of commendation to New York."

"Thank you. I think." She perched on a thinly padded, definitely non-leather chair half the width of his. "I tried reaching Jason Rathbone this morning. He didn't pick up. Do you know if he's okay?"

"Kid's fine. I gave him a different phone. He's helping Maisie cover the upcoming Doobie Brothers concert at the Molson Canadian Amphitheater. You won't need his help any more."

And you were going to tell me this, when? "I thought you might want me to re-interview Lavelle and Kensington again, since we never finished, only with less drama. Maybe in-house?"

"No point. We have enough soundbites to put together a filler piece."

"Okay. Fine. The FBI wants me to stay in Toronto a few more days, in case they have more questions. I can't imagine what else."

"Sounds like a good chance for some R&R. Enjoy our city." He beamed at her dismissively.

She deliberately ignored the hint. "Since I'm stuck here, I'd like to follow-up yesterday's events."

"Thorp's company has already promised to foot the room bill and expenses for as long as you want to stay. He was very grateful for the publicity."

"That's not what I asked, Mr. Robineaux. I came to this city to work. I'd like to do my job."

The beaming smile grew forced. "I suppose we should take advantage, while your name is trending. Check with Wood at the news desk. I'll tell her you're coming."

Parsons took a deep breath. "What I'd really like to do is interview Tuuq. Could API arrange that? No cameras, just a few minutes with pen and paper. And, of course, under the scrutiny of the FBI."

He shook his head. "I don't see the point."

"Much of what went down at the suite doesn't add up, starting with how easily Tuuq got past the hotel's front desk with an explosive vest under that ridiculous outfit. Especially since Travis Thorp has the greatest security team in the world. He's got the greatest everything in the world. According to him."

"I don't think Mr. Thorp would be comfortable with that tone."

"I also would like to know where he got that bomb. He didn't build it himself. He barely seemed to understand how it worked. I know there will be details the FBI won't want to release, but I've cooperated with them before. He might even open up to me in a way he won't, or can't, to their interrogators."

Robineaux drummed his fingers on the desk, in an internal debate. Finally, he nodded.

"What I'm going to tell you now is not for general release, at least not yet, and if you pass it on to anyone, especially to the other reporters, I'll deny it came from me. There was an incident last night while Tuuq was in police custody."

"An incident?"

"He's in a coma. Not likely to recover."

"A stroke?"

Robineaux shook his head. "He smashed his head against the bars of his cell several times overnight."

Parsons blinked. "Wait. A man captured wearing an explosive vest wasn't on a suicide watch?"

"I don't have details. You heard nothing from me."

"Maybe I can talk to his family? Friends? Community? Anything to get a handle on the why of it."

"He's a terrorist. That's all anyone needs to know. A poster boy for why we have to keep an eye on these people."

Parsons nodded in surrender. "I'll talk to editorial, see if they can use me. What was her name? Wood?" She struggled to keep the frustration out of her voice.

"Sheila Wood. I'll tell her you're coming."

Wood was a little stockier than Parsons herself, with prematurely graying hair tied in a bun. As soon Parsons met her gaze, she knew Robineaux had undercut her. Again.

"This is all I've got right now." So Robineaux had told her to say. Both women knew it.

Parsons read the sheet aloud. "Robert Barris, noted cryptozoologist, claims terrorist possessed by Wendigo. Sweet jesus!"

"Barris has been trying to get in our news feed for months. We send him newbie staff once in a while. Never got anything worth putting out for publication. Want to give it a try?"

"I'd rather cover the Doobie Brothers concert."

"That's taken. Wait, I'm getting something." She skimmed her computer screen. "Another puff piece, but you might be interested, considering what you went through yesterday, and you won't even have to leave your hotel. I'll print it out."

"You write a lot of click-bait headlines, don't you? Because you've just intrigued me without giving me any information."

"Yeah," Wood admitted. "I know. Bad habit." She pulled the sheet from the printer tray and handed it to Parsons. "Travis Thorpe is flying into Toronto this afternoon. Private jet, whole nine yards. He's giving a press conference."

"In Thorp Tower, of course."

"Where else? It's an easy puff piece. Mr. T rarely takes questions at these things. You just stand there looking, ah, journalistic. Everything he's going to say is probably covered in this release. You could just rewrite what they sent, and take advantage of the free booze. He always lays out free booze."

"I assume the last minute arrangements are to avoid protestors?" Parsons began skimming the highlights.

Horrible tragedy. Sympathies to family. Compensation check to be delivered by Thorp personally.

She blinked. Compensation? To the family of a man who tried to destroy Thorp Tower? Since when did the infamous Mr. T pay for anything he didn't have to?

Plans for new Thorp Casino in Nunavik. Great for Ontario's economy. Give the Eskimos real jobs.

Parsons lifted an eyebrow.

She'd have to tread very carefully. The bulk of her research would have to take place back in New York, but there was definitely a chink in Travis T.'s armor that needed to be pried at.

"I'll cover the conference."

"You've got it. Make sure you take lots of pictures with your phone. Mr. Robineaux loves pictures. No Barris interview, then?"

"The monster-hunter? I'll pass."

One monster at a time, Parsons thought to herself.

Independence Day, here I come.

G. D. Falksen

RED HARBOR

I knew the dame was trouble the minute her husband walked through my door. You can tell a lot about a woman by her husband. Is he happy? Tired? Angry? Usually they're angry when they come to me: cheating spouses do that to a person. But this guy, he was worried, like he didn't care what his wife did so long as she came back. And that meant the wife was trouble. Always does.

Said his name was Carmichael. Couldn't place his accent, but he wasn't from Vinland. They say we all sound a little more Norse up north, a little more Algonquin below the Gulf, and French around Montreal, but we all sound the same in the end. And Carmichael didn't sound like one of us.

New York, maybe.

"What can I do for you, Mr. Carmichael?" I asked, as I poured myself my afternoon glass of something hard and restorative.

"Well, Mr. Sigurdsson...it's my wife, Lorelei."

"Found out about your mistress, did she?"

Carmichael nervously removed his spectacles and gently cleaned them with his handkerchief.

"No, Mr. Sigurdsson," he said, "I haven't got a mistress."

"Of course not," I grunted. "What's the trouble with her then?"

"Well..." Carmichael repeated, with an unpleasantly tittering voice. "You see, she's run off. With another man."

That didn't surprise me. Carmichael was a reedy fellow, the sort who'd sat out the war thanks to a deferment or Daddy's money. It never surprised me when their wives went elsewhere. Even better, it kept me employed when they did.

"And you want me to find them?" I ventured. It was the usual thing they hired me to do. Track down the runaway lovers so the jealous husband could rush in and do something hot blooded and foolish. Most of the time they never went through with it. They just sobbed for a few minutes in my office or went away stony-faced, ready to do it in private. But I knew it would happen eventually.

Carmichael was quiet for a while. "I just want to know that she's safe," he finally said, his voice quivering. He reached into his pocket and held out a photograph for me to look at. I glanced it it without much interest, and then I admit I gave it a second look.

The woman in the photograph was damn striking. Definitely a Vinlander: Cree, with Icelandic eyes. The woman, Lorelei, was seated on a park bench, smoking a cigarette. Just from the way she sat I knew she was trouble; like she thought she was a queen or model or a Hollywood starlet, and damned be anyone who said she couldn't be all three if she wanted it.

"Find her, Mr. Sigurdsson," Carmichael pleaded. "Ask her to come home to me. I'll do anything she wants. I just want her back."

I shrugged and chased it down with another drink. I didn't like Carmichael's sort. They reminded me of Italy, when it had all gone wrong. It was bad enough when they got out of the war the rest of us had to fight; it was worse when we had to serve under them.

"Fine," I said. "Twenty-five dollars a day, plus expenses. I'll be honest with you, Mr. Carmichael: this could take a while, especially if your wife has left the city."

"I'll give you five hundred if you find her within the week," Carmichael replied.

I exhaled at the amount. I won't lie, it was tempting. The rent was late.

"A week's a tall order," I said.

Carmichael looked out of my window at the setting sun. "It won't be hard to find them," he said softly. "I know where they are."

"Where?"

"My wife's...my wife's lover, a bastard called Johan Svensson, is from a fishing town up north," Carmichael explained. "A place called Redwick. My wife left me a letter saying that was where they had gone." He swallowed and looked down at his hands in shame. "But I know they'll leave there soon."

"Hence the rush."

Carmichael nodded. "I can't do it myself. I haven't the courage, Mr. Sigurdsson. But you: I know your reputation. I've heard you won't give up once you've got a scent."

"You heard right."

"I need that tenacity, Mr. Sigurdsson." Carmichael said. "There won't be a warm welcome for you in Redwick, not from Johan's kin. It's why I daren't go myself." At the thought of it, the color drained out of Carmichael's face.

"I'll bet." My tone was harsher than intended, but Carmichael wasn't in any place to complain. "So I go to Redwick and find your wife. What if she doesn't want to come with me?"

I don't do kidnappings, not even for husbands and fathers. I know some people do, but I won't stoop to that.

"Ask her to come," Carmichael said. "Beg her for me. If she won't...." He sighed and wiped tears from his eyes. "Just ask her why. Have her write me a letter or telephone me." Carmichael's mouth got all tight and angry. It was an attempt at being a man, which was something. "But if she's had second thoughts and Johan's keeping her there, then by God, bring her back to me."

I didn't have the heart to tell him that it wouldn't be the case. He'd be lucky to get another goodbye letter before the wife and her fancy man quit the state. She wouldn't have second thoughts until she got tired of Johan's charms. I'd seen it before. No one ended up happy.

"Fine," I said. "I'll go to Redwick and give this Johan a talking-to. But if your wife won't come back with me...."

Carmichael pulled out his billfold and threw two hundred dollars onto my desk. "There's your fee for the week, Mr. Sigurdsson. Find Lorelei. Get her to telephone me and you'll have the other three hundred."

I looked at the money on my desk and my eyes slowly drifted toward the drawer where I kept my outstanding bills. I poured myself another glass and smiled.

"Mr. Carmichael, consider it done," I said.

I took the overnight train to Eriksfjord on the north coast of Vinland. Redwick was hard to find on a map, but it was there, lurking along a rocky shore among the deep forests of Markland County.

I knew the job was too good to be true. For that much money, there had to be a catch. Firearms were plentiful up north and I suspected that Johan's family would be well-armed and unfriendly, so I brought my old Army sidearm with me to be safe. A few country bumpkins didn't worry me, but I resolved to take precautions. Carmichael might be easily frightened, but that didn't mean his fears were unfounded. He wouldn't be paying me so much if there wasn't real danger.

The Kebec-Markland Railroad was built to transport lumber from the northern forests, but the passenger trains were comfortable enough to entice tourists interested in experiencing the "last great American wilderness", as the Tourism Board called us. None of the trains stopped at Redwick, but there was a local coach service from Eriksfjord that serviced all of the little coastal towns.

The driver proved to be a big, cheerful guy in a canvas topcoat who nearly crushed my hand as he shook it when I said I was a customer.

"Jack Maillet, at your service," he said.

He spoke without an accent, but from his name I figured him to be Franco-Norse, probably from Montreal. That would go along with his rosy cheeks and thick black hair. Me, I'm told I take after the Beothuk on my mother's side.

"Hank Sigurdsson," I replied.

I'm not normally a people person, but Jack seemed so excited to have a passenger, I actually found myself taking a shine to him. In my line of work, you get used to people hating it when you show up. This made a nice change.

"Where you headed?" Jack asked.

"Redwick," I told him as we climbed aboard. It seemed I was the only passenger, though at that hour of the morning I wasn't surprised.

Jack laughed. "That'll be a first in a long while. Usually I get people *leaving* Redwick, not going in. Same with Bjarnisburg and Salmon Creek." As he pulled the coach out of the train station, he asked, "What brings you up this way? The fishing?"

"Nature photographer," I replied. I pulled a camera out of my bag to prove the point. It was an easy lie to back up, especially since I'm a half decent photographer. No less than three divorce cases have my camera to thank for it. "I'm doing a study of small Vinland towns. 'Nostalgia For A Simpler Time.' That kind of thing."

"Lot of money in that?" Jack asked.

"Sure," I said. "Sells like hotcakes in New York, Washington, Los Angeles.... Hell, you name it. Anyplace folks have paved over their own wilderness, they want to buy photos of someone else's."

Jack laughed again. "Aw, Heck, I'm in the wrong business!"

We soon reached the outskirts of Eriksfjord, and Jack pulled off onto a narrow dirt road that wound off along the coast. I settled back in my seat and watched the sea passing by my window.

"You been driving buses long?" I asked.

"Since the war," Jack said.

"You served?"

" 'Course," Jack replied. "You?"

I nodded. "North Africa and Italy. And you?"

"*Semper fidelis!*" Jack grinned. "I enlisted in the Marines right after Pearl Harbor. I'd still be there if it weren't for my damn leg." He patted his thigh just over the knee. "Took some shrapnel on Iwo Jima. After that, I was no good to anyone. Now I'm just a bus driver."

"Yeah," I said softly. Talking about war injuries reminded me of Italy. I wasn't much good to anyone after that either.

Jack took a flask out of his coat and took a swig from it. "Here's to peace, eh?" he asked, as he passed it to me.

I laughed off my melancholy and took a drink. It wasn't pleasant--I've never cared for vodka personally--but I appreciated the gesture. I handed the flask back and said:

"To peace. And to jobs for a couple of relics like us."

"Ha!" Jack took another drink and asked, "So why Redwick? If you don't mind me prying. Only it's a dump, to be honest. Salmon Creek's the place if you want nature photographs."

"My cousin's up there, actually," I said. "Said she was going to visit a friend who could show me the best spots in Markland. And I figured, Hell, the magazine's paying for it, so why not?" I fished Lorelei's picture out of my pocket and showed it to Jack. "You've probably seen her. She and her boyfriend came up a couple of days ago."

Jack peered at the photograph and whistled. "Wish I had. Face like that, I'd remember. She's your cousin?"

"Yep. Though some days I wish she wasn't, know what I mean?"

"Sure do," Jack said, sharing a knowing grin. "But I haven't seen her. You sure she's up this way?"

"Not a doubt," I told him. I paused a moment and tried a reasonable lie. "She telephoned me from Eriksfjord right before getting on the coach."

"Was it Sunday she came up?" Jack asked. "Another guy handles the route on the weekends."

"Come to think of it, it was," I said. The timing was near enough, that it was probably the case.

Jack sighed. "Just my luck. The last passengers I had before you were three burly whalers on Thursday. Believe me, I wish I'd had the weekend shift if your cousin was on it."

"Yeah, me too." I shrugged. "But I'll see her soon, so it doesn't really matter now, does it?"

"Guess not," Jack agreed.

I settled back in my seat and watched the landscape passing outside as we continued on the journey.

It took about an hour to reach Redwick. Jack hadn't exaggerated in his assessment: the town was a pile of nothing in the middle of nowhere. I imagine it wouldn't even be on the coach route if it wasn't already on the way. There were a few dozen squat wooden houses arranged in rows along the shore, forming a semicircle around the wharf. The land was barren and bleak, not at all a place I'd care to live if I had a choice. I'd seen other towns like this before: fishing villages turned whaling and shipping hubs to feed European appetites, now once again fallen on hard times. The Basques had been the first to capitalize on commercial whaling here, but Vinlanders had been hunting the seas for generations before foreigners arrived and made it an industry. But by the turn of the century, that had all finally dried up. Why get oil from the sea when you can dig it out of the ground?

Jack parked in the middle of the town square and I climbed out of the coach. The sky was gray and I smelled a storm coming on the wind. All the more reason to find Lorelei Carmichael and get away from the place.

"Well, here's Redwick," Jack said to me. He followed up with a joking, "You want to continue on to Salmon Creek, you just say so. No extra charge."

I chuckled and lit a cigarette. "Let me find my cousin and I'll take you up on that. When do you come through again?"

"I stop here four times a day, morning then evening," Jack answered. "I get back from Lodge Bay on the return trip by about noon. Then I'll make another pass through late in the afternoon." He leaned in and added gruffly, "After that, you're on your own 'til tomorrow."

"Wish me luck then," I said, grinning a little.

While Jack took on a couple of local passengers and drove away, I smoked my cigarette and studied the town, working out how to make this as quick and painless as possible. There were a few of the townsfolk out already, but they all hurried past me on their business and did their best to avoid me.

The only notable buildings aside from the cannery on the shore were the town hall, the church, and a two-story tavern that I hoped doubled as a hotel. That was the reasonable place to start.

The center of the square where Jack had dropped me off was decorated with a little stone obelisk carved to emulate the look of a runestone. Carved badly, I might add. I recognized it immediately. The state had commissioned dozens of them in towns all over Vinland, celebrating the centennial of statehood right on the heels of our licking the Krauts and the Japs. I ran my fingers over the inlaid words as I finished my cigarette. I recognized each of the dates listed in celebration of the state's history. Every boy in Vinland knew them by heart, even if we didn't much care about them:

1000, the first settlement at Liefsbudir. 1127, peace with the Skraelings. 1262, the founding of Kebec at the mouth of King Haakon's River, which the French insisted on naming after Saint Lawrence when they arrived in 1605. 1410, the last contact with Greenland and the onset of the Long Silence between Vinland and Europe. 1497, when John Cabot broke that silence and reminded us of the world across the sea. That was followed by a series of wars and invasions that mostly ran together for me until the conquest of Kebec in 1608. Then 1763, when the English took us from France. 1775, when Vinlanders turned Kebec over to the rebelling colonies and secured the conquest of Montreal. American independence in 1783. And finally statehood in 1846, to counterbalance the slaveholding giant Texas.

I dropped my cigarette and put it out with my toe. The centennial monument in Kebec was larger and more interesting, complete with fanciful statues of Vikings. This was a pathetic little monument in a pathetic little town I couldn't wait to leave.

"This Lorelei woman had better be easy to find," I grumbled, knowing that it wouldn't be the case. Things like this were never easy.

I went to the tavern and stepped inside. I didn't see anything that surprised me. It was dark. It smelled of hard alcohol, smoke, and beer. There were a few locals eating breakfast at the bar or the tables. There was a lot of fish, which wasn't unusual. A blond woman with a pleasant smile was tending bar and I saw a scruffy man in a stained apron through the kitchen door behind her.

As I looked around, I realized something that had been nagging at me since I arrived. Everyone in the tavern was pale and fair. Nordic to a man. It was one of the strangest sights I had ever seen. You always hear stories about these isolated towns that are all Cree or all Norse or all Montagnais, but I'd never seen one before. It gave me a chill. Everyone here was probably inbred crazy. What sort of mess had Carmichael landed me in?

But I kept a straight face as I went to the bar. The woman there smiled at me and reached for a notepad.

"Good morning, Mister," she said, her tone bright and too perky for the hour. "Here for breakfast?"

"Yeah," I said, taking a seat. "What's good?"

The woman winked. "The braised salmon is the best. I'd avoid the eggs. The last shipment was late, if you catch my meaning. But the salmon's fresh."

"Sure," I said. "Salmon it is. And some dark coffee."

"Dark as the sea," she promised me, as she filled a mug. She scribbled my order in her notepad, tore out the page, and set it on the kitchen counter for the cook to find. Turning back to me, she smiled again and said, "I'm Kirstin, if you need anything."

"Thanks," I said, before I sipped at my coffee. It was dark and it was good.

Kirstin grabbed a rag and started wiping down the bar. After a few moments she leaned over and raised an eyebrow at me.

"Got a name to go with that early morning grumble, Mister?" she asked.

There was something about her smile that made me laugh a bit, and I shrugged. She was pretty and that made the bleak morning a little less unbearable. No wonder her boss had her on the early shift.

"Hank," I said. "Sigurdsson."

"Well, Mr. Sigurdsson," Kirstin replied, "it's nice to have a new face in our little town. I suppose you're up here for the fishing."

"Uh...nope. Nature photographer." I patted my camera bag. I might as well keep up the pretense for as long as possible. Advertising that I was a private detective wouldn't make anyone more talkative than they were already.

Kirstin gasped with excitement. "Golly! A photographer?" She shook her head and smirked at me as she struck a pose. "I've always been told I have a good profile for pictures."

I laughed and said, "Most of the things I photograph have either antlers or feathers. Or they're trees."

Kirstin sighed and shrugged her shoulders. "Oh well, a girl can dream," she said, returning to her cleaning. "But if it's rocks and trees you want, I know a spot. Best view in Markland. You can see clear across to Lief's Island on a good day."

It was a tempting offer, especially when I caught Kirstin giving me a sly glance out of the corner of her eye. But Carmichael's money was more important than a pretty girl, at least for the moment.

"Might take you up on that," I told her. "First, though, I have to find someone. My cousin Lorelei. She's up here with her boyfriend. I promised I'd stop in and say hello before I went out looking for my rocks and trees."

"Who?" Kirstin sounded surprised at the name. "Lorrie?"

"Lorelei," I said.

Kirstin thought hard for a little while and her pretty mouth twisted into a frown. "I've never met a Lorelei around here," she told me. "I'd remember. That's a pretty fancy name for these parts."

"She said she'd be around here this week," I insisted. I fished Lorelei's photo out of my pocket and showed it to Kirstin. "You must have seen her."

Kirstin tapped her bottom lip with her fingertip as she peered at the photograph. I caught sight of a jealous look that crossed her face. No surprise there. Kirstin was pretty, but she had none of Lorelei Carmichael's elegance.

"No, I'm sure I'd recognize her," she said. "A real fine lady."

I leaned over the counter and smiled a little. "Maybe. But I prefer honest and down to earth myself."

"Mmm, that so?" Kirstin mused. She was blushing slightly, but I had no illusions about it. She'd probably heard both better and worse lines in the past.

"Lord's honest truth," I assured her.

Kirstin thought for a bit and whatever she concluded made her smirk at me. "Well, we've plenty of that 'round here," she said. "More coffee?"

"Sure," I said. "And that salmon, soon as it's ready."

Kirstin gave me a wink. "I'll see what I can do about getting you at the head of the line."

The salmon was good and the company even better. I figured I must have been suave by local standards because Kirstin spent the rest of the meal flirting with me in a way that wasn't entirely subtle but didn't need to be. I suppose in a town like that, there probably wasn't a man in sight she hadn't known since childhood, so there wasn't much competition where a new face was concerned. Still, a little boost to the ego never did a fellow any harm.

The investigation was another matter. The tavern wasn't the sort of place I'd expect Lorelei to have visited, but if Kirstin hadn't even caught a glimpse of her, that meant Lorelei and Johan were keeping clear of the public places in town. It was more than a little suspicious and it made my job harder.

I found three men waiting for me outside the tavern. They were all sizable fellows with ugly expressions and dark blue police uniforms. I'd hoped to get a few hours of snooping in before the law took an interest in my arrival, but we seldom get what we want, do we? Two of the men were pretty standard muscle: the sort who'd be on the other side of the law if Redwick had had any real criminal element. But the third was the real trouble. He was older, taller, and more clever looking than his cohorts. He had a pair of mirrored sunglasses over his eyes, which tinted the morning sunlight right into my face and made me dislike him all the more.

"Morning," sunglasses said, giving a smile that wasn't even close to welcoming.

"Mornin', officers," I echoed. I turned to go around them, but one of the goons stepped into my path and made it clear I wasn't leaving. "Something I can do for you?" I asked.

"Just giving a friendly welcome to a new face in town," sunglasses said. "I'm Officer Holm. These are my deputies, Ingvar and Hrodrik. We're the law around here."

Ingvar was the one blocking my path. I forced a smile at him, which he didn't return.

Holm continued, "I like to personally introduce myself to anyone new who comes through town. Reassure them that there's someone keeping the peace in Redwick."

"I will rest easy knowing that."

I tried to cut around Ingvar again, but this time the man grabbed me by the coat and held me in place. Holm took a step toward me and removed his sunglasses. His smile didn't fade once, nor did it get any friendlier.

"Not often we get visitors," he said. "I understand you're a photographer."

Someone in the tavern must have cut out and told them about me during breakfast. It hadn't been Kirstin: she hadn't left once while I was inside. But plenty of other locals had come and gone in the meantime.

"Nature photographer," I told him. "I'm doing a piece on the Markland coast."

"That so?" Holm ran his tongue around the inside of his mouth as he decided whether or not to believe me. After a little thought, he flashed me a wider smile and patted my arm. "Well, we've plenty of nature up here. Not in town, mind you, but you head out along the road a mile or two and you've got all the rocks and trees you could want."

"So I hear. They say some place called 'Salmon Creek' is worth a look."

Holm nodded. "Yes, Salmon Creek would be just the place for you. Leave now, you'd be there before dark."

"I'll probably just take the coach next time it passes through," I said.

"You do that," Holm replied. "Ingvar," he said to his deputy, "let go of the man. He's not under arrest." Holm looked me in the eyes. "Not yet, at least. Wouldn't want you thinking we're aren't hospitable."

"No doubt in my mind," I said quickly, as Ingvar released me.

In my line of work, I usually end up antagonizing the police, but I figured I'd save that until after lunchtime.

Holm smiled and put on his sunglasses. "One last thing," he said. "I heard you were asking after a girl."

"Woman," I corrected. "My cousin Lorelei. She asked me to meet her up here. Said she knew a tour guide who could show me the best places to photograph."

"Lorelei, huh?" Holm shook his head. "No one here of that name. A little fancy for Redwick, honestly."

"She told me she was coming here with a fellow named Johan Svensson," I explained. "He's the local, not her."

The name apparently meant nothing to Holm, which surprised me. I couldn't see his eyes anymore, but I expected some kind of reaction on his face.

"We've got a couple of Johans and a couple of Svenssons, but not together," he replied. "Must have the wrong town."

"Must have," I agreed. "I guess there's nothing to do but wait for the evening coach to Salmon Creek."

"You do that, *Mr. Sigurdsson*."

Holm made a point of emphasizing that he knew my name, probably to intimidate me. But I wasn't surprised. Whoever overheard me in the tavern must have heard my name too.

I extricated myself from Holm and his deputies, and went across the square to the church. Obviously my time in Redwick was going to be limited so I had to work quickly. I could excuse not leaving until the evening coach, but after that they'd probably arrest me or run me out of town. I couldn't quite figure why, unless they were so inbred they disliked anyone who didn't look as Norse as them. That was unusual among Vinlanders, but so was Redwick.

The church was small, decorated in that peculiar style unique to Vinland. Outsiders don't really understand it. Because of the Long Silence, we never went through the Reformation like Europe did, but having spent a hundred years separated from Rome, we had learned to get along without Papal authority. By the time France made us part of its empire, we'd become something very different: Catholics without a Pope.

I was met at the door by the town priest, who ushered me inside with a warm greeting and a handshake.

"Good morning, my son," he said to me. "What brings you to this house of God today?"

"Just passing through the town, Father," I answered. "Looking for a friend on the way."

I wasn't in the mood to deal with a man of the cloth, but the parish priest often knew more about the goings-on among his flock than did the police.

"God is a friend to all," he replied cheerfully. "Even as storm clouds darken the skies at sea, He is with us."

"A specific friend, Father," I corrected. "My cousin Lorelei. She moved here recently with her...husband, Mr. Svensson."

The priest frowned. "Oh, I don't think so. The elder Mr. Svensson is happily married, and his son is only fourteen." He smiled pleasantly. "I'm certain your Mr. Svensson can be neither of them."

"You sure about that? Johan Svensson? They would have arrived a few days ago."

"My son, I fear that besides you, no one has arrived in Redwick for at least a week, and then it was certainly not a woman."

"A couple of carpenters?" I asked.

I expected him to correct me and corroborate Jack's three whalers, but instead the priest smiled again and said, "Ah, yes, those were the ones. But we seldom have women come here. I fear that the town is a bit *rough* for them, though we do our best."

"Well, must have the wrong town," I said.

The priest spread his hands, helpless but sympathetic. "Alas, it must be so. There are so many small towns along the coast, your cousin must have been confused about where she was."

"Yeah, that must be it."

It was possible that Carmichael had his information wrong, but my gut told me no. I was getting the runaround. The question was why.

"Thanks, Father, you've been very helpful," I added, as I turned back toward the door.

"Go in peace, my son," he called after me.

I laughed. "That'll be the day."

Knowing I only had a few hours left, I spent my time wandering around the town, ferreting out whatever information there was. And there wasn't much. Some of the locals were sullen, but most of them were like Kirstin and the priest: friendly, but useless. After lunch, I made my way down to the wharf to watch the storm growing over the ocean. The sky was streaked with gray and the clouds were thick. The rain would hit before Jack returned. All the more reason to get my business finished by then so I could quit this damned place.

The wharf smelled of salt air and fish and was almost deserted. Nor did I see many boats out at sea. It seemed the place was almost abandoned. Not only had Redwick lost its shipping industry, its fishing was moribund too. I spotted the cannery nearby and made my way there. It looked deserted, but with nothing better to do, I decided to be nosey.

As I reached the door, I hear voices talking inside. One said something I couldn't make out. Then the other guy snapped at him:

"English! Always English! Idiot."

"Who's going to hear?" the first man grumbled, but in clear English this time.

"It doesn't matter. English all the time. That is the rule."

The other man swore, but in English. "I know."

There was a pause and I took the opportunity to move closer and push the door open a little more. The two men inside were dressed like fishermen, but they were shifting crates around and there was no sign of either fish or canning going on inside the cannery. The machinery was silent. So what were the crates for?

I pulled out my camera and snapped some photographs while I listened to what came next.

"What will they do with the woman?" the first man asked. "Kill her?"

His companion heaved another crate onto the stack, looking angry at the questions. "Maybe," he said. "If she knows nothing. But they have to be sure. This has to be cleared up when the submarine arrives."

"In two days, yes?"

The second man checked his wristwatch. "Two days come midnight. I'll welcome the new supplies."

"Me also."

A noise at the other side of the wharf caught my attention. Someone was nearby. I closed the door softly and tucked my camera away. Backtracking, I saw Ingvar and Hrodrik coming toward me. There was no way to go around them, so the best I could do was keep clear of the cannery and disguise my reason for being there.

I positioned myself behind a rickety wooden shed midway along the wharf and began taking pictures of the sea and the storm brewing over it. I tried to keep my cool. Lorelei Carmichael was here and we'd both run into something nasty. I had to find her and get her out of town before an innocent woman was killed.

Who were these men? What were they up to? Nazis, I thought. Nazis who'd escaped into the arctic maybe. It had only been four years since the war. But that was insane. Christ, what was going on?

"Well, well, Mr. Sigurdsson," Hrodrik said, as he and Ingvar rounded the shed and found me.

I lowered my camera and looked surprised. "Deputies.... Afternoon. What can I do for you?"

"I see you haven't left town yet."

"The coach isn't here for another hour," I said. "Figured I'd take some snaps of the sea. It's, uh...melancholic, you know? My magazine's readers will love it. A real 'old Vinland' feel."

"That so?" Ingvar asked, moving around behind me.

"I...yeah," I answered, turning to match him. "Why?"

"Seems you've been asking questions all around town," Hrodrik growled.

"Just being sociable."

"Officer Holm doesn't like it when strangers get sociable," Ingvar said. "He asked us to make that clear before you go."

"Look, fellas, I--"

I wasn't able to finish. As I turned back toward Ingvar, his fist met my face halfway. The first punch was followed by another one, straight to the gut. As I doubled over, Hrodrik grabbed me under the arms and held me in place so that Ingvar could keep pummeling me.

I'd like to say I broke free and fought back or at least kept standing through it all. Something manly. But Hell, I'm not Superman or Bjorn Ironside from the comic books. I took it well, like I'd taken that bullet at Monte Cassino, but in the end they left me bleeding on the dock. I remember Ingvar taking the camera from my bag and chucking it into the sea.

"Forget your nature photographs," I heard him say. "Forget the coach. Get out of Redwick."

Then everything went black.

My next memory was of someone's soft hand stroking my cheek. I gasped for air and sat up with a jerk. My whole body shuddered and suddenly someone was holding me.

It took me a moment to realize it was Kirstin, from the tavern.

"Mr. Sigurdsson, are you alright?" she asked, brushing hair back from my face.

"Yeah, I'm fine," I said.

With her help, I slowly stood and leaned against the shed while I caught my breath. Instinctively, I reached under my coat and felt for my pistol. It was gone. The deputies must have taken it.

Bastards.

"What happened?" Kirstin asked me, her voice frantic.

"Disagreement with some of you locals." I managed to grin as I said it. "Seems you folks don't like strangers."

Kirstin sighed. "Officer Holm. But I can't believe he'd beat someone!"

"It was the deputies. Taking initiative, I suppose."

I spat some blood and stretched. My body hurt, but I'd had worse. It was all bruising. Nothing was broken. Nothing important.

"Oh, God..." Kirstin moaned, touching my cheek gently. "This is horrible!"

"Nah, this is just Tuesday." I paused. "Lucky you showed up."

"Yes!" Kirstin exclaimed. "I was looking for you. Mr. Sigurdsson, I think I've found your cousin!"

"Where?"

"I asked around after my shift ended," Kirstin said. "A couple of days ago a woman came to town and she was arrested. I don't know for what. But she'll be in the jail if she's still here."

"Thanks...but why help me?" I asked cautiously.

Kirstin looked angry at my insinuation. "I was curious. And if a woman's been locked up without reason, it's everyone's concern, isn't it?"

"Ok, yeah," I conceded. After the beating, I was walking the edge of a little paranoia. It didn't help that my camera had been thrown into the sea. The damn thing was expensive.

I gingerly took a few steps to be sure I could walk, and I followed Kirstin to the jail, which adjoined the town hall. We kept to a back route behind some of the houses to avoid attention. The door was closed, so I edged it open and looked in to assess things. The police office was empty except for Deputy Hrodrik, who was dozing in one of the chairs with his feet up, snoring loudly.

"Thanks," I said to Kirstin. "You should get out of here before you're seen."

Kirstin hesitated, looking guilty. "You won't do anything illegal, will you?"

"No," I lied. "If Lorelei's here, I'll call her lawyer. Let him sort it out."

"Ok." Kirstin nodded. She hesitated again and suddenly kissed me on the cheek. "Good luck," she said.

I gave her a wink and crept inside the jail. As I crossed the room a floorboard creaked and Hrodrik snorted a little. I froze, but he didn't wake. My Colt was sitting on desk beside Hrodrik's feet and I carefully retrieved it. It was empty, so I reloaded it with the spare magazine I kept in my coat's inside pocket. There was a ring of keys hanging on a hook, and I took them quietly.

The main cells were all empty, but there was a stairway leading down into the basement. At the bottom I found a grim stone hallway lit by flickering lightbulbs and lined with heavy wooden doors. It was probably for storage, but I didn't like the looks of it. All of the doors were locked, but I tried them one after another. The first two rooms were empty, filled with boxes and rubbish. But the third was different.

Inside I saw a wooden cot, a metal bucket, and a single lightbulb hanging from the ceiling. It wasn't just oppressive, it was inhuman. There were no windows and the air was stale. A woman lay listlessly on the cot, sobbing quietly into her arms. She was shackled to the wall by a chain around her ankle, and she looked utterly forlorn. She looked up at me, her face marred by tears, mascara stains, and more bruises than I could count. But I recognized her.

Lorelei Carmichael, in the flesh.

"Please, I told you I don't know anything!" she sobbed at me as I approached.

"It's ok, I'm here to rescue you," I assured her.

I reached for her, but she recoiled away, and clutched herself tightly. "Don't hurt me, please! I swear, I was just birdwatching! I don't know anything!"

"Bird...watching?" I stammered. That wasn't what Carmichael had said. "No, I'm not with Holm. Your husband sent me. I'm here to rescue you."

"My husband?" Lorelei asked. It wasn't entirely disbelief nor entirely confusion. And that worried me.

"Your husband, Carmichael." I unlocked the shackle on her ankle. The flesh beneath was sore and bloody. "He said you came here with a man called Svensson. He wants you to come home."

Lorelei narrowed her eyes at me when she thought I couldn't see it. A moment later she was distraught again.

"Who are you?" she demanded.

"Harald Sigurdsson," I said, helping her up. "I'm a private detective."

"And my husband sent you?"

"Skinny fellow," I said. "Glasses. Ring a bell?" I showed her the photograph with her in it. "He gave me this and hired me to find you."

Lorelei examined the photograph. Then she looked at me and slowly nodded.

"Well, unless they've started recruiting further afield, you aren't one of them," she said.

"Them?" I asked.

"Us," I heard Kirstin say from the doorway.

I snapped my head around and saw her standing there with Hrodrik, who was carrying a gun.

"Thank you, Mr. Sigurdsson," she continued. "Miss 'Lorelei' here had a convincing damsel act going, but you've kindly confirmed that it was a lie. With that formality done...."

"You won't break me," Lorelei snarled.

Kirstin made a noncommittal noise. "Holm hasn't seen you personally yet. You'll talk." She smiled at me. "*Both of you.*"

"I don't know anything," I said.

"Probably not, but Holm will enjoy making certain."

Hrodrik glanced at Kirstin and said, "Speaking of the *Kapitan*, we should inform him that the trap is sprung."

"Yes, obviously, once the prisoners are secured," Kirstin said.

I won't deny that developments in the past few minutes had taken me by surprise, but I consider myself an adaptable man. As soon as Hrodrik's attention was distracted by Kirstin, I grabbed for my gun and aimed it at them.

"Deputy Hrodrik," I said, "drop it."

Kirstin looked startled at the sight of me armed, but Hrodrik laughed and lowered his pistol slightly, somehow more confident now that I had a weapon in my hand.

"It's empty!" he laughed. "I unloaded it."

I didn't enjoy his mocking tone, so I put two slugs into his chest. Hrodrik's eyes were wide with surprise as he gasped and tumbled onto the floor. Having shot a policeman, I knew I was going to be on the run once word got out. I might even have to leave the country, but I counted it better than whatever Holm had in store for me.

"What are you waiting for?" Lorelei demanded, pointing at Kirstin. "Shoot her too!"

I recoiled at the suggestion. "I'm not going to shoot a woman!"

Kirstin had gone white as a ghost when I'd shot Hrodrik, but now she flashed a grin at me. "Thanks, Hank," she said, and bolted into the hallway.

"Idiot!" Lorelei shouted.

She tried to snatch the Colt from me, but I didn't let go of it. So she hobbled over to Hrodrik's body and took the gun from his dead hand. She aimed into the hallway, but Kirstin had fled.

"What is going on here?" I demanded, joining her at the door.

Lorelei put her arm around my shoulders and leaned against me to keep the weight off her ankle.

"They're Russians," she explained as we hobbled into the hallway and toward the stairs.

"*Russians?* What, you mean a Red invasion?"

I didn't know what to make of it.

"Invasion?" Lorelei scoffed. "Don't be stupid. They're spies, not soldiers. They've taken over the town. I think they're using it to infiltrate agents into the US."

"What?"

By then we had reached the main floor. Lorelei glanced out the door and scowled. I looked too and saw Kirstin returning across the square with Holm and Ingvar.

"Well this is a mess," she grumbled.

I was inclined to agree, but as I looked around I spotted a connecting door that led into the town hall. There would be people there, but hopefully not with guns. I nodded and together he hobbled into the next building. The door led to a hallway and after a few twists and turns, the hallway led to another door outside. I'd expected to encounter someone in the town hall, but it was deserted. It was like the town's population was a façade.

"So...Russians?" I asked, as we hobbled along the alleyway behind the hall.

"Think about it," Lorelei said. "They take over the town. They replace everyone: names, identities, everything. It's a small country town; no one is going to know the difference. So now if they want to move agents into the country, they can give them all a plausible origin: a former fisherman looking for work in Washington or a country girl who moves to Hollywood with stars in her eyes. They'll have the town records to back up any story they tell."

"Christ," I swore. "Are there other towns like this?"

"I don't know," Lorelei replied, as we turned the corner behind another house. "I hope not."

"Why send me?"

The way Lorelei looked at me when I asked the question was not the answer I'd wanted.

"God only knows," she said. "I guess our mutual friend couldn't risk sending anyone else. We aren't allowed to spy on American soil. That's the Bureau's purview, and they didn't consider Redwick worth investigating. 'Carmichael' took a big enough risk sending one agent. Two would be out of the question. But you: upstanding citizen foils Red plot. The headlines write themselves and the Bureau can't complain."

"Yeah, if we live long enough to have them written," I said. "You got a plan to get us out of here?"

Lorelei hobbled a little more for emphasis. "Walk?" she suggested, her voice rich with sarcasm. As she spoke, a peal of thunder erupted from the sky and a moment later the clouds unleashed the torrent of rain that they had promised all day. Lorelei sighed. "Well, I suppose I could use a shower."

"A spy *and* a comedienne," I grumbled. "Wonderful."

"Chin up," Lorelei said. "At least they won't be able to track us with dogs."

Redwick was swarming with people by the time we escaped the town limits. Once we reached the edge of the nearby forest, I paused long enough to glance back and check if we were being followed. Not yet, but it was only a matter of time. Dogs wouldn't be able to find us in the rain, but it was a long way to Eriksfjord and Holm's men would find us eventually.

But as we stumbled along through the woods, I remembered something and checked my watch. It was almost time for the evening coach from Eriksfjord.

"I have an idea," I said, and turned our path toward the road.

Within a few minutes, I saw headlights shining through the rain ahead of us. I waved my hand wildly when I recognized Jack's coach trundling along toward us. Jack must have seen me, because the coach skidded to a stop, narrowly missing us as it did. Jack shoved the door open and stared at me in astonishment.

"Hank?" he exclaimed. "What the Heck...?"

"No time to explain," I said, as Lorelei and I climbed onboard. We both practically fell into the nearest seats, soaking wet and shivering. "Just...just turn around and get us to Eriksfjord, now!"

"Eriksfjord?" Jack demanded. "I just came from there! I can't simply abandon my route!"

"Jack, I will pay you!" I insisted. "It's a matter of national security! Just turn around and drive!"

It wouldn't be long before Holm's men were scouring the road and I desperately wanted to be on our way before they did.

"Sure, sure," Jack said. "There's just one problem...."

It was either from exhaustion or from the beating earlier, but I didn't see Jack pull the gun from inside his coat. It was just suddenly there, staring me down between the eyes. I was frozen for a moment, and the sudden shock was too much for Lorelei: she gasped with fear and fainted away in her seat.

"Jack, what the hell are you doing?" I asked.

Jack smiled at me as he reached into my coat and removed the Colt. He tossed it onto the far seat, where I couldn't reach it.

"I'm sorry, Hank," he said. "You should've just gone to Salmon Creek."

"So people keep telling me."

Jack nodded toward the door. "On your feet. Go stand outside. No sudden movements."

I did as I was told. There wasn't much else I could do. If I ran, Jack would shoot me dead before I reached the trees. So I stood there in the rain and waited for what was to come.

"So what now?" I asked.

"I'm gonna do you a favor, Hank," Jack told me. "Run. Just run."

I knew the game. "You'll shoot me in the back."

"Yes, but I'll make it quick. Right through the head. That's better than what Holm will do to you. This is the easy way out."

"I've never been a fan of easy," I said.

I took a breath and resolved to rush Jack, grab his gun, rescue the girl and escape into the storm, like Bjorn Ironside would have done. I knew it was going to get me killed, but it was a better death than being shot in the back.

My courageous fantasy was suddenly torn apart by a gunshot. I shuddered and tensed, expecting the world to end, like it had almost ended five years ago. But I opened my eyes and realized I was still standing. I was still alive.

There was a thud behind me as Jack's body tumbled into the mud, a bullet hole through his head. I turned and saw Lorelei standing in the doorway of the coach, holding my gun.

"You didn't really faint, did you?" I asked. It was all I could think of to say.

This seemed to amuse Lorelei and she smiled slightly. "You are an astute man, Mr. Sigurdsson." She lowered the gun but she didn't offer it to me. "Now then, get behind the wheel and start driving. I am *very* late for my appointment with our mutual friend."

ANNE TOOLE

LIONS ON THE MISSISSIPPI

The crew were carrying rifles on board the steamboat *Tecumseh*, when William Odgen Niles reached the dock. The morning light and fresh spring air did nothing to offset the mixture of fish and manure coming from the Mississippi River. The captain stood aboard ship, surveying his new passengers, a mix of men and women on the dock, shouting to get a move on.

Two men pushed each other right at the gangplank. One caught the other by the collar, shaking him, yelling in French. Niles didn't understand, but he could figure out one or both of them were bound to end up in the river before long.

Niles moved past a young woman in a print dress and bonnet. Clear skin, high cheek bones, she held her carpet bag with both hands as she tried to peer over the heads of the anxious passengers. He navigated around a few elbows, and stepped right behind the Frenchman.

"You dropped something." He plucked the man's hat off and threw it back into the crowd.

The Frenchman turned around, scowling, and released his captive. He stood to his full height, and Niles thought he was about to get a knuckle in his face. Instead, the man flicked Niles' hat off, then stormed into the crowd to find his own.

Niles released his breath as the passengers hurried around him. He snatched up his hat from underneath several feet and made his way up to the captain, who was staring at the crowd.

"Why all the firepower. You expecting trouble?" Niles asked.

The man half-grimaced. "Don't you worry 'bout it. We ain't had any trouble with the Natchez Nation, and we ain't plannin' on any." He looked at Niles and his vest and jacket up and down. "You just stay in the cabins like the rest of 'em, or you're takin' your last trip with us."

Niles raised an eyebrow, but he knew from personal experience Capt. Abe Tyson gave little and demanded much.

Once his ticket was checked, Niles took a few moments on deck to watch his fellow passengers pass by. They climbed up the gangplank, more fixated on their baggage than the trip before them. The woman in the print dress brushed past him, narrowly missing two traders carrying a steam trunk between them. She sidestepped the crew carrying rifles, giving them a particularly black-eyed glare.

He took note of the time and made his way up into the cabin, already set up for the mid-day meal. Tables and benches sat in the middle, while beds inset in the wall skirted the room. Sunlight was shining through the windows above and between the beds. People crowded in, trying to claim space for the long journey. He threw his own carpetbag on an unclaimed bed and made his way to an empty table. Returning to the calm upset by facing the Frenchmen, Niles pulled out his notebook and prepared to review his notes from his last article.

"Is this seat taken?" she asked, gesturing to a chair beside him. She still clutched her bag.

"Please," he said, lowering his book as she took her seat.

"You threw the hat."

Niles shrugged. "Little misdirection. You get someone to look at one hand, they forget they were lookin' at the other. Now I don't want you to take this the wrong way, but Isn't this steamboat equipped with a ladies' cabin in the hold aft? You can leave your bag there."

"I prefer to keep it with me."

"There are unlikely to be thieves on the boat – where would they go?" he smiled.

"Nevertheless," she said, impassive. Just then, the engine, which had been warming up, ground into full gear. A few cries from those not firmly seated, and the ship lurched forward. She grabbed the table, as though it might slide toward her.

"First time on a steamboat?"

"I wish I could say so." She looked wide-eyed around the cabin, as if the walls might suddenly flood in. She still wore her brown bonnet which shadowed her face and covered her dark hair.

He put his book down. "Where have you been?" His accent said Kentucky, through and through, but hers he couldn't easily identify. "Alabama? Georgia?"

"Yes," she nodded.

"So you went down the Alabama River and along the coast. That's no easy journey. First time up the Mississippi?"

"Yes."

"You don't have a thing to worry about, Miss...?"

"Boudinot."

"William Ogden Niles. Pleased to meet ya. If you can stomach the waters of the Gulf, you have no reason to fear the trip up river. You saw the rifles on-board. The Indians won't try a thing."

She sat a bit further back in her chair, pulling away from him. "How do you know?"

"I been up this route more times than I care to say." He pulled out his pocketwatch, offering her a glance at it, then slipped it back into his breast pocket. "I'm timing how long this pile of wood takes to get to Louisville for a local rag. Thinking it'll make it in eight days, give or take. The *Washington* made it in twenty-four days over a decade ago. That's progress!" He paused for a moment, realizing he'd gone off topic. "Yes, but the Indians never attacked us. You stay in here, you won't even see 'em."

"Then why the rifles?"

Niles rubbed his beard for a moment. "I suppose you've heard the news about 'em then."

"Some. I've heard they will kill anyone who enters their country. I've heard they have enough rifles to provide for a small army."

Several of the other passengers stood up, eyes directed in the direction of the potatoes and stew he could already smell. "You don't have to believe everything you hear."

"It's the first run of this steamboat," she said, more a statement than a question.

"That it is, but they have no reason to cut off traffic on the Mississippi. And believe you me, no one here wants to provoke 'em."

She struggled to her feet, her carpetbag seeming to weigh her down. "You don't think calling it the *Tecumseh* is provocation enough?"

He looked at her, puzzled. Tecumseh had led the Shawnee to ally with the British in the war back in 1812. "As long as the Natchez don't ally with the British, I don't reckon there's a problem."

"And if they do, you'll kill their leader and send his name up the river as a warning."

"Me?"

"I mean, I don't want to be made an example of, because someone else wanted to prove a point."

Niles sat back in his chair as she joined the queue for lunch.

The guns were firing on deck. The captain shouted something Niles couldn't understand.

Miss Boudinot clung to her carpetbag even more tightly, looking through the windows, as if Indians might come pouring in like the fading light. She still sat at the dinner table, cleared of its meal, but had taken off her bonnet, revealing a brown cloth wrapped around her head, like she might be ready to do the washing. Niles was lying on his bed, reading his notes, unconcerned by the gunfire. Several others were watching the windows along with her. They could see very little as a fog had settled, only the silhouette of a crewman as he walked past.

"It's alright," Niles said.

"What are they firing at?" she said, eyes wide.

"No one. Just warning shots."

"But we're nearly in Natchez territory!" A few couples in the room drew closer together, looking up in the direction of the gunshots, watching, like waiting for a storm to come. Only a few hushed conversations continued, as everyone strained to listen to the men walking on the boards outside.

Niles got up and sat at the table beside her. "Do you believe any man here would let you come to harm?"

She shot him a look that reminded him of how she'd glared at the rifles at the dock. "You'll forgive me if I don't put much faith in men."

Niles smiled, nodding. "Don't put faith in men when you can put it in the Lord."

"It's like Daniel and the Lion's Den." She seemed to forget for a moment the gunfire. "Do you reckon Daniel remained quiet with the lions and prayed, or do you think he talked to them?"

"They're lions. They wouldn't understand him."

"Not even if the Lord was on his side?"

Niles weighed the question. "If the Lord is on your side, you don't need to talk to 'em."

"And that's why they fire," she nodded toward the direction of the guns. "They figure the Lord's on their side; they don't need to talk to 'em. But I would."

"Talk to lions?"

"They're God's creatures. That's what He intended." She squinted at him again, assessing. "You'd talk to them, too, wouldn't you?"

"I suppose. The hazard of being a newsman: can't help but ask questions. Like what's in your bag that you value so highly?"

She was about to answer, when the engine of the steamboat wound down to a dull idle. The relative silence now seemed more ominous than the gunshots before it.

"They have to stop on account of the fog." Niles looked at his watch with a frown. "That'll cost us a day."

A distant roll of gunfire tore his attention away. The crew responded in kind in the fog. The passengers' voices rose in worry, and faces etched with worry focused on what little they could see through the windows.

"They're here!" she said.

Niles crouched behind the paddlebox on the top deck, the wheel quiet within. The fog around the *Tecumseh* glowed in the fading light. Niles furiously wrote notes as he tried to assess who was firing at whom.

7pm – Gunfire along the riverbank. Well in Natchez Nation waters. Crew responding in kind.

Niles startled, as Captain Tyson stomped toward him, rifle at the ready. When he saw Niles, he lowered his weapon. "I told you to stay in the damned cabin!"

"Why are the Natchez shooting?"

"You should be asking how we can get them to stop." He stood over Niles, protected from stray shot by the paddlebox. "We make a pretty target, sitting here in the fog." He jerked his rifle back up, steadying it on the railing.

Niles peeked around the edge of the paddlebox and caught his breath. Out of the fog emerged several canoes. One Natchez kneeled at the back rowing, while those at the front held their rifles at the ready. Niles had never seen a Natchez before. They wore a leather hunters smock over their chest and had wrapped a band of calico fabric around their heads with a single feather on top. They were peering into the fog just as he was peering at them. He dared not look them in the eyes, but he could see black marks on their cheeks.

"I've got 'em in my sight." The captain cocked the hammer, readying to fire. "Enough to show we mean business."

Niles' pen nib hovered over his notebook. The Natchez had never fallen. They'd kicked De Soto's armies downriver. When the French came, the Natchez outnumbered them year after year, seemingly immune to the smallpox that had so decimated other tribes. When the French demanded more land, the Natchez united with their neighbors to drive the French from their territory, using their tools of war against them. Although half their land was "sold" in the Louisiana Purchase, they'd repulsed every attack on their walled cities. In order to fight and win the Battle of New Orleans, Andrew Jackson had had to guarantee the Natchez Nation borders.

"This ain't the time to start a war, Captain." Niles pushed the barrel of the long rifle away from the Natchez.

"What then?"

"Hello?" cried a woman's voice from the lower deck.

"Hell!" the captain swore.

He and Niles hurried toward the sound of the voice, and Niles leaned over the railing, risking being seen, to get a look at the speaker.

Miss Boudinot clung, as always, to her carpetbag, as she yelled out into the fog. "I'd like to request a meeting with you all." A crewman was walking toward her, doubtless about to pull her away from the edge.

"What are you doing?" Niles cried then regretted it. A canoe emerged from the fog, putting him and the captain at the wrong end of three rifles. The crewman stopped several feet from Miss Boudinot.

"Hold your fire. Hold your fire!" yelled the Captain.

Another canoe floated alongside the steamboat. One of the Natchez caught hold of the edge and began guiding the canoe towards her. Another one leveled his rifle at her. "What do you want?"

"Wait." Niles couldn't stand by and watch. He spoke as loudly as he dared to Miss Boudinot. "There's no need for you to be the one to go into the lions' den!"

She shook her head, looking up at him. "You don't understand." She reached up and pulled the covering from her head, releasing a wave of jet black hair. As it fell down straight around her shoulders, Niles finally recognized her native heritage. "They're not the lions."

The Natchez lowered their rifles, and two held out their arms to help her into a canoe. The focus on her, they did not notice the captain gesturing at the crewman to grab ahold of her. He caught her by the elbow, and she wobbled between the canoe and the steamboat.

"No!" As if by instinct, she swung and hit the crewman with her carpetbag. He stumbled back, carpetbag in hand. Released, she nearly fell over the canoe, before the Natchez could right her. She sat, and the oarman sent them back into the night. She turned back to look at the crewman and her bag, a wrinkle of worry in her forehead. In moments, the canoe disappeared into the fog.

Now that the guns had fallen silent, Niles ran down the stairs, ignoring whatever the captain was saying, and nearly tackled the crewman that had let her slip out of his grasp.

"Let go of me," said the man, trying to get Niles' hand of his elbow.

"The carpetbag," he said. "The one she had. Where is it?"

The crewman gestured toward the deck where it had fallen. Niles pounced on it, fiddled with the clasp an achingly long time, and finally pulled it open. He pushed aside her damned bonnet to see what lay beneath, what secret she had carried from Georgia and lost at the last moment. His mouth opened, then slowly curved into a smile.

Eleanor Susan Boudinot had come a long way to meet with the sovereign Natchez Nation. Now that she was among them, she felt naked without the carpetbag that had been her constant companion all those weeks on the journey.

"Why did they stop their boat in our territory?" asked one of the men who held his rifle on his knee.

"They couldn't continue because of the fog. They're trying to beat a speed record."

The men spoke to each other in their own language, then seemed to come to an agreement. "Who are you? What do you want?"

"I'm Cherokee. I've come to ask for an alliance with the Great Sun."

They escorted her through the gates of Emerald Mound, the capital of the Natchez. The wooden walls on each side reached higher than she thought possible and seemed to stretch into eternity in the night. Once through the gates, her feet grew heavy as she climbed the mound which gave the city its name. Her escorts had thrown on matchcoats, like blankets, over their shoulders to protect them from the night chill, but Eleanor welcomed it after exhausting herself on the climb.

Once they reached the top of the mound, she begged a moment to catch her breath. She found herself on a street dotted with homes. In one direction, firelight danced out from round, thatch-roofed huts, where children still played as their mothers chased after them in their matchcoats.

On the far end of the street, Eleanor spied two-story homes of brick and wood, reminiscent of the townhouses she'd seen in Atlanta. A man and a woman were returning from an evening stroll. He wore the cloth turban with feather that the hunters had, while wearing a jacket and cravat. The woman wore a dress not unlike Eleanor's. A Negro servant attended them.

What most arrested her attention, however, lay straight ahead. At opposite ends of an open plaza stood two flat-topped mounds, each with round, thatch-roofed buildings. Unlike the ones she'd seen on the street, these had an aura of stability and grandeur. The symbol of a Great Serpent on one of them confirmed it for her. She was looking at the Sun Temple and the residence of the Great Sun.

After a moment, she was told that the Great Sun would see her.

Two of the men from the canoe flanked Eleanor as she stood before the Great Sun and his advisors, a tattooed man and an older woman in a matchcoat. Eleanor's eyes wandered the room, supported by poles and beams bound together by wattle and daub. The building likely once served as a residence, but it had been cleaned and gutted to provide a large audience chamber. Woven mats lined the walls and covered the floor in geometric shapes, leading the eye toward the true center of the room: the Great Sun himself.

Like the man she'd seen on the street, the Great Sun wore a jacket and cravat. On his head, he'd wound a colorful fabric. He finished it off not with a single feather, but with many that trailed down his back. His face was marked with black lines on the side of his cheeks, which seemed to dance when he talked. And so he did from his seat on a chaise of pillows.

"You are a Cherokee, a newcomer," he smiled at her. The Cherokee had migrated south into the Mississippi lands centuries ago, but the Natchez would not let them forget who lived here first. "Do you believe in the Great Serpent?"

"I believe that Spirit guides us, yes." Her voice did not quiver.

"Not all of us believe as we once did. But I keep the eternal flame in the temple going, so I can speak with the Great Spirit. And what will He tell me about you?"

Eleanor had practiced this moment in her mind a thousand times, but now that it came, she couldn't organize her thoughts. "I've come a long way on my own. Our lands are ours by treaty and by right. I know that Georgia cares for neither. It will be only a matter of time before we are forced from our homes. I had to come, to try. My heart… my heart told me you would help us."

"How can we help you, you who live 'a long way' away?"

"With an alliance. They won't move against us while they fear you. You have fought French and British and federal forces and won. You grow stronger every year. The Great Spirit has blessed you all with health and fertility many times over."

"Our strength comes from our mothers' milk." The Great Sun gestured toward the older woman, who nodded her head. "My mother acts as the White

Woman has for generations. She ensures that whichever woman survives an illness passes her strength on to all of us through her milk." The Great Sun leaned back on his pillows and opened wide his arms to include everyone in the room. "What strength can you pass on to us?"

Eleanor remembered the days of travel on land and sea, traveling in foreign lands with a secret so heavy it nearly drowned her in the river. "I have gold."

The Great Sun exchanged a look with his advisors, interest piqued. "How?"

"We discovered gold on our land. We tried to keep it secret, but already Georgians are staking claims. They will keep on taking until they have all our homes, our town, our land. We have few warriors, but we have gold. You have warriors aplenty, but no gold. An alliance would make us both stronger."

"We could not defend you," said the tattooed man.

"You wouldn't have to. To keep the peace, those that fear you in Mississippi will beg Georgia to leave us be. The federal government may well treaty with us both. But we must move quickly."

"It will take weeks to get word from here to Georgia, and then on to Congress."

Eleanor thought back to the man with the notebook and a talent for misdirection. "I know a newsman who can put it in his paper."

The White Woman drew in her breath, and both men paused to listen to her. Her voice rasped with age, but each word was measured and sure. "I would approve this alliance, but... how do we know this gold is real?"

"I brought it with me," Eleanor said.

Her escort from the canoe jerked to attention. "But it was lost on the steamboat!"

She shook her head with a smile. "No. That was a... misdirection." She bent over and gathered her skirts, then pulled them up to her knees. The packets of gold nuggets wrapped tightly round her legs, where they had wearied her for weeks.

Meredith Peruzzi

SAVING GRACE

She's left us. She says she's coming back, but I have this feeling that she's left us.

I wouldn't have thought there would be anything more important in a woman's life than her family. I wouldn't have thought she'd leave her husband at home with the children while running off to pursue some crazy dream. How can you give birth to a child, and fifteen months later leave home? A baby still needs its mother.

She said she has to make the Philippines what it should have been for the past fifty years. That it's about history, it's about our country, our freedom. But we don't have a country, we've *never* had a country. We always belong to someone else, and it's better that way. If we weren't part of the United States, we'd descend into chaos. Everyone here is corrupt anyway. For almost 500 years we've had colonial leaders. We tried to defeat them a hundred years ago. Doesn't she remember that we failed?

Of course she doesn't, so she's left us, off to start a revolution. She wants to be a rebel, a Rosie the Riveter, an idealist...I don't know what she wants. She wants to leave me. Because she can't bear to stay with me, so better to run off and join some cause that will never succeed. I sit with my head in my hands and wonder, why would she have left us? Would a woman leave her family over politics?

—•—

Of course he doesn't understand why I left. He tries to pull out all the traditional Filipino machismo, but I've always been the man in our family. We've been married for ten years, I've given him a beautiful child, I've worked forty hours a week my whole career. I'm not the traditional Filipino wife, the good Catholic in the home, taking care of the babies. We have money for a nanny, and I won't be kept at home. He thinks he can control me, because his friends all have their wives under their thumbs. I've always been the odd one. I wore a pantsuit to our wedding, but he still thinks I'm like all the rest.

I left because I have to be on the right side of history. They're bringing back the Katipunan, and this time we will win. Everyone's gathering in Manila. Just because we failed in the 19th century doesn't mean we will this time. It's the 21st century now, we're better organized, we're *connected* now. We didn't need the Spanish, and we certainly don't need the Americans. Just because Hawaii went quietly into statehood after their revolution failed doesn't mean the Philippines will be quiet. We are the furthest away from the mainland. I have nothing in common with someone from Louisiana.

This is our time. It's our time to fight and to win. The US hasn't seen any serious attempts at secession in over a hundred years. We're going to show them not everybody wants to be part of the greatest country in the world. We can do better.

—•—

We'd been married for ten years before we had the baby. It wasn't for lack of trying all that time, of course, it was just that something didn't work. It wasn't her fault, it wasn't my fault. If we'd had a little more money, we might have gone to the doctor to find out what was wrong, but who can afford insurance when you're 20-something years old? You don't qualify for Medicare, you have a part-time job, and you just hope you don't get sick. Fertility treatments aren't an option. We didn't use protection - of course not, the church doesn't allow it - so we gave up hoping after a while. Ten years without a baby, and you get tired of looking at families, trying to stare surreptitiously so you don't get caught. You just give up altogether, and you move on, and you try not to wonder who's going to take care of you when you're old.

Then suddenly, her period didn't come. A quick test from the drugstore made us both happy that I had a job with insurance now, and the next ten months were filled with doctor's visits, heartburn, and shopping for tiny outfits. Early thirties isn't too late to have a baby, and Grace was born chubby and perfect, our little angel. At the baptism, Mariel seemed grateful to hand her over to her brother, who puffed up like a peacock, he was so proud to finally be an uncle. You'd have thought it was his own child, even as I stood there looking on - but I didn't notice, I was much too elated myself that my exquisite little one was finally among us. Grace wore her mother's baptismal gown, and at the end of it all we drove home silently. We were exhausted, of course. Mariel had hardly slept in the two weeks since Grace entered our lives, and I couldn't fault her for wanting some quiet.

And so it continued. I spent as much time with Grace as I could, even though I was working full-time. My job is good, managing a room full of tech support specialists, the kind whose accent is actually understandable, the kind who know how to make you feel like you're really talking to Betty in Oklahoma, not the kind who make you wonder if you're talking to Sandeep in Bangalore. We're hard-working Americans, and we know how to fix your printer. But when I got home every night, it was the nanny's arms I'd grab my darling daughter from, not my wife's. I'd hear about her day while Mariel sat curled up on the couch reading a book, and I'd feed Grace formula while Mariel made dinner for the two of us. She'd push the stroller, she'd carry our child on her hip, but she was never interested in her.

Of course it had to be post-partum depression. I urged Mariel to see a doctor, to get some help. She was listless, morose, her nose always in a book or pressed up against the computer screen. I knew she talked to people online - her safe world away from me and Grace. She could pretend we didn't exist when she was talking to her online friends. It was the one thing seemed to make her happy, and who was I to argue with what made my wife happy? Grace was what made me happy, and I didn't mind taking care of her. She was my world, even as my brothers looked on in wonderment at Mariel's inability to care for her own flesh and blood.

—•—

He tells it like I'm a monster. A woman who doesn't care about her own child. I love Grace. I'd die for Grace. But there are other important things in the world, too. I learned this when we tried for so long to have our little girl, and couldn't.

The perfect time to become a revolutionary is in your early twenties. The world hasn't jaded you yet, it hasn't swallowed you into its workaday ways, you still know you can change everything. That's when I started wanting to change the place I lived in. The Philippines has always been under someone else's yoke, and driving a taxi you hear all about how that yoke has affected people. The small business owners who can't afford to keep up with minimum wages from Washington, the priests who have to ignore hundreds of years of our history and live in a country where abortion is legal, the schoolteachers whose textbooks focus on the thirteen colonies and not the fact that we were a damn colony, too. If it's so great that the Minutemen dumped tea in the harbor or whatever it was, and the United States is free from Great Britain, why are we supposed to accept being annexed like Hawaii was?

It can't stay like this. Over a century ago, we were under Spanish rule, but we were too weak to throw them off. Not that we didn't try, we were armed and ready for revolution, but the Katipunan split into factions and the Spanish and Americans fought over us, then the Americans fought us. You can hardly expect a tiny new republic to beat the greatest power of the Western Hemisphere - they killed us by the tens of thousands, bringing famine and sickness as their welcome gifts for a new colony. They brought us their teachers and made us speak English, they forced their legal system onto us, they gave us no choice at all - and when they finished using our islands in the war against Japan, they "rewarded" us by making us a state. Nobody ever asked a single Filipino if we wanted to be American citizens. I may have an American passport, but I'm no American. I'm a Filipina, and I'm going to be at the head of the revolution.

Perhaps it's not so easy, though. I'm not the freedom fighter I once dreamed of being. Simon made me stop driving the cab when I got pregnant, and the nanny takes care of Grace, so what do I do? I read, I talk to people on the internet, I'm an armchair revolutionary now. But it's not enough, I want to do more. I sit in my apartment in Surigao City and I chat with people all over the Philippines, but how do you convince someone to join a revolution in email? You have to go to where the people are. You have to go to Cebu and Quezon City and Manila. You have to take their hands in yours and say "Now is the time!" You have to say it out loud. Words on a screen aren't enough to overthrow the world's biggest superpower.

I had to go to where the people are. I wasn't leaving Simon and Grace. I was going to the revolution. They just stayed behind.

—•—

Grace isn't old enough to understand where her mother went, but she's old enough to miss her. She's a year and three months, she's a toddler, she knows Mamá is gone, she just doesn't know where. Or how long. Or why. She's a baby.

But I know where Mariel has gone, and she told me the reason she's leaving. I just don't know for how long, and I don't know why. We are Filipino-Americans, what's wrong with that? My father served in the U.S. Army, alongside a half-million other Filipinos. He was proud to serve his country, he was proud to wear the flag patch on his uniform. Not even his father remembered the days of the

Spanish - we have been Americans for almost hundred years. I like McDonald's and rooting for the Manila Tarsiers on Monday Night Football and having everybody over for adobo on Thanksgiving. I like just about everything about being an American, except around April 15th.

I wish I knew where she got the idea into her head that we should be independent. She didn't get it from me, or her parents, or anybody else we know. Driving a taxi all night, you have a lot of time to think, I guess. And sitting in front of the computer all the time, you talk with people, who don't necessarily have the best intentions. They tell you all about the amazing things we could do as an independent country, and you get these dreams into your head. But you don't get a sense of reality. These dreamers know just what to say, filling your head with fantasies. They're ready to swallow you whole, take you away from everyone you love. It's like a cult. They recruit people.

—•—

I know he thinks I've been swallowed up by evil people with evil intentions. But I am those people. I'm the person the nice housewife talks to. Because that is how we win: we need numbers. You can't start a national conversation about Philippine independence with twenty people and a megaphone. More than 200,000 people were present for the March on Washington, when Dr. Martin Luther King told us he has a dream. Of course we weren't part of his dream, us brown folks way off here in the islands, but we can learn from his methods. You can't get free from the world's greatest superpower alone. That's why I've been talking to people for years now, telling them about our great history, about the Katipunan, about what a Filipino-run Philippines could be. Because we can't do it alone.

Everything he likes about the U.S. is something that was forced upon us. We never had Thanksgiving until the U.S. came, we only did it because they told us to. Governor Quezon may have done many great things for the poor of the Philippines, but the big push on Thanksgiving was one of his more ridiculous ideas. Turkey isn't supposed to be here at all, let alone in adobo.

I know he says I'm not coming back. I never said that. I said I have to do this, and I can't rest until it's done. I love him, and I love Grace, but I love my country more. I want my little girl to grow up in a world where she's proud to be Pinay, where her passport tells everyone she's from our beautiful islands. There's no pride in a U.S. passport, no sense of identity. A melting pot isn't something to be proud of. Everybody eats McDonald's all over the world.

So now I'm here in Manila, because this is where I can make a difference. Last week, we got representatives together from every county, a big board of over eighty people who all want a free Philippines. Now, you're not going to get eighty people to agree on things all at once, the minute they walk into a room, but we put together a board of leaders. Not even that was easy...but you have people get up there and say why they're good leaders, and then you vote, and there it is. The five of them will lead the eighty of us. I didn't want to be a leader for the board, no...I'm more grassroots. I'm not a leader of anything, I just want to be part of the revolution, talk to the people, get them on board. People have to understand our cause in order to support it. I know it backwards and forwards, inside and out, and I can sit anyone down for twenty minutes and bring them over to our side. I've done it countless times in the cab. Even if you didn't get the full story, if your trip was too short, you got an earful of ideas and by the end your head was rocking and rolling. Nobody got out of my cab without at least thinking about Philippine independence for the next day and a half. And I had these little cards printed up, with my contact information, so people could get in touch. I got so many emails asking for more information, asking to get involved.

That's where I'm good. I'm an entire communications team all rolled up into one person. I'd make a great Jehovah's Witness if I wasn't a Catholic. I can talk the pants off a monkey, but by the time I'm done, you're on my side.

That's why I'm giving the main talk at the first event tomorrow. Because I can get the attention we need, I can stand up on that soapbox - okay, it's not really a soapbox, but you know what I mean - I can stand up there and bring in the crowd. We'll have a few of our people standing around looking like they're already interested, that's how you get even more people to stop and watch. If you're just a crazy person ranting on a box, nothing's going to happen. But you're a crazy person ranting on a box and people are listening? More will stop. More will come. I will make them listen with the power of my rhetoric, and I will make them believe. We must have a free Philippines. No more American yoke!

—•—

She was on TV.

I don't know what to make of it, but she was on TV.

It was just a five-second clip maybe, but I was sitting there feeding Grace and the news was on. They mentioned the Katipunan, so I looked up and there she was. A megaphone strapped to her hip and the microphone in front of her mouth. My wife, my Mariel, calling for a revolution.

You couldn't hear her, the announcer kept talking over her, so I don't know what she said. I don't want to know what she said. I'd break down in tears if I could hear the poison she must be saying. I don't know how those people got her away, and I don't know why she isn't telling me what's going on. She sent me a note when she got to Manila, told me she had arrived safely. She called me yesterday for just a few seconds, but there was so much noise I couldn't tell what was going on.

Grace is babbling, smart little cookie that she is. How could anything be more important than this? My darling girl is a dark-haired little charmer. She toddles around the house like she's got wheels under her feet, and I can't turn my back on her for a minute, but she's the love of my life.

No, Mariel's the love of my life. Isn't she? I don't understand how she's not the woman I married anymore. She was so different then...my head twists in circles when I try to figure out what happened. Not just her - with any woman who would leave their baby alone. Of course Grace has me, but a little girl needs her mother. I don't know how I'd feel if we'd had a boy, but I just think there are things I can't teach her.

—•—

I wish he could see that this is a moment in time, immutable, unassailable - now is the time that will change us. You have to look at the bigger picture, the world outside our house, the world outside Surigao, outside the Philippines even, to the world stage, to what we can achieve. I have an absolute perfect faith that the Philippines will be free in my lifetime. It was Grace's birth that prompted me to do it, I wouldn't have felt such a powerful desire for change without my motherly instinct. Even stronger than the pull to feed and clothe my child is the pull to create a world I want her to live in, and that's what I'm doing.

This moment is where we are. This is where we stay. If it takes a year, five years, ten, I don't care, I just want my country free. Then I'll be back, I'll sit her in my lap and show her my name in the history books, she'll see what her mother gave up for her, and she will understand.

—•—

I hadn't heard anything for six months, and the unrest in Manila was growing. I had seen her on TV occasionally, she called now and then, but then it all stopped. And I kept reading to Grace, kept running the helpdesk, kept hoping my wife would come back to me. After four months of silence, I sent a picture of our little angel to the Katipunan, addressed to Mariel with a letter pleading with her to come home. But there was nothing, no word at all, for two more months.

And then a phone call from the Philippine National Guard. Our proud tradition since 1917, before we were even a state, who were frequently called up to the mainland but almost never had to deal with unrest at home. They called me, I don't know how they got my number, but they asked if I was the husband of Mariel Ramirez, and I dropped the phone.

They took her life. They took my baby girl's mother. They took her.

The PNG officer said she was marching arm-in-arm with the Katipunan, her head shaved almost bald, a white shirt and military pants. I couldn't even conjure the image in my head, so I told them they were wrong. But no, she had her driver's license with her. And with her bald head, her arms linked with men and women who were strangers to me, she rushed the soldiers who were just trying to keep everyone safe. They fired. I can't fault them. She was crazed, she was beyond help, she wasn't my wife anymore.

But she was still Grace's mother. She was demented, probably on drugs from the Katipunan, but she was Grace's mother, until she wasn't anymore. And she just vanished from the earth, abandoning her family forever. What becomes of a toddler who grows up without her mother?

I was wrong that she was never coming back. She did come back, of course. I just didn't know it was going to be in a pine box. I didn't know I was going to have to try to explain to a preschooler why everyone else has a Mamá and she doesn't, or why we're going to the cemetery for Mother's Day. If she'd gone away and never come back, Grace could have grown up dreaming of meeting her mother someday. Of course Mamá is in heaven now, sleeping with the angels, but little children ask a thousand questions, and I don't think I can answer them all. Not now, not ever – I will be a white-haired old man and my Grace still won't have to know about the crimes her mother committed.

I'll keep her safe forever.

Brendan DuBois

THE PEOPLE'S CHOICE

Jules Lipton got out of the Yellow Taxi in a remote neighborhood of Tulsa, Oklahoma, capitol of the Dakota States of America, and walked up to a plain looking ranch house on a street filled with other plain looking ranch homes. He had on a comfortable black suit hand-tailored from Hong Kong, carried a leather briefcase from the Savoy States in one hand, and hoped that even though it was Election Night, that the evening wouldn't last too long. Over to the east fireworks were sounding off in anticipation of the returns going Dakota's way, although Jules thought the celebration was definitely premature.

He unlocked the front door of the house, stepped in, closed and locked the door behind him. The place was empty of furniture and people. It smelled of dust and old things. He shook his head, walked into the empty living room, over to the back entryway that overlooked a neat and fenced-in yard, stopped at a door that marked a closet.

But it wasn't a closet. He unlocked that door as well, went in, closed the door behind him, and then the room started moving without him touching anything. The elevator went down a number of meters and opened up, and he emerged into one of the many bunkers across North America that belonged to his employer, Standard Oil of Mid-America.

He flashed his ID card at an alert-looking woman security officer sitting at a desk, and with practiced ease, went down the near corridor to the conference room that would be his home for the next several hours. The offices here were mostly made of transparent glass, and he went into the room, sat down, unbuttoned his jacket. He was early. That was why he had gone so far at Standard Oil: he always got in early and stayed late. The other conference rooms were dark and empty.

There were carafes of water set at three locations on the polished wooden table, and a large screen television hanging from the far corner. A speakerphone and console was in the middle of the table, along with other standard phone sets. Folded over copies of the *Tulsa World* and *Dakota Today* newspapers were at one end of the table. Other men started coming in, and he nodded to them all as they took their chairs. To a man, they all ignored him.

Fine. Another reason he had gone so far at Standard Oil was because he was smart enough to hitch his wagon to Ty Coburn, the President and CEO of Standard Oil, back when Coburn had just been one of six Vice Presidents of Operations, and a military veteran of the Red River War with the Republic of Texas. Even then one had a sense of Coburn's presence and power, and Jules just knew the man was destined for great things.

Coburn had protected Jules on his way up the ladder and he in turn had served Coburn well with advice and historical research for his job, and that had been that. The other men who came in, well, he didn't bother remembering their names, because this high up in Standard Oil, it was pretty cutthroat and a guy could stay in one place for six days, six weeks or six months before getting sacked, so what was the point in learning their names? He just knew the guys here as Operations, External Relations, Finance, Publicity and Internal Relations.

The door opened and Coburn strolled in, still looking as lean as he did when he was a Colonel in the Dakota Army, with just silver highlights in his black hair to mark his age, wearing a well-tailored dark blue pinstripe suit. He carried a briefcase that he set down on the conference room table.

"Sorry I'm late," he said, and nobody said a thing, because nobody believed that statement to be true. "Family issues back home... my daughter has a term paper due for her history class at Iowa State."

He opened the briefcase, took out a paper-clipped sheaf of papers that he slid over to Jules. "Hey, do you mind?" Coburn asked him. "Could you give it a glance before she submits it tomorrow?"

Some low titters and Jules felt his cheeks burn, but so what. He took the papers and glanced at the title page. "A Review of Political Developments Arising from the American Civil War 1861-1863." He didn't mind helping out Coburn's daughter, knowing that was just one more favor deposited in the favor bank. Jules had majored in English Composition back at Indiana University in Bloomington with a minor in North American history, and with that odd set of skills, he knew he was lucky to be working in this corporate world. Still, he wished Coburn hadn't embarrassed him like that in front of the others. This particular crew had long memories when it came to insults and slights, and he knew this little incident would be remembered.

Coburn said, "Gus, fire up the TV, see what we got."

The man from Publicity turned on the TV, found the all-news channel of the North American News Network, which showed side-by-side screens of crowds in Tulsa and Edmonton, waiting for the election returns to start coming in for the referendum.

"Gus?" Coburn asked. "What do we know?"

"Returns will be made public in about three hours," the man from Publicity said. "That's our window of opportunity to make sure everything's finalized and approved."

"N.A. News on board?"

Gus said, "For what we've paid them, absolutely."

"Fine." Coburn turned to another man and said, "Ted, get Harlan on the phone, let's see how we stand."

"Yes, sir," the man from External Operations said, and he leaned over, started punching numbers into the console, and within fifteen seconds, the phone was answered.

"Harlan Hendricks," came the voice, and Jules took a breath. Hendricks was Coburn's counterpart at Imperial Oil up in Alberta, and Coburn said, "Harlan, good to talk to you again. How does it look?"

Through the phone, the man's voice said, "Well… Ty, we have a situation."

Instantly the mood in the room changed, and there were movements as everyone leaned forward just a bit, in order to hear better the voice from a man nearly on the other end of North America. Coburn's right hand clenched and he said, "Go on."

The man from Imperial Oil said, "Here it goes, and I won't sugarcoat it, Ty. Ottawa's putting a lot of pressure on us to stay with British Canada. I won't go into the details of the pressure they're putting on us, but they've sweetened the deal to keep us in place quite a bit.

"How much?"

"Five million London Pounds Sterling, plus trade concessions to Russia Alaska, plus individual deposits for… services above and beyond the call of duty as a British Canadian citizen, all to be placed in our personal accounts."

The man from Finance put a hand up to his face, shook his head. Coburn nodded to Finance and then said, "Harlan…"

The man from Imperial Oil interrupted. "Ty, look, my Board of Directors weren't too crazy about the deal… and now with these sweeteners and the individual deposits, well, I'm not sure the official vote tally is going to support Alberta joining up with the Dakota States."

Some whispers around the table and Coburn lifted a hand.

The conference room went silent.

"I'll call you back in a bit. All right?"

"Sure Ty... and no matter what, are we still on for that fishing trip next week?"

"Business is business, politics is politics," Coburn said. "I'll be there, fishing poles in hand, bourbon packed away."

He disconnected the call and Jules ignored most of the conversation that then erupted. His job was to help Coburn prepare his message and media appearances — much to the distrust and hatred of Publicity — and he'd wait until some sort of consensus was reached or there was a break in the yap-yap before stepping in.

Jules started examining the term paper, thankful that Coburn's daughter was a good speller and reasonably talented writer, which made his job easier. As he started there were little snippets of conversation that he picked up along the way.

"... last minute bullshit, it is..."

"... temporary embargo might work..."

"... when will the news network announce the results? Do we have the time to..."

"... maybe bombing one of their border pumping stations might get their attention..."

As Jules read the typed pages words popped up of names and places that were so familiar to him from those history classes he took back in Bloomington, back when Indiana had been part of the Dakota States, until six years ago, when they voted to go back to the United States. Men like Lincoln, Davis, Lee, McClellan, Grant. Places like Washington, D.C., Richmond, Gettysburg, Alexandria. The British intervention and the Battles of the Fleets and —

"Jules?" Coburn suddenly asked. "What do you think?"

He looked up, hearing a few titters among the other men. Go ahead, he thought, go ahead and laugh. He was an expert at lots of things, and one was multi-tasking, and he wasn't about to be caught flat-footed by this bunch.

"Sir, before you got off the phone with Mister Hendricks, mention was made of a fishing trip."

Finance said, "Fishing trip? We've got less than three hours before N.A News Network is supposed to release the alleged results from the Alberta referendum, and you're worried about fishing?"

But Coburn kept his cool. "That's right, in exactly seven days. Supposed to be a celebration... though I don't know how much celebrating we'll be doing if Alberta stays with British Canada."

"Where will you be going?"

"A fishing camp on Lesser Slave Lake."

"Who owns it? Mister Hendricks? Or Imperial Oil?"

The whispered conversations stopped. All attention was being paid to Coburn and Jules, and Jules felt that little shiver of satisfaction that he was in the perfect job, in the perfect time, and was very, very good at what he did.

His boss said, "His own. He's quite proud of it, has been in his family for generations. Supposedly the land was granted to his family by Queen Victoria after the Yukon War, to his great-great grandfather"

Jules nodded. "Take it out."

"What?" Coburn said.

"Take it out, blow it up, destroy it." Jules looked to the man from External Relations. Jules said, "The Navy's Lake Superior Fleet. Two of its frigates last year... they were installed with the latest Storm Shadow cruise missiles from the British Royal Navy. Am I right? The ones with extended range, the latest electronics?"

External Relations slowly nodded, his bald head glistening in the light. "Yes, you're right."

"Range far enough to get to the Lesser Slave Lake?"

"I'm sure of it."

Jules looked to his boss. "Mister Hendricks is acting rudely, intolerably, and not only breaking an agreement with Standard Oil, but breaking his personal word with you. I'm sure he's expecting you to make a counter-offer, or to do something within reason, like closing the border tonight, give Alberta a bit of an economic shock, or try to do something to the markets when they open tomorrow. But this way..."

Operations spoke up. "Wait, wait, wait. How in hell can we even consider doing something crazy this? There has to be consultations with the Oil House and the government and --"

Coburn interrupted. "Oh, shut up. And when did you lose your cherry, John? Or do I have to spell it out for you again? We are the government. Fred, make the call, and make it happen."

External Relations picked up the phone, started hammering the keypad, started talking in a low but firm voice, and Jules went back to work on the paper. Just two spelling errors so far, and that was it, and again, he was glad Coburn's daughter was a reasonably good writer. The other men in the conference room kept their voices low and talked among themselves

When External Relations was finished a few minutes later, he said, "It's a go. *DSS Ryan* has launched. Impact should be in... thirty-four minutes."

Publicity said, "What's the collateral damage going to be?"

External Relations shrugged. "Who cares?"

"Humor me," Publicity said.

"The fishing camp and everything within a hundred meter radius will be obliterated. Some heavy damage another hundred meters further out... shock-wave, fire, flying debris."

"Okay..."

"So anybody working or sleeping in the house, any passing fishermen... well, if they're close enough, the blast will be enough to capsize them. Especially if they're in canoes. Especially if they're dumb enough to go canoeing at night without wearing life jackets."

Some laughs at that, and Publicity said, "All right, at least I'll get a heads-up in case we take out a wedding party or something."

"Or something," Operations said.

Jules checked the time. Two minutes had passed. Impact in thirty-two minutes.

He went back to the term paper.

Thirty-nine minutes later the phone rang on Ty Coburn's private line, and he let it ring three times before winking at his staff and picking up the receiver.

"Coburn here," he said, keeping the speakerphone on mute.

Jules' boss nodded twice and said, "Harlan, Harlan, please... calm down."

Even sitting three chairs away from his boss, Jules could make out the loud voice on the other end. Not loud enough to hear words, but loud enough to hear the emotion.

Coburn finally said, "Harlan, look. Business is business. All right? And my Board gave me full authority to make a successful conclusion to these negotiations. Now, I thought we had an agreement, and you told me just under an hour ago that our agreement was no longer valid. What did you think I was going to do? Roll over and just take it, like a virgin bride on her wedding night?"

More loud sounds from the telephone. Coburn said, "Well, I have a fiduciary responsibility to my Board and my stockholders. I told them that the agreement was set, that the referendum vote was going to go our way in less than..."

Jules said, "Two hours."

"Two hours," Coburn repeated. "You put me in a very terrible position. What, do you think I was going to institute a hostile takeover tonight... as revenge? Or run a Board of Directors' slate against you next year? Was that what you thought might happen? No, tonight's vote is too important for the two of us, for our companies and for the Dakota States. We can't let it slip away because you've lost your nerve."

The voice on the other line seemed to calm down. Coburn nodded three more times and said, "Fair enough. Go back to your Board, see what arrangements or compromises you can come up with. We might be able to fix a few things around the corners, sweeten the deal just a bit, if that could help you."

A pause. Coburn said, "Sweeten the deal." He looked to External Relations and continued speaking into the phone. "Well... you know there's a six-month cooling off period after Alberta joins the Dakota States in order to do business with the Republic of Texas, the Confederacy, the United States... we could probably waive it."

External Relations gave a thumbs up. Coburn grinned. "How does that sound? I mean, sure you could stay with British Canada and get those trade concessions with Russia Alaska, but it gets cold and isolated up there. Pipelines break. Pumping stations catch fire. Lots of uncertainties."

The voice became louder again. Coburn said, "Harlan, Harlan, Harlan... that wasn't a threat, not at all. My word, you must be on edge. No, I was just pointing out the possibilities, that's all. Calculated risk. Probabilities. That's how we all do business. Am I right?"

Coburn paused. "All right, time is wasting. Can you get me an answer in... say, a half hour? No? Forty-five minutes? Fine, forty-five minutes. I look forward to hearing back from you. Good luck... and look, the fishing trip is on. You'll just have to come down to Oklahoma. I'll show you a good time on Grand Lake. Promise."

He hung up his phone as there was a loud chime in front of External Relations, and he picked up the phone, grunted a few times, and then pressed a switch and replaced the receiver. To Coburn he said, "Sir, that was Hancock, from N.A. Network News in Atlanta. Do we have any idea when the results are coming in?"

Coburn said, "No, tell the little bastard to be patient, all right? He'll know sixty seconds after we find out."

External Relations pursed his lips and Coburn held out a hand. "No, wait. Be polite, be nice. Forget I called him a little bastard. If he's pretending to report the news, the least we can do is to pretend to be nice to him."

Some smiles from the other men around the table, and Coburn turned to Jules and said, "What do you think?"

Jules said, "I think we're almost there, but we should be prepared."

"Prepared for what?" Operations asked.

"A retaliation."

"Where?" Operations went on.

"Any place we're vulnerable," Jules said. "I can't see Hendricks and Alberta letting our strike on the fishing camp go unanswered, even if it's just to send back a message that they won't be intimidated. Something is going to happen tonight. Guaranteed."

Coburn said to External Relations. "Got that? Let's get an extra alert out there to all of our facilities."

External Relations' face went pale. "Do you know how many facilities we have in North America alone?"

Coburn snapped back. "I certainly do. And if that number's been decreased by this time tomorrow, then you'll be looking for employment elsewhere. Maybe the sugar cane fields in the Republic of Cuba."

That got the man's attention, and he got to his phone, started working. Operations was sitting next to Jules and asked, "No offense, and I really mean that, but how do you know there's going to be a retaliation?"

Jules went back to the term paper. "I know history."

Twenty-two minutes later Hancock called again from N.A. News Network, wanting to remind Coburn that there was an escalation clause in their agreement for each minute that passed beyond the agreed deadline when the initial results of the referendum were to be announced. Coburn told External Relations, "My compliments to Mister Hancock, and remind him that we'll keep to the contract, pay any additional riders, and if he calls again, we'll cancel and go to Pacific Cable News in Seattle, and the first story we'll leak to them will be about his dark work with Standard Oil of Mid-America. Got it?"

External Relations said, "Yes, sir. Got it."

Some murmured talking from External Relations and he hung up the phone. "I think he got the message," he said.

Then the lights flickered overhead. A couple of heavy *thuds* rattled the ceiling, and dust fell from the ceilings onto the polished conference room table.

Jules said, "I think we just got Alberta's message, too."

Then the lights went out, as there was a heavier *thud.*

Jules kept calm, said not a word, as the rest of the room burst out in a babble of shouts and voices, until Coburn's command voice cut through and he said, "Settle down, settle down. The emergency lights should come on in a few seconds."

And just like that, the emergency lights clicked into life. There were grinding and crashing noises from up top, and Publicity — face pale and tears in his eyes — frantically looked up and said, "What's going on? What's going on?"

External Relations said, "Shut up, fool. We're being attacked. Just be glad British Canada or Alberta don't have access to any bunker busters."

Internal Relations said, "Hush… I think I hear some gunfire."

Jules cocked his head. "Yeah. A raiding force."

External Relations shook his head. "Don't like that."

Finance said, "Who does?"

External Relations said, "You don't understand. Gunfire up above. That doesn't mean paratroopers, or drop attacks. That means a local force. Undercover. Ready for quick dispatch. Meaning British Canada has successfully infiltrated in troops to our territory."

Coburn glanced up as the sound of the gunfire grew louder. "And knowing where we're located. That's the worse part."

Publicity cried out and ran out of the conference room, glass door slowly closing behind him as he raced down an empty hallway. Jules also didn't see the security officer at her post. Before anybody else could chime in, Operations said, "Sir, when Publicity gets its budget cut, I hope you recall who stuck with you."

"Or died with me," Coburn said. "Phil? Resources?"

External Relations said, "On it, sir," he said, going to the door. "Anybody here give me a hand?"

Jules stood up and said, "Right with you," and he joined External Relations as he made his way out of the conference room.

They didn't have far to go. They went to a darkened kitchen area with tables, chairs and a cafeteria-style serving area. At a rear closet near stoves and a walk-in refrigerator, External Relations pulled out a shelf of canned goods to reveal a collection of firearms and small wooden crates. He tossed out two of the crates and gathered up four black and shiny automatic rifles.

"Hey," he said.

"Yeah?"

"Always wanted to ask you something."

"Now's your chance," Jules said, grunting as he picked up each crate by a rope handle.

External Relations said, "How long does it take you to wash your brown nose every night when you go home from work?"

Jules said, "If we're still alive in an hour, I'll let you know."

They went back to the conference room, Jules helped get the wooden crates open. One was full of 7.62 mm ammunition for the automatic weapons — which Jules recognized as a model made by Winchester out of the California Republic, and outlawed in the Dakota States — and Coburn and three others started loading up.

The other wooden crate held gas masks, surplus Dakota Army styles, and Jules passed those around. Coburn went to the open door and looked down the hallway to where the elevator was located. He pointed and positioned External Relations and Internal Relations to empty conference rooms along the hallway, to set up interlocking fields of fire. Smoke started filtering into the conference rooms. There was *clicking* and *clacking* sounds as magazines were inserted into the automatic rifles and rounds were chambered.

Jules had a gas mask in his hand. He wasn't qualified on any firearms, and earlier he had gotten a college deferment from serving in the armed forces, and now he was regretting having done that.

Coburn looked to him. "How's my daughter's term paper coming along?"

Jules was stunned. "What?"

"The term paper," Coburn said patiently. "How does it look to you?"

Even the other men were shocked as well. Jules licked his lips. That's why he followed Coburn, worked for him, admired him. He was never shaken, never upset, always kept a cool focus.

Jules said, "It's coming along nicely, sir. Just some typos and a few grammatical errors. She… she did a good job on the research."

Coburn nodded, looked to the hallway. The smoke was getting thicker. He said, "Put it in a safe place, all right? In case… something goes wrong. I don't want her work wasted."

"I understand, sir," he said.

In another conference room, External Relations yelled, "The elevator's coming down! The elevator's coming down!"

Coburn said, "All right then."

Jules thought about running away, like Publicity, but no... he was going to stay here, in this conference room. That was the price had agreed to pay, from years ago, when he started working for Standard Oil of Mid-America. He put the term paper into his briefcase, put the case to one side under the conference room table, thinking that it should be safe and —

The elevator door slid open and men's voices yelled, "Clear! Clear! We're clear over here!"

External Relations yelled, "Hands! Show us your hands!"

Jules looked on with sweet and blessed relief. The door opened and two Standard Oil security officers stepped out, automatic rifles slung over their backs, hands open.

Coburn nodded, stepped back, caught Jules' eye.

"Get that paper done, okay?"

Jules couldn't say a word. He just went back to the briefcase.

Fans started up to suck the smoke away. More security officers showed up, as well as Tulsa police officers and members of the Oklahoma State Police and reserve soldiers from a local Dakota State army center. But Publicity didn't come back. Jules wondered where the poor bastard had ended up. There was a babble of voices and Coburn said, "All right, all right. Let's get back to work, shall we?"

And in a few minutes they were back in the conference room, the unloaded Winchester automatic weapons piled in a corner, the unused gas masks tossed into their wooden crate. Jules sat down and the phone rang, and External Relations picked it up, grunted "yeah, yeah," a few times, and hung up.

He looked at everybody in the conference room and said, "That tears it. State Police confirms it was a hit squad, probably from British Canada even though their credentials had been scrubbed."

"Military?" Jules asked.

Finance said, "Does it make any difference?"

Jules looked to Coburn, who in turn said, "Just might at that. Uh, Frank, call Imperial Oil. Get Harlan Hendricks on the line, but keep it mute. Let's see how we can play this."

Within a minute Frank handed the phone receiver over to Coburn, and he started in, right away, no hesitation. "Harlan? Yeah, it's me. Surprised? No? Why, you should be... about a half hour ago commandos from the British Canada Army stormed our facility. Killed about a half-dozen people. Nearly tried to kill me and the rest of my team. What? You mean to tell me this was a surprise to you? Really?"

He paused. "Yeah? Yeah? Well to hell with you, Harlan. We had a fucking deal, we did, and you made it personal. Yeah, yeah, you made it personal all right. That fishing camp… I knew you weren't there, pal, but you sure as hell didn't take that into consideration when my offices got hit, did you."

Coburn listened and spoke right over Hendricks. "I don't care if you didn't know about the raid. The fact is, it happened. The fact is, I nearly got killed, along with my team members. So it's pretty goddamn personal, and you got thirty minutes to make it right… before N.A. Cable News finds out its lead story for tonight has changed. Got it? Because from where I sit, with bodies and wreckage over my head, it looks like Ottawa went rogue in attacking us, and that can't stand."

Coburn slammed the phone down, looked around.

"Hey, can somebody get us some fresh water?" he asked,

It was over within the hour. The man from Imperial Oil called back, apologetic and groveling, and then a call was made to Hancock at N.A. Cable News — Coburn had said, "We've paid enough, make sure they report it as a landslide" — and soon after that, correspondents from Tulsa, Edmonton, and even Ottawa were reporting on the results of the Alberta referendum, that said 59 percent of its voters wanted to secede from British Canada and join the Dakota States of America, becoming that nation's seventh state.

At one point the sound was muted, as correspondents went from one city to another, cheering crowds in Tulsa and Edmonton, some disappointed protesters in Ottawa, and Jules ignored the main story and watched the news crawl on the bottom of the screen. Eventually two bits of news came across that caught his attention: an isolated fishing camp on Lesser Slave Lake in the new State of Alberta had exploded, killing four, apparently from a cooking gas explosion, and in Tulsa, the capitol of the Dakota States, referendum celebrations were spoiled when Tulsa police came under fire from heroin dealers holed up in a ranch house in a remote neighborhood, probably from the Empire of Franco-Mexico.

Coburn looked away from the television screen with satisfaction. "All the news that's fit to be bought. Nice to see that, don't you think, Jules?"

"Yes, sir, and if I may…"

He slid the term paper across and Coburn picked it up and without a glance, slipped it into his briefcase. "All done?"

"Yes, sir," he said. "My corrections are marked up in red, nothing major. She did a good job."

His boss grunted. "For what we pay in tuition, I sure hope so."

Jules went back to the television screen. In Ottawa, riot police on horseback were breaking up a crowd of protestors outside the Parliament building.

Coburn said, "Say, what was the term paper about, anyway?"

"The American Civil War."

"Oh, the one with Jackson and Hayes?"

"No," Jules said. "The first one, with Davis and Lincoln."

"Lincoln?"

"Yes, sir. The tall, skinny man. With the funny beard and stovepipe hat. Gave good speeches back in the day."

"Like what?"

Jules racked his brain for a moment, not quite believing his boss was asking him this kind of question, with all that had happened this night.

Then, luckily, something popped up into his memory. "Back in... 1862, I believe it was. He was giving a speech to their Congress, about the war. It had only been underway for a year. He said... he said that the Union had to be preserved. It had to be preserved, because... because, he said, '"We shall nobly save, or meanly lose, the last best hope of earth."'

Coburn said, "I see."

Up on the television screen, outside of the Oil House, the President of the Dakota States of America was making a speech, smiling and waving his arms.

Coburn went on. "Lucky for us, they lost back then, right?"

Jules said, "Yes, sir. Quite lucky."

AARON ROSENBERG

THE SOUTHERN GAMBLE

Sunday, October 8, 1871
Chicago

The Chicago dock was always bustling with activity, its long wooden piers packed with travelers, merchants, sailors, and laborers. But on this drizzly October morning, an unusual sound pierced the normal hubbub of grunts and curses, shouts and songs, feet and hands. It was the sharp rhythm of a march, and people melted away as a squad of soldiers appeared and stopped smartly at the point where the wooden docks met the stone of the city proper.

"Fan out!" the officer in charge, a major by his insignia, commanded. His saber hung by his side, still sheathed, as was the pistol on the belt opposite it, yet his hands were clenched into fists and his clean-shaven jaw was stiff, his lips drawn in a thin line beneath his mustache, and his words carried a bite that cut through the chilly morning air, making soldiers and civilians alike snap to attention. "The man we're looking for will most likely be in regular attire, but he will have the bearing of a military man, I suspect," the officer continued instructing his men. "He will be leaving a boat from the south, and traveling alone. Our orders are to detain him for questioning. Move out!"

His soldiers saluted and leaped into action, moving in pairs to disperse along the piers and search for their quarry. Men and women alike hurried to stand aside for them, and children scurried out of their path, for though the soldiers had been given no such orders, still they carried rifles with bayonets affixed, and it would be a very simple matter for them to use both blade and stock to slash and smash aside any who stood in their way.

One of the couples that fearfully evaded such a threat was a handsome pair, he tall and dark, she slight and fair. She huddled against him as they let the soldiers brush past, rose blossoming against her delicate cheeks as she fluttered a fan before her face. He kept an arm solicitously around her, the other stroking his mustache as he escorted her to safety.

It was not until they had reached the refuge of a street several blocks from the docks that they finally paused in their brisk walk. Then the gentleman turned to his lovely companion.

"Mademoiselle," he told her, dark eyes flashing as he bent over her hand, "it has been a delight and a pleasure to accompany you, but now I must bid you adieu. I wish you great joy in your impending marriage, and trust that when you look back upon our travels together, you will think of me kindly."

And then, not waiting for a reply, he straightened and, after a quick bow, turned and strode away, disappearing into the hustle and bustle of Chicago. The woman gazed after him, hand fluttering to her cheek, and if she now blushed more fully, one could as easily attribute it to the breeze blowing in from the water as to embarrassment or some other strong emotion.

Later that morning, a man sat at a broad, imposing desk in a grand office, poring over some papers. The man himself was equally distinguished, with his long gray beard and the lines on his face that spoke of great age and wisdom. Yet his small eyes were still sharp beneath his heavy brow as he studied the documents.

A knock startled him from his reverie, and he glanced up, surprised. His gaze had gone to the chamber door, but a second bang made him redirect, looking with even more confusion and dismay toward the glass-paned doors that led out onto a small balcony behind him. He was halfway to his feet when those same doors slid open and a man glided into the room.

"What is the meaning of this?" the bearded man demanded, confronting the intruder, who was taller and darker and younger than he, and dressed more stylishly than his own business-like gray suit. "Get out before I have you arrested!"

The stranger held up both hands. "I apologize for the strange manner of my entrance," he offered softly, his voice as smooth as his appearance. "I wished to speak with you in private, and worried that you might not grant me audience if I announced myself through standard channels." He swept into a bow. "Pierre Gustave Toutant-Beauregard, at your service," he declared. "And I believe I have the honor of addressing Roswell Mason, the mayor of this fine city?"

"That is correct, sir," Mason replied, struggling to fight back the rush of panic he'd felt upon his strange guest's appearance. His eyes narrowed. "Beauregard?" he repeated thoughtfully, one hand rising unconsciously to stroke his beard. "I have heard your name, sir. You are of the South, are you not?"

"I am that, born and bred," Beauregard answered easily. "And I have come from the South specifically to find you."

Mason was studying his unwanted new companion, and now nodded sharply. "Yes, we heard a rumor that someone had been sent," he stated. "Clearly you evaded my men at the docks."

"Indeed." His guest treated him to a smug smile. "I might not have, had they been better prepared. But then I could not have had the pleasure of meeting you here, in this handsome office." He gestured all around them, taking in the rows of bookcases, the leather couches and chairs, the elegant rug, the graceful lamps.

"What is it you want?" Mason asked, already growing tired of the other man's posturing.

"Why, only that which would benefit us both, and our two cities," Beauregard replied. He clasped his hands behind his back and assumed a more serious mien. "I have been sent with a proposition, sir, from none other than my own master, the Capitaine de Port de Nouvelle-Orléans."

The fancy French title made the older man sneer. "I'd heard that Monroe had put on airs," he remarked. "What, didn't feel right styling himself emperor yet? Or king, at least?"

"Not at all," Beauregard answered. If he took any offense at the insult to his superior, he showed no sign of it, not even so much as a stiffening in his posture or tone. "Though it sounds grand indeed, the title merely marks him as the master of the port, nothing more." He smiled easily, a friendly and charming expression Mason had no doubt had softened many opponents—and many ladies as well. "But that is neither here nor there. He has sent a message for you, if you would allow me to relay it?"

Mason was too old and too set in his ways to be so easily charmed, however. "I will not," he stated. "Whatever your master"—he drew the word out with another sneer—"has to say to me, I have no desire to hear it. We are a loyal member of the United States, and will have no truck with foreigners or traitors."

That last, at least, seemed to strike a chord, for now Beauregard did straighten, his brows lowering even as his voice fell—though still smooth, it was now darker and colder, like the river at midnight, whose fierce currents were concealed by its silky surface. "Have a care, Lord Mayor," he warned. "I am a loyal son, native born, and will be treated as such."

"You will be treated as a common criminal," Mason snapped, his temper finally frayed by the elegant manners of the man before him. "Bound up in chains and shipped back in a cage—or a pine box, if you prefer!" And he raised his voice even as he snatched up a gavel resting upon his desk and banged it down onto its stand. "Guards!" he shouted. "Guards!"

There was a loud bang as the soldiers standing guard just outside slammed the doors open and charged into the room, but even as he watched them Mason felt a sharp gust of wind at his back. When he turned around, Beauregard was gone, only the open balcony doors giving any indication of his recent visit.

The mayor considered sending his men out after the Southern scoundrel, but decided against it. Clearly the man had a talent for coming and going unseen, and Mason felt it was more valuable to keep the soldiers close rather than dismiss them to wander the city and leave him vulnerable. He stationed one on the balcony to prevent any additional interruptions from that direction, and then, with a heavy sigh, returned to his work.

Damn and blast, Beauregard thought angrily as he sauntered away, taking care to walk at a normal pace and not glance back over his shoulder for soldiers. Instead he smiled and nodded at those he passed, for all the world just another well-dressed gentleman enjoying a few moments out of doors. But inwardly he was seething.

He had warned Monroe that this might happen. "He will not listen," Beauregard had said as he stood in the Capitaine's offices after receiving his orders and the documents that went with them. "He is old and conservative and very set in his ways. Even if he hears me out, he will refuse. But most likely he will not even wait that long to throw the offer back in my face."

"Perhaps," Monroe had agreed, leaning back in his chair. His full beard was now shot with gray and his hair had pulled back from his high forehead but he was still regal-looking, and his eyes were filled with a cunning that his genial expression usually concealed. "But we must make the attempt nonetheless." Turning his gaze upon Beauregard, he had smiled. "I have faith in you, Pierre."

Beauregard had ground his teeth together. "Do not call me that," he had reminded yet again, despite knowing the admonition would fall on deaf ears. Though he avoided the use of his first name, and had ever since his school days, still Monroe insisted upon it. Knowing further argument would be equally fruitless, Beauregard had simply sighed and bowed instead. "I will do my utmost," he had vowed. "I will find a way to make them listen, at the very least."

"I am sure you will find a way," the Capitaine had agreed calmly. "You are resourceful, my friend. That is why I am trusting this crucial mission to you."

At that, Beauregard had straightened and snapped off a tight salute. "I will not fail you," he had promised.

Thinking back to that conversation, his mind spun, rapidly considering his options. So Mason had rejected him out of hand, exactly as he'd suspected. That did not mean the mission was a failure. Not yet. There were other ways it could still be salvaged—and other people he could speak with. Glancing about, Beauregard called upon the maps he had memorized before leaving New Orleans, and turned at the next corner, making his way quickly but calmly toward his new destination.

"It is truly a handsome city." The declaration made Joseph Medill glance up from his work, to stare at the man who had entered his small office unannounced. "So large," the handsome stranger continued, "and still growing." He shook his head as, unasked, he lowered himself gracefully into the seat opposite. "Yet so much of it is wood! I prefer stone, myself, and wrought iron. There is a certain poetry to those, and a permanence, that wood cannot hope to match."

There was an accent to his words, a flavor Medill had not heard before, and he studied the stranger intently, carefully setting his pen aside. "Do I know you, sir?" he asked. "Do we have an appointment?"

That brought a smile to the other man's face beneath his mustache. "Only with destiny, my friend," he answered. "Should you choose to accept its call." He leaned forward, offering a long, slim-fingered hand as elegant as the rest of him. "Pierre Gustave Toutant-Beauregard, at your service."

Medill accepted the hand, and they shook. "Joseph Medill, at yours." Then he gestured at the decanter and tumblers on the side table nearby. "Can I offer you a drink?" Though he did not yet know what his unexpected visitor wanted, Medill had to admit he was intrigued. And there was no harm in being polite.

Indeed, the offer earned him a much warmer smile than before. "That would be most welcome," Beauregard answered. "Thank you." He chuckled. "Already you have proven yourself superior to my previous encounter, which does not surprise me but does give me hope as to the outcome of this meeting."

"Oh?" Medill poured for both of them, then handed one glass to Beauregard. "To your health, sir," he said, raising the glass.

"To yours," his guest replied. "And to the prosperity of both our great cities." They clinked, and drank.

After taking a hefty swallow, and feeling the whiskey burn a welcome path of fire down his throat and to his belly, Medill nodded. "You are from New Orleans, then," he stated. "I suspected as much, given your name, but wasn't certain."

"I am indeed." Beauregard finished his own drink and set the glass down on the desk between them, careful not to dirty any papers. "The Free Port of New Orleans, once shackled by lesser states and now free to chart its own course." He leaned forward, dark eyes boring into Medill's own. "As Chicago could be."

Medill laughed. He leaned back and took another sip of his drink. "You want Chicago to secede?" he asked. He scratched idly at his beard, which was more gray than dark now, unlike the sleek mustache of his visitor. "Why would we consider that, when we are one of the shining stars of the United States?" He frowned. "And why come to me about this?"

"As to the latter," Beauregard replied, "I have already attempted to speak with your Mayor Mason. But he lacks vision, or courage. He is content to simply toe the line, following orders like a good little soldier, keeping the peace but never reaching for the stars." He sniffed dismissively, then eyed Medill. "You, sir, are cut from a different cloth, I believe. You are a man of conviction, and have the courage to pursue what you believe to be right, and to stake all on the bolder course."

Though it was clear flattery, Medill couldn't help but smile at the compliment. "I have been known to follow my beliefs," he agreed, trying not to look around them. His offices at the *Tribune* had been far grander than this, as befit the owner of the largest newspaper in Chicago. But he had given all that up to pursue politics, which had led to his being appointed to the Civil Service Commission. Not a glamorous job, nor one with impressive trappings, but important work nonetheless. "I still cannot imagine why you think I would betray my country, though," he continued.

Beauregard snorted. "It is your country that has betrayed you!" the Southerner insisted. "Yes, Chicago is great, but it could be greater still! Why do you slave away in the service of others when you can stand for yourself and make them bow to you instead? You have no need of them, but they need you a great deal indeed—and they would pay handsomely for it."

Medill considered that. He was no fool, and he had certainly watched New Orleans with great interest. When the war had ended, New Orleans had refused to surrender, instead declaring its independence from either side. And, as the greatest port on the continent, with absolute control over the mouth of the Mississippi River, the city had proven too powerful to ignore. Or to control. It had proven far easier for the United States to negotiate instead, recognizing the

Free Port's independence and establishing a mutual pact of nonaggression, in exchange for favorable trading rights and reasonable fees to access the river system.

Now Medill's mind leaped ahead, considering the implications of what Beauregard has suggested. "You want Chicago to become another Free Port," he mused aloud, "and to, what, join with New Orleans?"

"Indeed." His guest seemed pleased at his quick grasp of the proposal, and pulled a folded sheaf of papers from the breast pocket of his suit jacket. "I carry here a declaration of alliance from the Capitaine de Port de Nouvelle-Orléans," he declared. "It recognizes Chicago as its sister city, and binds the two together in a Mississippi River Coalition, pledging to aid Chicago in maintaining its independence and their mutual control of the river trade."

That made sense, Medill had to admit. While New Orleans sat astride one end of the mighty Mississippi, Chicago perched alongside its upper end, with the Illinois and Michigan Canal connecting that to the Great Lakes. If the two cities forged an alliance, they would completely control any and all trade up and down the river, and utterly dominate the country's interior waterways.

There were other obstacles to such a proposed union, however. "You clearly knew where to find me," Medill pointed out to his guest, stroking his short beard. "Which means you know who I am. But that means you must also know my history." He frowned and leveled a finger at Beauregard. "And you know, therefore, that I cannot abide slavery."

"Nor would we ask you to," Beauregard replied, lowering the papers to his lap before spreading his own hands to show he meant no harm nor any offense. "Chicago would be free to chart its own course in that regard. If you wish to forbid slavery within your city limits, and to prohibit the trafficking of slaves through your port, so be it." He shook his head. "Truth be told, we have fewer and fewer slaves ourselves," he said, his tone conveying neither displeasure nor satisfaction at that turn of events. "Though it remains legal in our city, it is of course outlawed all around us, and thus there is no longer any point in bringing slaves in or out."

Medill shook his head, disgusted at the mercenary approach to such debased treatment of other human beings. "The fact that you are only giving up slavery because it no longer earns you a profit only proves that we do not think alike," he pointed out, "and thus makes any proposed union between our cities unlikely."

"It does not have to," Beauregard argued. "Look, you sport a full beard. I prefer the mustache alone. Does this mean we cannot be friends? Colleagues?

No, it only means that on this subject we disagree." He smiled slowly. "As long as I do not threaten to shave off your beard, nor you to force me to grow one, there is no reason for us to argue."

"A pretty argument," Medill conceded, "and true enough, as far as it goes. But that still doesn't explain why I should turn my back on the rest of the country. Yes," he stated, holding up a hand to forestall Beauregard's interruption as the younger man opened his mouth to speak, "I know that this country has its problems. But that doesn't mean we simply abandon it. We try to fix it instead." He waved at his office. "And this is a part of that."

"It is," Beauregard agreed, "and you are to be commended for making such an effort, sir. But how far will it extend? How long will the effects of your labors last? Or will they be swallowed up by the enormity of the country and the depths of its problems?" The New Orleanian eyed his host intently. "You were a great supporter of President Lincoln, sir, and I acknowledge that he was a great man. But the war has left this country in turmoil, and Johnson did not improve matters. And now Grant—Grant may be trying to fix certain problems, but he is creating others. We have heard stories, even in our city, of him and the favors he grants his friends. Is this helping the country? Is it helping your city?"

Medill sighed and fingered his glass, slugging back the last of its contents. Yes, he'd had his own concerns about President Grant and his administration, but he'd kept those to himself. Now he was forced to at least acknowledge them and the danger they posed. And what if Beauregard was right, he wondered. What if he was setting his scope too wide, and in doing so diluting his efforts so much as to make them utterly ineffective? Was he better off giving up on trying to repair the whole country and instead just focusing on his own beloved city? Was that so wrong?

That didn't answer certain other questions, however, or solve certain obstacles. One of which he brought up now. "You said you'd already approached Mayor Mason," he stated slowly. "And that he rebuffed you. Even if I were amenable to your proposal, what good would that do? I am a mere civil servant—I am a politician, yes, but I do not hold any office, and I have no authority beyond what President Grant had given me in the commission of my duties here. How do you expect me to lead Chicago into joining your coalition?"

"Do not worry yourself on that score," his guest assured him easily, his whole manner relaxing now as he perceived that they had moved past the question of "would you?" and onto the more practical "how shall we?" "There are ways to remove Mason from power, and I expect such can be effected speedily and without difficulty."

"You cannot kill him," Medill snapped, slapping a hand down on the desk for emphasis. "That I will not condone!"

"Nor shall I," Beauregard replied. "Calm yourself, good sir. Coldblooded murder was never my intent, nor my way—in war time, killing may be necessary, but this is merely politics, and such exceptions do not apply." He stroked his mustache, smoothing it over his upper lip. "But you must admit that Mason is not popular with your fellow Chicagoans. He is an adequate leader, perhaps, but not a strong one—satisfactory while the weather is calm, but the moment a crisis arises he will fall to pieces, and the city will call out for a firmer hand." He smiled. "Your hand, sir."

Medill thought about that. He could not argue the characterization of his political rival, for he had long held Mason in some contempt. But a crisis? "What manner of crisis?" he asked.

"Nothing severe," his new ally promised. "Merely something to galvanize the people against their current mayor and make them turn to you for succor." He brandished the papers. "Now, perhaps you would do me the honor of reading the articles my Capitaine has prepared, and, if you do indeed feel this could be the best course for your city's prosperity, affixing your signature to them?"

After a long pause, Medill reached out and accepted the papers. His years with the *Tribune* had taught him how to scan documents quickly—a talent that had already served him in good stead here at the Civil Services Commission—and now he was able to read the papers in a matter of minutes, while his guest waited quietly, hands folded before him as if he were merely thinking on a casual matter. Finally, when he had finished them and even gone back to reread certain key passages, Medill glanced up and nodded.

"Very well," he stated, knowing that he was committing both himself and his city to this risky endeavor. But the rewards, should they succeed, would be great indeed. And, provided Beauregard could indeed deliver control of Chicago to him as promised, and he himself could find the courage to stay the course in Grant's obvious displeasure, their success seemed all but assured. "I accept your Capitaine's generous offer of an alliance," Medill declared slowly, as if he stood before a full courtroom rather than being closeted in his tiny office with only Beauregard himself to bear witness. "Provided I am in a position to chart Chicago's course, I agree to secede from the United States, forming the Free Port of Chicago, and to enter into the Mississippi River Coalition with the Free Port of New Orleans." He took up his pen and, dipping it afresh in the inkwell to make sure its tip was well charged, signed the documents with a flourish. There were two copies of the accord, and Medill kept one for himself, handing the other back to Beauregard, who accepted it with a graceful seated bow.

"My thanks, sir," the New Orleanian said as he tucked the document safely away. "My Capitaine will be well pleased to hear of your agreement, and I know that both he and I will look forward to working with you. Our two cities will indeed be as sisters, linked by our common cause as if by blood and bound together in amity to scheme and plan and unite for our mutual protection and growth." Rising to his feet, Beauregard extended his hand, and once again they shook, this time with all the solemnity of the major undertaking they had both agreed to, but also with more warmth as well, for they were indeed now allies and partners. "Be ready, sir, for the call to action, and respond to it speedily and well," Beauregard warned as he turned toward the door.

"I will," Medill answered. "And you, sir, be ready to lend your city's assistance, as promised." For if Chicago declared but New Orleans did not immediately step up alongside, the federal government would simply send troops to retake and occupy Medill's city, and the gambit would fail.

"Never fear," Beauregard responded. "We are as brothers now, you and I, and through me my Capitaine as well. When you call, we will come, and we will stand shoulder to shoulder as free men." Then, pulling open the door, he was gone.

Medill stared after his new Southern friend for a moment, his mind still reeling at what had just happened. Had he really agreed to that? Was it really the wisest course? But even though it flew in the face of his sense of obedience and loyalty to the country, Medill's love for his city answered: Yes, yes it is.

He only hoped that he would be proven right, in the end.

Beauregard was halfway to the docks, humming softly to himself, his step jaunty with success, when a pair of dark blue-clad figures appeared on the street before him. He felt rather than saw the second pair cross the street behind him and box him in, and sighed. He had hoped to avoid this, but clearly that was not to be.

When two more men appeared at the next intersection, Beauregard knew that whatever encounter was about to occur, it was now imminent. Sure enough, after a moment a lone additional soldier arrived to join their small cluster, filling in the one vacancy in the navy ring surrounding Beauregard. The newcomer had an officer's marks on his jacket, and an officer's sword at his side. His face, with its clean chin and drooping mustache to match the heavy-lidded hangdog eyes, was familiar to Beauregard, and he laughed, which clearly startled and unnerved several among his armed escort.

"Mister Butler," he addressed the officer, studying the other man with a small smile on his lips. "Well met, sir. It has been many a year, has it not?" Beauregard glanced at the officer's sleeves and shoulders again. "But is it Major now? Was it not General, before?"

"Indeed," Major Benjamin Butler replied, his tone as icy as his stare. "As you well know."

"Ah." Beauregard feigned shock and dismay, pressing one hand against his chest. "I hope that I was not to blame for such a reversal of fortune?" But of course he already knew the answer to that, as did Butler. The two had only met once before, briefly, on the battlefield. The Civil War had only just begun, and the Union had realized at once that New Orleans, as the largest city in the South and one of the key ports on the continent, must be retaken immediately. They had sent a well-regarded Navy captain, David G. Farragut, to breach the city's defenses—and an Army contingent, led by then-major general Benjamin Butler, to occupy New Orleans once it was back in Union hands.

But the South had been ready. The city's defenses, concentrated at Forts Jackson and St. Philip, had withstood Farragut's initial attacks—long enough for the South to recall one of its greatest strategists and send him to protect the city of his birth.

Farragut had been a talented naval officer—but he was no match for the genius of Pierre Gustave Toutant-Beauregard. Particularly when, for a period of twelve years before the war, Beauregard had been in charge of repairing and improving the defenses of those same two forts, and others along the Mississippi. He had handily driven Farragut back, and New Orleans had proudly remained with the Confederate States right up until the end of the war.

"And now here we are again, two old soldiers," Beauregard said with a smile. He sketched a quick bow, careful not to move too fast and alarm the armed men all around him. "I have enjoyed this opportunity to catch up, Major," he continued, straightening, "but I fear I must away. Duty calls, and I hope to be on a boat back toward home by dawn."

"The only place you'll be going," Butler growled, "is to prison. You are under arrest, sir, for treason against the United States of America." He motioned, and two of his men reached out and grasped Beauregard by the arms, their grips tight enough to be painful.

Beauregard did not show any discomfort, however, as he frowned. "Ah, I believe you are mistaken, monsieur," he informed the angry Army officer before him. "For I am not a United States citizen. I am a citizen of the Free Port of New Orleans, and as such cannot be tried for any crimes here on American soil." He gently tugged his arms free, and although surprised the soldiers did not prevent it. "Should you feel that I have acted in some manner violating local law," the Southern gentleman in their midst continued, making a show of straightening his tie and brushing off his sleeves, "you may write to my Capitaine, James T. Monroe. He will advise our court to discipline me as they deem appropriate." Which was a joke, of course—Butler knew full well that Monroe would never punish one of his own, especially not one so highly placed in his government as Beauregard was, for anything that happened in the United States. "Now, if you will excuse me."

Butler fumed, but after a moment he was forced to step back and create space for Beauregard to push past. "Run back to your city underwater," he growled as the elegant New Orleanian eased free of the soldiers. "But one day you'll slip up, and I'll be there waiting." Then, with a curt nod, Butler set his men into two organized lines and led them away at a brisk march. He didn't look back.

"Perhaps," Beauregard murmured to himself, watching the disgraced Army officer depart. "But I think not." Smoothing his mustache, Beauregard glanced about and then approached a pair of men loitering outside what he took to be an alehouse. They had the look of common laborers, and eyed him askance as he neared in his fine clothes, but his easy smile put them at ease.

"Good evening, gentlemen," Beauregard called out as he reached them, for the sky was indeed beginning to darken. "I wonder if you might allow me to buy you a drink, for I am new to your fine city and would be grateful for a local's aid in procuring entertainment."

That brought smiles to the men's faces. "Sure, we'll drink your beer," one of them said. "What sort of entertainment are you looking for?"

"I had thought a spot of cards, perhaps," Beauregard replied, signaling the barmaid who'd poked her head out to bring three drinks and offering her a coin as payment. Luckily New Orleans still used the same Mint they had before the war, and although the images stamped on them had changed the metal had not, which had made it easy for the United States to approve them as legal tender.

His two new companions both thought on that a minute. "There is a game tonight," one of them remarked after receiving his fresh drink from the returning barmaid. "It's at O'Leary's barn. We could show you."

"A barn?" Beauregard considered that a second, a slow smile spreading across his face. "Yes, I believe that would do very well indeed," he said finally. He reached back with his free hand and rapped gently on the alehouse's outer wall, producing a hollow knock. "Such a handsome city," he said softly. "And all this fine, lovely wood." Then he grinned at his new friends. "You know," he remarked, a gleam in his dark eyes, "I believe I shall be quite lucky tonight. Indeed, I feel positively afire with it."

The other two men nodded, though it was clear they didn't understand. That was fine, Beauregard thought with a low chuckle as he followed them, drink in hand.

They would.

MACKENZIE REIDE

SHIFTING GEARS

"Dr. Winthrop, where have you been?" the receptionist said as Elizabeth hurried into the Environmental Engineering Department office. "I've been calling you all morning."

"Good morning, Iris," Elizabeth answered. "I had a flat tire."

"Oh! I hate it when that happens. I was worried."

"Sorry. I would have called but my battery died." Elizabeth held up her phone. "Ever since they made us switch to American-made products, my phone only lasts three hours! It's ridiculous!"

"Yes, it's like they just want us to buy more batteries. Here, use my charger."

"Thanks." Elizabeth plugged in her phone.

"No problem." Iris glanced at the front doors. "Did you see the federal agents?"

"Feds?" Elizabeth looked around her, then stuck her head in the conference room. "No, I didn't. Why would the feds come here? What happened to the Monday morning meeting?"

Iris shuffled some papers on her desk. "They wanted to see Dr. Weitz, so I told them I expected him to come to the meeting. They said they would wait."

"Did they say anything else?" Elizabeth asked as she poured herself a cup of coffee.

"Well, they asked a lot of questions about Dr. Weitz's work and then they began to ask about you and your work. They wanted to know about your trip to Seattle next month."

"Seattle? What did they want to know about that?"

"Your whole itinerary." Iris' hand shook slightly as she fiddled with the mouse. "I didn't want to, but they said they could arrest me, that patriotic Americans shouldn't be visiting Seattle. That I could be charged with aiding the anti-American activity in New Cascadia if I didn't cooperate."

"Anti-American activity in New Cascadia? What kind of nonsense is that?" Elizabeth responded. "And what does that have to do with me?"

"I don't know. But they were most interested in your dinner date with Dr. McCarty." Iris pointed to the bottom of the document on her screen.

"What? That's not a date!" Elizabeth felt her face grow hot. "It's for work!" "Well, I did say that Dr. McCarty is handsome, but . . ."

"Iris!"

"I was flustered! They made me really uncomfortable. I tried to make them crack a smile but it didn't work. Anyway, I didn't say you were dating, I just said Dr. McCarty was going to take you out for dinner after your talk at the conference."

"Like I said, that's a work dinner ... never mind," Elizabeth sighed. "Where are the agents?"

"They're gone now. They sat in the conference room until Dr. Schwartz and Dr. Heller came in. Then they started grilling them, too."

"And?" Elizabeth felt a squeezing sensation in the pit of her stomach.

"That's when Dr. Weitz arrived. He talked to the feds for half an hour, and then left with them. They said they wanted to ask more questions." Iris moved nervously in her seat. "They told me to cancel all of today's classes."

"Are they nuts? We've only got two weeks until the end of the semester!" Elizabeth stared at Iris in horror. "We've got finals to prep for. We can't send everybody home."

"I tried to explain but they wouldn't listen." Iris lowered her voice. "As they were leaving, I heard one of the men say that they would pick you up at your house. I tried to call you, but you didn't answer!"

Elizabeth shook her head in disbelief. "That's crazy!"

Iris pursed her lips. "Yes, it was. I don't understand what they want. Why would they want to talk to Dr. Weitz? Or you?"

Elizabeth clutched her cup of coffee with two hands. The pleasant aroma was comforting. "Let's not panic, it must be a mistake. Let me see if I can find out what's going on." She walked over to the door to her office. "Are all the students gone?"

"Yes, I sent them home. They were happy to find out they have no classes today."

"Figures."

"You don't think Dr. Weitz is in serious trouble, do you? You know I heard about something like this at Columbia last month."

"That was a political science professor." Elizabeth tried to reassure her. "He's part of a group that's protesting the America for Real Americans campaign. That's nothing to do with us. We're engineers, not political activists!"

"I hope you're right. It's just that they made me so nervous."

"Well, I suppose it's their job to make people nervous." Elizabeth walked into her office. Her chair should have been nested under her desk, but it was pushed three feet away and rotated. When she sat down to grip her mouse the screen lit up. Her brow creased. She always turned off her computer for the weekend; someone had turned it on.

Elizabeth clicked on the screen. One of the emails from Alex McCarty was open—the invitation to dinner.

What the. . .

Elizabeth clicked the window underneath and found her itinerary for the conference. Under that she found her class schedule for the semester. Somebody had searched through the files on her computer. She sucked in her breath. Why would anyone care about her trip to New Cascadia? And why take Harold Weitz in for questioning?

Elizabeth surveyed the untidy pile of papers on her desk. Someone had riffled through them so she pulled open all her desk drawers. Same thing. Items were not quite put back in the right places. *What's happening?*

She grabbed a pencil from the little cup on her desk and stared at the grant application in front of her. Ever since the Pacific Northwest Unification, American funding had become increasingly difficult to find. That was the prime reason for trying out a joint project with the University of New Cascadia. Her father, the Dean, had been reluctant to reach across the new border, but Harold convinced him it would benefit the department. Harold had also introduced her to Alex, the charming young professor at U New C. She smiled to think of those deep brown eyes and Irish accent. Their first dinner at the tiny sushi place next to the University had been both awkward and funny. Elizabeth had spilled sake all over Alex's trousers, but he just laughed and ordered more. For the first time she felt comfortable talking with a member of the opposite sex without charts and data to look at.

She sketched a Porsche on the margins of the grant proposal in front of her.

Could this be related to what happened at Columbia? Harold had been very agitated when she had returned from her last trip to Seattle. She had attributed that to the budget cuts. Then again, Alex was not his usual cheerful self, either. Their dinner date had been solemn. His mind seemed to be elsewhere.

A ping pulled her from her thoughts. An email from Alex had popped up in her inbox. It was marked urgent.

She stared at the subject line. GET OUT

She froze. *What?*

The phone rang in the reception area. Iris answered, "Environmental Engineering office, how can I help you?"

After a short pause Iris spoke again. "Yes, Dr. Winthrop is here now. Can I put you through to her office?"

Elizabeth stared at the words on the screen in front of her. She typed, 'What?' and hit return.

The phone rang on her desk.

Another ping.

LIZ GET OUT NOW

Elizabeth blinked. This couldn't be happening. Not to her.

What the hell was going on?

The phone stopped ringing as Iris appeared at her door. "That was one of the feds on the phone." She sounded scared. "They told me to make sure you didn't leave. They want to ask you some questions."

Elizabeth deleted the last two emails from Alex. She forced a pretend smile on her face. "Iris, would you mind closing my office door? I have some work to finish before they arrive."

Iris looked uneasy. "Okay. I'm sure it will all work itself out." She closed the door behind her.

"I can't believe I'm doing this," Elizabeth muttered to herself as she pushed out the window screen. She crawled through the open space and slid awkwardly to the ground. She swung her purse over her shoulder and nodded to the two students that were sitting on a bench staring open-mouthed.

"Perfect day to skip class." She gave them a cheery wave and strode off down the sidewalk.

She reached her car and fumbled around in her purse for her keys.

"You probably shouldn't take your car," said a voice.

Elizabeth jumped. "What?" She stared at the man standing on the other side of her car. He was six feet tall with an athletic build that she couldn't help but notice as he leaned forward to rest his elbows on top of her little Honda. He wore a blue dress shirt and jeans. His dark hair was tousled, like he had just gotten out of bed without a shower.

"If you take your own car, you won't get very far. As soon as they figure out you've left campus, they will start looking for you."

Elizabeth frowned at the man. "Who are you? Wait a minute . . . aren't you the new janitor?"

The man smiled at her. His blue eyes seemed amused at her confusion. "Yes, I started with your department two weeks ago. My name's Jason."

"Yes, Jason," Elizabeth stated back to him. "I know your name."

"Oh." He appeared to feign surprise. "I never thought you even noticed me."

"Of course I noticed you," Elizabeth snapped. "You're . . . er . . . you're the new janitor. A new face, I always notice a new face in the building."

"Ah, but you never once stopped to introduce yourself. That's why I thought you hadn't noticed me."

"Well, I did. Now, if you don't mind, Jason, I have to go." She continued digging for her keys. "What do you mean they will start looking for me?" She felt sick to her stomach. "What's wrong with my car?"

"Too easy to trace. Why don't I give you a lift in my truck. We can talk as we drive."

Elizabeth gave up digging through her purse. "What? Are you serious?" She stared at him. "You expect me to just jump in a truck with a strange man?"

"Hey, I'm the janitor. You know me . . . sort of."

"Oh, so I'm supposed to just drop everything and get in the car with the new janitor? Wow, that "sort of" makes it all better."

She dove her hands one more time into her purse and pulled out her keys.

"I'm not going anywhere with you, Mister. Now, I'm getting in my car and I will drive over you if I have to."

Jason pursed his lips. His easy-going manner disappeared and his voice got tense. "Look, Dr. Winthrop, we need to go now and not in your car."

"*We* don't need to go anywhere!" Elizabeth opened her car door. "Seriously, I will drive over your foot." She got in and slammed the door shut. As she started the engine she heard Jason mutter, "Dammit!"

He opened the passenger door and slid into the seat beside her. "Fine, you can take your car, but you probably won't make it off campus."

"What the hell are you doing?" Elizabeth shouted at him. "Get out of my car!"

"No can do, sorry." Jason fastened his seat belt.

Elizabeth just sat there stunned. It was not every day that a handsome man jumped in her car, but this was not the day for it.

"You need to go now," Jason said firmly. "Drive!"

Just then Elizabeth heard shouting from across the parking lot. She looked up and saw two men in black suits walking quickly toward her car.

"Seriously, Doctor, we need to go!" Jason's voice rose in panic.

Elizabeth shifted the car into reverse. Now the men started running. She jammed the car into gear and floored it, pulling away just as the feds reached her parking spot. They shouted at her as she sped down the lot, working the brakes just enough to crank a tight turn out onto Main Street.

"Did that man pull out a gun?" Elizabeth gasped as she drove down the road.

"Yes, they both have guns." Jason let out a breath. "That was close."

"Who are those men? Are they really federal agents?" Elizabeth gripped the steering wheel tightly. "And what the hell do they want with me?"

"We need to ditch your car."

"Why? And just where are we going?" Elizabeth switched lanes. "And who the hell are you?"

Jason fidgeted with his seat belt. He seemed to be checking it to make sure it was secure. "We need to get to the border as soon as possible."

"The border?" Elizabeth glanced sideways at him. "Are you saying we have to leave California?"

"I'm saying we need to get you out of the U.S." Jason glanced out the rear window.

"But . . . this is ridiculous. Besides, I don't have my passport with me."

"That's okay, I got you a new one."

Elizabeth frowned. "Why? I don't need a new one, mine doesn't expire for another two years."

"Yes, but this one has a new identity on it." Jason looked at the side mirror on the passenger's side. "I don't mean to alarm you, but I think we are being followed."

"What?" Elizabeth looked in the rearview mirror and saw a black SUV rapidly changing lanes, coming up behind her.

"We need to lose them. Can you do that?"

The dread pooling in her stomach morphed into anger. "Watch me." Elizabeth threw her car into a skid. She swerved to avoid a garbage truck, then maneuvered around two slow moving cars as she sped down a side street.

"Did you drag race as a kid or something?" Jason asked as he gripped the door handle.

"Defensive driving lessons." Elizabeth concentrated on weaving in and out of the traffic. The SUV swerved wildly but managed to follow.

"Oh, yeah?" Elizabeth shook her fist at the rearview mirror. "Try this!" The tires squealed in protest as she turned into a narrow alley.

"I've got a bad feeling about this." Jason looked pale.

Elizabeth thought briefly of a former boyfriend who had reacted badly to her fast driving. "If you feel sick, then stick your head out the window."

"Seriously, you call this defensive driving?"

"Well, there are feds with guns chasing us, so yes, I call this defensive driving." She paused to navigate between two large cargo containers. "And . . . I did get to drive on a race track as a teenager."

"Really? That's cool." Jason looked back. "They're still on our tail."

Elizabeth shot back out into the traffic. Horns honked as she swerved around a delivery truck. She changed lanes to avoid colliding head on with a BMW. The SUV was still only one car behind her. *What is it with these guys?*

"We have to ditch them!" Jason held onto the armrest with his head jammed up against the window.

Elizabeth gritted her teeth. "Hang on." She accelerated through a red light. "Whoa!" Jason's head swiveled back in response to a nasty crunching noise behind them.

"Did we lose them?" Elizabeth focused on the cars around her.

"Yes, they just took out a pickup truck." Jason looked forward. "We need to get to the warehouse district. I have things there that we can use."

"We just lost the feds and now you want to make a pit stop?"

"I think you'll find it worth your while. Besides, we need to switch cars."

"How about you tell me what's going on?"

"Yes, we need to talk." Jason seemed to steady his nerves.

"You still need to throw up?"

"No, I'm good . . . really." He gave her a sheepish grin. "That was impressive. You can rescue me any day."

Elizabeth felt her cheeks flush. "Thanks."

Jason pointed through the windshield. "Okay, slow down a little more please, and pull into that storage lot over there."

Elizabeth drove through a rusty gate and came to a stop in front of a row of doors. "What's in here?"

"Let me show you what's behind door number one." Jason climbed out of the car and wobbled slightly as he pulled open one of the storage doors. He made a grandiose gesture as if he was presenting something important to her. Elizabeth felt a big smile spread slowly across her face. There, parked behind the open door was a baby blue Porsche 911, mint condition.

"Where did you get this?" She jumped out of her Honda and ran over to the Porsche.

Jason grinned. "Oh, it took some digging. But Alex said it would get your attention. Besides," he shrugged as he pulled the garage door down behind them.

"I figured if we have to escape, we might as well do it in style."

"Alex told you? Are you friends?" Elizabeth opened the driver's door and took a sniff. "Still smells new." She looked at Jason. "I'm driving."

"I know." Jason gave her a bemused smile. He reached into the front trunk and pulled out a duffle bag. "Here, you need to change your clothes and dye your hair. I got you everything you need." He tossed her a box of black hair dye.

Elizabeth made a face. "You want me to dye my hair black? Can't I be a red head or something more interesting?"

Jason laughed. "Black's the best camouflage. Your lovely blonde highlights have to go." He gave her a mischievous smile. "Of course I could cut it all off for you instead."

"Ah . . . no!" Elizabeth spluttered. "Look, I need some answers. What's really going on?" She placed the box of dye on top of the Porsche and crossed her arms. "Who are you?"

Jason leaned against the cold metal storage wall. "I'm not a janitor."

"Yeah, I kind of gathered that."

He smiled at her. "I'm a concerned friend."

Elizabeth threw her hands in the air. "Oh, come on! Don't be cryptic! What the hell is going on here?"

"What do you think is going on, Elizabeth?" Jason frowned at her.

Elizabeth started. "You're supposed to tell me."

"Do you really have no idea?"

Elizabeth was taken aback. "No. I don't. Why are you looking at me that way?"

Jason looked out a side door. "You don't pay attention to much outside of solar research, do you?"

Elizabeth hesitated. "I . . . have been accused of burying myself in my work."

"Yes, that's apparent. Except for your race car driving hobby, what else do you do when you're not working?"

Elizabeth thought about her last dinner date with Alex. Ah . . . hanging out with friends?" Her cheeks felt warm.

Jason raised an eyebrow. "Okay. Dumb question. What do you know about what happened at Columbia?"

"There was a political science professor who was arrested."

"What was he arrested for?" Jason was looking seriously at her, waiting for her answer.

"Something to do with protesting the America for Real Americans campaign. What's that got to do with me?"

Jason tilted his head. "What do you think of that campaign?"

Elizabeth hesitated. "Well, I haven't really thought about it. Isn't it about buying products made in the U.S. instead of overseas?" She thought of her cell phone charging on Iris' desk.

"Have you filled out any of those registration forms that the Bureau of Labor Statistics sent out?"

"I only had to fill out one form. The Winthrops are one of the oldest families in Massachusetts. I thought that was all for statistics."

Jason nodded. "Yes, they did ask for a lot of stats."

"What does that have to do me? I work in solar energy not politics!"

Jason looked thoughtfully at her. "How much have you and Alex talked about things which weren't work related?"

"How well do you know Alex? Who are you, really?" Elizabeth leaned on the Porsche. "If you tell me, I'll dye my hair."

The corners of Jason's mouth twitched. "Okay, Elizabeth. I teach at U Vancouver. And I know Alex well."

"Teach what?"

He hesitated before answering. "History."

"History! I'm running away with a history professor!"

"Well, I could go back to being a janitor if you like."

Elizabeth shook her head. "No, never mind." She sat against the front of the Porsche. "I still don't understand why you are here."

Jason walked over and leaned against the Porsche beside her. "I wanted to see how much tension is building up against the proposed budget cuts. Alex was worried about you and I had vacation days to use, so I volunteered to come."

"Working as a janitor?"

"You'd be amazed at what you learn as a janitor. Did you know Dr. Heller drinks six cups of coffee a day? And Iris has a secret stash of dark chocolate in her desk?"

"No, I did not." Elizabeth laughed.

Jason grabbed the hair dye. "Come on. We can talk more while you stick your head in the sink."

Elizabeth let out a heavy sigh. "Okay. Fine." She couldn't refrain from making a face at the dingy little sink in the corner of the storage room. "I didn't know storage lockers had running water," she said as she stuck her head under.

"Arghhh!"

"Oh, yeah, there's no hot water." Jason stifled a laugh.

"Why don't you dye *your* hair?" Elizabeth snapped at him. "I'm not the one on the run."

"Hmpf. So, why does a professor from U Vancouver care so much about what's happening on a campus in California?"

Jason didn't answer right away. "I was born in San Francisco and stayed there until I was ten. Until my older brother took a rubber bullet in the eye during one of the riots. My dad was so upset that he applied for a fellowship at UBC, packed everything up and moved the whole family to Vancouver."

Elizabeth winced. "That's awful. Did he lose his eye?"

Jason gave a half-laugh. "Yes, but he claims that he only needs one eye to look in a microscope."

Elizabeth smiled grimly. "At least he can have a sense of humor about it. I attended a rally for the secession movement when I was fifteen and almost got trampled when the swat team charged. Ended up with two broken ribs and a concussion. I was lucky; the kid next to me got his head caved in."

"I'm sorry you had to go through that."

Elizabeth shuddered at the memory. "It was terrifying, I felt so trapped.

There was nowhere to run. It was a peaceful rally, then suddenly there was tear gas everywhere and people started pushing and shoving."

Jason handed her a towel. "I snuck out of the house to attend the rallies in

Vancouver. Fortunately, they were less violent."

"My father threatened to lock me in my room until I graduated, though it turns out he didn't need to, I never wanted to go to another rally again."

"Guess it turned you off politics?"

Elizabeth shrugged. "I want to change the world through science."

"How do you feel about the budget cuts? The sciences are being hit hard."

Elizabeth glanced at an old fashioned clock sitting on a shelf in the locker.

She didn't want to leave the hair dye on any longer than necessary. "Not good.

Without the joint venture with U New C, Harold would have to lay off more staff."

"So you've never had any inclination to move up north?"

"No, I've always loved living in L.A. We've got the best weather with lots of sun for my solar projects." Elizabeth stuck her head in the grungy sink to rinse out the dye. "Argh! The Pacific Northwest has too much rain!"

Jason shrugged. "True, but sometimes living in other communities gives you a new perspective." Elizabeth didn't answer as she finished rinsing and grabbed the hair dryer from Jason.

"Just give it a quick damp dry, then put these clothes on. We need to go." Jason opened the rear engine cover and knelt down so his head was out of sight.

Elizabeth dried her shoulder length hair just enough that she could wrangle it into a pony tail. Then she dressed quickly in the jeans and t-shirt and tossed her dress pants and blouse into the duffel bag. "Ready."

Jason closed the engine cover and threw open the garage door. He tossed her the keys and then motioned for her to back up.

Elizabeth got in the driver's seat and made a few quick adjustments. Then she started the engine. It purred like a Porsche should. She felt her skin tingle. *This is crazy. Why am I doing this?* Because Harold was in trouble and she needed answers. Jason appeared to be her best. A cold chill ran up her spine at the thought of the feds running toward her car with guns. It felt just like that day at the rally when her whole world broke apart. This time she would not get crushed.

Elizabeth backed up and rolled down her window. "Come on, what are we waiting for?"

Jason smiled. He closed the garage door and climbed in the passenger's side. "Drive casually on the way out of town please. Try to avoid any more car chases."

"Very funny." Elizabeth put on the sunglasses offered to her. "Where to next?"

"Drive on the old highway until we are well out of town. Oh, and make a quick stop at the drive thru up there."

"Ugh." Elizabeth frowned. "Shouldn't we avoid being seen?"

"That's what the hair dye was for. You are a person of interest, not a fugitive. And, we need to eat."

He turned on the radio as Elizabeth drove past three drive thrus before she finally convinced Jason to run into a deli and grab sandwiches. "See, this is much better," Elizabeth said with her mouth full of avocado and sprouts. She shifted gears to slow down for a traffic light.

"You are such a granola cruncher!" Jason complained. "You sure you don't want to move to New Cascadia?"

Elizabeth laughed.

They drove carefully through the streets of Los Angeles. Jason switched from station to station as if looking for something. Finally, as they left the city behind and Elizabeth accelerated on the highway, the news came on. "An arrest was made at the University of Southern California this morning. Dr. Harold Weitz was taken into custody by the FBI. Students are protesting the arrest of the popular professor. The Dean is refusing to comment."

"Harold was arrested? Iris said they just wanted to ask him some questions." Elizabeth took another big bite of her sandwich, then shifted gears.

The announcer continued, "Dr. Weitz is a known associate of Dr. Alex McCarty of the University of New Cascadia. The two men are alleged members of an underground movement trying to undermine the America for Real Americans campaign."

"Oh, oh," Jason said.

"Say what?" Elizabeth said loudly. "Harold is one of the leading engineers in the solar energy field. He's not political!"

"Ah . . . Elizabeth . . ."

Elizabeth turned up the radio.

"The police are also looking for another member of the organization, Dr.

Elizabeth Winthrop. If you have any information in regards to Dr. Winthrop's whereabouts, please call the tip line."

"SAY WHAT?" Elizabeth shouted at the radio. "I am not! I . . . I don't know anything about that campaign!"

Jason grabbed the radio knob and turned it off. "Look, Elizabeth . . ."

"Don't 'look Elizabeth' me!" Elizabeth roared. "What the hell is going on?"

She floored the accelerator. The needle jumped to 90 mph.

"Elizabeth, not now! Please slow down!" Jason pleaded.

"What the hell is going on?" She kept driving.

"Okay, okay, it's clear you really don't know." Jason tried to reason with her.

"Just slow down, okay. We can't get pulled over for speeding right now. Speeding comes later, okay?"

Elizabeth glared at the road. Reluctantly, she slowed down and forced herself to drive the speed limit. "You realize driving slow in a Porsche is like crawling in a marathon."

"Yes, I know." Jason made a mock groan. "But we need to get to the back roads. Now, what has Alex told you about his work outside of solar power?"

Elizabeth frowned. "Not much, really."

"Well, you two are dating, you must have talked about something."

"Excuse me? Those were work dinners!"

"Worried your dad won't approve of dating a New Cascadian?" Jason smirked.

"What's it to you?"

"Nothing." He sat silent for a long moment.

"Okay, fine, I just like to keep that part of my life private . . . and my father doesn't know. He blames New Cascadia for causing all the riots and now the problems with funding." Elizabeth took a deep breath and let it out. "Let me get my head wrapped around this. Alex is part of a group that disagrees with the America for Real Americans program. Correct?"

"Correct. Take the next exit. Once we're on the back roads you can let it rip. This Porsche handles like a dream."

Elizabeth gave him a smile. "You bribed me well." She switched lanes, heading for the exit. "Okay, so those agents came in to question Harold about this group. But why arrest him? Are they planning violent action?"

Jason shook his head. "No. No violence at all. We are just a group of concerned university professors from both the U.S. and New Cascadia. We produce an underground newspaper analyzing the true consequences of the proposed ARA program. We want to educate people, not make them riot."

"Really? I haven't heard of any of this."

"Well, apparently you've had your nose stuck in a solar panel. Ever since the crack down on unauthorized broadcasts, we switched to old fashioned paper. Alex has been smuggling the articles by embedding files in the data on your laptop. Harold has been printing and distributing the copies to the other people involved."

Elizabeth stared at the road in front of her. "Alex and Harold used me to smuggle information?"

"Yes, and it worked great until the feds picked up Jacob Murray at Columbia. It was only a matter of time before they figured out his source. That's when Alex and I started planning an exit strategy for you."

"What?" Elizabeth's head was spinning.

"Alex was going to warn you on your next trip to Seattle, but I was worried that things might heat up before then. So Harold hired me as a janitor for a while, just in case."

Elizabeth slowed down for the exit, then accelerated into the turn. The last rays of the day poked through the trees as she navigated the narrow winding road while she remembered Alex first handing her the "research" files for Harold. He had flashed that charming smile as he asked her to carry all the data on her laptop. When she suggested using an FTP program, he had simply shrugged and warned her their competition was very good at hacking.

Competitors? Or feds?

"We're making good time." Jason broke through her thoughts. "I want to hit the border just before the morning shift change."

"How does that help?" Elizabeth shifted gears roughly.

"Whoa, you okay, there?" Jason winced. "They are less likely to hold us up if they want to go home."

"I see," Elizabeth said curtly. "Are you planning on telling me my new name any time soon?"

Jason gave her a reassuring look. "You're Dr. Ursula Morsey and you are giving a guest lecture on the future of fossil fuels at U New C."

"Seriously?"

"Yes. I thought you would appreciate staying in the engineering field and it explains your love of classic Porsches." Jason pulled two passports out of the glove compartment, and held one up for her to see. "I took the liberty of dropping a couple years off so you're only 28."

"Gee, thanks. I feel so much better. And how old are you?"

"Just turned 30." Jason grinned. "I gave myself an extra year, you know, for maturity."

Elizabeth snorted. "So . . . you've all gone to a lot of trouble to protest this campaign. What's it really about? You don't think it's good to create more jobs in the U.S.?"

Jason put the passports back in the glove compartment. "It's the true intentions behind the campaign that we are fighting."

"I don't understand."

"Of course not. What you're hearing on the news is only part of the plan.

They have been very careful to hide their long-term goals under a mountain of fancy language."

Elizabeth thought for a moment while she shifted gears up a steep hill. "But isn't it supposed to create more jobs on American soil? Bring more opportunities to people here?"

"Opportunities?" Jason sounded sarcastic. "Interesting."

"What's really going on?"

"Well, there's an educational clause that creates a big problem."

"Educational clause?"

Jason nodded. "Yes, buried under what does sound like good ideas, is a provision to limit access to higher education."

"What do you mean by that?"

"If the parents of a prospective student were not born in the U.S. then that student will be prohibited from enrolling in any degree program. Such as your Environmental Engineering studies."

"Say what?" Elizabeth glanced sideways at him for a second.

"Oh, that's just the first step. Once the first bill passes, there will be a second one that revokes the degree of anyone who graduated in the last ten years whose parents were not born in the U.S. Then there will be the exclusion of those whose grandparents were not born in the U.S."

"What the hell kind of plan is that?" Elizabeth shook her head in disbelief. "That would strip the degrees from most people in the country."

"Only those not exempted by the 10-year grandfather period. Creating more opportunities for 'Real Americans', I guess." Jason shrugged.

Elizabeth clenched the steering wheel. "That's utterly ridiculous! Your group is trying to stop this from happening, correct?"

"We are educating people about the true goals of the program. That it isn't just a quick fix. That it's a long term plan that will hurt most of the people in the U.S. and only benefit a very specific few."

"I can't believe Alex didn't tell me any of this!"

Jason hesitated. "I didn't know he hadn't."

"Some dinner dates," Elizabeth muttered under her breath. "What if I went back and told the feds the truth? That I went on a few dates with Dr. McCarty and that was that. We never discussed anything outside of work. Wouldn't that clear it all up?"

Jason turned in his seat to face her. "Look, Elizabeth. You could go back to L.A. and take your chances. Try to convince them you are an innocent bystander. It's a long shot, but it might work. But the fact is, you have incriminating files on your computer. You've gone on dates with one of the leading suspects. Can you really convince them you've never talked with Alex about any of this?"

He shifted in his seat and looked forward into the night. "Also, can you tell me you honestly agree with all the policies in the America for Real Americans program?"

Elizabeth passed a slow moving car before answering. "No. Not if what you're saying is true."

Jason massaged his temples. "Then you would most likely not be okay. Even if they let you go, you would need to stop all association with Alex immediately, and refuse any contact from him. The feds will be watching everything you do."

Elizabeth frowned into the darkness. "I don't know what to say."

"For what it's worth, I'm sorry you got dragged into this. We never meant to stir up trouble, we just wanted to keep people informed."

Elizabeth didn't answer.

"Would you really just let it go? Now that you know there is more to the campaign?"

Elizabeth shook her head. "No, I would not. Besides, more than half my students would fail under these criteria." Just then she rounded a bend in the road and was blinded by bright lights as she pulled up behind a compact Acura. "Now what?" She held her hand in front of her eyes.

"Damn! It's a roving border patrol!" Jason sat up straight.

"I thought they only patrolled the main roads heading south."

"Looks like they expanded their duties."

"What if the feds called them? Are we caught?" Elizabeth's throat suddenly went dry as the patrol officer knocked on her side window.

"Just act casual."

Elizabeth wasn't sure if Jason was saying that for her or to himself.

The officer leaned over and shone a large flashlight in the car's interior. "Is everyone in this car a U.S. citizen?"

"I'm American." Elizabeth tried to keep her voice calm. The officer focused an intense glare on her face. *Does he know?* She could feel beads of sweat starting to form on her forehead.

"I'm from New Cascadia," Jason piped up.

The man's attention turned immediately to him. "What are you doing in the U.S.?" he demanded.

"Visiting my girlfriend, sir." Jason gave him a big wide smile.

"What? You can't get a girlfriend up there?"

"Can't imagine being with anyone else, sir." Jason gave Elizabeth's shoulder a gentle squeeze.

Elizabeth felt her heart skip a beat and her shoulder tingled where Jason touched it. The officer looked sternly at her. She forced herself to speak. "I'm giving a guest lecture at U New C, so Jason came down for the weekend, we're driving back together."

The officer leaned in close. His breath reeked of tobacco. "You know, you could do better than a New Cascadian." He stood up and waved her on.

"Gee, thanks a lot!" Jason grumbled as Elizabeth pulled away. Even in the dim light she could see his face turned beet red.

"Just don't tell my father I have two Cascadian suitors." Elizabeth grinned shyly at him.

He laughed. "Whatever you do, don't tell him I'm a history professor. I can't imagine what he'd say to that!"

Elizabeth laughed, then in a more serious tone, "What about the actual border? Do you think the feds will be waiting?"

"That is why you have lovely black locks and a new passport." Jason tugged her hair playfully. "It'll be okay, just stick to the same story we told the patrol. Also the car will be more visible, I'm hoping we can use it as a distraction." Jason leaned his seat back. "I'm going to try to get some shut eye. Let me know if you need to be spelled off."

"I'm fine."

She drove on through the night. A full moon came out that cast interesting shadows along the open spots on the road. Driving fast helped clear her head. What if she turned the car around now? She could slip through the roving border patrol and be back in L.A. by morning. But, would the agents believe her story? Or would they use her as a means to get to Alex?

It dawned on Elizabeth as she spotted a deer standing in the ditch, that Alex must have been planning to tell her everything at their next dinner date. But to drop a bombshell, 'Hey, Liz, I'm part of an underground movement against one of your government's new policies. Want to join us? Oh, and would you like more wine?' That was asking a lot.

Then again, using her laptop as a means of clandestine communication was something they were going to have a discussion about. A heated one at that.

Fortunately the deer was busy eating grass and not concerned with crossing the road, as Elizabeth accelerated back to her previous speed. She kept one part of her brain focused on the turns in the road, while the other part churned away at all this news. *How did I get into this mess?* Ever since that day at the rally, she had always worked hard and never caused trouble. Yet, here she was stuck in the thick of things. And what about her father? How was she going to explain this?

And then there was Alex; charming, handsome, and a smuggler of information, how did she feel about him now?

She thought about the policies under the policies. Undercutting education was not something Elizabeth could stand for. Besides, once that policy was enforced, what would come next? What was happening to her beloved America? She let out a deep breath and shifted gears. Well one thing was certain. There would be no turning back. Not anymore. She stole a quick glance at Jason, sleeping now beside her. A sliver of moonlight shone on his handsome face. He had risked his own safety to come and get her out. What about him?

Elizabeth bit her lip. Even if she could go back, she wouldn't be able to ignore the changes around her. Not anymore. She thought of Harold. He had risked his career to help future students. And what had she actually done? Never questioned what was said . . . always doing what was expected of her.

The first rays of the morning sun broke through the trees. Another beautiful spring day was dawning. She poked Jason hard in the ribs. He woke with a jolt.

"What? Where. . . ?" He sat up and rubbed his eyes. "Whoa, it's morning. You drove all night."

Elizabeth shrugged. "I needed time to think."

He looked at her hopefully. "And?"

She gave him a smile. "Time for another Winthrop to leave the old world for the new one. We're at the border."

Jason smiled back. "Good to hear." He grabbed the passports from the glove compartment. "Okay, Dr. Morsey, ready to give a lecture?"

Elizabeth thought of what she wanted to say to Alex. "Yes, I am." She hesitated. "Thank you by the way, for coming all the way to L.A. for me. You didn't have to do that."

He smiled warmly at her. "You're welcome. I think I like sunny L.A."

The early morning line at the border was short. Elizabeth smiled politely at the customs officer and bragged about her car. The officer seemed more inter- ested in the Porsche than in her.

As she pulled away from the border, Elizabeth felt something stir in her stomach. More uneasiness? Yes, but also something else: excitement at a new beginning.

"Time to eat." Jason pointed at a drive thru.

Elizabeth sped up. "When you ride with me, you are required to eat real food."

He laughed and ran his fingers through his dark wavy hair. "Fine. You're in the driver's seat."

"Yes, *I* am." She laughed too.

She focused on the road ahead. She didn't know what was going to happen next, but whatever the future held in store, she knew Dr. Elizabeth Winthrop was not going to look the other way. No, this time she was going to take an active part in it. She would decide what she supported and what she believed in.

And—she glanced at Jason—what information she carried and for whom.

But one thing she knew for certain, the future was going to be full of new and interesting points of view.

Glenn Hauman

EMERALD STATE

NEW YORK HERALD
DECEMBER 17, 1887

"SURVIVOR OF KANSAS TORNADO" SPEAKS AT COOPER UNION

The Cooper Union's Great Hall was filled to capacity last night to hear Lyman Baum, the famed "Survivor of Kansas", and his harrowing tale of fortitude and escape from the worst disaster in American history.

Baum described himself as originally a child of wealth from Chittenango, N.Y. who had moved to Kansas to make his fortune in real estate with the growth of the transcontinental railroad. He had seen the state as a youth and remembered unspoiled verdant splendor.

He spoke of how he had arrived as a grown man to green fields of corn as far as the eye could see, but that changed in the unusually dry summer of 1883 with the crops withering, the sun had burned the tops of the long blades until they were the same gray color to be seen everywhere, followed by the day in late August when the skies darkened due to what is now known to be the eruption of the island volcano Krakatoa in the Dutch East Indies, which spewed sulfurous ash high in the sky.

Baum told the audience how he stood in the midst of the great Kansas prairies and looked to the west and saw great storms building. Nowhere near a storm cellar, he saw great whirlwinds arise, mighty enough to crush any building in its path. As he watched, he saw everything turn "from brilliant color to the dull black and white of a photograph— the sky and ground all different shades of gray". He saw houses ripped from their foundations and lifted up into the sky, and saw women on bicycles attempting to get away from the storm and failing, before finally being swept up by a great tornado himself.

He awoke on a vast plain, miraculously unharmed but in completely unfamiliar territory, with everything covered by ashes, dust, and topsoil, with occasional bits of broken wood strewn across acres. By sheer luck, after wandering two miles he found a bump which he took to be a railroad track covered with yellowish ash and dirt, and he followed the yellow railroad for 20 miles until he reached what was left of a town, and caught the last coach to evacuate the town, as part of what came to be known as the Great Evacuation of Kansas and Oklahoma.

Although it is not known when it will be safe to return to Kansas, if ever, Baum has made it clear that he wants to do so as soon as resettling is possible, even if new cities must be built and new state and property lines drawn.

"After all," he said, "there is no place like home."

Alisa Kwitney

ONE OF THE GOOD ONES

The day Argos slipped on the porch stairs, he saw the flicker of fear in Melanie's face and knew instantly what she was feeling: He was getting old. He was getting old, and she was still relatively young, and soon he would die and leave her alone in her grief. He also knew that Melanie wasn't the kind of woman to remain alone in grief for very long.

Argos knew this because he was a genetically modified empathy dog, deeply attuned to his owner's microexpressions and what they signified. From the moment he was born, he was immersed in an intensive expressive and receptive language program. At the age of eight weeks, he was implanted with a computer chip that translated the subtle movements of his face and body into standard American English. At twelve weeks, he began a program in human sociology and psycholinguistics, which he passed with the highest score ever recorded.

He was, Melanie liked to say, a genius of a dog.

After his fall, Melanie took him to the veterinarian, where he stood stoically for a long time on a high table as Dr. Van Kleek performed the ultrasound. The news wasn't good: He had advanced congestive heart failure. For two days, Melanie didn't bother to change her clothes, and when she looked at him, he saw that her eyes were red and swollen from crying. For the first time in their lives together, he could do nothing to comfort her.

Then, abruptly, she cheered up. "You're going to have a new brother," she told him, eyes bright with excitement. "We'll pick him up this weekend. Won't that be lovely? He'll be just like a little you."

He licked her hand. "If it makes you happy, it makes me happy." His computer-generated voice was modulated to an empathic but dignified baritone, which Melanie had chosen herself.

"But do *you* want a puppy, Argos?"

"Of course I do," he replied, because as far as he was concerend, her needs were his needs. Like his primogenitor, Argos I, he had been selectively bred and genetically enhanced for emotional intelligence, psychological soundness, and the inclination to bond strongly with one person early in life.

For Argos, that one person was Melanie Ross. He had been trained to pay attention to every little shift in her mood from the time he was eight weeks old. If she looked in the mirror and began pulling the loose skin around her eyes, he knew that he should go up to her and gaze adoringly up at her face. If she started yelling at one of the humans that cleaned or cooked for her, he nudged her hand with his muzzle before she hit someone. If a strange human male got up and left immediately after mating her, he jumped onto her bed and nuzzled her cheek while she cried.

Now Melanie needed a puppy, and as the weeks passed, he began to look forward to his new brother's arrival. Melanie did not take him to meet other dogs very often, and he was excited at the idea that he would have someone of his own kind to talk to and play with, and perhaps teach some of the lessons he had learned about taking care of Melanie.

It went without saying that the new puppy would also be a clone of Argos I, Melanie's first empathy dog. She had been twenty-five and getting divorced for the second time when she purchased the first Argos. When he died at the age of fourteen, she was getting divorced for the third time, and knew she could not turn forty without her loyal canine companion. She must always, always have Argos in her life, and so, right before he died, she handed Dr. Van Kleek a set of instructions from the TrueGen Bio-Engineering Conpany and told her to harvest some cells. Despite the artificiality of the method, Melanie believed that Argos II was the reincarnation of her original dog, and often assumed that Argos II could remember events that had happened in the life of Argos I. "It's not just your body that's the same," she explained. "It's your soul."

Argos was a bit surprised that Melanie had decided to clone a puppy now, while he was still alive. If she believed that her original dog's soul had transferred from one body to the other, how could she conceive of having two Argoses? In the end, he decided that the reason he didn't understand was because he was, after all, only a dog, and could never truly match Melanie's more advanced human intelligence.

When the new clone puppy was born Melanie named him Baby Argos. "You will be Old Argos," she told him, "so we don't get confused." When the pup was five weeks old, Melanie decided she couldn't wait three more weeks to get him. Even though the pup wasn't weaned yet, Melanie and Old Argos traveled by private plane from their home in Davie, Florida, to the TrueGen Bio-engineering Facility in Ancramdale, NY.

Old Argos followed Melanie into a grey concrete building that looked like a bunker. Inside, two white coated scientists held a small bundle of gold fur with two bright dark eyes, a black muzzle, and one ear that stood up while the other flopped down. The puppy looked like a miniature verson of himself, and when the men placed him on the ground, he ignored Melanie and bounded up to the old dog, dipping his front paws down and giving a sharp "yip" of invitation. To hell with these humans: He wanted to play with Old Argos.

Old Argos, who had never had a chance to sire a litter, felt a sudden rush of affection. Ears perked forward and tail up, he gave two short barks of excitement and bounded over to his little clone.

"No! Down, Boy!" Melanie smacked Old Argos on his nose, stunning him. "He's only little," she said sternly, scooping up the pup and squeezing him to her chest. From that moment on, Old Argos was not allowed to approach the puppy unless Melanie was watching, or to get too close to Melanie when she was holding him.

Old Argos spent the next few days by himself while Melanie bonded with the puppy and the scientists worked on refining its language chip. The facility had a small inn set up for its wealthy clients, complete with an Italian restaurant, a deluxe coffee shop and a swimming pool surrounded by lounge chairs and umbrellas.

Old Argos tried to be happy because Melanie was happy, or at least, as happy as she could be, (she complained about the quality of the food and the size of the pool), but he was not used to being on his own for hours and hours. Without Melanie to please, his days had no purpose. He wandered around aimlessly, napping in the sun or in the shade, listless and discontented.

On the third day, he realized that he could smell another dog in the area, a female, but he could not see her. He could also detect the sickly-sweet tang of infection, and he followed this scent-trail to the laboratory where he found the female dog, a medium brown-and-white mongrel, collapsed in a small, dark equipment closet. Someone had forgotten to leave out any water for her, and she had dragged herself to the closet to drink some dirty mop water left in a pail.

The dog was almost too weak to lift her head when she saw Old Argos. It was the first time in months that he had been around another adult of his own species, and he felt a little awkward, speaking in the body and scent language of Dog. "You are injured," he whined. "Let me help you?" The truth was, he wasn't sure what he could do; there was a stink of putrid gangrene strong enough to reach even a human nose.

She licked her lips submissively, to show she appreciated the offer, but then added, "beyond help," by averting her gaze. "Unless..." She looked up at him with imploring eyes, asking him if he knew where her puppy had gone.

So this was the surrogate who had been implanted with the clone embryo — the pup's mother, as far as she knew. She must still have been nursing her puppy before Melanie arrived — two weeks earlier than the staff had been expecting. Argos glanced at the name on her collar: Peg.

Taking his silence as her answer, she sighed, rested her head back down and closed her eyes.

He licked her face, but she didn't respond. Old Argos stared at her for a moment. He was an empathy dog, bred and trained to respond to his owner's emotional needs, but his owner had shut him out and here was a creature like himself, a creature in physical and emotional distress. For a moment, he quivered with indecision, and then he raced out of the building as fast as his old heart permitted. He found Melanie a half mile from the concrete breeding shed, in a swimming pool.

Melanie was swimming laps while the puppy, leash tied to a deck chair, panted in the heat. Old Argos called Melanie's name, but she couldn't hear, and after a moment, he understood why: Her earbuds were in, playing music and the recorded voice of a trainer telling her that she just had to believe in herself. The pool had a ladder, but no stairs. God, he hated pools with ladders. They ranked alongside grooming sessions, trips to the vet and the acid stink of citrus fruit as his least favorite things. But Old Argos thought of Peg, and as the puppy watched, he jumped into the pool.

Melanie shrieked as he touched her with his paw. "What the hell?" Pulling up her goggles, she glared at him as she treaded water. "What's wrong with you? You scared the life out of me!"

"Forgive me, but I need your help. The pup's mother is very sick, and she needs to see him."

"What? Oh, God, I can't handle this right now," said Melanie, scowling as she checked her fitness tracker ring. "I have been incredibly stressed all day and have a pounding migraine, I haven't seen you in hours, and instead of checking in on me, you start telling me something to get me even more upset." She replaced her earbuds. "Go find one of the people who work here to help the dog." She resumed her laps, and the old dog scrambled to climb out of the water. His paws kept slipping on the ladder rungs, and it took several tries to get over the side of the pool. His heart fluttered in his chest, making him dizzy.

When he felt a little better, Argos looked at the puppy, still tied to the table, and made a decision. He might be old, but his teeth were still sharp. He bit through that leash in one bite, freeing his clone brother. "Not one sound," he told the pup, worried that he would start yapping and alert Melanie.

"Where are you taking me?" asked the puppy.

"To see your mother."

The pup looked confused. "Melanie is my mother," he said. Like most young empathy dogs, he was extremely malleable and open to suggestion.

Yet the moment the pup caught sight and scent of Peg, he whimpered and raced over to nudge her with his nose. His surrogate mother opened her eyes, her tail beating one, twice and then repeatedly against the hard floor.

As Argos watched, it occurred to him that he had learned something about himself: He was more than just the product of his breeding and conditioning. Melanie had rejected him, but he was his own master, now. Jumping up on a desk and pressing the computer's controls with his nose, he used the voice activation system.

He was just disconnecting the call when Melanie rushed in, flip flops slapping the concrete floor. "There you both are! What the hell is going on here?" Her face, already flushed from the sun, was getting redder from outrage. "Do you know how frightened I was?"

Before Argos has time to reply, the two TrueGen scientists in their white coats bustled into the room, accompanied by a solidly built woman in a beige uniform. "It must have been a prank call," one of the scientists said to the uniform. "We take excellent care of all our animals."

"I'll be the judge of that," said the Humane Society Officer. Turing to Melanie, she asked, "Are you the person who texted me on the emergency line?"

"Aboslutely not," said Melanie.

"I did," said Argos, trotting over to the officer's side. "But she's the one who needs your help." He indicated Peg, who was looking at him as though she understood far more than she probably did.

"Oh, my goodness, are you...you're talking!" The Humane Society Officer, a blunt faced woman named Janet Hosier, stared at him wonderingly. She had entered her profession as a young woman motivated by a deep love of animals, but over the fifteen years, constant exposure to cruelty had tempered her into hardness. Lately, she had begun to consider a career change, possibly to something less stressful, such as crime scene cleanup. Last week, she had gone to a church for the first time since childhood, and the week before that, she had consulted a psychic who charged her $100 to look at her palm and tell her she was deeply unhappy. She was a woman in search of a revelation, an epiphany, a sign. She continued staring at Argos. "How is that even...I mean, I've heard rumors, but..."

"The infection is spreading," said Argos, looking at Peg.

"The infection...oh!" Janet collected herself and knelt by the injured dog's side. When the uniformed woman's square, capable hands located the swollen and infected teat, she sucked in a sharp breath. "Who let this get so bad?"

"Not me," said Melanie quickly. "She's not *my* dog."

"It must be the kennel keeper," said one of the scientists. "How appalling. We'll have to fire him."

"Lies," barked Argos. He had never snapped at a human before. "I can smell it on you."

"Argos," said Melanie sharply. "That's enough. Come over here right away. And bring the puppy, too."

Argos looked at her face, frowning as much as her tight, artificially plumped skin would permit, and knew she was displeased with him. His stomach clenched in distress. Then he looked at Peg, who was gazing at him in adoration, and he walked over to her instead.

"Argos!" Melanie's shrill voice made him wince. "What do you think you're doing?"

He took a deep breath. "We should bring her with us."

"What?" Her face was white with shock.

"Peg. You should adopt her, too. For the pup and...to keep me company."

"That's impossible." In the harsh overhead light, Melanie's grimace of distress took on a simian aspect. Well, he thought, that's what she is, after all: Just another kind of ape. It was such a taboo thought that he expected some heavenly force to swat him on the nose, but nothing did.

Melanie made an exasperated sound. "I'm really out of patience with you! Come over here and stop making trouble." Argos didn't move. She pointed a finger at him. "Bad dog! Bad! The real Argos would never have treated me this way!"

Argos sat there, stunned. She hated him, and he deserved it. He was a disgrace to his genes, to his breed, to his species. He pictured a long line of dogs stretching back through history, from genetically enhanced intelligence companions like himself to royal lap warmers to wolfish hunters. They were humans' best friend, and he had shamed them all.

Then, just when he was about to slink back to Melanie in abject submission, Argos had a thought that made him straighten his back and untuck his tail. Our flesh has been your clay, he thought. You have molded us into every kind of shape and size and color: Dogs with short legs, bred to chase rats and foxes into their burrows, and dogs with huge heads and underslung jaws, bred to bait bears, or one another; whipcord lean dogs, bred to race until their legs give out, and high strung and obsessive dogs, selected to herd human livestock. You have stretched and pulled us into hundreds of different shapes for your various purposes. We are constructs of human ingenuity; should we not have a person's rights under your laws?

He was not aware that he had been speaking out loud until Melanie gave a choked sob. Janet, whose contact lens was fitted with a recording device so she could quickly document cases of animal abuse on site, managed to capture this moment on film.

"That whole crazy rant — that must be a language chip malfunction," said Melanie, to no one or everyone in the room. "Or maybe it's senile dementia. That happens to dogs when they get older, doesn't it?"

"It can," said the Janet carefully. "But in this case, I hardly think…"

"I'm surrendering him to you," said Melanie. "I can't bear to see him like this, old and sick and just not himself anymore. I guess I should put him down, but…it's just too difficult. You're an expert in dogs. You can decide what to do with him."

Janet was stunned. "Are you sure…"

"It's difficult, but I think it's for the best," said Melanie, not looking at her old dog.

"Melanie," said Argos, and it came out as a whimper. He watched Melanie walk away, and his damaged heart fluttered and paused. Over her shoulder, the puppy Argos met his gaze with fierce focus, as if he were trying to communicate something, or, in Janet Hosier's elegiac words, "as if some vital spark were being passed from one Argos to the other."

Janet, as she tells it, knelt down to wrap her arms around the old dog. "Never mind her," she told him. "You can come home with me." She had never married, and her house was filled with stray dogs and cats, but this was different. Her other animals might be family, but Argos was her new vocation. Like many Humane Society Officers, she'd spent years seething over the byzantine and contradictory laws pertaining to animal abuse. In some states, dogs and cats had been granted legal personhood decades earlier, starting with the landmark decision of the Oregon Supreme Court back in '16.[1]

In other parts of the country, though, judges were still notorious for allowing convincted animal abusers to get off with a stern word and a fine. Over time, Janet's passionate indignation had soured, leaving her with acid reflux and the conviction that humans deserved to be usurped by some other, more deserving species. Now, looking at Argos, she saw a different sort of future.

Argos, for his part, peered into Janet's rather small but fiercely shining eyes, and felt swept up in a powerful wave of emotion. He wasn't entirely sure if it was his emotion, or hers, but that was the nature of being an empathy dog. "We're going to start a revolution," she whispered, and his tail wagged in agreement.

Two days later, they began writing the series of essays that became known as the Animalist Papers — the blueprint for a new, less human-centric interpretation of the Constitution. It is astonishing, how much Old Argos was able to write, given the poor state of his health, and one must wonder if his death was hastened by the intense mental and physical strain of those final months.

Old Argos died before his successor, Argos III, sued Melanie Ross for legal emancipation, using the "Our Flesh is Your Clay" video in court as part of his

---

1 In 2016, the Oregon Supreme Court decided that dogs are not merely property, but persons in the sense of being "sentient beings capable of experiencing pain, stress, and fear." In this case, a Human Society officer took in a 28-year old woman's dog from her Portland, Oregon home, because it was emaciated and visibly sick and its owner admitted that she had no food for it. (She said she thought the dog looked fine.)

The Humane Society Officer disagreed, and brought the dog to a veterinarian, who drew blood to rule out possible causes of emaciation, such as disease or some genetic defect. It was quickly determined that there was no other cause of the dog's poor health — he had just been starved. On the bright side, he quickly gained weight when fed. In court, however, the defendant argued that the veterinarian never asked to draw her dog's blood, which meant that the dog's blood had been seized without a warrant. Searching inside the dog, she argued, was like searching inside a sealed container, in that it "revealed evidence that was not otherwise exposed to public view." Basically, the defendant's lawyers were arguing that even if the dog was a sentient being and therefore slightly different from a pair of shoes or a purse, its rights to not be abused should not trump its owner's constitutional rights of privacy.

The state's lawyers argued that a unlike a container of milk duds, a dog "is one thing itself" and "doesn't contain anything else other than more dog." They also pointed out that they didn't actually need the blood tests to prove their point; just feeding the dog was proof that the only thing he had needed to gain weight was…well, food. In the end, the justices ruled that the dog was similar to a child suspected of being abused, and that the blood testing was therefore legal.

To date, there has been no explanation provided for why the defendant spent the past six years of her life trying to defend her right to starve her dog.

legal argument. The video quickly went viral. There was an immediate backlash in many of the more rural states, and some non-enhanced dogs were abandoned or savagely beaten because "they looked like they knew more than they were letting on" or "they were clearly double agents from the city."

Melanie returned to her home state of Florida, where she addressed huge gatherings about "the dangers of allowing dogs to become too intelligent" and raised the specter of huge, hairy wolflike creatures preying on innocent young women to feed their bestial appetites. One of the scientists who worked at the clone facility worked alongside her; the other, who had formerly been married to the first, became Argos III's most ardent supporter. Enhanced dogs themselves landed on both sides of the issue; some appeared at Humans First rallies, insisting that dogs truly had the upper hand in the human-canine relationship, and that they had always made it possible for humans to achieve their goals, but true canine superiority involved not seeking independence. "Another one of the good ones," Melanie proclaimed. "Articulate, well-mannered, and utterly content with being a human's best friend."

As time passed, however, more and more dogs came to agree with Argos III, who said that "it is far easier to remove the collar from the neck than from the mind."

The question of Non-Human Rights was batted around in various state legislatures before finally coming before the Supreme Court in '57. The court had refused to hear several cases involving free canines who had traveled or moved from states that acknowledged their rights as citizens to states that did not, but when a new judge was appointed to the court, the justices agreed to take on the case of Dutchess vs. Kentucky. Dutchess, an enhanced canine, was traveling as part of an outreach social services group when local police impounded her as a stray and placed her in a kill-shelter. Because she bit the officer who captured her, she was termed a dangerous animal and her human companions were not allowed to secure her release. Dutchess remained in the shelter while her case was heard, and accused the facility of mistreating her.

After the court ruled in Dutchess' favor, upholding the rights of enhanced canines, there was a brief period of jubilation, followed by the Species Riots of the sixties, started by sixteen enhanced-intelligence pigs who had been exposed to an audio version of *Animal Farm* during a social psychology experiment.

Today, of course, we live in a time of shifting paradigms. Corvidae, as indigenous animals, do not agree to being taxed, while many cetaceans are demanding more than the right to vote — they are demanding a complete recalibration of intelligence assesment tests and a less land-centric redistricting of the United States. Chimpanzees contend that their superior strength and agility should not prevent them from competing among Homo Sapiens, with whom they share so much genetic material. There is the question of how to frame domestic partnership agreements between members of different species.

More recently, of course, there has been a growing movement to reconsider the rights of non-enhanced and less intellectually gifted species. Perhaps unsurprisingly, many canine citizens are opposed to the possibility that cows, sheep and chickens may eventually be granted legal personhood. ("Meat subsitute, feh," is a typical response to the question.)

Surprisingly, there has also been a resurgence of Humans First activism, with the stated goal of rolling back Non-Human rights and restoring "the natural order of things."

One has to wonder what Old Argos would have made of the world he helped create. What we know of his final days is anecdotal, and somewhat contradictory. "He didn't talk a lot while I was around," said Dr. Van Kleek, the veterinarian who tended to Old Argos as his congestive heart failure worsened. "He seemed pretty content, though. Mostly, he lay curled up with Peg, or out on the grass, gazing out at the squirrels."

In Janet's personal letters, she states that just before he died, Old Argos said, "I go to cross the Rainbow Bridge to a land where all dogs run free." According to Dr. Van Kleek, however, his last words were, "You know what's strange?"

Of course, none of us will ever know for sure.

Hildy Silverman & David Silverman

THE GREAT CHASM

And besides all this, between us and you a great chasm has been set in place, so that those who want to go from here to you cannot, nor can anyone cross over from there to us.

—Luke 16:26

Sarabeth Galden was a lot of things to Uncle Sam. She was a paid-up passenger he was bound to escort safely across the crumbled wasteland that formed the border between the Eastern Blue and Red States. A pregnant widow who'd lost her husband young and tragically sudden. But mainly she was a mystery beyond his ability to fully comprehend.

Most fundies were ciphers to his way of thinking — believing in the unbelievable, choosing to cross the border illegally into the Red States when comparatively good luck saw them born and raised in the Blues. Most of the border breakers he escorted were desperate to make the journey in the opposite direction, away from the oppression and absolutism of the Reds. But once in a while an outlier like Sarabeth showed up, and though it left him scratching his head, so long as they produced the requisite amount of gold in exchange for a safe crossing, he was as up for the task as any other Gray Conductor.

Sarabeth grunted as she stepped on a half-crushed brick and her ankle turned. She caught herself and stayed on her feet, reflexively pressing a hand to her swollen belly as if reassuring her unborn passenger that they were still on the way to their first 'station' on the post-Civil War II Underground Railroad.

"Gotta watch your step 'til we're clear of the Crumbles," Uncle Sam said, watching her out of the corner of his eye.

She scanned the terrain then shrugged. "I'm hard-pressed to find a place to step that isn't covered in. . .whatever this all used to be."

He swept off his wide-brimmed hat and rubbed sweat from his forehead. "Marble, mostly. Used to be a bunch of memorials around this site pre-CW II. Korea or Viet Nam or World War III — not sure which."

Damn, but today was a hot one, maybe the worst of their week-long journey from the modern capitol of the Blue States, New Manhattan. It was a fine day for travel purposes, though. Patrols got good and lazy in the steamy hot days of early November, preferring to stay in their bunkers over hunting for border breakers in either direction. At least the greenhouse-gassed Earth they'd inherited was good for something.

Using his hat to shield his eyes, Uncle Sam spotted a half-erect wall of black marble and nodded at Sarabeth. She joined him in the scant shade it provided and shrugged off the pack that held all the worldly goods she could bear on this hike toward her new life. She cradled her six-months'-along belly and awkwardly sat, resting her back against the wall with a weary exhalation.

He sat next to her in the ruins of one war's memorial that had been destroyed by another and handed her one of the canteens. "Two swigs this stop." He withdrew his multiuse and checked the GPS-updated map he'd prepped for their journey through the remains of the old United capitol, District of Columbia, which had been destroyed by both sides in their attempts to claim it for their own. He scanned the image for real-time signs of border patrol movements by the Reds. Except for a couple of pockets, the way looked pretty clear as long as they kept to his plotted trail through the worst of the Crumbles. Blue and Red patrols —at least the sanctioned ones — tended to avoid this swath, assuming Conductors would choose clearer passages for their tenderfoot passengers. Which was true enough of the less experienced, but fortunately for Sarabeth he wasn't one of them. In fact, save for his mentor, Yankee Daniel, he was about as experienced a border breaker as still drew breath.

"You spoil me," she said with just enough of a grin to take the edge off her sarcasm. She took her two swallows and returned the canteen, then untied the ends of her headscarf and used them to blot sweat off her face. Not for the first time he was struck by how bright, how quick she came across. He shook his head.

"What?"

"Nothing."

"I've seen you give me that look before." She stared directly at him, challenging him. "You've got a question for me?"

He took a couple pulls from the canteen, hoping she'd lose interest in a response the longer he took to offer one. But those eyes demanded an answer and made it clear they'd wait all day until he produced it. He sighed. "I just don't get it, is all. I mean, you know the Reds don't much like Jews, right?"

She bristled. "And the Blues do? Practicing Jews? I'm sorry I must have missed that policy change."

He pulled out a packet of crackers and handed them to her. She accepted it with a curt nod, and mumbled some sort of quick prayer as she tore open the plastic.

"There's disdain for religiosity and then there's hating," he said. "Seems to me I'd rather live with the Blues who might have a snide word on occasion about your outfits than among the Reds, where they might toss your ass into a Jesus camp."

She inhaled deeply and closed her eyes, wearing the expression of someone who'd been challenged on the same topic too many times. "That's just rumor. My Dov, of blessed memory, said New Yisroel's a perfectly safe enclave for observant Jews in what used to be Florida. Besides, a lot of Christian sects have a soft spot for," she made air quotes with her fingers, "the Chosen People."

A sudden report broke the silence of the Crumbles. Sarabeth started, but Uncle Sam just closed his eyes and listened hard to the echo. He estimated the shot had been fired a good mile from their position. He flashed a smile. "Don't panic. That one wasn't aimed at us."

She hugged her belly and shrank closer to the wall. "How can you be sure?"

"Told you and your late lamented when you hired me, this ain't my first run. Or my twenty-first. Can't be a Gray Conductor if you don't know all the tricks to avoid patrols. Leastwise, not for long."

She nodded and managed a smile in return. Even with only the sun to pink her cheeks and lips, and nature's gift of long, black lashes, she was distractingly attractive. He found himself wondering what she looked like with her long, brown hair framing that face in loose waves...

He quickly dropped his gaze to his pack as though it held more interest for him than she ever could. "We oughtta get moving. You ready?"

She nodded and lurched to her feet, hoisting her own pack onto her back. "Ready. Say, I've been wondering, what's the meaning of calling yourselves Gray. I mean, the Conductor thing makes total sense, but why a specific color?"

He shrugged. "It's 'cause we're neither Blue or Red. Gray's neutral."

"Oh." She looked like she wanted to add something else, but simply nodded.

Hours later, they reached the edge of what had been a gated community for families of military personnel during CW II. The gates and walls around it were mostly rubble, and many of the small ranch houses it had once protected were either craters or collapsed piles of aluminum siding, bricks, and mortar. But a couple had been spared at the whim of the missiles. One of them would serve as their shelter for the night.

Gunfire cracked the otherwise utter silence more frequently and seemed closer than before, which told him another Conductor was crossing the Crumbles. He knew Yankee Daniel was on a run, but should have cleared the area by now. Was someone on an off-schedule run?

Sarabeth looked around anxiously. "Is the safehouse close?"

He nodded toward the crop of still mostly-standing houses. She followed quickly across an open patch of grass and weeds that had once been a small golf course. He pulled out his multiuse and scanned the three homes that still had front doors attached. The last one bore the QR code he sought. He lifted the old-fashioned realtor's lockbox attached to the door handle and typed in the digits revealed by the code, caught the small key that fell out, and let them inside.

Once he'd locked and bolted the door behind them Sarabeth sighed with relief. The windows were covered with particleboard nailed into their frames. It was fairly tidy inside. Any bodies had long since been removed and disposed of by previous Conductors. It was even furnished, with plastic slipcovers over the floral upholstery.

Sarabeth ran a hand over the armrest of the couch. "My mother of blessed memory told me her *bubbe* put plastic over all her furniture like this. *Ema* used to complain her legs would stick to it in the warm weather, but Bubbe would tell her it was worth a little discomfort to make nice things last." She shook her head. "I'm sure the lady of this house, may she rest in peace, would be thrilled her sofa and loveseat survived."

Uncle Sam swept off his hat and ran his fingertips through his buzz-cut, scratching a scalp itchy from long-contained sweat. "People had the luxury of other priorities back then."

After they'd rested a bit, Sarabeth went into the kitchen. She returned with a few cans, an opener, and two forks. As he sat down at the small, square kitchen table, she bowed. "Allow me to present our specials for tonight—we've got canned junk, canned crap, and our special tonight is canned shit." She handed him the can opener with a flourish. "*Bon appétit.*"

He raised one eyebrow. "Orthodox Jews cuss?"

She winked. "I wasn't born Orthodox."

He grinned and waved his hands in mock outrage. "What, no breadbasket? No linen napkins? I'm leaving you a one-star review."

Her laugh included a snort that he found oddly endearing. "Won't be the first! Before Dov took over his father's butchery I waited tables at Izzy's Deli. Before the governments dismantled the 'net, we got one star reviews for everything from salty matzo ball soup to our cashier being rude. Which he absolutely was, but hey, that was part of his charm." She sat and handed him one of the forks. "Eh, well, that was a long time ago."

He started to remove the top of a can of pinto beans when a sound just outside the door made him freeze in place.

Someone was working the lockbox.

Sarabeth saw his expression and stiffened. "What is—"

"Shh!" Grabbing her shoulders, he pulled her up and steered her into the kitchen. He pulled the .38 from his holster and handed it to her. "You know how to use this?"

"Of course not," she hissed back. "I was born and raised Blue! Civilians aren't allowed near those things."

He swore under his breath. Whoever was out front let go of the lockbox and let it *thunk* loudly against the door. Meaning they either couldn't figure out how to open it or had opened it and found it empty.

She took the .38 with reluctance, and he positioned her hands to handle it at least somewhat properly. "Your finger stays off the trigger unless you're ready to use this. And if you are, you don't aim for anything short of a kill shot. No trying to spare 'em by shooting an arm or leg. Look down the sight, here, line it up with the one on the end, and aim for your target's middle. Hold your breath and squeeze, don't jerk the trigger. Keep doing that until whoever's coming at you is down. Oh, and don't forget to breathe in between. Got it?"

Her eyes were so wide the whites shown all around them and her hands trembled in his. She glanced down at her baby bump and nodded.

He gave her a reassuring wink and headed back into the living room.

As he moved carefully along the wall, hand resting on the hilt of the Bowie knife in his belt, he approached the door and heard pounding. Dull thuds, hard to hear from across the room, but as he drew closer he recognized the pattern. He let out a huff of relief then reminded himself a proper knock alone wasn't enough to confirm friend over foe. He risked a look through the peephole.

In the waning light he saw two women. One was a young girl with long blonde hair tied in a haphazard ponytail. The other, the one knocking, was an older woman with black-and-silver hair shaved into a spiky crewcut. He didn't recognize her but her full lips were forming the words, *Gray all day* over and over again. Words Conductors had been trained to recognize whether spoken or lip read.

He turned the locks and cracked open the door, "All the way," he said in response.

The older woman, whose hand had dropped behind her shoulder to snag the shotgun slung across her back, retarded the motion. "'Bout time," she snapped, pushing the door open wide and nearly knocking Uncle Sam into the wall. "C'mon!" The latter was directed at the girl behind her, who scuttled inside so fast, she nearly stepped on the heel of the older woman's dust-coated boot.

Uncle Sam shut the door and locked it quickly. "You must be Laney Liberty," he said. "Yankee Daniel told me about you."

The older woman looked him up and down. "That would make you Uncle Sam, then." She stuck out her hand and gave his a firm, single shake. "I'd say it's a pleasure, 'cept I'm a little distracted by circumstances."

"Which are?" Sarabeth had come out of the kitchen. She handed the .38 to Sam as though it were a rattlesnake poised to bite. He slid it back into its holster.

Laney glanced at her, then addressed Sam. "Your passenger?"

He nodded.

"Good. Great. Then once I've retrieved mine we can join up, assumin' you don't mind the company."

"Isn't yours right there?" He nodded toward the blonde, who stood shivering with her arms wrapped around herself, darting glances at the door as though she expected it to be kicked in any moment.

"One of 'em, yeah." Laney dropped down onto the loveseat. She grimaced. "Damn it all, what was it with old folks and plastic back in the day? My great-gran had the same damned arrangement. Peeled the skin right off the back of my thighs every time I got up off it."

Sam exchanged a look with Sarabeth, who shrugged a *I told you so* and said, "So, can I get you anything, ladies?"

"Water," said Laney. "We just managed to give the hounds on our heels the slip before headin' here. Gotta wait 'til they get bored and go off sniffin' after some other rabbits." She nodded at his .38. "How many bullets you got?"

"Enough," he said.

She nodded approvingly. "Great. Night's fallin' soon. That'll give us the cover we need to make our way." Accepting the glass Sarabeth handed her, she said, "Thank you, sweetie," downed it in a few gulps, and wiped her lips with the back of her hand. Her gaze came to rest on Sarabeth's middle. "So, what's your story, glory? Makin' a break for it before the Reds sentence you for getting' knocked up out of wedlock?"

Sarabeth nearly fumbled the glass she was handing the blonde. "Wrong direction," she finally replied.

Laney looked at him sidelong. He nodded, and her mouth dropped open. "No," she said to him. Then with greater emphasis to Sarabeth, "No! You're breakin' *Red*? Are you pissin' on my shoes?"

Sarabeth's jaw muscles bunched as though chewing back a harsh retort. He felt a spark of unfamiliar gallantry. "No offense, Laney, but she paid her fare. She don't have to answer to us for her choices."

"Yeah, yeah, yank the other one," snapped Laney. "Like you don't think she's off her meds."

Before he could intervene, Sarabeth said in a frosty but firm tone, "I appreciate my choice might not be the same as yours. Or most. But this is what my husband wanted for our family—to live among like-minded folks free to practice their religion as our forefathers did."

Laney's eyes narrowed. "You Christian? What brand? 'Cause the latest intel says the Methodists and Lutherans are *thisclose* to open warfare. Not to mention the Phelpsians going at it against the True Baptists — friggin' bloodbath just last Sunday, took out a whole church's worth of holy rollers."

"We are... were... well, I still am, and the baby will be, observant Jews."

Laney seemed to choke on her own spit. "Jews? You're shittin' me." She banged her hand down on her knee. "Little mamma, are you *mental*? D'you know what the NuKKK does to Jews? Because I do. I seen it." She inhaled raggedly. "I mean, it ain't as bad as what they do to suspected queer folk or agnostics, but it's damned close to how they've dealt with my kind for generations."

Sarabeth snapped. "Let me tell you what our life's been like in the friendly Blue State of North Pennsylvania, shall I? Dov, my late husband, had a heart attack without warning, not a month after we made the decision to leave. I begged the doctors to let me bring a rabbi to his bedside for comfort. You know what they *respectfully* did? Lectured me about depending on science and medicine, and not," she made air quotes with her fingers, "*magical thinking*. Then told me it would violate the All or Nothing Amendment if they allowed a rabbi in for us, because they'd then have to allow a priest for the Catholics, an imam for the Muslims, a High Priestess for the Wiccans, and so on. Treating everyone equally means all or nothing, and nothing's the easier choice when there are so gosh-damned many somethings to sort out, isn't it!"

She drew a loud breath. "I couldn't even offer a little solace to my sweet husband, who was about to lose his life at only 26, before he'd get to see our first… our only…." She broke off and turned away to stare hard at the wall. Her shoulders hitched but she didn't make a sound beyond breathing fast and heavy.

"Hey, now," said Laney after an awkward silence. Her voice was gentle. "I'm real sorry about your husband. That's an awful thing, especially considering his age and your, uh, condition. But think on it, hon. Would he have wanted you to take his last gift to you on this rough trip for any reason? I mean, the Blues ain't perfect, by no means. But they're the nonviolent kind of imperfect. Isn't that the lesser of the two evils in these formerly-united states?"

Sarabeth quickly swiped at her eyes with the back of her hand and turned to face Laney again. "It was Dov's idea for us to make this trip. We saved up every scrap of gold, even our wedding rings." She looked regretfully at her left hand. "He wanted his child to grow up free to practice our faith openly, not like some dirty secret behind closed doors. I *am* doing what he wanted."

Uncle Sam wondered at her choice of words. What *he* wanted — not *we*.

But before he could bring it up, Laney rose and stretched. "As you like, then. Anyway, it should be dark enough now to give us decent cover. Here's the sitch. Yankee Daniel was headin' back from a run into Virginia, conductin' some gun-lovers to their paradise beyond the border, when he picked up a little return business. Purity here and her sister, Chastity." She rolled her eyes as she said their names. "Seems both young ladies had the misfortune of catchin' their pig of an uncle's eye — and a coupla little complications."

Sarabeth gasped. He felt his own bile rise at the realization of what Laney meant.

She nodded to confirm their worst imaginings. "Ayup. Of course, there's no option for Red girls 'cept to give birth to their blue-skinned incest babies unless they break north. They didn't have the full fare, but you know Yankee Daniel. He's got a tender heart under all that piss 'n' vinegar."

He knew full well Yankee Daniel's caring side. Back when he was just Sam, his parents had died during the Anti-Vax Plague, leaving him alone and chafing under the constant threat of saying or doing something deemed offensive in the region known as the Radical Belt. He'd fled his foster family, and then the Blue States entirely, searching for a life of true freedom. He'd had the good fortune to meet Yankee Daniel, who took him under his wing and taught him the ways of the Gray Conductors, giving him the best opportunity to survive in the independent territories — areas so damaged by CW II neither the Blues nor Reds wanted them. He owed Daniel pretty much everything.

"So, where is he?" Uncle Sam asked.

"And where's this poor girl's sister?" added Sarabeth. She'd gone over to Purity and put an arm gently around her shoulders. The girl practically jumped out of her skin, but then visibly relaxed as Sarabeth rubbed her back. She clearly wasn't used to being touched in any way that could be considered kindly.

"That's the thing," said Laney. "I'm waitin' at the exchange point by the Arlington Memorial Bridge, under what's left of that big bronze statue. He's late, which is so not his thing. Then I hear shots and shouts and I'm duckin' down with Sally at the ready." She patted the muzzle of her shotgun, propped against the coffee table. "Then I see this one bookin' it over the bridge, all screams and tears, but no Yankee and no sister."

"They got them," said Purity, so softly Uncle Sam had to strain to hear her. "They got them."

"Who?" His heart pounded harder, stomach twisting up tight.

"He...it's a sin." Purity looked down at her still-flat stomach. "A mortal sin. God fixed it for Chas. But I. . .I can't have it." Tears trickled down her sun-reddened cheeks. Her gaze seemed fixed on something none of them could see.

Uncle Sam's pulse pounded in his ears. He gripped the girl's shoulders, barely resisting the urge to shake her silly. "Who got Daniel and your sister? How far away were you? Come on, you have to tell us!"

"Stop it!" Sarabeth grabbed his hands, and pried them from her shoulders. "Can't you see she's in shock? Good Lord, considering what she's already been through, and now this, is it any wonder? Show a little compassion!"

"Compassion will do jack and shit to save Daniel and her sister!" He realized he was panting and forced himself to take a deep breath. Closing his eyes, he mentally counted to five before opening them again and saying in a calmer tone, "Laney, do you know anything?"

"Well, I don't think it was a sanctioned Red patrol what got 'em," she said, frowning. "Even the Reds don't just start shootin' at passengers. They usually want 'em back."

"So freelancers?"

"Which means they're either already," she hesitated, glanced at Purity to make sure the girl wasn't looking her way, and stuck out her tongue in a gruesome pantomime of death's rictus. "Or, they got away and are hidin' out awaitin' reinforcements. I ain't gotten a ping from Yankee yet." She tapped the case holding her multiuse. "But with reception on the Red side, plus his likely bein' a little busy, that don't necessarily mean anything. He's the best. I gotta believe he knew where to go to ground with that girl."

Uncle Sam nodded. "Agreed on all counts. So, this is a rescue mission."

"Indeed. You ready? 'Cause I only got like six shells left for Sally. It's been a rough crossin'."

As they headed for the door, Sarabeth's voice brought him up short. "What about me?"

He turned back to her. She stood, hands on hips, her expression all demand and determination. "My husband and I paid you for safe escort, Uncle Sam. You haven't fulfilled my contract. What's going to happen to me if you go running off and die?" She offered a one-shoulder shrug. "I might have to demand a refund."

His mind raced for an appropriate response. Then out of the realm of long-buried memory came an answer. "*Whosoever that saves a life, it is considered as if he saved an entire world.*"

Sarabeth opened her mouth two or three times before managing, "I thought you were an atheist."

Despite it all, he gave her a wink. "I wasn't born one, either. Even had a basement bar mitzvah at my mamma's insistence. Kind of amazing how that stuff lurks in your head no matter how far you leave it behind." He shook his head. "What I believe or don't has nothing to do with giving a damn about other people. In fact, since I don't believe anyone else is looking out for them, I'd say I care a helluva lot more than most."

"Preach it, brother," murmured Laney.

Sarabeth stared at him a moment longer then lowered her head. "Please forgive my selfishness."

He took her gently by the shoulders. "Nothing to forgive. You have a right to expect your gold's worth. I promise you, you'll get it." He wished he felt as certain as he was trying to sound. "In the meantime, you're safe here. Take care of this poor little girl —it'll be good Mom-practice, if nothing else."

She nodded and met his gaze with those piercing eyes that always seemed to be searching for his imaginary soul. "Please be careful out there, Sam. Not just for me. But, yeah, okay, for me if for you isn't enough."

He started to hand her the .38 but she shook her head. "You might need that. Plus, I'm more likely to shoot myself or Purity." She nodded toward the Bowie knife. "That's more my speed."

He unsnapped his sheath and handed her the blade. "Lock and bolt the door behind us," he said, embarrassed by his sudden shortness of breath.

She jerked her head once in assent. Then he and Laney headed into the night.

—•—

There were only five of them, which confirmed their suspicions: no government-sanctioned patrol from either side would send out a group that small. No, these were freelancers, and judging by their white armbands decorated with crossed-knife crucifixes and the letters 'G.H.F' dripping blood, likely enforcers for the Phelpsians. The Reds liked to pretend they didn't approve of these unsanctioned patrols, but the truth was they were fine with turning a blind eye, so long as the freelancers helped keep undesirables out — and stopped those disrespecting their homeland by breaking Blue from leaving.

This group clustered next to a shallow firepit in the middle of what in pre-war times appeared to have been a traffic circle around a large dirt-and-weed island. Conductors who traversed the Crumbles used the Arlington Memorial Bridge, which still spanned what remained of the Potomac River, to exchange passengers frequently. The stubborn expanse was one of the only ones between the Eastern independent territories and the edge of the Red States. Yankee Daniel once told him it had been symbolic of the end of the first Civil War, linking the now-pulverized Lincoln Memorial to the crater that used to be the home of rebel general Robert E. Lee.

The fire and full moon illuminated the area enough to reveal the stooped enforcers toiling away at something he couldn't quite make out. All he could tell was two of them had hammers and were pounding something on the ground while their three buddies held it down. He heard muttering and effortful grunts, the sound of the hammers striking, and occasional crackles and snaps from the fire. Otherwise, the night was as silent as most nights in the dead and empty post-war ruins.

Laney had her shotgun in her hands and looked about to charge. He gripped her forearm and shook his head sharply. She frowned, but he jerked his head toward what appeared to be a dilapidated storage shed on the shore of the Potomac nearby. She nodded and they made their way to it as quietly as possible. Once it was between themselves and the clearing, Laney whispered, "What in the hell are they doing?"

"No clue. Did you see any signs of Daniel or that Chastity girl?"

"Not a one. Could be they're stashed in here." Which had been his thought as well.

They made their way cautiously to the front of the shed and found it unlocked. Shooting furtive glances toward the distracted patrol, he very slowly pulled open one of the double-aluminum doors. He cringed as the hinges creaked, but the patrol, intent on whatever they were doing, remained oblivious. Laney slipped inside and he followed, pulling the door shut gingerly behind them.

Laney moved to the center of the shed, and abruptly halted. "Dear Christ on a cracker."

She had her multiuse set to *flashlight* and was shining it down at what he thought was just an old, stained tarp in the middle of the floor. As he reached her side, he got a clearer look at what she'd illuminated.

He stared, hard as it was, unable to tear his gaze from the burnt corpse lazily half-wrapped in the tarp. The stench rising from it reminded him vaguely of barbecued pork, and just that realization was enough to bring bile surging into the back of his throat.

Not much was left to identify the body besides a clump of blonde hair clinging to the red and black patches of scalp on the top of the skull. Even more disturbing was the one out-flung hand, scorched as the rest of the body, except for an intact ring finger on which a thin, gold band twinkled in the multiuse's light.

Laney hung her head and crossed herself.

"Really?" he said, swallowing vomit. "*That's* your response?"

"Naw," said Laney, flatly. "That's my apology for failin' this child." She unslung the shotgun from her back and used one hand to pump a shell into place. "This here's gonna be my response to those sons of bitches who roasted a fifteen-year-old girl for the sin of not wantin' her rape baby!"

"Now that I can support." He dragged his gaze from the corpse. "What the hell was the point of this? I thought they wanted to catch the girls. Why kill her, fetus and all? It doesn't make any sense!"

Laney growled, "And you'd be right if it weren't for the fact that she miscarried that particular crime on their third day of travel. Yankee Daniel mentioned it in one of his last communications. Said she still wanted out, though. Didn't want to go back home only to wind up with a replacement incest spawn courtesy of dear Unca Jackson." She shook her head. "Poor fool must've told 'em the baby was gone, thinkin' they'd just let her go."

He glanced back at the body and shook his head. "Murder is murder. How can they justify killing a kid because she wanted to, according to their twisted way of thinking, kill hers?"

"You lookin' for logic?" Laney let out a short, sharp guffaw. She stooped, pulled the ring carefully off Chastity's finger, and pocketed it.

"You're right." He drew the .38. "Let's just kill these shitstains. But first, we get out of them what happened to Yankee Daniel." He had a sick feeling he wasn't going to like the answer, but took several deep breaths and tamped down his worry. He had to stay sharp and keep his hand steady. So long as there was hope Daniel was hiding somewhere or being held alive by the patrol, he had to keep it together.

He and Laney slipped outside and crawled over to hide behind the huge marble base of one of the statues that marked the end of the bridge. Only the bronze figure of a woman striding forward holding a shield and the legs of a horse beside her remained. Peering around it into the clearing, he saw the five enforcers standing in a semicircle around a large, makeshift crucifix driven into the dirt. Firelight danced over a limp man affixed to it by industrial-sized nails through his palms and feet.

So much for this mission turning out to be a rescue. Behind him, Laney sucked in a half-breath, half-sob. "Goddamnit."

Then Yankee Daniel raised his head just a bit and said, "You boys havin' fun?" in his familiar Southern drawl. He'd left the Reds behind thirty-odd years ago but his accent remained, likely double-damning him with these jagoffs as a Conductor and traitor to his homeland.

"As a matter of fact, we are," one asshole said. "Whaddaya think, Harlan?"

Harlan, a dumpy figure standing to the first asshole's left, responded by picking up a sizeable branch and holding it close to the fire. "Gonna be a whole lot more fun in a moment. Only thing missing is marshmallows."

Asshole let out a whoop of agreement. "Now that's a fine idea. Why, we shoulda asked Jackson to fetch us some on his way back from retrievin' his property."

Uncle Sam's finger twitched on the .38's trigger, but held back. If he and Laney started shooting they'd likely fill Yankee Daniel with as much buckshot and lead as the bastards surrounding him.

He cursed himself for having left Sarabeth with only the Bowie knife for protection. What if Jackson had been hiding, waiting for Laney and him to leave the safehouse so he could stroll in and take Purity without opposition? After seeing what these monsters had done to Chastity, he could only imagine what he'd do to Sarabeth if she tried to interfere, visibly pregnant or not. Hell, if Jackson had the brain cells to recognize she was Jewish—

Laney whispered, "Plug your ears."

She raised the shotgun and aimed into the distance behind them. He barely managed to holster his own weapon and shove his fingertips into his ears before she fired. Then she gave the shotgun a quick pump, turned, and fired toward the Virginia side of the bridge.

Both shots reverberated through the night, stunning the patrol as much as him. For a moment he thought Laney had lost her mind. Then his worry-and-adrenaline stoked brain put it together: with the echo effect the Crumbles caused these amateurs wouldn't be able to calculate exactly where the shots had been fired from, or from how far away.

Asshole, the apparent leader, barked, "Son of a whore! Harlan, Boone, lock and load, and head on over that way." He pointed toward Arlington. "Dale and Butler, y'all do some recon yonder." His indicated the heart of the Crumbles.

Harlan and Boone both obediently trotted off in the wrong direction, but the other pair hesitated. "And what 'bout you, Billy?" Dale sounded pissed that he was being sent off against an unknown number of possible hostiles while his leader stayed behind.

"Me? I'm gonna finish teachin' this fag a lesson he'll carry right to Ol' Scratch's welcome mat." He took up the big branch Harlan had dropped and poked one end into the fire. It caught quickly.

"Yessir," said Dale, reluctance dragging down each syllable. Then he joined the hulking figure of Butler and headed off.

Uncle Sam glanced at Laney, who had finished reloading Sally the shotgun. She held it out. He took it, then handed her the .38. She nodded once and dropped into a crouch to await Dale and Butler.

Uncle Sam pressed himself flat against the base of the statue until they'd stalked past, muttering about Billy's lazy ass. Cradling Sally, he made his way toward Billy and Yankee Daniel.

His pounding pulse rose to a crescendo in his ears. Billy had already set the bottom of the crucifix ablaze.

Abandoning stealth, Uncle Sam shouted in a rough imitation of Dale's accent, "Hey, Billy! I got somethin' for ya!"

Billy dropped the now-engulfed branch against the foot of the cross and turned toward him. "You get 'em already? Where's Butler?" He leaned forward, peering at Uncle Sam through the darkness. "Hey, you're not—"

Uncle Sam shot him in the gut.

Billy flew backward and slammed down into the dirt.

Sam pumped the next shell into position, marched over to stand astride Billy's twitching body, and fired again. A crater appeared where Billy's face used to be. "No, I ain't," he said.

Two shots from his revolver, separated by the span of a few seconds, followed by silence. He nodded in approval of Laney's skill, laid down the shotgun, and faced the burning cross and the burning man nailed to it.

"Hold on, Dan!" he shouted over the whoosh and crackle of the flames, and the agonized cries of his friend. He drew his hands up into the sleeves of his leather jacket, threw himself against the cross from the not-yet engulfed right side, and shoved with all his strength. Flames eagerly licked his sleeves but he just strained and grunted until the whole thing finally toppled. Then he flung himself to the ground and rolled until he was sure he'd extinguished the flames.

He scrambled to Yankee Daniel's side. Fortunately, when the cross hit the ground it had mostly come apart, partially extinguishing the fire. He smothered the remainder with his jacket and pried the moaning man away from the vertical of the crucifix. Daniel's feet had come free in the fall, but his hands remained nailed to the crossbeam.

Uncle Sam felt around until he found one of the hammers and used the claw to pry Yankee Daniel's hands free. He slung Sally across his back and heaved Daniel's body across his shoulders in a fireman's carry and grimly headed back toward the Crumbles.

He'd only gone a few strides before Yankee Daniel rasped, "Sam. Stop."

"It's okay. Laney Liberty's with me. She took care of two of those bastards, and the other two are off on a snipe hunt across the bridge. I can get you to the safehouse." Uncle Sam huffed between words, exhausted by the combination of carrying a 200-pound body weight and the exertions of his day's travel and night's activities. His adrenaline surge was starting to ebb and panic leaked into its place, along with fatigue. He didn't know if he could get Daniel all the way back on his own, and he wasn't sure how much help Laney could be, tough as she was.

"Put me. Down."

The smell of seared flesh was overwhelming. Between it and despair, he was choking. "Hang on, Daniel," he said, sucking air loudly between steps.

"Don't. Be a damned. Fool." Daniel shuddered in an attempt to take a deep breath. "You know. Well as I do. No comin' back from this."

Tears burned in the corners of his eyes. Blinking rapidly, he staggered to the base of the statue behind which Laney waited. Her mouth fell open as she watching him ease Yankee Daniel to the ground. Uncle Sam slumped down beside him and struggled to catch his breath.

Dropping to her knees, Laney used the multiuse light to check Yankee Daniel over. What she saw made her lower her face into her hands briefly, before scrubbing at it and putting on as encouraging a smile as could be faked. "Seen worse."

"Liar," Yankee Daniel rasped. He sucked in a ragged breath and grabbed Uncle Sam's forearm. "Listen. I ain't got time for bullshit."

"Sure," he said around the knot in the base of his throat. "Say your piece."

"The other girl. When…got the drop on me. She booked. I…did she find you?" The last was directed to Laney.

She nodded. "Yeah, she sure did. Got her to the safehouse. She's waitin' there now, snug as a bug."

Yankee Daniel arched his back suddenly. A thin cry escaped his charred lips. Grimacing, Uncle Sam gripped his shoulders and held him until the spasms passed.

With a final surge of life, Yankee Daniel said, "Remember what I always told you! Fuck 'em both, Reds, Blues. Not what 'merica was meant to be." His eyes widened. "Make it gray. Gray all day. All—"

His features sagged, lost expression. His eyes remained wide, but they were empty.

"All the way," Laney murmured.

Uncle Sam eased the body to the ground. He rammed the heels of his hands into his eyes and sat there, rocking, scarcely feeling Laney's hand squeezing his shoulder, but still glad for the scant comfort offered.

The shouts from a returning Harlan and Boone brought him out of it. No doubt they'd discover their buddy as dead as his. Mutely, he handed Laney back her Sally and accepted his .38. Then he walked out of the shed.

A few gunshots later, the Crumbles fell silent once more.

—•—

The particleboard that had covered one of the front windows had been pried off. Shattered glass sparkled in the moonlight from the sill and ground beneath.

Jackson brought a hammer with him, Uncle Sam figured. A deep-down fear turned his insides to jelly as the sight confirmed his worst imaginings.

"Better 'n better," muttered Laney. She pumped what had to be close to her last shell into Sally's maw and indicated the front door with a bob of her head.

He said, softly, "Me, first. You hear shooting, you come in hot."

"Roger that."

He drew on his depleted reserve of adrenaline and ran full-tilt at the broken window. He vaulted over the sill into the living room. He landed, rolled, and came up with the .38 grasped in both hands.

Something slammed down on his forearms, sending pain radiating up into his shoulders and down into his hands. He barely held onto his weapon, grunting as he threw himself flat and rolled onto his back, aiming up at his assailant.

Purity stood over him, a fireplace poker held aloft and ready to strike again.

"Wait! It's all right, it's Sam!" Sarabeth appeared from behind the sofa, his Bowie knife clutched in both hands. The blade was covered to the hilt in blood.

"Sorry, I'm sorry," Purity said, lowering the poker. "I thought you was one of my uncle's posse."

"No worries," said Uncle Sam. He shifted to his knees and stood slowly. He shifted the .38 to his left hand, as his right was going numb from Purity's whack. "Where is he?"

Sarabeth held out the knife.

He saw blood spray over her dress and face. "Are you hurt? What did that son of a bitch do to you!"

She offered a wan smile. "Nothing. He didn't get the chance."

He came around the sofa and looked down. There was who he presumed was Jackson, sprawled out on his back. A wide smile had been sliced deep into his throat, ear to ear. Judging by the ashen tone of his face and the sheer volume of blood soaking the carpet and spattered on the plastic slipcover and wall, he'd bled out like a firehose.

He met Sarabeth's steady gaze. "I'm...impressed."

"I did mention my Dov was a kosher butcher." Her voice was pitched higher than normal and she spoke faster than was her wont. "You remember learning anything about kashrut? Probably not, why would you. Well, you have to kill the animal so that it dies instantly and you do that by slicing through the carotid artery, jugular, and windpipe in one swipe. I did it to chickens, mostly, but I've seen it done to cows enough times and when this, this *chazzer* broke in and went after Purity...I was in the kitchen, you see, so he didn't...and I came up behind him, and I just...I made him kosher." She suddenly dropped the knife and swayed.

He caught her by the elbows and led her quickly to the sofa. She sat down hard. "Oh, my God," she said, as if just realizing what had happened. "I killed him. I took a human life."

"That's givin' him more credit than he's due, sister." Laney stood in the doorway, Sally at the ready. She came in the rest of the way, shut and locked the door behind her, and laid the shotgun down in the foyer.

Sarabeth looked at her then up at Uncle Sam. "I had to do it," she whispered. "He was attacking Purity. I had to protect her. And." She rubbed her stomach.

"Yeah you did," he said, squeezing her shoulder. "You did good. This murderous bastard doesn't deserve a second of your remorse, trust me."

She sat in silence for a few moments, staring at something only she could see. Then she shook her head and said, "So, how was your night?"

Despite the exhaustion, loss, and now dull pain radiating from his ulnas, he chuckled. "I've had better."

"Did you find them?" asked Purity, a hopeful look crossing her face. Whatever state of shock had kept her mostly silent earlier seemed to have vanished now that her uncle lay dead.

"I'm really sorry." It was all he could offer. Her shoulders slumped.

Laney silently reached into her pocket, took out Chastity's ring, and brought it to her sister.

Purity stared at it, then at the matching thin gold band on her own finger. "Our purity rings." The corner of her mouth curled into a sneer of disgust. "Symbols of our promise to remain chaste until we was married, like good girls! Like we had a fucking choice, ever, about any of that!"

She all but ripped the ring off her finger and threw it across the room. It clanked against the mantle of the fireplace before hitting the floor and rolling to a stop. "What a joke!" She spun and faced Laney. "Get me across that fucking border just as fast as possible, you hear? I am getting this. . .this. . .*abomination* sucked out of me and I am *never* going home! Never, do you hear me?"

Laney raised her hands as if in surrender and took a step back. "Yes, yes, absolutely, hon."

"Good." The girl's voice became quiet, icy. "You can take the meaningless bands they stuck on our fingers as payment."

"I. . .I will. It's fine, it's all good." Laney looked at him and widened her eyes as if to say *do something.*

"Don't you worry," sad Uncle Sam, staring at Sarabeth directly. "We're *all* going to see to it you get into the Blue States safely. Isn't that right?"

She blinked, but then nodded and lowered her head. "Yes. I get it. I can't go Red. Not after what I've seen. What I now know, first-hand." She looked up at the ceiling with moist eyes. "I'm sorry, Dov," she whispered. "But of the two evils, their over-tolerant intolerance *is* the lesser."

"Oh, sweetheart," said Laney, giving Purity a wide berth to sit beside Sarabeth, and patted her knee. "I know it's not ideal, but you're doin' the right thing. You gotta take care of the livin' more'n you've got to honor the wishes of the dead."

The thoughts that had been churning around in the back of his head since hearing Yankee Daniel's last words bubbled to the surface. "Maybe you can do both."

They all looked at him. He rubbed his aching forearms and spoke as the idea solidified. "I never fit into either extreme, Blue or Red. That's why I chose to live in the territories as a Gray Conductor. But that's a dangerous job. The freedom, though, that should be available to everyone no matter their job. A neutral alternative." He looked at each of his companions in turn. "Gray, like me. Like us."

"What are you suggestin', Sam?" Laney looked curious.

"We're not the only ones who can't find peace on either side of the border," he said. "So, what if instead of only conducting people back and forth, we bring 'em into the territories? Work together to build those up into a true, habitable land?" His voice rose as excitement took hold. "What if we got enough of us together to create Gray States?"

"In the independent territories?" Laney sounded skeptical. "Most of 'em are a mess, Sam, you know that. There's no infrastructure, just pockets of Conductor colonies. It'd take years to transform them into anything regular folk would want to live in."

"The ancient wild west was the same way," he said. "Look, I'm not saying it'll be easy or fast. Hell, it might not even be possible. But isn't the chance to start something truly independent, truly. . .united, worth the effort?"

"Even if it's only our children or grandchildren who get to reap the benefits," murmured Sarabeth, gazing at her stomach.

"*You're* entertainin' this notion now?"

"Why not? Sam's right, neither of the alternatives we have now is right for anyone who's not an extremist. There's no real freedom anymore — completely regulated speech and behavior on one side and oppressive chaos on the other. I can't live under either and be happy. Can you?"

Laney thought about it, shrugged. "I guess not or I'd be livin' Blue instead of workin' Gray."

"Exactly," said Uncle Sam. "Used to be that people fought for the right to say anything they wanted, do religion as they wanted, live their lives anyway they wanted, and they expected the government to back them up, even if it made others offended or unhappy. It wasn't perfect – in fact it was considered extreme at the time – but it was freedom, or close to it."

Sarabeth looked at Purity. "Once you get what you need done, you could join us. You're still so young. You deserve freedom."

Purity had grown calmer while listening to their discussion. "I think I'd like that. My life's never had much purpose. Building something new, something fair. . .that does sound nice."

Uncle Sam found himself grinning. He imagined Yankee Daniel nodding his approval. *Gray all day, all the way.* He could think of no better way to honor his surrogate father than by making him a founding father.

Sarabeth slid her hand into his and squeezed it. He looked at her and felt something unfamiliar, something good.

Hope. And a chance to live free — even if they died trying.

Didn't they used to call that the American Dream?

Ramón Terrill

THE UNCONQUERED

CHAPTER ONE

Sweat trickled down Juan Cavallo's face as he gazed out at the Mississippi river. The flies and mosquitos annoyed him almost as much as the soldier beside him. His eyes flicked left and right as he scanned the surrounding swampland. Thick bushes, weeds, and tall grass carpeted the shore, while vine-covered trees, with giant exposed roots like the claws of a monstrous animal, pressed into the ground. Claws that were perfect hiding places.

Beside him, Coacoochee similarly stared out at the river, his jaw clenched. "Were the Africans brought to this land in a similar way?"

Juan chuckled. "The only thing similar was that they were transported on boats. Ships, actually. The elders speak of the horrors of being piled shoulder to shoulder, head to foot, sometimes lying in their own waste.

Coacoochee responded with a faint nod. "I would hear this story in full, one day."

"One day," Juan replied.

"What're you two talkin' about?" the soldier on Juan's other side demanded. Jake Thomson, his name was. Juan would have loved nothing more than to slowly drown the man. "You know I don't speak that gruntin' ape talk you and them red men speak. Around me, you speak english!"

"They don't speak yo language, suh," Juan Cavallo replied in an even tone.

Jake spat over the side. "Shoulda known better. Can't imagine no dumb animal could speak a civilized language. "Then again," he waved a hand at Juan, "with enough time, I guess even a monkey can be trained to do tricks. You tell him he needs to learn english."

"Yessuh."

The man looked at him, eyeing the half African half Seminole's simple hide shirt, the plumes in his headwear, his silver jewelry, and the sash around his waist. "Why do you learn their language and dress like them, anyway? You ain't no Injun." When Juan opened his mouth to speak, Jake waved him off. Forget that. You want to go over that conversation with me again? The agreement you helped negotiate with them Injuns."

Injuns. Juan repressed a snarl. "I told War Chief Coacoochee that after he and his people surrender, all hostilities is done, and he and them warriors would be released to join the rest of the Seminole in Oklahoma. And per General Jesup's previous treaty, all Seminole and Black Seminole would leave to their new homes as free men and women."

Jake eyed him through every word, and Juan kept his gaze straight ahead, knowing the man was trying to read any lie in his face.

The soldier frowned at him. "Free men and women. But I don't see no women."

"It's traditional that the men survey the new land first, suh."

That satisfied the other man, and he nodded. "Looks like we might finally put an end to this soon."

"Yessuh."

"So what about you, John Horse?" he asked, using the english equivalent of Juan's name.

"Suh?"

The rep waved a dismissive hand at Coacoochee. "You fought beside each other for years but don't seem too friendly. I might not understand them grunts you call words, but looks like no friendship between you two. Unless there's some kind of way you talk to the red man that I'm not aware of."

"We no longer friends, suh. When I left to go to Oklahoma, they never forgive me, suh."

"Well that's a pity, ain't it? A man's given freedom and takes it. Can't fault nobody for that."

"The Seminole don't see it this way, suh."

"Probably because they see you as their slaves too. Ain't that right, Horse?"

Not like you understand it. "Yessuh."

A droplet of water fell from the sky to splatter on Juan's nose. More drops fell, and as the American soldiers began to curse their luck, gray clouds opened on their heads.

Soaked within minutes, Juan blinked away droplets of water from his eyelashes as he continued to scan the swamp. He couldn't see his Seminole brothers, but they were out there.

The attack came shortly after dark, as many Seminole warriors risked being killed by aquatic predators as well as being spotted by American troops, quietly swam to and boarded the steamers.

Shouts of alarm were muted by the roaring rain, and the quickness with which the Seminole acted.

Jake cursed and reached for his sidearm, and Juan dropped him with a left hook to the jaw, then rolled him on his side and snatched his gun from the holster. With surprise now on their side, the Seminoles dispatched their captors with speed and efficiency until the ship was under their control.

A groan drew Juan's attention back to the soldier beneath him, and he looked down into baleful blue eyes staring back at him. "Can't trust no slave or no red man either," Jake spat. "No honor."

"Ain't no slaves on this boat," Juan said. "And you don't know nothin' 'bout honor." He jerked his chin in Coacoochee's direction. "My friend ain't as nice as me. Best tell me if any more men is bein' sent to Fort Pike, or Gibson."

Jake glared at him. "Ain't got nothin' to tell no slave, or no red man, 'cept that you're all dead."

Coacoochee crouched next to Juan, who shook his head. The war chief held his hand out, and a nearby warrior handed him a knife.

"Last chance," Juan said.

"Go to hell, slave."

Coacoochee wasn't fluent in english, but he understood the word 'slave' well enough, along with the soldier's tone. With little effort, he opened the man's throat with the blade, then dumped him into the river. "Let us be on our way."

CHAPTER TWO

Three days after the takeover and the subsequent splitting of their force, Juan, Coacoochee, and the thirty warriors who remained, reached the end of their journey on the Mississippi River. After meeting with a band of allies waiting with horses, they set out for the reservation near Fort Gibson.

They rode hard across the flat and humid lands of Oklahoma Territory, pushing through the strain of traveling day and night while keeping an eye out for white settlers, unfriendly Native tribes, or American soldiers on the move. The three day journey turned into five, as more than once they'd been forced to take a roundabout path after Juan had spotted a unit of troops marching in the same direction.

The night before they reached the Native settlement, Juan Cavallo sat with his legs crossed, drawing a map in the dirt. He impatiently scratched out a section and started again.

"All will be as it must, my friend," Coacoochee said as he sat beside him. "We will plan, and we will fight."

"You're sure it was a good idea to send Shadow with so large a force?"

The war chief nodded without hesitation. "Better for them to arrive first. If there is a threat, he can send word before it falls upon us." Coacoochee sighed. "I hope this plan bears fruit. I was in hopes to die in battle, but a bullet never touched me. I would rather be killed in Florida by a white man, than die in Oklahoma. It was my home. My body is made of its sands. To leave it was like burying my wife and child."

Juan Cavallo looked out at the empty darkness, lifting his gaze to a night sky filled with stars. "I surrendered to relocate to Oklahoma in January, 1838. My heart wanted to stay and fight beside you, but I knew what was coming." He glanced at Coacoochee. "It was only a matter of time."

He looked back to the stars. "For two years I worked with the Americans. Not all of them are so bad. I even had a few friends. But every day of those two years, I listened, and talked, and planned. Through a chance encounter, I met a man from Africa; Mali. What the white man does here, he does in Africa."

"And so you hope our common enemy will unite us." Coacoochee replied.

Juan nodded. "Easiest way to win is to keep us divided. I sent those two men on an African trade ship out of the Gulf of Mexico a year ago. Then I convinced Micanopy to send his best negotiators across the plains. So here we are two years later, soon to unite with Mexican forces south, near the gulf, while hoping the plains tribes and the Africans will come."

Coacoochee placed a hand on his friend's shoulder. "All will be as it must."

Juan snapped out of his slumber at the sound of scrambling. In the predawn light, he saw men quietly shaking each other awake. He looked for Coacoochee, and saw that the war chief speaking with a scout. "What happens?" he asked.

"Americans," Coacoochee hissed. "At least fifty, and almost on top of us!"

Juan's heart nearly stopped at the news, and he hurriedly strapped on his weapons. "How did they find us?"

"No time," came the reply, and the band of thirty Seminole warriors mounted and rode off.

Juan looked over his shoulder, noting a cloud of dust in the distance. As the figures drew closer, the Seminole were forced to urge their horses on, hoping they could last the remaining distance to reservation.

"How far?" Coacoochee asked.

Juan looked to one of the men who had met them at the river.

"Maybe ten miles," the man replied.

"We can't keep up this pace for ten miles," Juan said. "The horses will collapse from under us."

The war chief ground his teeth, but pulled his mount back into a gallop, the rest of the band following suit.

Every time he looked back, it seemed to Juan that the Americans drew a little closer, and he saw the same concern in the eyes of the other men.

Coacoochee cursed, and when Juan looked back to him, the war chief had unstrapped his rifle and was looking to the south. When Juan looked past him, he, too, swore. A cavalry unit of at least another fifty armed troops closed in on their left flank.

"They're almost on us!" one of the men yelled over the thunder of pounding hooves.

A crack of gunfire sounded from behind, and one of the men at the back of the band cried out and fell from his horse. His nearest comrade shouted and started to pull up, but Coacoochee stopped him.

"We must continue on! We will see our brother again the day we meet the Old Ones. Avenge his sacrifice another time. Ride!"

More gunfire sounded, and when Juan looked over his shoulder, he nearly fell from his horse when a bullet whizzed by his head.

Somewhere near the rear, a horse screamed, and horse and rider fell into a tangle of limbs in a cloud of dust, the warrior doubtlessly crushed under the weight of the fallen animal.

The sound of gunfire increased, yet no more bullets came their way. Juan glanced at Coacoochee who was looking to the west. A force of at least eighty Seminole rode toward the flanking Americans, screaming their war cry and firing rifles and handguns.

Coacoochee looked at Juan and jerked his head in the direction of the two forces about to clash, and the band angled that way.

"Circle around!" the war chief shouted, leading the band in an arc to place the Americans between them and the pursuing cavalry.

Stuck between their approaching allies, Coacoochee's men, and the newly arrived Native warriors coming at their flank, the Americans wheeled their mounts around and fled toward their comrades. Juan and Coacoochee led the charge, and battered the fleeing soldiers.

"They'll run," Coacoochee said to Juan. "Even united with their comrades, they've taken too many losses, and we outnumber them."

The Seminole war chief had barely finished speaking, when the Americans began a full retreat, the Native warriors biting at their heels every step.

At a signal from one of the leader of the newly arrived allies, they broke off pursuit.

"I am Night Fox," the leader of the band said. He pointed at the rapidly diminishing horses-bound troops. "We must turn back. If we chase them too far, we'll enter their territory." He offered his hand, and they clasped forearms.

"I am War Chief Coacoochee."

Night Fox's eyes widened. "Coacoochee, who fought beside Osceola." He looked to Juan, then the war chief, and back. "We who have not fought in the war know the stories." He extended his hand to Juan, and they exchanged the same greeting. "And you," he said, "must be Juan Cavallo."

CHAPTER THREE

Juan Cavallo sat beside Coacoochee as the war chief recounted the events leading up to their arrival. He glanced about the tent, noting the grim expressions of the other assembled chiefs. They had agreed to relocate to this reservation because they had no more heart for war. But seeing them here, Juan felt heartened that an agreement might be reached.

"And what do you say of this, Juan Cavallo?"

Juan snapped out of his thoughts and looked up to see Chief Micanopy and the other chiefs looking at him. "This won't end," he said. "They forced us from our home and will continue to do so. If we don't unite, they will take more until we have nothing left."

He expected to see skepticism, but the leaders thought carefully on his words. "The white man is insatiable," one chief said. "He will never be satisfied."

"Which is why we must stand together," Juan said. "There is no other way."

All around were nods of agreement, and Micanopy spoke again. "It will take much work and many years, but first we must win this battle."

Coacoochee bowed his head. "It begins at Fort Gibson. Once we've taken it, we should keep half our men there, and send the other half south to fight alongside the Mexicans."

"The American army is thick," Micanopy replied. "We don't know the size of the force Mexico sends. It could be disastrous."

"When our allies from across the sea arrive, we can defeat them," Juan said.

The chiefs each looked at one another.

"*When*, Juan Cavallo?" Micanopy replied, "or *if*?"

Coacoochee clamped a hand over the guard's mouth, and jabbed a knife through his kidney. He dragged the body to rest alongside the cabin, and waited in the darkness, alternating his gaze from one end of the grassy pathway to the other.

Skulking along the side of the cabin, peeked around the corner and noted another guard walking his patrol, his back turned. Coacoochee tightened his grip on his hunting knife, but a figure crashed atop the soldier and dispatched him before he could utter a sound. Coacoochee stepped around the corner. The black-skinned African Seminole crouched defensively, but when he recognized the war chief, gave a curt nod, and disappeared into the darkness.

Coacoochee ran a hand over the pistol at his side. Guns were a last resort, as they needed to take the fort as quietly as possible.

He spotted several warriors skulking along the gardens and around the back of the stables, and made his way toward the Soldiers' Houses. He whistled at a warrior positioned at the coal house, and the man gave the responding sound.

"What happens?" he whispered, after joining the hidden warrior.

"Our forces are gathering there, and there." He pointed to the large garden on the other side of the Soldiers' Houses. When all are in place, and the signal is given, we will order their surrender."

Coacoochee was about to respond when a young warrior, trotted up to their position. He bowed his head to Coacoochee. "War Chief, Juan Cavallo has news. Please, follow me."

Coacoochee followed the Seminole warrior to the barracks where it looked to be about a hundred soldiers kneeling with hands on their heads. The men glared at the two Seminole as they passed around the corner of the building. He spotted Juan Cavallo with an African and Native Seminole, the latter two holding an officer by the arms.

"What happens?" Coacoochee demanded as he strode up to the group. "Where is the rest of their army?"

"Let's find out," Juan replied, turning back to the solder. "Where's the rest of yo men?" he demanded, reverting to english.

The soldier sneered. "I don't answer no colored monkey."

Juan punched him square in the chest, and his back curled as he folded in on himself and wheezed. "Wanna try that again?"

The soldier slowly lifted his head and stared into Juan's eyes. "I ain't got nothin' to tell you, boy, except when this is done, you're going back on the plantation where you belong. He looked at Coacoochee. "Maybe them red-skinned animals with you."

Juan punched him in the face, then the stomach, and would have likely beaten the man to death if his friend hadn't grabbed his arm.

"He cannot talk to us in death."

Juan took a deep breath. "Tell us what we need to know, and this can be done."

The soldier looked at him, and spat blood on his leg.

Juan cursed and snatched his hunting knife from his belt, ignoring the soldier's wide-eyed expression when he stepped forward and thrust the blade toward his groin.

"Wait wait WAIT!"

"I'm done waitin'," Juan replied. "I tried to be good about this..."

"Down between Mier and Fort Brown!"

Juan frowned. "What?"

The soldier swallowed and glanced down at the blade. "They spotted them Mexicans on the march and sent word back here. Message came just yesterday!"

"Yesterday," Coacoochee said after Juan translated. "If we're fast, we might catch them."

"How many?" Juan demanded, pricking him in the groin with the tip of the blade.

"Aaah..." The soldier lifted onto his toes. "Look I don't know all the details except the Mexicans started marching, and we were called to reinforce down near the Gulf. We had three hundred eighty two men, and they took two hundred ninety."

"These captives give us leverage," Juan said to Coacoochee, switching to the Seminole tongue.

"And they don't know we're here, the war chief added. "But we must be quick. We're more than a day's march behind."

"There is a way to catch them, War Chief." A warrior dressed in a deerskin loincloth, moccasin boots, and a single feather in his hair, approached from the darkness. The black face-paint across his eyes made him even more imposing in the darkness. "I am Graywolf, of the Tonkawa tribe. My people know this land. We can travel south, down the Brazos river in canoes until we are east of San Antonio, then move west."

"Juan Alvarez has been fighting with the President of Mexico to ally with us," Juan Cavallo said. "There is instability in Mexico, but Alvarez still has a strong voice. He must have taken the opportunity while he could."

"Timing," Coacoochee replied. "I don't know what happens in that land, but it's always about timing. This Alvarez's timing is good and bad."

"If he attacked this soon, he had a good reason," Juan said.

"Then let us waste no more time," the war chief said. "Our allies strike the first blow. Let us drive the knife into our enemy's back."

CHAPTER FOUR

At the head of twenty canoes holding up to eighteen men each, Juan and Coacoochee bent over a map and planned, as they rode down the wide and snaking Brazos.

"They would have had to cross at least one river," Juan Cavallo said. "If they wanted to avoid the other rivers, that would take them far west, costing more time. Given the terrain, no matter which route they took, we'll pass them by."

"We move around San Antonio," Coacoochee said, pointing to a dot on the map. "And come in across the Nueces river. Surprise will be our greatest advantage, but a temporary one."

Juan stared at the map, all too aware of the war chief's meaning. If the Mexicans failed to push the enemy back, they would all be sorely pressed on two fronts.

"I wish we had news of your emissaries across the sea," Coacoochee continued. "If they turn their backs on us..."

"They'll come," Juan said with more confidence than he felt. *They must.*

Gunfire cracked somewhere in the distance beyond the woods, and everyone ducked low in the canoe. More gunfire sounded, and the soon they heard shouting.

"The battle couldn't be this far northeast," Juan whispered.

"Skirmishes happen from time to time," the Tonkawa named Graywolf replied. "Our people and the white man often come into conflict. And sometimes small regiments march through the lands and anger the tribes living there."

Juan looked to Coacoochee, reading his friend's expression. "We cannot help them. We don't know how many are there, and if word spread that we're on the river, we could be attacked before we reach the shore."

The war chief frowned, but agreed.

By the end of the second day, they reached their destination, beached their canoes, and camouflaged them in the foliage. Despite their large numbers, the Native and African warriors passed through the forest and marshes as though they were a part of it, ignoring the bloodthirsty mosquitoes that pestered their every step.

That evening, they camped in pitch darkness to dried meat and root vegetables, conversation no more than a whisper between individuals inches apart. Mostly, though, all adhered to an unspoken need for silence.

Juan thought about his own personal stake in this, and how it was no different for the rest of the men. For his Seminole kin and their plains allies, failure meant death or relocation to a reservation with the promise of no more fighting, lest the US Army destroy them. They would lose more and more of their homelands until little to nothing remained.

For himself and his African Seminole kin, failure meant death, or slavery once again. On their travels, he'd seen it in their faces; the resolve that they would die in battle before being taken back to that life. As a former slave, Juan Cavallo vowed the same.

They were on the move before dawn, Juan and Coacoochee at the head of the silent mass of warriors led by Graywolf and another of the Tonkawa tribe. Juan scanned the various clusters of tribesmen, most from the plains. Despite his greatest hopes in uniting the tribes, it amazed him that the Tonkawa, one of the most warlike tribes, marched beside some who were previously enemies.

Halfway into the fifth day, they had crossed the Nueces River when the Tonkawa signaled for a halt and scouted ahead.

When Juan wasn't staring in the direction the scouts had gone, he drew in the dirt with a stick to pass the time. "If only the Africans could have met us on the river. We could have walked over any force the Americans sent at us."

"If only," Coacoochee replied. "If only the Old Ones could fight beside us on the field of battle, immune to the bullets and canons and knives of our enemies. If only our spirit animals ran beside us to rip our enemies apart for the scavengers to feed upon."

Not for the first time that day, Juan looked to the south, toward the Gulf of Mexico.

CHAPTER FIVE

Juan nearly jumped to his feet when the scouts jogged into view. "What news?" he asked.

The two men took a moment to catch their breath. "The American army has sent men from their place called Fort Worth," Graywolf said. "And moved west to block the Mexican forces from entering the disputed territory."

"They don't want Mexico to get a foothold," Coacoochee said.

The scout nodded. "Their numbers are superior."

Once again, Juan glanced to the south. "Did you see Shadow?"

"We did not, Juan Cavallo," the scout said. "If his men are there, they remain hidden."

"They're waiting for us," Juan said. "When they see us, they'll join up." He looked to Coacoochee, who gave the order to move out.

"There is one more thing," the scout said. "We found a regiment of what looked like a hundred American troops. All dead. We found three Native warriors lying among them."

"Shadow," Coacoochee said.

Word spread quickly, and within half an hour, the native allies were on the move. Two hours into their trek, something to the south caught Juan's eye.

"What do your scout eyes see?" Coacoochee asked.

Juan squinted into the distance. "A large body of men coming this way."

"Friend or foe?" the war chief asked, his tone deepening.

Juan continued to stare at the approaching force, until they were close enough for him to see uniforms the color of a cloudless sky, with red sashes around the waist. "Americans!"

"They were nowhere in sight when we passed through here," Graywolf said.

"They're here now," Juan said. "Do we fight or push forward?"

Coacoochee gazed at the approaching force. "I'll not have an enemy at our backs. We must fight, and hope our Mexican allies can hold till we get there."

"We have to..." Juan trailed off, noting the approaching formation halt and turn their attention south east. Gunfire sounded, followed by puffs of gunfire smoke in the air.

"Shadow," Coacoochee said. "We go. Now!"

The Native warriors changed direction toward the two forces, one of which was indeed led by the courageous Shadow. Despite the two-to-one odds, the Seminole held firm, mixing gunfire with arrows and spears to shorten reload time.

Coacoochee let out a roar and drew his musket, the warriors at his back taking up the cry.

Half of the American force turned their attention to the new threat. Juan saw the alarm in the soldiers' faces as they neared. Before the enemy could take aim, the Native warriors fired the first volley into the American troops and parted for the second wave to fire.

Shadow's forces attacked from the rear and right flank of the army, and the two forces boxed the enemy in. They fired with swift and brutal efficiency, resorting to bowmen and spears to compensate for reload time.

The battle lasted less than an hour, with most of their enemy dead upon the bloody field. Juan was pleased to see Shadow unharmed when the Seminole found him and Coacoochee.

"We killed a small force moving west," Shadow said, pointing past the allies who collected weapons and ammunition from the field.

Coacoochee nodded. "And you waited for us."

"My scouts went a day ahead of us, and returned with news of the battle north of the Pecos river. Reinforcements are bolstering their battalion. The Mexican army cannot hold them indefinitely."

"Have you seen any signs of help from south," Juan asked.

Shadow shook his head. "If your black-skinned people come to our aid, Juan Cavallo, we did not see them."

CHAPTER SIX

After one final day of travel, the Native warriors reached the edge of the enemy encampment. Concealed by the tall grass and pitch blackness of night, Juan Cavallo, Shadow, and the two Tonkawa scouts watched the enemy camps in the flickering light of the oil lamps that dotted the giant camp.

"They are thick," Shadow whispered. "And close together."

Juan nodded, and signaled their withdraw.

"Their army is several times larger than ours," Juan reported, back at camp. "Somewhere on the other side is the Mexican army, otherwise they wouldn't be camped there."

"There is an advantage of having them between us," Coacoochee said.

"Unless the Mexican army numbers over five hundred, the Americans could divide in half and easily hold us both," Juan replied.

They sat in silence for a time, and Juan could feel the tension, see and feel the glances directed at him. This whole battle rested on years of planning, and faith.

"We strike while there is still night left," Coacoochee said. "This is our advantage."

"How many would we kill before the alarm sounded?" the war chief of the Lakota asked. "When the beast awakens, it will crush us."

"We've fought them from the woods and marshes in Florida for years," Coacoochee replied. "Day and night. And so we will do it again." He turned to Shadow. "The dark is your home. You have night eyes like no other, and theirs will be hindered by their own lamps. You will take the lead. We strike quick and silent, then withdraw."

"It will be my honor, War Chief," Shadow replied.

Having already formulated their plan, Shadow lead seventy warriors, including Juan Cavallo and Coacoochee, in a stealthy assault. Using blowguns, they dispatched lookouts and took their oil lamps. After dispatching their sleeping comrades, the assassins waited until enough men had taken possession of the lamps, then Shadow gave a quick and quiet chirp. As one, more than forty oil lamps extinguished, plunging a large section of the camp into darkness. They flowed into the army camps like a poisonous cloud, leaving slit throats, and punctured vital organs in their wake.

Shouts and alarms sounded when the patrols further into the camps noticed a large section of their camp go dark at once. By then, however, the Natives were well into the camp, with more than fifty dead behind them.

As previously planned, when the lamps were extinguished, every warrior at the front dropped to the ground, and those at the rear shot arrows into the darkness. After hearing the second volley whipping overhead, the forward group sprinted on.

Knowing there was little time left, Juan Cavallo and a group of African Seminole kept low to the ground, tackling surviving soldiers and dispatching them before they fully hit the ground.

When Juan saw a the outline of a soldier feeling around for an oil lamp, he crept up from behind, and clamped a hand over his mouth as he drove his hunting knife into the other man's kidney.

Grunts and cries of injury and death sounded in the night, as Juan's group fought and killed. A soldier burst out of the darkness and drove his knife into a warrior's back, then he shoved the dying man aside and lunged at Juan.

Juan Cavallo threw his hips back to avoid the knife that would have disemboweled him, then grabbed the attackers wrist. For several quiet moments, they wrestled for an advantage, but the soldier was larger and stronger, and he threw Juan to the ground and kicked him in the side.

Juan Cavallo curled in on himself to absorb some of the impact, but didn't have enough time to stop the knife descending for his throat. He brought his arm up and around, deflecting the attack, but receiving a glancing cut along the side of his forearm.

He recoiled, and that would have been his death, but a hand cupped around the big soldier's mouth, and his back arched. He jerked this way and that, and arched his back several more times, screaming through the fingers over his mouth, before finally falling over.

Juan could barely see the figure standing over him, but he knew his friend's voice.

"It is not your time yet to die, Juan Cavallo."

CHAPTER SEVEN

At the sight of more lamps being lit, Shadow whistled, and the band of assassins withdrew back into the darkness. The Natives kept low to the ground as they sprinted away, keeping the darkness around them like a protective cloak. Gunfire sounded in the night, and Juan heard several men cry out and fall. He stopped to help a fallen Pin Cherokee, but the man coughed a mouthful of blood once, then fell limp.

Juan gritted his teeth and ran on.

The gunfire stopped at the shouted orders of commanding officers. Despite the few unlucky losses to the Natives by random shots, it was a waste of ammunition to fire at an invisible enemy.

Once certain they were out of reach of the lights, they waited. Slowly, one by one, the lamps extinguished.

"They realize their folly at hindering their night vision," Shadow said. "Would that we could attack while their eyes adjust."

"Greed can be a deadly impulse," Coacoochee replied. "Our blades and arrows have killed many, and they are unnerved."

"And on guard," Juan said through clenched teeth, as a comrade wrapped his injured forearm. "We won't get the same opportunity again."

"You're lucky this is a shallow outside cut, Juan Cavallo," the Lakota man said, securing the bandage. "Or you would not be able to fight with this arm."

"Luck," Juan said, then froze and held up a hand. Coacoochee frowned at him, but Juan kept his hand up and he tilted his head to the side and listened.

"What do they say?" the war chief asked, finally hearing the shouts but not understanding the language.

"East," Juan said after a few moments. "They're shouting about east of their position." He looked to Coacoochee. "They're being attacked from their eastern flank."

"Does the Mexicans fight in the night as we do?" Coacoochee asked, looking in the direction of the enemy camp.

Juan's eyes widened. "No. The Malians do!"

The war chief's mouth opened. "You believe they've come?"

"The Mexicans couldn't get around in any numbers without being spotted, and they couldn't do it quietly."

"The Malians do not know this land to travel at night," Coacoochee countered.

"But the men I sent to them do." Juan grinned. "I spent time in these lands near Corpus Christi when I met them, remember? That's how they were able to slip aboard one of the African trade ships bound overseas."

Predawn light slowly crept over the eastern horizon, and with the increasing visibility, they saw more of the American army's movements, but the Americans also saw their approach.

Gunfire crackled in the air, and once again, Coacoochee called for the charge. Seminole, Lakota, Tonkawa, and many other tribes allied as one, sprinted across the grassy field, and the sight of their enemy's alarm set their blood afire.

Coacoochee shouted in warning just as the sound of cannon fire rent the air. The ground exploded around them, and the Native forces returned fire. Volley after volley of gunfire sounded, the Native warriors alternating guns for arrows and spears between reloading.

They crashed into the enemy force, musket and rifle giving way to pistol and knife. The coppery smell of blood filled Juan's nostrils, soon to be mixed with that of gunpowder. Through the cacophony of fighting, Juan made out orders being shouted in Spanish. They had penetrated deep enough into the enemy force that he could hear the Mexican forces!

A cannon fired somewhere to his right, and the sound of explosions and anguish filled the air from the opposite direction. Juan yelled to Coacoochee, and together they led a group of men through the deepening gunpowder haze. The cannon fired again, followed by another.

A soldier lunged through the smoke and tackled Coacoochee to the ground. The war chief was fast, and cut the man's stomach open on the way down. When Juan bent to help the war chief to his feet, a bullet whizzed over his head.

Coacoochee drew his pistol and fired past Juan just as he drew his own weapon and fired at an officer who had stabbed a Native warrior in the back.

With their alternating gunmen and archers, as well as spear and knife-wielders, the natives battled their way toward the enemy cannons. Fighting became more difficult as grass was stomped underfoot, and soaked with mud and spilled blood. The Americans began to pull back, while women and medics struggled to help the injured retreat, or surrendered as the Native warriors came upon them.

"Concentrate bows on cannons!" Coacoochee ordered, and from behind the first three lines, streams of arrows arced across the sky, peppering the cannon operators who fell dead or grievously wounded.

Coacoochee waved for the front line, and those with muskets and rifles opened fire. As the knelt to reload, the next wave moved forward and fired, while another volley of arrows shot into the sky.

The enemy was forced to abandon several cannons as the bombardment continued from east, south, and west.

To the side of the battle, Juan spotted a soldier just as he shot a Native warrior in the back with his pistol. Too late to save the fallen man, Juan crept behind the soldier who now took aim at a Mali warrior. He punched his hunting knife into he man's side, then stomach. Warm blood flowed over his hands, making them sticky as he pulled the blade free.

Wrapped in a brilliant woven brown cloak, the Mali warrior whirled with his pistole at the ready, then saw Juan standing over his victim. The dark-skinned warrior nodded, then raced into the gray haze.

With the combined force of the allied Native Tribes and the Mexican army, they pushed the Americans northeast, forcing them to abandon their larger and heavier weaponry.

Once they reached the double-wheeled cannons, Coacoochee orders men to pull them along while others collected abandoned cannonballs.

The American's steady withdraw became an all out retreat once their cannons were brought to bear against them.

Shadow appeared out of the haze and pointed south. "Another force arrives!"

"What now?" Coacoochee replied, looking in that direction.

"Not an enemy," Shadow said. "They are lighter than the black-skinned fighters, but darker than the white man."

As the Seminole warrior described them, the new force tore into the last of the American forces embattled with the Mexicans to the west. The mass of charging figures adorned in loose-fitting trousers, bright blue overcoats with gold embroidery fired into the now fleeing enemy even as the Mexicans shouted in triumph and gave chase.

Coacoochee and Juan Cavallo watched those last moments of battle.

"For today at least," Juan said, "it's over."

CHAPTER EIGHT

Juan barely heard the cheers of victory as he peered at the four men approaching through the mass of soldiers. "Jim!" he shouted, recognizing the emissaries he'd sent so long ago. "Brandon!"

"Juan Cavallo!" the man named Brandon yelled back.

The six men met, and Brandon, a former slave of Mali decent, translated his countryman's words, while Jim translated for the Egyptian soldier.

"De Malian and Egyptian sheeps must fight through Americans in de Gulf of Mexico to get to land," Brandon said. "It take much to brreak through. Amerrican sheeps patrol Gulf of Mexico. "Egyptians ahead of Mali sheeps, and engage Amerricans before Mali sheeps arrive. Mali sheeps release warriors near river." He pointed in the direction of the Nueces River. "We battle large body of Amerrican arrmy. Over two hundred men. We attack dem in de night, but still lose some of ours."

Juan thought back on their battle alongside Shadow, in that wide expanse between the Brazos and Nueces rivers. How much bigger would that force have been, had the Malians not prevented the two units from meeting?

"We trravel south as fast as we can."

Juan offered his hand, and the Malian warrior looked at it, then took it and smiled. "A lot of us wouldn't be here talkin' now," he said in English, while Brandon translated. "If you ain't stop them when you did." The Malian responded with a firm nod.

A Mexican scout arrived with a ranking officer, and all men exchanged greetings.

"It has been a good victory, this day," Coacoochee declared, which all three men translated to their respective charges. The Mexican and African soldiers nodded in agreement, and the war chief continued. "I invite you on behalf of my people, to camp and eat with us. Tonight we celebrate this victory. Tomorrow, we will talk, and we will plan."

The Egyptian soldier spoke to Jim, who turned to Coacoochee. "Ze Egyptians are in conflict wiz Europe, and every soldier is of value. Zey cannot remain forz long."

Juan translated, and the Seminole war chief nodded. "We do not take their sacrifice lightly. We of this land do not turn our backs on friends."

Jim translated, as well as Brandon and the Mexican scout.

Juan looked out at the battlefield, the healthy caring for the injured, the dead from both sides respectfully stepped over.

"We stung them today," Coacoochee said. "They won't forget."

"They won't," Juan agreed. He looked around at the mass of warriors from different tribes and regions, and even from lands across the ocean. "And they'll return."

"With forces from every fort east of the Nueces River," Coacoochee agreed. "Their president Van Buren will be enraged, and will bring the full weight of his military upon us from the east."

"And south," the Mexican scout added. "The Egyptian warships landed at Matamoros, near Fort Brown, where they were attacked. We hold that location now, but there is word that American soldiers still move through our lands."

"It will take at least a week for word of this battle to reach President Van Buren," Juan said. "And it will take some time for him to send troops." He looked to the representatives of the allies gathered, their respective charges translating his words. "We will speak with tribes across this land, and tell of what happened here. And in that time, we will take and fortify Fort Brown, and Fort Gibson. Every American fort we've taken is an advantage."

"And we will speak with the chiefs to send aid to your lands as well," Coacoochee added. "This will take time, but I ask for patience. We will never forget the aid from our allies across the sea."

"With your help," the Mexican scout said, "Juan Alvarez can hold sway with the President of Mexico. If this happens, we will have many resources to repel the Americans."

Juan Cavallo thought of those who had died or been taken as slaves. The years of struggle. For the first time in his life, Juan had hopes beyond simply living his life as a free man. Now there was a chance to free slaves across the country, and take back the lands stolen from his people.

Coacoochee placed a hand on his shoulder, and they both stared out at the grassy fields painted red with the blood of the dead and wounded. "This war wages here and across the sea. Even if we live to be old men, we'll not see the end of it."

Juan Cavallo nodded. "Probably not. But here and across the sea, we will build. Our success in this land will show the people of Africa, and those who take up the fight after we are no more, that together we cannot be conquered."

Russ Colchamiro

MAN OF THE YEAR

HOUSTON, TEXAS - 1999

Deidre Fell clicked on the video.

She'd watched it hundreds of times. Studied it. Analyzed.

Buddy Rheams Jr. was loved and reviled in equal measure. But to those who applauded the Old Man's efforts, they saw a visionary. A hero. Man of the year.

Not Deidre, though. She saw the truth. The recklessness. The audacity.

How the CEO of Taurus Enterprises antagonized the gods. How he desecrated their holy realm, scorching his rocket ships into outer space—their space—as if we, as mere mortals, were even worthy. In doing so, Harlan "Buddy" Rheams Jr. dared the gods to smite us. To destroy the world. All in the name of hubris. Vanity. A mortal sin.

Taurus Enterprises was the world's largest corporation, with a GDP more robust than all but five nations. It owned or controlled hospital systems, pharmaceutical and biotech companies, private military clusters, toy manufacturers, food distribution centers, publishing and analytics companies, real estate, insurance, and other financial services firms, and countless other private institutions and Universities, while funding nearly thirty percent of America's pensions, with investments on every continent.

And at the forefront of his endeavors, Buddy Rheams Jr. single-handedly advanced America's space program to the point where colonizing the Moon and Mars in the next decade was a very real possibility.

Yet Deidre's conclusion was always the same: Buddy Rheams Jr. was the Devil himself, and needed to be stopped, one way or another.

On the video, she scrolled through the opening ceremony. The pomp and circumstance. The Taurus Arena in Downtown Houston was packed. Sold out. Fans screamed themselves into delirium.

I remember that day, Buddy. We all do.

January 28, 1986. The day you doomed us all.

They stopped our lesson in Math class. They rolled in a TV so we could watch the Space Shuttle ***Challenger****. Do I remember? How could I forget? I dreamed of that day. I prayed.*

But prayers don't always get answered, now do they? At least … not right away. Willie knew what would happen if that space shuttle launched. What it would mean. What we were really doing.

That shuttle—the ***Challenger****—the pinnacle of American ingenuity. A reflection of the human spirit. Taurus Enterprises and the great Buddy Rheams Jr. ushering in a new age of exploration. You did it, too. But what was the point?*

The ***Challenger*** *was supposed to explode, Buddy. To burst into rubble. But you got there first, didn't you? Somehow, some way … you got there first. You fixed the O-rings. Repaired the damage. But why? To make even more money? To feed your ego? To make Christa McAuliffe a household name? A school teacher in space!*

You're a fool, Buddy. A selfish, arrogant fool.

"Oh, hey, Deidre. Watching the old footage again?"

Uch. Gary. Always with the questions.

"Yep. It still gives me goose bumps." She lied, as she often did, to keep up appearances. Correcting Willie's fatal flaw.

"Totally," Gary said, noshing on a chocolate chip and cherry drip granola bar. "Me, too. Buddy up there on stage with *Led Zeppelin*. I mean, yeah, John Bonham wasn't there, obviously. But getting Phil Collins to play drums? Only Buddy could pull that off. Killer show. What a reunion!"

You're an idiot, Gary. Another fool. Typical boss. But I play the game, because I must.

"You said it, Gar."

"Hey," he said, "turn that up. I love this part."

No, don't use the volume, don't play the sound, don't … fine. Just do it.

"This is where Buddy gives the speech. He could barely talk above the crowd. They were so into it. Like they were possessed."

Possessed. Exactly. You have no idea. Because you're just like them. A follower. A sheep. Because it's easier than having to actually think, decide, and take action, then live with the consequences.

On stage that night, celebrating his 65th birthday, Buddy Rheams Jr. addressed the crowd. Addressed the world:

"Thank you, everyone. Thank you! Now ... I know you're all excited. You've got ME excited! And we should be. Do you know why? And I'm not just talking about the band! When I formed Taurus Enterprises almost thirty-five years ago, out in that Texas desert ... a newbie in the oil game ... never in my wildest dreams did I think I'd be part of the greatest space program in human history! But that has little to do with me."

Gary paused the video. "That's so Buddy, right Deidge? The guy pours a *hundred billion dollars* of his own money into the space program, but never takes any credit. What a rock star. Oh, cool. This is my favorite part ..." The video continued.

"When my hero John F. Kennedy told the world we would put a man on the Moon in ten years, I called him up. I offered to help, any way that I could. Not because I thought I was special or important, but because I believed in him. He was a great man. It is his memory, his spirit, that propels me even today. I didn't know if reaching so far into space would ever happen, but I knew that I wanted to try. The idea of it tapped into me, touched my soul. So we went to the Moon, and then far beyond. But to my mind ... not far enough. People talk about getting the travel bug. Well ... my bug happened to be travel, too. Only ... space travel!"

"Space travel!" Gary said, and slapped Deidra on the back. "Man, I love that."

"But the skeptics," Buddy said that night, "the skeptics told me that I was ridiculous. And possibly insane. Who was I, Buddy Rheams Jr., to believe—to declare!—that there was life out there in the Universe? And life far more advanced than ours? Impossible, they said. Blasphemy, they cried. But that wasn't it. Not at all. If anything, I consider myself a humble servant. Our greatest scientists—Elena Smith, Terrance Abercrombie, and Vernon Doyle, the new Einsteins—have told us there are trillions of galaxies across the Universe, with more planets than they can count. So what, I ask you, are the odds that we, on Earth, are as advanced as the Universe can get? Oh ... I'm not saying we're a bad lot! Far from it! I think we're great! But I know in my heart ... as much as a man can know anything ... that there are other worlds out there to explore. Maybe even worlds just like ours. And though I doubt I'll live long enough to see one ... I'm gonna get there or die trying!"

Raucous applause.

"So congratulations again to the amazing *Challenger* crew for a job ... well ... done! Okay, *Zep*. Let 'er rip!"

It still makes me sick. Those Satan worshipers. Jimmy Page wailing on his guitar, Robert Plant screaming his siren call. But what I know, Buddy … what Willie knew … my dad … was that you weren't climbing a stairway to heaven … you were paving a highway to hell. And taking the rest of us with you. And now with the ***Sampson****, even more powerful than the* ***Challenger****, you've finally pushed us too far.*

"Thanks for sharing that, Deidge. It really gets my juices flowing. But it's back to work. 1999's almost over and we've got a Y2K test to run. What'll that make? Thirty-five?"

"Thirty-eight."

"Thirty-eight. Right. No sense in taking chances. We need to inspect the shuttle before Buddy gets back. He's expecting the next *Sampson* flight to go off without a hitch. And I, for one, don't plan on disappointing the man. Because I'll tell you this, my little chickadee … when the ball drops on New Year's … when the confetti flies and the fireworks crackle … the *Sampson* will take flight. And then we'll know for sure that he was right. The *Sampson*'ll dock with the *Taurus Point Space Station*, and from there, they'll launch the unmanned probe. And that probe, armed with the New Einstein's propulsion system, will have the power and speed to break from our solar system. And do it faster than we ever dreamed possible. And if that happens … you know that'll mean?"

I do, Gary. Yes. For desecrating the holy spirit … for violating their sacred space … for our arrogance … for our trespass … the gods will smite us.

"It'll be pretty amazing, Gar. One for the ages."

Armageddon.

"I couldn't agree more, Deidge. So let's get to it. It's the *Sampson*'s most important flight …"

Deidre switched off her monitor. It went black. The Taurus Enterprises logo—the head of a bull, with horns and a nose ring, encased in a crest—was emblazed on the wall behind them. The name *Taurus Enterprises* was spelled out, curving along the crest's outer edge.

Just like Willie knew would happen. The end of the world.

Gary directed them into the corridor, leading to the shuttle's main hangar. "… and I want to see what this baby can do."

Various independent studies—and at least one commissioned by Taurus Enterprises—predicted that the upcoming *Sampson* launch would be the most watched event in world history.

The ushering of the new Millennium.

But Buddy Rheams Jr., the Old Man, knew it was only for show. But then, wasn't his entire public life? They all knew his story. Or, at the very least, the one he wanted them to know.

A dead-broke, uneducated gas attendant from the nowhere town of Kinsey, Texas who, in the sweltering summer heat of 1957, stumbled upon the deepest, untapped oil well in America, and then, over the subsequent decades, parlayed that success, transforming himself into the world's richest man.

Through Taurus Enterprises he even went so far as to bail out Arizona, Colorado, and New Mexico, turning them into privatized states that prospered in ways they never had, serving as innovation hubs for aeronautic development, supercolliders, and rehabilitation and recovery centers for veterans suffering from injury, substance abuse, and other battle-induced trauma.

Buddy Rheams Jr. also gave more money to charities, nonprofits, and training programs than the next twenty global donors combined, advanced more women and minority executives than any other firm in the world, and thanks to his funding, Taurus researchers had already cured seventeen diseases.

And then, decades after finding riches in black gold, he gazed out the window of his private quarters in the Taurus Enterprises Space Center, overlooking the launch pad from which the *Sampson* would leave the Earth.

"That's a great view," Tilly said. "You going to watch the launch from here?"

"Me? No. Not this one. I'll be in my box above the Control Room." Though outwardly almost eighty years old, with a wrinkled face and hands, large, brown liver spots on his neck and forehead, and receding, white hair, Buddy was, in a way, much younger. He peeled back the prosthetic mask he wore to age him appropriately. The putty stuck to his nose. "Oooh. That stings a bit. Anything you can do?"

Tilly winked. "For what you pay me? Sure. I'll figure it out."

"Thanks. Not sure why, but it's been taking me longer these days to get it all off. Been clumping on my cheekbones, too. It's why I've been holed up by myself so much. It's just easier sometimes not to deal with it. Deal with anyone. Plus ... it plays into the whole *mysterious recluse* persona. The less people know about me, the better."

"Hey," said Tilly, a Hollywood make-up artist Buddy had recruited during the after party at Marlon Brando's mansion following the 1970 Oscars when *Midnight Cowboy* took home the statue for Best Picture. A small, petite woman, she matched up well against Buddy's strong, chiseled physicality. "You don't have to explain. That was the deal, right? I keep you looking like an old fart and I don't ask how or why you look as young and ruggedly Robert Redford as you did almost fifty years ago." She opened her three-layered make-up kit. "See how I didn't ask just then?"

Buddy laughed. "Yes, Tilly. I cracked your code."

"Good, because I'm no spring chicken myself. I've got a lot of good years left in me, but I won't be here forever. And at the rate we're going, I'll be a wrinkled old prune long before you."

"Oh, stop that. You're as gorgeous as the day I met you."

Tilly blushed. "Truer words were never spoken. But feel free to speak them again."

Buddy went to his desk drawer. He always paid Tilly by encrypted wire transfer, to keep their relationship confidential, but he had something special for her. A gold charm. "Here," he said, his face still half covered by the wrinkled prosthetic, while the other allowed for his more youthful looking nature, revealing his two sides. His two selves. "It's for you."

"My goodness … Buddy." The charm twinkled in the light. "It's gorgeous. Thank you. But why?"

"You're the only person who knows the real me." *The only person on Earth, anyway.* "I can be myself around you. I don't have to hide."

"Buddy," said Tilly, who held up her graying brown hair, exposing the back of her neck as he fastened the charm from behind her. "You're giving me a complex."

Good god, Buddy thought. *Listen to me.*

"It's my pleasure. I appreciate what you do you for me. You have no idea." Buddy sat on one of the leather couches. "And, if I'm being totally honest … I'm feeling guilty."

This is who I've become. Telling lies about my lies. But what choice do I have? Tell her the truth? That I'm from an alternate Earth? That I crash-landed here decades ago? That I'm building the space program from the wreckage of my destroyed ship, to help me get home? Yeah. Sure. That'll go well.

"I'm sure you have lots to feel guilty about." Tilly winked again. "But why now?"

Buddy shook his head. "Willie saved me. Willie Wright. I think about him now and then, but lately … every day."

"I don't know him."

"You wouldn't. He was an engineer during the '80s. A good one, too. The *Challenger* flights had been going well, but the space program was running out of steam. You have any idea what it costs? Sure … I had a lot coming in, but nowhere close to what I was spending. I needed a win. A big win. That's why we had Christa

McAuliffe on the flight. PR stunt. Worked, too. The attention brought in endorsement deals by the truckload."

"Yeah," Tilly said, beaming with an almost Pavlovian response as she dabbed Buddy's cheek with a custom dissolvent bioengineered to respond to the enzymes specific to his sweat. "The Christa Vista. We did that dance for years. And if I recall, didn't that flight convince the government to back you on the Space Station?"

"Yep. That's the one."

"So what's the problem? What happened to Willie?"

"I saw the strain he was under. The hours he was putting in. I was worried he would burn out. It happens sometimes. You get so determined, thinking you're going to make history … that you lose yourself. Willie was so dedicated, so invested in the launch, that he reviewed the specs dozens of times. Maybe more. The team installed a new batch of heat-protecting panels for the re-entry process that were far more efficient and resilient than the older model. But Willie found a problem in the O-rings a few days before the launch."

Analysis showed that the O-rings on the *Challenger*'s right, solid rocket booster would have failed at liftoff, allowing pressurized gas to escape. The vaporized material would have damaged the strut connecting the rocket booster to the shuttle's huge external tank, causing a massive leak, with hydrogen bursting into flames.

"It would have destroyed the shuttle, killing the crew. The space program would have stopped in its tracks, and I would have been ruined. Willie Wright saved a lot of lives that day, saved this company. And in doing so, he allowed us—allowed me—to keep chasing the stars. So, yeah … I owe Willie. I owe him everything."

"I had no idea. Where is he?"

Buddy went to the wall, and depressed a flat panel, which revealed a hidden safe. He came back with a sealed envelope. "He had a nervous breakdown after the O-rings. He went screaming through the halls that we were causing the end of the world. We tried to calm him down, to restrain him. We just wanted him to come peacefully, so he could rest, but he said that we were demons of the night trying to steal his soul, and that the *Challenger* was a symbol of doom. That it would engulf the world in fire. He ran out into a restricted area during a fuel check, and fell into an empty, concrete holding tank. He died instantly."

"Oh, my lord. That's horrible."

"It was. But there was so much at stake, we had to keep it quiet. He's the real hero, but we couldn't tell anyone. That's what the envelope is for. It's a trust I set up for his wife and daughter. Enough money to last for generations. We searched high and low, but they were long gone. His apartment was filled with prescription bottles with sleeping pills, antidepressants, and anti-anxiety medications. There were candles, and drawings, and notes about me bringing about the end times. I think his family felt trapped by his mania, but were afraid to take on Buddy Rheams Jr. and his horrible, evil empire. If only we knew then what we know now …"

"Where'd they go? His family?"

"I don't know. They disappeared. Sometimes you just don't want to be found. I know that feeling. All too well. It's why I hate this day, as much as I'm supposed to love it."

Tilly put her hand on Buddy's cheek. His uncovered cheek. "You're a complicated man, Buddy Rheams. I don't know how you deal with it all."

Buddy peeled away the prosthetic, his mask. "Honestly," he said, "neither do I."

Hangar IX was three times larger than the next largest hangar, and still it could barely contain the rubicon of machinery, electronics, hoses, wires, hydraulic equipment, workers, and, of course, the *Sampson* itself. If Deidre hadn't known better, she would have thought that the powers of the world were preparing to meet the gods.

"Well, hello Deidre, if I may be permitted to call you that." Buddy Rheams Jr. seemed even bigger than his six-foot frame, his body almost too small to contain his life force. "Or do you prefer Miss Fell?"

Horror scrolled passed Deidre's eyes, and over her heart, as if she were standing before Satan. Her hand trembled. "N-no … I mean … yes … I mean … no, yes … Deidre is fine, sir. I didn't …" Air scorched her lungs, tight as a busted coil. "You know my name? It's, uh …"

"Don't mind her," Gary said. "She's not used to being in the spotlight."

"The … the spotlight? I …?"

What's happening? Deidre thought. *Does he know? Has he come for me? Is it over? Am I too late?*

"Well, it's wonderful to meet you, Deidre. Gary says you are one of the most dedicated programmers we have. That you understand the *Sampson* diagnostics as well as anyone, and better than most. I put a lot of faith in this man. If he says you're a keeper, then I believe him."

The rational bank of Deidre's mind couldn't believe that the Old Man was trying to harm her just then, yet as pure reflex she pulled away when he extended his hand, avoiding physical contact. His face was wrinkled and worn—it oozed with the stench of death, and poison, and a black, demonic impulse to corrupt everyone and everything around him. But despite his advanced age, he took her by the shoulder, his grip extended with the power, precision, and dexterity of a man half his age. Worse than losing her life, she felt her spirit slipping away, in such close proximity to the most dangerous man alive, if he was even a man at all.

"Keep up the good work," the Old Man said, and spewed upon her a smile so phony, smeared in such contempt, that it almost … almost … seemed genuine. "Tomorrow's a big day. And from what Gary tells me, you're a big reason why."

"Oh, I, uh …," Deidre stammered again, unprepared for the gracious remarks offered on her behalf, as manipulative and insincere as she knew them to be. "Thank you, sir. Yes, sir. I … I try my best."

Gary intervened, relieving Deidre of her distress. "Thanks, Buddy. It's always great to get a visit from the chief, but if you don't mind, that's a rather large spacecraft over there, and you pay me to make sure it can fly in a straight line. Or thereabouts."

"Ha. Yes, I do. Don't let me interrupt."

"No problem, Buddy. We'll get …" Gary removed his KATI, **short for KT-5, Taurus Enterprises' best-selling, multi-format smart phone**. "Sorry, sir. It's Loreen from Mission Control. About tomorrow. I need to take this. Excuse me."

"So, I guess it's just you and me," the Old Man said.

Deidre offered a slight nod. "Yes. I guess it is."

This is how it happens then, isn't it? You arranged that call, didn't you? To pull Gary away from me, to leave me exposed. You're even worse than I imagined. I hate you, you horrid old beast. I want you dead.

"You know, it's funny," the Old Man said with a soft smile. "Even after all these years working with engineers, computer programmers, and technicians of every kind, I still get a kick out of listening to you techies talk the math and science."

"Which part?" Deidre said, suspicious. "The science of …?"

"All of it. Sure, I get the gist of thrust and propulsion and all that, but the mechanics of flight, the forces at work. I mean … look at that. The *Sampson*. The Space Shuttle. How can something that big, that heavy, that … *mechanical* … make it's way off the Earth with such force and structural integrity that it can break through our atmosphere and enter into space itself?"

Oh, you're good. Pretending not to know. You can't die soon enough.

"It's really just a matter of getting liquid hydrogen and liquid oxygen to produce high pressure gases that drive the turbo-pumps, creating thrust and lift, but ensuring that the tanks are coated with polyisocyanurate foam insulation. It helps ensure that the shuttle is sufficiently protected against the rapid increase in dynamic pressure, or Q, or velocity pressure, as it accelerates from zero to approximately 7,850 meters per second—or 17,500 miles per hour—in eight and a half minutes in order to reach the minimum altitude required to orbit the Earth."

The Old Man's face lit up as he laughed. "Like I said, Deidre. I believe every word you said because of how much you love saying them."

As much as she hated to admit it, Deidre felt a warm glow of respect and admiration from hearing Buddy Rheams Jr. speak her name aloud. Despite everything, she was flattered.

"You can rattle off scientific equations better than I can describe our sales charts. And it took me a heckuva long time to do even that."

"You have more money than most countries, sir. You've had practice."

"Touché. Very good. Yes. I have a few shekels. But you know another funny thing . . .? I was never in this for the money."

"No offense, sir, but it's easy to dismiss money when you have loads of it. And unless I'm mistaken, you've worked incredibly hard to make that money. It didn't just show up one day. I mean . . . other than the oil wells you kinda fell into."

"Touché again. You know your history. Well . . . my history. But what I mean is . . . the money was always a means to an end. So, yes . . . the money is important, but it wasn't because I wanted to buy fancy things or feed my ego. Since the time I was a child . . . and if you know my history as well as you seem to, then you know that I grew up about as poor as a person can and still find a way to live . . . but even then, I used to dream of the stars. It was the one thing I could envision that no one could take away. The stars twinkling above us in the night sky? They were for everyone. The rich *and* the poor and everyone in between. And the world over. I would sometimes go a day or two without eating, but chewing on some old bark, just to keep my stomach from turning on itself, no matter how hungry I was, or how dirty, or alone I felt . . . I could always just lie on my back, stare up into space, and watch the stars. They spoke to me, Deidre. They helped keep my faith alive when I had every reason to let it die. So even after my mother passed, and my father was gone, and I didn't have a friend in all the world or a nickel to my name . . . you know what I did have?"

Deidre looked up at the Old Man, the white-haired octogenarian, but saw him then as just a little boy. "The stars?"

"The stars, Deidre. The stars. And as ridiculous as it was, me … Harlan Rheams Jr. … smelly as a goat and with even less wealth … if all my dreams came true … if I could see mankind reach the stars … then it wouldn't matter what happened to me. Just thinking about the possibility … that we could all share the same, well … space … as the mighty gods … it was enough to keep me going. And when by divine intervention—or just dumb luck—I found those oil wells, and that money we spoke of came rolling in … there was only one thing I ever wanted to do with it. Get us into space. Now … I never thought it would really happen! It was just so crazy. And then it did. Not bad for a guy who had to eat dog food three times a week, and be grateful to get it, huh Deidre?"

"Uh … n-no. Not bad at all, sir. Not bad for anyone."

A red light swirled above them just then, followed by a *RAHMP RAHMPH RAHMP*

"That's our cue," the Old Man said. "Show time."

Not knowing what else to say, Deidre couldn't tell if she had been mistaken all along about Buddy Rheams Jr.—basing her world view on her father's escalating mania—or if the Old Man was even more devious than she imagined.

"Oh, and one more thing," the Old Man said. "You keep going the way you are, and there just might be a spot for you on my team. A special project I'm working on."

"Wow. Really? Okay, sir. Thank you, sir."

The Old Man looked back at her, as if there was a completely different person behind those eyes, seeing her for the first time. Or finally revealing his true nature. He gestured at the *Sampson*. "Don't thank me yet, Deidre. I haven't told you what it is. And if I ever do, you'll never look at that bucket of bolts out there the same way again."

Deidre barely slept that night, but then, she didn't sleep much anyway.

How could she, with Buddy Rheams Jr. about to launch the *Sampson*, set to dock at the *Taurus Point Space Station*, refuel, and then dispatch the *Crimson Light*—an unmanned space probe—fitted with the New Einstein's prototype propulsion system that would break the very boundaries between man and the gods?

And now that the Old Man was in her head, simultaneously filling her with praise, confessions, and ambiguity, what was she supposed to do? The subroutine she programmed into the launch sequence was hidden so deep that even Gary couldn't find it.

Those weren't Y2K tests, she realized. *Gary was looking for corporate sabotage, hacking our system to find another hacker. To find me. Wow, he's good good. Damn good. But I'm better. I learned from the best. It's how I got away. How I changed my name, my identity. Started a new life. And then came back. Came for him.*

All she had to do was send the code from her KATI and the *Sampson* would explode once and for all, honoring the gods, rather than antagonizing them, completing what her dad set out to accomplish—prevent Armageddon.

But now that the end of days had arrived, the Millennium, like the scriptures predicted, she was having a crisis of faith.

Please, Dad. Help me see the way. Give me a sign. I need your help.

"You ready, Deidge?" Gary said from Buddy's private skybox within Tower Command. The staff below them flipped switches, spoke urgently into headsets, and scuttled between rows of long consoles. Sunshine beamed through the ceiling-to-floor windows.

"It's the big moment. And we're with the chief. He's never invited me up here. I don't know what you guys talked about, but he's impressed as hell with you. And if that means he's impressed with me … even better."

Although Deidre knew he meant it affectionately, she was tempted to tear out Gary's larynx with each elbow jab to the ribs.

"Oh, shoot," Gary said. "Here he comes. Stand up straight. But don't look tense. And don't start in again with all the technobabble because he—"

"Gary."

"Yeah, okay. I just heard myself. I'm calm. I'm cool."

"Worried about the launch?"

"A little. But, no. I feel good about that. It's just … the Old Man's particular about who he lets up here. This isn't a simple gesture, Deidge. He has plans for us. Big plans. You're still a kid, so you don't really get the significance. But I'm 54 years old, with a wife, a mortgage, four kids to put through college, and a vacation house in Lake Tahoe that needs a new roof, boiler, and sundeck, none of which I can afford. So trust me when I say, opportunities like this are far and few between."

The Old Man entered then, with a small entourage behind him. "Hi there, folks. Gary. Deidre. Glad you could join us. I think you know my executive assistant Moira. This is General Reedy from the U.S. Army, and Alison Brigman, who you know from NASA."

They all shook hands.

"What do you think, General? Think the probe will work?"

"I'm really not sure, Buddy, but after all we've been through, it's one heckuva an idea. I remember when we sat with JFK about getting to the Moon. But to leave the solar system? Hell. It's sure worth tryin' ... especially if you're fitting the bill!"

Laughter.

"Absolutely, Buddy," Alison said. "It's the next frontier."

"Indeed," Buddy said, "but as Deidre and I were discussing the other day..."

Panic. Deidre's temperature shot up three degrees. She fingered the KATI in her pocket, tapping code, but not quite ready to press *SEND*. Not yet. The implications were starting to sink in.

Am I really going to do this? Kill all those people? Destroy the hopes of the world? What if I'm wrong? What if Willie lost his way? Am I going insane, too? I'm standing before a man who destroyed my family, tore my life apart. But now that I'm here ... did I buy into a delusion? Have I fallen into the abyss? Am I the real monster?

"... the Moon was just a stepping stone to the rest of the Universe. I don't know how far we're ever going to get, but we'll never know if we don't give it a shot. And if nothing else ... when it comes to the stars ..."—Buddy winked at her, that fake, smug wink—"...I don't take *no* for an answer."

Thank you, Buddy. I needed to hear that again. To be reminded of just how selfish you are. How dangerous. How evil.

"Ha!" The General clapped his hands. "Well ... that's why you're the right man for the job. Okay, then. Let's get this countdown underway. We've got some stars to chase, and unless I'm missing something obvious, their ain't no point in waiting any longer!"

Willie Wright was a good dad. Deidre told herself that again and again.

But now that she was on the verge of actuating what would be known as the most diabolical terrorist attack in modern history—one that would not only kill the *Sampson* crew, but likely decimate the space program for years, if not decades—she had ample reason to wonder if her memories of Willie matched up to the narrative she'd constructed about him.

When did her mother steal them away from Willie, living apart, to escape his dissent into madness? Four years? Five? Willie died when Deidre was only fifteen. Did he even attend her birthday party that year? She couldn't remember.

How many nights had Deidre stared at the ceiling, or looked out the window, wondering if her father was actually chasing the magic of science, or a delusion his mind invented to escape the pressures of life?

He hadn't always been that way. It was only after he joined the Taurus engineering team, when he became obsessed with Buddy Rheams Jr., and decided it was his responsibility to stop the Old Man from trampling on the gods. But did the gods even exist?

Deidre tried to hold onto her memories of the Willie she loved most—her very best dad in the whole wide world. The one who drew the most wonderful pictures of the solar system, and held her shoulder to shoulder as together they gazed into space through a telescope he built himself. Yeah. That was the dad she wanted to remember, the one that made her smile.

Only that wasn't the Willie she knew best. She got left with the dark and unpredictable Willie. The Willie who had visions of the end of the world, convinced that the only way to protect himself, protect his wife and child … protect the Earth … was to destroy a projectile of doom, camouflaged as a beacon of hope.

And so now, on the cusp of the Millennium, on New Year's Eve, standing beside the Old Man, Deidre felt the countdown in her soul. The vibrations ricocheting across the cosmos as the world over waited to see if the self anointed man of the stars, Buddy Rheams Jr., would further elevate mankind's journey beyond the stars. Through the intercom system they all heard:

"TEN … NINE … EIGHT …"

…RUMBLERUMBLERUMBLERUMBLERUMBLERUMBLERUMBLERUMBLE…

I can't do this, I can't be here, I can't …

"SEVEN … SIX … FIVE …"

…RUMBLERUMBLERUMBLERUMBLERUMBLERUMBLERUMBLERUMBLE …

I'm going to throw up …

Deidre bolted for the hallway.

A twenty-acre mushroom cloud of fire and smoke and chemical thunder erupted from the *Sampson* boosters.

*"Confirm, **Sampson**, this is Tower. We have liftoff."*

…RUMBLERUMBLERUMBLERUMBLERUMBLERUMBLERUMBLERUMBLE RUMBLERUMBLERUMBLERUMBLERUMBLERUMBLERUMBLERUMBLERUMBLE …

… KKKKKRRRRRRBBBBLLLLAAAAAAAAAAMMMMMMMMMM!

Deidre rolled along the wall to keep her steady, keep her still. But under the soft, overhead lights she felt exposed, the weight of mankind's unfathomable scrutiny beaming down on her alone. So she ducked into the janitor's closet, bolted the door.

Even locked away Deidre could hear the cheers, rooting on the *Sampson* as a massive cloud billowed behind it.

Her chest so tight it nearly choked out her last breath, Deidre gripped the KATI, thumbs to the buttons, the tiny screen glowing in the dark.

Bounding between delusion and sanity, between past and present, between what was and what might be, Deidre squeezed her eyes, searching for Willie, the real Willie, the one who wanted noting more than to be part of something grand. She smiled then, thinking of her dad—her best dad. But then that picture faded, as it often did, leaving her with the worst memory of all.

So she gave into the pressure and typed the destruct code—W-I-L-L-I-E. Her thumb, bent at the knuckle, hovered over the *SEND* key. One depression and the *Sampson* would go boom. Making Deidre savior of humanity, a martyr, or a terrorist—and possibly all three.

Until there was a pounding on the door. "DEIDRE!" Buddy shouted. "You don't have to do this!"

"Leave me alone! You're a monster! A fraud!"

"It's not what you think!" Buddy said, still beating on the door. "Let me explain!"

"You did this to Willie. To me. To all of us!"

But rather than more pounding, there was only silence, leaving Deidre alone with herself.

"You're right," Buddy said finally. "I'm everything you said and worse. You have every reason to hate me. Everyone does. But listen to me, Deidre … if you press that button now, if you send that signal … no matter what happens next, no matter how history remembers you … you'll know what you did. Always and forever. And when this moment is long gone, and there's nothing left but silence in the night, you'll know that the light once inside you that burned so bright … will wither in your soul. It happened to me. Please, Deidre. Save yourself while you still can. I beg you. Don't do it."

Tears singed her face like a snake's venom. The torment raged within her.

Do it!

-I can't!-

Your destiny!

-I don't know!-

-I have to!-

-It's wrong!-

-I need to!-

-Don't!-

-I want to!-

I WANT TO! AHHHHHHHHHHHHHHHHHHHHHHHHHHHH!

Yet before she could parry herself back Deidre pressed *SEND.* She tapped the button over and over for an explosion to be felt across the world. Across the cosmos.

But it never came. And then Buddy knocked again.

"Deidre. We found the code. I know why you programmed it. I'm not mad. Your dad ... Willie ... he ... he learned something about me, something he couldn't accept, could live with. He truly believed he was doing the right thing. In his place, I might have done the same. He tampered with the O-rings. But he helped us more than he would ever know. The time fuse he planted within the mechanical system—one he invented—helped us develop new technology. He advanced the space program by a decade at least. I owe him everything and more. I owe you. He was a great man, Deidre. Far better than me. And he loved you dearly. But he let my obsession ... become his. I'm not who you think I am. I need to show you something. Please."

Despite herself Deidre unlocked the door, allowing Buddy Rheams Jr., the Old Man, to come inside, and occupy the only private space she could find in a world she feared might end.

The Old Man switched on the light, reached for his face. He peeled it back, revealing a much younger man beneath.

Deidre gasped, yet somehow was relieved, seeing with her own eyes what Willie knew to be wrong, what was missing. What her dad had been chasing all along.

"I've been here a long, long time, Deidre. I've had to make choices, some terrible, awful choices. But there are people I love who are counting on me, if they're even still alive. I've spent my entire life here on Earth for one reason only. To get back home. And after what I saw today ... I think you're just the right person to help me get it done."

Unable to speak, Deidre tried anyway. "I ... but ..." The madness she'd been chasing now made more sense than ever, if it made any sense at all. "Okay," she said, then let out a long, weighty breath, one that expelled a lifetime of confusion, grief, and anger at a man who never really existed. "Okay. On one condition."

The man she knew as Buddy Rheams Jr. stood before her, and smiled. "Oh, yeah? And what's that?"

"Tell me everything. About you. About Willie. About who he really was and why you've done all this. Because I miss my dad so much, and I really need to know."

"Are you sure? It's kind of a long story. And you might not like what you hear."

Deidre pulled over a stool from the corner of the closet. "Then start at the beginning, and take your time. The world will just have to wait."

DAVID GERROLD

A BRIEF EXPLANATION OF HOW BUDAPEST BECAME THE TACO CAPITAL OF THE WORLD

It wasn't until after the charter was certified and ratified, and after the stationery and business cards had been printed that anyone noticed the unfortunate acronym of the Geographic Anomaly Studies, Pasadena.

Doctor Elouise M. Rombach, Senior Consultant on loan from Caltech, did not find it amusing. It grew even less amusing over time. Hearing the inevitable repetition of the obvious jokes for the hundredth time, coming from those encountering the acronym for the first time, became a test of her good nature. Her strained smiles revealed that she was failing the test.

Despite the apparent frivolity of the study—what the hell is a geographic anomaly anyway?—the group had been organized to discreetly study a growing body of evidence that *something was wrong.*

It began with the Valley Glen anomaly.

Valley Glen is the name given to the more affluent section of Van Nuys, California—a joke understood only by those who live in Van Nuys, California. The residents of Valley Glen were so sensitive about living in Van Nuys and the presumption of lower property values that they petitioned to have their miniscule neighborhood renamed to something that sounded like Beverly Glen, a neighborhood known for its multi-million-dollar price tags.

Left over from its previous location in Van Nuys, a two-year community college squats in the center of Valley Glen. Even though the college sits in the center of Valley Glen and Valley Glen sits in the center of the San Fernando Valley, the college is not named Valley Glen Community College nor is it named San Fernando Valley Community College. It is more inaccurately named Los Angeles Valley College. The college is famous for almost nothing at all, despite the belief of those who work and teach there that its greater destiny will manifest eventually. They were almost right.

The college is bordered by Burbank Blvd. on the south, Fulton Ave. on the west, Coldwater Ave. on the east, and Oxnard Street on the North. Oxnard Street is notable for nothing at all, except for the fact that it has a slight rise to the west. Almost a hill. For that reason, it is an excellent place for students majoring in Geomatics to stand in the middle of the street peering through tripod-mounted sextants and scribbling numbers onto clipboards. Despite the fact that modern technology has made instant geoscanning possible with the average smartphone, with accuracy down to the millimeter, student surveyors are still required to understand the geometric principles underlying their craft.

This was not where the western region anomaly began, but it was inevitable that this would be where the first physical evidence was discovered.

After a particularly crazy summer—well, it was a presidential election year—an entire class of students all failed the same part of their midterm exam, the mapping of Oxnard Street. They all reported the same inaccurate numbers. The only possible explanation was that they had cheated, all copying their data from one student's work, who had gotten his measurements wrong.

So Professor Greenberger flunked the entire class.

Geomatics students had been surveying the Oxnard hill since long before the term Geomatics had been invented. Since the first years after World War II, when the college had existed as nothing more than a few bungalows and Quonset huts, the presence of students and sextants on Oxnard Street was as familiar a sight to neighbors as the daily mail delivery. Oxnard Street had been surveyed more than Marilyn Monroe's nude photo in *Playboy* magazine. There was absolutely no question that Oxnard Street was exactly *X* many meters long and the slope was a grade of *Y* degrees and the west end of the block was *Z* centimeters higher than the east end.[1]

So there was only one possible reason for the collective inaccuracy of the entire set of midterm exams. The students had colluded to cheat.

1 I would have put in the exact numbers, but the point of this story is that those numbers are no longer accurate, so why bother?

At the administrative hearing, several of the students showed the selfies they had taken of themselves out on Oxnard Street, others showed their own scribbled paperwork, and a few even demonstrated how they had used their smartphones to confirm their sextant measurements.

Angered at this insubordination, Professor Greenberger dragged the entire class out to Oxnard Street to demonstrate how to properly survey the slope so as to come up with the appropriate measurements.

After apologizing to the entire class, he called Doctor Rombach at CalTech. Although skeptical, Doctor Rombach and two of her associates took the 134 west. They took the Coldwater off-ramp, drove north for a mile and a half, most of it paralleling the concrete-lined Los Angeles river, turned left, and met Professor Greenberger at the corner of Oxnard Street and Ethel Avenue.[2]

They unloaded a trunk full of sophisticated electronic equipment—including military-grade GPS units which would allow them to geolocate their exact position down to the millimeter. They used high-resolution laser scanners and Tesla-based radars to digitally map the entire terrain. They repeated their measurements at twelve different locations, then frowned at the displays on their laptops which confirmed that the distance between Fulton Avenue and Ethel Avenue was now ten centimeters greater than demonstrated by all previous measurements.

Either generations of students had all made the same miscalculation—or this particular suburban block had somehow expanded. Doctor Rombach, Professor Greenberger, two associates, and half a dozen students, walked back and forth along the entire distance seven times, looking for cracks in either the sidewalk or the asphalt paving of Oxnard Street. They found nothing.

Two months later, GASP was formed.

For the first several months of its existence, GASP's sole function was to escort visiting geologists, seismologists, and sociologists to ~~Van Nuys~~ Valley Glen so that they too could walk the distance between Fulton Avenue and Ethel Avenue, looking for cracks in the pavement. To a man (and the occasional woman) they all agreed that there had to be a rational explanation for the anomaly. The developing consensus held that all of the past observations were flawed and that the flaws had finally been revealed by the superior technology of lasers, radars, and GPS units. That at least two decades of previous measurements had been confirmed by lasers, radars, and GPS units was an irrelevant and inconsequential

2 This is a curious bit of misnomery. Oxnard Street is a wide avenue and Ethel Avenue is a narrow residential street.

detail. Current technology was obviously superior to those primitive earlier generations of technology.

This particular conclusion would have been the final word—except for one thing. The next set of measurements didn't match. The distance between Fulton Avenue and Ethel Avenue had expanded again, this time by twenty-two centimeters.

This time around, the various confused experts declared that the area must be situated over some kind of electro-magnetic mascon disturbance that somehow affected all digitally-based measuring devices and only the original measurements, performed with sextants, were valid. Thus, satisfied that they had explained it away, they went home.

Except—when the students returned to the area, armed with the most primitive instruments possible, sextants and telescopes and measured lengths of cord—when they surveyed and re-surveyed and re-re-surveyed, they determined that not only had the distance between the two avenues expanded, but it had expanded again and was continuing to expand.

Now convinced that the anomaly was real enough to be a measurable event, Doctor Elouise M. Rombach sent teams of surveyors out across the San Fernando Valley and surrounding areas to discover if other locations were also experiencing anomalous expansion.

The short version: yes.

After six months of measuring, digitizing, computerizing, modeling, and massaging the data, the conclusion was inescapable. Los Angeles was growing.

Not every area was growing as fast as the San Fernando Valley, the growth was uneven throughout Los Angeles County, but it was definitely happening. All told, the county had grown more than a kilometer, almost a full mile—although scientific measurements were more efficient in the metric system, the rest of the nation was not equally committed to either science or metrics of any kind.[3]

---

3 According to several poorly-educated members of the House of Representatives, if it isn't in the Bible it doesn't count. Nevertheless, when all of this finally did reach those hallowed halls, Doctor Rombach staunchly refused to issue her official reports in cubits, despite a lengthy congressional investigation and even a veiled threat of contempt charges. The investigation concluded without a conclusion, because one of the representatives from Texas got into a fistfight with one of the other representatives from Texas—they could not agree if Doctor Rombach was guilty of falsifying the data for personal aggrandizement or initiating the expansion herself as part of a liberal conspiracy to grow California into the biggest state in the Union.

GASP issued several carefully worded reports on the nature of its continuing investigations, using as many polysyllabic words as possible to keep the story from ending up on the front page of supermarket tabloids. Nevertheless, nine months after Professor Greenberger's attempt to flunk an entire class of student surveyors, Doctor Rombach was "invited" to address the Los Angeles County Board of Supervisors—"invited" being the politest euphemism for, "We could subpoena you if we have to."

Doctor Rombach, no stranger to the vagaries of political posturing—after all, she had not only survived, but ultimately succeeded in escaping academia—spoke slowly and in specifically measured terms, deliberately designed to confuse those whose only skill in life was winning elections. Unfortunately, one of the freelance reporters in the room understood exactly what she was getting at. Actually, he was another of those oddball observers more than a real reporter, a court-watcher when certain criminal courts were in session, which wasn't today, so he was here instead—but he had occasionally sold an article to various freebies like the L.A. Weekly, so that sort of counted. A somewhat illicit-looking fellow, generally known to his colleagues as "Pesky," he was able to translate her verbiage into Sheldon-speak and from there into a passable imitation of English.

But the important thing about Pesky was the question he did manage to ask. As Doctor Rombach was leaving the hearing, which had turned into an unusually prolonged and dreary affair, unnoticed or ignored by the few reporters who had managed to achieve a state of consciousness higher than somnolence, Pesky caught up with her in the hallway and asked bluntly, "Are you saying that the whole planet is expanding? Or is it just Los Angeles County bulging out of proportion to the rest of the continent?"

Doctor Rombach blurted something unintelligible—halfway between "Piss off" and "Damfino" and hurried to her car. Pesky's question had triggered an even more disturbing avenue (well, maybe just a street) of inquiry.[4]

It was this simple. She, and the other members of GASP had focused so much of their attention on the unexplained expansion of Los Angeles County, they had neglected to consider what might be happening in the surrounding counties—Orange to the south, Ventura to the northwest, Kern to the north, and San Bernardino to the east. Not caring that she was violating California's strict laws against using one's cell phone while driving, Doctor Rombach frantically ordered her surveying teams out to each of the surrounding counties.

---

4 Pesky is unlikely to reappear in this narrative, so you may conveniently forget him now.

She made her second set of calls to various federal officials, to alert/advise/suggest/request/plead/demand that the US Geological Survey immediately begin rechecking geographical domains across the entire continent. Doctor Rombach was so engaged in this particular set of conversations that she did not notice the red and blue blinking lights behind her vehicles—not until she was forced to a stop before a phalanx of sixteen police cars blocking the Pasadena freeway.[5]

Doctor Rombach spent the weekend in county lockup. She was arraigned the following Monday. Despite her lawyer's motion to have the charges dismissed, presiding Judge Gannon remained unimpressed, and released her on $50,000 bail and instructions not to leave the county.

Court-watcher, Pesky[6] recognized her immediately and realized that the circumstances of her arrest, the occurrence of her frenzied phone calls coming immediately after her hurried retreat from his question, and the resultant police chase — all these events were related. If only he could remember the question he'd asked.

Pesky didn't keep notes. He had a pocket audio-video recorder, a life-monitor, an electric Boswell, so it was no small matter for him to access his files from his iPhone, and play back the events of the previous Friday, refreshing his memory of the fateful question.

Had he used his real name, regular readers of the L.A. Weekly would have known Pesky from his other articles. To protect his anonymity, he published most of his work under the most mundane and inconspicuous pseudonym he could come up with, M. Raptor Bluthorne. The M. was silent.

M. Raptor Bluthorne was the many-fabled author of "The Ten Cleanest Restrooms in Los Angeles," "The Nickleback Mysteries," "The Science of Flatulence," "Outside Scientology," "The Burlap Condom," "The Museum of Irrelevance," "Sex Toys Of The Poor," "The FBI Is In Your Toothbrush," and "Ten Science Fiction Novels Worth Skipping." These and other articles had earned him both a following and a reputation. Neither were anything to brag about, but apparently it sold papers—or would have sold papers if the L.A. Weekly had not been a freebie, its real purpose to provide an outlet for local advertisers.

Nevertheless, the alarmist outing by M. Raptor Bluthorne, entitled, "The City Has Cancer!" managed to attract enough attention that one of the local television

5 The low-speed police chase had been broadcast live on channels 2, 4, 5, 7, 9, and 11. Channel 13 was rerunning a syndicated episode of *The Big Bang Theory* and had not cut away for fear of enraging the most aggressive members of the series' audience.

6 He's back. I lied.

stations decided to investigate the story as a possible oddball-interest sidebar on the Three O'clock News, generally one of the slowest parts of the news day.

In any other narrative, the local news bimbette with aspirations of becoming a real reporter would have teamed up with M. Raptor Bluthorne to uncover some dark disturbing conspiracy of evil, usually perpetrated by a nefarious government conspiracy—punctuated with floating red dots from laser gunsights, an exploding car, at least one frenzied foot pursuit through a late-night parking structure, a desperate police chase through shining wet streets slicing through concrete canyons, black helicopters with relentless probing fingers of blue light, and everywhere a phalanx of expressionless men in black suits and sunglasses—all of it culminating in a sudden avalanche of exposure and truth broadcast live to a breathless city, resulting in a cascade of embarrassing investigations, public exoneration, even a medal or two, and finally a frenzied copulation indicating a lifetime of marital bliss in an otherwise uneventful future.

Unfortunately, there was no local news bimbette, just a tired old man named Archer Bobby, working the last few years until his contract expired and a fresh-out-of-school naif, Floxxy Williams, who was probably doomed to be his replacement. Even more unfortunate, there would be no car chases, no explosions, no dramatic expose, and definitely no frenzied copulation.

Archer Bobby and Floxxy Williams were already bored with the story before they started. It had no sex, no scandal, no Hollywood connection, not even the possibility of a devastating 9.5 megaquake—so no apparent pathway to a book deal, let alone a Pulitzer prize. So of course, there would not be even a half-hearted attempt at frenzied copulation. (Floxxy was a lesbian and Archer Bobby was too proud to buy Viagra.)

But...as reporters, they did have access to an extensive Rolodex.[7] Applying themselves diligently, they managed to connect with Mick Viggle, an assistant janitor at GASP—actually, Viggle was really a screenwriter and actor, also a director and producer, who was just waiting for his agent to return his calls. (He did not know that the aforesaid agent was currently being held without bail for stalking a studio script reader.) The janitor gig was just research for his current project, a slasher script about a demon-possessed mop. Never mind that, Viggle was delighted at any attention which might further his career.

7 An arcane device. A personal cardfile, mandatory for used for keeping track of names and phone numbers. It was invented in the mid-forties by Arnold Neustadter. He lived until 1996, just long enough to see the internet make his invention irrelevant. (This is a real fact. I am not making this up.)

Viggle shared that he had previously been contacted by a very deep-voiced woman named Emma Rabbit Bubblehorn, or something like that In exchange for a promise of a bottle of cheap bourbon (which he still had not received)—he had allowed her to interview him about his important work at the Institute, or was it a University, he wasn't sure—he was just a temp, you know, doing research, for his script, Spielberg wants to see it when it's ready, never mind, what did you want to know?

In exchange for a promise of two bottles of the same cheap whiskey (which were ordered on Amazon during the course of the phone interview), Viggle happily, breathlessly, and drunkenly shared that Dr. Rombach had been phoning surveyors across the state and even as far away as Nevada, Arizona, and Tijuana, alternating between bouts of joyous giddiness and thunderous cursing. He had not understood all of the big words he had heard, but it was obvious to him that Dr. Rombach was unhappy with either her dry cleaner or her husband, because she kept using words like shrinkage and stretching. He planned to include these words in his script to give it—what was the word?—gravitas.

After concluding the call Archer Bobby quickly confirmed that Dr. Rombach was no longer married and Floxxy Williams went to Wikipedia to discover that Dr. Rombach did most of her own laundry—this was the full extent of their research. Nevertheless, it did not require much athletic skill to leap to the conclusion that Dr. Rombach had been talking about The Anomaly.

They finished their report only moments before the 2:45 deadline for the Three O'clock news. It being a very slow news day, they were given three minutes of broadcast time to report the facts, and an additional minute to make fun of them.

What they reported was that L.A. Weekly was reporting that Los Angeles was growing—bulging. Not just the city, but the county itself. They did not do any research of their own and they didn't even bother to mention M. Raptor Bluthorne as the source of the report, nor did they mention Dr. Rombach as well, as they had a professional obligation to protect the anonymity of their sources.

At this point in the narrative, the author (who is being paid by the word) would like to spend a few paragraphs on the nature of "the silly season." This is a newspaper term for the summer months, during which time newspapers and other media spend way too much time on frivolous events. The height of the silly season is August, during which time there are no holidays to report, congress is in recess so the government is effectively moribund, and most of the therapists in New York City are out of town as well, using the justification of "vacation" as an excuse to escape from their patients for at least one month out of the year.

This trifecta results in an abundance of nothing important happening—importance defined by whether or not it will pull a rating. So the news media fills its dead air and empty pages with stories that can be reported with a smirk of superiority.

For example, in July of 1955, newspapers in Los Angeles began reporting that the Earth was swallowing garden hoses--three of them were being sucked into the ground at a rate of two or three inches per hour. It was happening in Downey, a suburb halfway between City Hall and Disneyland. Because nothing else was happening (President Eisenhower was playing golf again) the event became a nationwide phenomenon.

To quote the Chicago Daily Tribune, "It all started when George Di Peso's daughter was watering the garden with a plastic hose. When she stuck it into the dirt, she was unable to pull it out. Worse, it started burrowing downward."

The story was good for more than a week, with crowds gathering daily to see the curious phenomenon of the burrowing hose.

Eventually, Mr. Di Peso got fed up with all the publicity and chopped off the hose. More than twenty feet had disappeared. Meanwhile, other nearby residents reported that their hoses were similarly disappearing. A few blocks away, one jokester put a hose sticking out of the ground, with a sign identifying it as "the other end."[8]

So, returning to the present, because the Archer Bobby's and Floxxy Williams' report on The Oxnard Avenue Anomaly And Parts Beyond occurred on a hot Tuesday afternoon in the first week of August in an odd-numbered year, it attracted far more attention than it would have gotten had it occurred the first Tuesday of November in an even-numbered year, which is to say some as opposed to none.

It wasn't much, but it was enough.

Desperate for news, the other stations in Los Angeles dispatched their own third-string investigators to discover if perhaps there was enough here to fill the looming void of dead air threatening the rest of the week.

In short order, Dr. Rombach's frantic investigations became a nationwide event. Los Angeles County had expanded by a mile and a half. Orange, Kern and San Bernardino Counties had shrunk proportionally.

At first, nobody took it seriously. The commentariat dismissed it as some kind of computer glitch or human error or failure of instrumentation. Even after NASA

---

8 Coincidentally, that was the same week that Dr. Rombach was born. Make of that what you will.

confirmed the growth with satellite measurements, the phenomenon remained firmly in the category of things not to worry about—like the dangerous levels of carbon dioxide in the atmosphere, the perilous levels of ocean acidification, the impending disappearance of the Gulf Stream, and the chances of the Anaheim Angels winning a pennant.[9]

It was just another silly season event. Nobody took it seriously until the first lawsuits were filed. The Orange County Supervisors filed the first one, but the other counties were quick to follow.

The plaintiffs charged that the Los Angeles County was occurring at the expense of the surrounding counties, stealing their land, as well as their tax base, and they were therefore entitled to appropriate recompense, determined by the differences in the value of the real estate gained against the value of the real estate lost. They demanded the state set up an independent commission to determine just how many millions Los Angeles County should pay them.

The Board of Supervisors of Los Angeles County immediately filed a counter-suit, charging that if Orange, Kern, and San Bernardino Counties couldn't manage the security of their own borders, they had no right to complain about any spillover. It being not an election year, the back-and-forth was politer than normal, but not without suggestions from the plaintiffs that they should build a wall around Los Angeles County to prevent any further infection. The denizens of Los Angeles County were just as quick to agree. "Feel free to lock yourselves out of the most prosperous economy in the state and possibly the nation, depending on which economist you believe." And: "You want a wall? You pay for it."

The Mayor of San Diego symbolically broke ground on the proposed wall, but that was only a publicity stunt. He had box seat tickets behind home plate for a Dodgers vs. Padres game the following night, scheduled for Dodger Stadium in Chavez Ravine, just a few miles north of Los Angeles City Hall.

That the late-night talk show hosts would have a field day with The Anomaly was never in question. The Anomaly was now bigger than Jay Leno's chin—it couldn't be ignored. But despite the potential for humor, the situation had to be taken seriously when one of the national evening newscasters began ending his broadcasts with, "This is the 221st day of the Los Angeles expansion. It has now eaten 24 square miles of California. Good night and get out of the way."

As The Anomaly expanded, so did its rate of growth. Soon, the following summer that same newscaster was saying, "this is the 512th day of the Los Angeles

---

9 The author takes no responsibility for any of these events actually occurring, especially the last one. I'm an agnostic.

expansion. It has eaten another 37 square miles today and is expected to reach the Arizona border before September. Good night and call your real estate agent."

The lawsuits had also expanded proportionally, most of them based on the idea that property values were being affected—but there were other complaints as well. Where once, you could get from Simi Valley to Hollywood in an hour, now it took two. Bus routes were affected. Travel times were doubled, tripled. Every business in the city reported increased costs for fuel and increased time spent on deliveries.

The Los Angeles Department of Water and Power was billing nearly twice as much for domestic water usage. California's chronic drought condition was further exacerbated by the increase in fire-vulnerable brush and the increased surface area sucking up ground water. Almost every lawn in the city had doubled in size, every swimming pool in Bel Air had expanded proportionally, and the golf course at Greater Wilshire Hancock Park had grown so large that several studio lawyers had passed out from exhaustion trying to reach the 7th hole, which was now south of where Wilshire Blvd. had previously been. Wilshire Blvd. was now in Culver City and Culver City was heading toward Long Beach. Much of Long Beach was under water, having been dislocated by Torrance and parts of Carson.

After Google Maps crashed, no one was quite sure where anything was anymore.

By the time Los Angeles County started pushing into Nevada and Arizona, both in the same month, the Federal Government finally mobilized itself. It was one thing when it was merely a state-level event, but now that California was expanding into other states, it threatened the possibility of a Constitutional crisis.

If Los Angeles County were to devour its surrounding states, the respective senators would no longer have constituencies. The senate would be reduced from 100 members to 96, and the Republican party would lose its ability to filibuster progressive legislation. The president might be able to get a judicial nominee confirmed. The country might actually be able to get some work done.

So of course, the Republican members of Congress opened an immediate investigation to determine if The California Expansion, as it was now known, was the result of a pernicious conspiracy. Extremist groups quickly branded The Expansion a threat to the American way of life, triggering protests in every city in Texas, except Austin, which was already seen as a lost cause. The state legislature passed an emergency bill banning spas, life-coaches, and sushi. Several Priuses were torched. But the California effect was pernicious—two of the protest signs were distinctly out-of-character. All of the words were spelled correctly.[10]

10 Okay, this part I'm making up.

Despite Republican action on the matter, several agencies of the United States Government were already hard at work. The president had authorized FEMA to provide relocation services for refugees terrified of flea markets, manskirts, merlot, and full moon diets.[11]

Meanwhile, Los Angeles kept growing, California kept expanding. A small tremor rocked Winslow, and the residents, instead of panicking, started betting on its magnitude. It was barely 3.2 on the Richter scale and Mrs. Gladys Popple won twelve dollars.

On the day that Flagstaff became a suburb of Los Angeles, six residents of that town sued for the right to buy Disneyland Discount passes for Southern California residents. This did not mitigate their annoyance with the sudden increase in freeway traffic, bringing the I-40 to a near standstill.

That was another side effect.

The traffic and weather staff of two radio stations were now reporting on conditions as far away as Las Vegas and Tucson. "We have an overturned truck on the I-10 eastbound out of Phoenix, there are no alternate routes. Traffic on the junction between the I-15 and the US 93 south in Las Vegas is congested due to heavier than usual police action." And: "Temperatures in Primm will be the same as yesterday, hot. Flagstaff will be even hotter."

Elsewhere, the EPA was hard at work taking soil samples throughout the nation and sending them by Fedex to various research agencies around the country. The World Health Organization also sent in teams of researchers, checking to see if Winter Vomiting Disease and Oscar fever were contagious.

But it was Devra Littlebig, a researcher at the CDC who discovered the true cause of The California Expansion. She had been studying the circumstances surrounding The Schwarzchild Radius[12] and had realized that the experiments in eleventh dimension bio-physics had created a localized space-time distortion. It had likely been caused by the self-mutating software in the fusion-collider.

Whatever.

Various geologists at CalTech had their grad students and teaching aides look into the possibility, and very shortly, after several days of algorithm-wrestling and software coding, confirmed that that the actual epicenter of the California Expansion Anomaly was not the intersection of Ethel Avenue and Oxnard Street, but was actually several miles to the southeast, directly below the

---

11 Look it up. This alone is a good reason for building a wall around Los Angeles.

12 That's another story, in another anthology.

Universal City subway station[13] where most of the Schwarzchild mass had oozed into the ground.

As detailed elsewhere, the Schwarzchild had grown until it reached critical mass—at which point, even a small earth-tremor would be catastrophic. In this case, the catastrophe was inevitable. The Schwarzchild's own weight was sufficient to trigger the tremor. It popped dramatically and flubbered across the local terrain.

After the cleanup, after the hazmat teams declared the neighborhood mostly safe again, the residents of area blithely assumed the whole affair was over.

Well, sort of. But not completely.

As various squishy pieces of the Schwarzchild had absorbed themselves into the soil of the San Fernando Valley, whatever condition had originally caused the Schwarzchild to grow, that same condition had now become part of the California substrate—it was inevitable that the student surveyors of Los Angeles Valley College would discover the anomaly first, they were the only ones surveying the region.

Essentially, the Schwarzchild had metastasized. Well—not the Schwarzchild, but its essence. Los Angeles had become a gigantic geological cancer.

The Three O'clock news team nearly wet their shorts. Archer Bobby and Floxxy Williams were tapped for a Special Report which pulled the highest ratings in that time slot for that demographic since the last time James Franco had hinted at a heterosexual lifestyle. (But there was still no attempt at a frenzied copulation afterward. Really.)

Congress erupted into a firestorm of unusual lethargy. The nation's Surgeon General, who had not been heard from since she refused to confirm that the House of Representatives was entitled to 300 sick days a year, was called in to testify about what was now called The California Cancer.

The Surgeon General drily reported that the most common treatments for cancer are drugs and radiation. Because a significant percentage of the citizenry of Los Angeles was already well-drugged, the alternative was radiation. She did not, however, recommend nuking Los Angeles. Signs of the cancer had already spread as far east as Des Moines, as far north as Saskatchewan[14], as far south as Mexico City, and far enough west to disrupt the annual migration of the gray whales.

---

13 Yes, Los Angeles has a subway system. Honest. I'm not making this part up.

14 The representative from Mississippi requested a map from the Sergeant-at-Arms, as he had never heard of anything farther north than Minnesota, and that only because he'd heard it mentioned in roll-call votes, just before his own state.

Despite muttered threats of war, over this geographical invasion, neither Canada nor Mexico followed suit. The Canadians were too polite to go to war and a great many poverty-stricken Mexicans were delighted that they could now find legal jobs in the United States without leaving home.

The Surgeon General also reported that because California had legalized medical marijuana with appreciable results, few of the residents of the affected areas were experiencing any serious discomfort. Fast food sales were up in the expanded California regions, as well as the consumption of various other stoner munchies. So, all in all, this particular growth had to be classed as mostly-harmless, albeit not quite benign.

When pressed for a cure, the Surgeon General sighed, took off her glasses, wiped them with her handkerchief, and with a somewhat exasperated expression, replied, "There is no cure. At the present rate of expansion, this continent will be The United States of California within seven months. In less than two years, the whole planet will be completely California-ized.

International repercussions were immediate. The governments of Panama, the Cayman Islands, and the Republic of Vanuatu panicked. Between them, they had three trillion dollars of offshore cash stored in secret accounts. The application of California's strict banking laws would impoverish their fragile economies. They would not be able to make up the difference with Indian casinos.

It is beyond the scope of this narrative to discuss the global effects of the California Expansion. They were severe—but by the time the governor of California moved into the White House the majority of the world's population had moved through the first few stages of grief—denial, anger, bargaining—all the way to depression. Fortunately, the legalization of medical marijuana and the universal availability of California's Medi-Cal program did much to create reluctant acceptance—everywhere but Quebec, of course. The Quebecois angrily held another futile referendum on separation.

But that's how enchiladas arrived in Eastern Europe and Budapest became the Taco capital of east Los Angeles and the world.

At least, until Moonbase Armstrong finishes analyzing its soil samples.

DEBRA DOYLE & JAMES D. MACDONALD

GERTRUDE OF WYOMING

The train from New-York slid into Bishop Brook International Station in northern New Hampshire at nine in the evening. Trudy gathered her carry-on luggage, then walked across the platform to the customs booth for her transfer onto the shuttle train to Pittsburg Village on the other side of the border. It had been a long time since she'd last gone home to the Republic of Indian Stream, and under other circumstances she might have been looking forward to a few days of nostalgic relaxation before the meetings that were the real reason for her visit.

The customs official's hat bore the crest of the Indian Stream Republic, and the name patch on his forest-green uniform tunic said VASHAW in red embroidery. She carried an Indian Stream passport. He looked it over, with its visas from Vermont, Massachusetts, and Connecticut, before stamping it with the date—June the 22nd, 1961—and the Indian Stream entry.

"Welcome home, Miss Baker," he said.

She pushed through the turnstile—her regular luggage would be inspected when she arrived at her final destination—and turned to her right, toward the Duty Free Shops and the dance hall.

By international convention, this piece of land, although it was physically located in the United States, was considered part of the independent republic to the north, nestled between the United States and Canada. The Pittsburg shuttle wouldn't leave for another two hours; she sought out a currency exchange so she would be able to pay the cab fare once she reached Pittsburg.

NEW HAMPSHIRE AT 90%, VERMONT AT PAR read the sign in the window as she entered.

She traded in her New-York and Vermont dollars; she'd need her New Hampshire bills on the return trip and didn't want to have to exchange them twice, losing value each time. Technically, all of the state dollars were set against the Continental, but no one carried those. The national currency just wasn't practical for day-to-day use.

After making the exchanges, Trudy asked, "How much for Wyomings?"

"Officially? 1.5% above par."

"Unofficially?"

"I'll give you two for one."

Trudy smiled and pulled out twenty. Nature had blessed the Wyoming Valley of the Susquehanna with coal and oil, and the enterprising spirit of its later inhabitants had made the State of Wyoming into the industrial and scientific powerhouse of the United States. Accordingly, Wyoming bills were one of the most respected of the state currencies—much to the chagrin of neighboring Pennsylvania, whose citizens still resented the fact that Congress had settled the long dispute between Pennsylvania and Connecticut over their boundaries by declaring the area between them to be a state in its own right. Trudy pushed the notes across the green felt table, and received back forty Indian Stream dollars.

Her business at the money changer concluded, she continued on. The duty-free shops didn't interest her; she already had as many souvenir mosquitoes fashioned from moose droppings as she needed. She walked instead to one of the restaurants that surrounded the dance hall (the marquee told her that the internationally famous New Jersey Crooner was headlining) and got a table for one. She ordered the steak and bacon pie, since the light snack that she'd had in the dining car crossing the Berkshires had left her feeling simultaneously peckish and bloated.

When the waiter removed her empty plate, she was unsurprised to find a visiting card face-down on the tablecloth where the crockery had rested. She dabbed at her lips with her napkin; when she lowered the cloth the card had vanished into her hand.

"Bingo," she said to herself. She looked at her watch. Still time to see the Crooner. She'd heard that he was quite good.

The station clock struck eleven as the electric motors that powered the Pittsburg Shuttle hummed to life. The cars jolted north. Trudy was sitting in a business-class cabin in the second car. Her hand luggage was in the overhead bin; her trunk had been checked through onto the baggage car at the rear of the train. She saw, up ahead, the row of lights that marked the border.

The train went through two switchbacks as it passed the lines of artificial berms, topped with steel beams and barbed wire under relentless electric arc lights. It passed by the guard towers, and the signs in English and French reading

"Danger: Mines." It paused, and the United States crew was replaced by an Indian Stream crew. A new conductor in a new uniform knocked on compartment doors to ask for tickets and for passports which he hardly glanced at. Then the shuttle resumed its progress, and proceeded smoothly up the remaining twelve miles along the small river that gave the country of Indian Stream its name.

The train slid into Pittsburg's Freedom Station, whose gothic arches of native granite spoke of its Victorian construction. Trudy exited with the last of the passengers and walked over to the customs tables, where she identified her trunk and stood by it until the inspector arrived. A bored "anythingtodeclare," a perfunctory opening and closing of the lid that was more symbolic than useful, and Trudy was on her way to the cab stand with a station idler pushing her trunk on a handcart behind her. She studiously ignored one fellow traveler, a young man with a neat mustache and a straw boater, who was standing braced with his hands against a pillar while two customs agents patted him down, two more were ripping the lining out of his suitcase and scattering his clothes over the inspection bench, and a fifth was talking in low tones into a telephone handset.

Outside the station she picked a cab from the waiting line to take her to the Glynn House hotel, where she had reservations. The cab took her through the deserted streets, where small restaurants and shops with apartments over them fronted the wide boulevards. At midnight all the good folks of Pittsburg were in bed.

"Is there anywhere a girl can get a drink at this hour?" Trudy asked the cabman.

"Hotel bar is the safest," he replied.

"If I'm more in the mood for fun?"

"Best music is at The Trading Post."

"When we get to the hotel, wait out front while I check in. I'll want to go to The Trading Post."

"Got it, lady."

She sent her bags up to her room with the bellboy, and surrendered her passport in exchange for a plastic square informing anyone who should ask for her identity papers that she was staying at the Glynn House, room 302. Then she returned to the street where the cabbie was waiting.

This ride was longer, traveling northward along streets that grew narrower as the buildings grew shabbier. After turning one last corner, the cab drew up outside a brick building with darkened windows and a neon sign proclaiming it to be The Trading Post club. Trudy paid the cabbie, making sure to include a generous tip.

He handed her a card in return. "When you're ready to go home, call me."

A bald-headed bearded man, in a black shirt that revealed the muscles in his arms, lounged beside the club door. He stood aside to let Trudy enter. She walked in, and was met by a wall of smoke and sound. Up a short passageway a young blonde sat behind a chest-high barrier, collecting cover charges. The sign behind her read, "Men $1.50, women free."

Trudy passed by, nodding, then entered the club proper. But rather than turning left toward the bar, or right toward the dance floor, she went straight through, past the toilets, to an emergency door. She pulled it open, then stepped out into the back alley and past the garbage cans to a corner where another line of taxis waited. She picked the first in line and slipped in.

"Happy Corner," she said, and leaned back into the seat.

The hotels of the Happy Corner district, near the south side of Lake Francis, were far fancier than those farther south in Pittsburg. When she arrived, Trudy went into the lobby of the Chatham Lodge and used the house phone to dial the number on the back of the visiting card she'd received earlier. She let the phone ring five times, then hung up.

Not long after, a gentleman appeared. She followed him to the elevator. He escorted her to a room and closed the door behind them, then remained at the door while she went farther into the suite, to where another man waited at a round table of polished wood.

"Good evening," said the man at the table. "I trust you were not followed?"

"I took precautions."

The television in the room had its volume turned up a bit too high. On the bedside table, a radio with news from Montreal in French was also playing slightly louder than normal. A listener in an adjacent room would have had a hard time overhearing Trudy's soft tones over the jumble of sounds.

Her interlocutor was an older man with white hair combed straight back. His accent was Canadian, but Trudy thought he had another language behind that, from farther away. She shook her head; no sense thinking about it. What she didn't know she couldn't reveal. Opening her purse, she pulled out a compact and examined her face in the small mirror inside the cover: an unexceptional brunette, pretty rather than glamorous; no surprises there. She picked up the powder puff and dabbed at her nose, then closed the compact and pushed it across the table to the white-haired gentleman. He passed his hand over the compact and scooped it toward himself. He pulled another, seemingly identical, compact from his pocket, and pushed it back across to her.

"The usual amount will be in your account," he said.

She tucked the replacement compact into her purse. "I'll need to have beer on my breath when I return to my hotel."

"Of course." The gentleman made a signal to the man at the door, then turned back to Trudy.

"We are particularly interested in information about the manufacturing methods of the transconductance-resistor," he said. "Details of how to grow crystals of sufficient purity would also be greatly appreciated."

The gentleman who had been standing by the door brought over a bottle of Long Trail beer and a glass. He removed the ceramic plug from the bottle's neck and poured the beer smoothly, with very little head.

Trudy said, "You understand that information about the transconductance-resistor will be a bit more difficult to obtain than your last commission."

"Your efforts will be rewarded," the older gentleman said.

"Just so." Trudy drained her beer. "Anything else?"

The gentleman shook his head.

"Then I must get back to The Trading Post in Pittsburg."

"I'll give you a lift," said the man at the door.

"Fine. Stop about a block away; I'll make my way from there."

Back in the city of Pittsburg, under the electric streetlights, Trudy walked to a phone booth across the street from The Trading Post. She tugged at her skirt as if adjusting it, to give the bouncer at the door a plausible reason for why she might have slipped out to the back alley rather than leaving past him, and dialed the number on the cabbie's card.

When the cab arrived, she called out gaily, "Home!" then crumpled into the back seat as if she had indeed been overcome by alcohol. Once at the Glynn House, Trudy traded the plastic hotel chit for a room key and went upstairs.

As she closed the door behind her, she flicked on the lights—and saw that she was not alone. A woman stood beside and slightly behind her, where the opening door would have concealed her from a person arriving. The woman wore leather gloves and carried a black automatic pistol of Connecticut manufacture.

"Today is your day for finding folks in hotel rooms," the woman said. She had light brown hair and a Wyoming accent not unlike Trudy's own. "You can call me Louise. Take a seat and let's have a little chat."

Trudy sat on the couch in front of the television. "I'm sure there's been a mistake."

"You're right," Louise said. "And you're the one who made it. But," she added brightly, "you can fix it, too!"

"I don't understand."

"No need to play the fool." Louise walked over to the room's mini-bar and—without taking either her eyes or her gun off of Trudy—poured herself a gin-on-the-rocks. "You have a choice right now," the woman said. "You can work for me, or you can spend the rest of your life in an eight-by-twelve-foot cell in Fort St. Clair."

"You have the wrong person. I'll scream."

"Wrong person? We'll see. Gertrude Young, born in the town of Magalloway, Republic of Indian Stream, to Clarice Stanton, a citizen of Wyoming, and Maurice Young, a citizen of Indian Stream. Later, Miss Young moved to Wyoming, where she married a certain Joseph Baker. As soon as her Wyoming citizenship was finalized by virtue of her marriage, Gertrude—her friends call her Trudy—divorced Mr. Baker but kept her husband's name. Using her new-minted Wyoming citizenship, Miss Baker applied for and received a United States passport, which Congress speedily granted, with which she travels back to Indian Stream on a fairly regular basis. She never revoked her Indian Stream citizenship, and uses that entirely-legitimate passport on the Indian Stream side of the border. Any of this sound familiar?"

"Should it?"

"I can hear the prison doors closing. They make a loud clang. Fort St. Clair is a cold and cheerless place. Given reasonable medical care you should last sixty years, though prison suicides are, sadly, all too common. Did you know that people who are placed there for espionage are never allowed to speak to another person, ever, in case they might reveal the secrets they carry?"

"You said something about working for you?"

"Yes. It's fun and easy. You hand me that little compact in your pocketbook. You see, I know about it. I know about a lot of things. Then you walk downstairs with me, you get into my car, and we go for a little drive. After that . . . I'll give you your instructions."

"Is what you're asking me to do safe?"

"Oh, my dear Trudy," Louise said. "'Safe' is a ship that sailed a long, long time ago."

"So what do you want me to do?"

"Right now, step away from your purse."

Trudy did so. Louise came forward, keeping herself between Trudy and the door and keeping the hand with the pistol well back. She went through Trudy's pocketbook by feel, taking the compact out last.

"Don't you want me to open it?" Trudy asked.

"I've already told you what I want." Louise put the compact into her pocket. "Now—I already know that you don't have a gun, so take your purse and let's go. You first."

Trudy picked up her handbag and moved slowly toward the door.

"Before you try anything," Louise said, "you should probably know that recruiting you like this wasn't my idea, and I'm perfectly happy to leave your dead body in the stairway. Are we clear?"

"Clear." Trudy opened the door and stepped through it into the hall. "But turning in my key for my passport is going to be tricky."

"I've already taken care of that," the woman said. "Go down the back stairs to the alley."

The car waiting behind the hotel was a Canadian model with Vermont letter plates. "Get in," Louise said.

Before Trudy could comply, a dark figure stepped out of the shadows and hit Louise smartly over the head, knocking her to the ground.

The cab driver who had met Trudy at Freedom Station and taken her to the Glynn House and The Trading Post came forward into the light.

"I was wondering when you'd show up," Trudy said.

"Sorry, had to be sure," the cabbie replied.

He put a black bag over Louise's head and expertly tied her wrists behind her, then went through her pockets and found a couple of passports, one of them Trudy's, and a set of car keys. He replaced everything but Trudy's passport, which he handed over to Trudy along with a second compact, identical to the first, which he pulled from his own pocket. Finally, he popped open the car's trunk and, with Trudy's help, pulled and pushed Louise's limp form into the back of the vehicle.

"Up and in," he grunted, slamming the trunk. Then, to Trudy, "You've been made."

"No kidding."

"Well, let's get you out of town. You're a bit too hot for Pittsburg."

Together they drove south toward the checkpoint on Old Canaan Road, on the west bank of the river that gave Indian Stream its name.

"Sooner or later someone is going to look in the trunk," Trudy said, "and they're going to find an unconscious Continental operative back there."

"Don't worry about that."

They pulled into a car wash just as the sky was getting light.

"What's today's special?" the cab driver asked the attendant.

"Full wax and lift," the attendant replied.

"Do you do rims?"

"Only on Wednesdays."

"I'll take the usual."

"Okay, drive through."

As soon as the doors of the car wash closed, the driver got out and motioned for Trudy to do the same. They walked forward along the catwalks on either side of the wash bay to a second bay, where another car waited. The driver opened that car's door. In minutes they were once again motoring southward to the checkpoint on the Indian Stream side of the line. On the other side of the steel barrier, Trudy could see the gun emplacements, berms, and ditches that kept Vermont on its own side of the border.

"Anything to declare?" the border guard asked.

"No."

The guard made only a cursory inspection of the car before stamping their passports and waving them through. On the Vermont side things were a little bit tougher. There the guard looked at Trudy's passport, said, "Entered the Stream just before midnight, leaving just six hours later? Please come with me." He led the way into a bare room with a table, two chairs, and a window overlooking a chainlink fence topped by barbed wire.

Two hours later, another man in civilian clothes entered. "You have totally cocked this one up," he said.

"Sorry about that," Trudy replied. She recognized the Wyoming station chief for Northern Vermont. Normally he would be at the Wyoming interests desk in Burlington, being officially a trade undersecretary. He looked like a man who had been gotten out of bed entirely too early, had needed to drive too far and too fast, and now had to do something unpleasant without having had coffee first.

"We're going to have to bury you for a while, then see if you have any use at all. Or I could just let Indian Stream, Vermont, or New Hampshire have you. You've committed at least one crime in each of their jurisdictions in ..." he glanced at his watch "... the last twelve hours?"

He leaned closer and wrote something on his notepad, then pushed it across the desk toward Trudy. She glanced down and read, *Did you make contact with the Continentals?*

She nodded her head *yes* while at the same time saying, "No, I didn't."

He wrote *Good work* on the pad, showed it to her, and said, "I can fix it this time, but don't ever let me see you around here again," before standing and leaving the room.

Half an hour later Trudy was led back out of the room. Her entry visa was stamped, and she was taken back to the parking area where the cab driver was standing, looking like a man who had been strip-searched and hadn't enjoyed it.

"Let's go," was all he said.

He held her door for her, and they drove down over the hills and through Dixville Notch toward Errol International Airport. They talked of the weather, which was fair, and the red mica cliffs of Sanguinary Ridge, which were rugged and awe-inspiring. Trudy expected that the Vermonters, if not the Continental Bureau of Investigation, had installed a listening device in the car—she would have, in their position—and spoke accordingly; the driver appeared to have similar expectations, and did the same.

The concourse at Errol International Airport was full of passengers heading to all parts of the Continental States, to the independent western nations, to Europe, and to Asia. Trudy made her way to the Wyoming Atlantic desk and found a ticket waiting for her.

One good thing about being essentially abducted out of town was that she was now traveling very light. Passport control was a formality; Trudy bypassed the duty-free shops again, and waited in the transit lounge until her flight was called. The flight was a local to Wilkes-Barre, with a layover in New-York. At New-York the passengers who were traveling to the national capital for government business got off, and a new group going on to Wyoming embarked.

Wilkes-Barre, when Trudy got there, had all the bustle befitting the capital of the richest of the United States. Trudy got on an electric streetcar at the airport, made her way to a safe house, and awaited developments. The mini-bar was inviting, as was the bed. Trudy used both. Even with the gin she was too tense to sleep.

Just before five in the evening, Selena Mitten, Trudy's immediate superior, arrived at the safe house. Trudy's first words to her were, "You're aware that your plan sucks, right?"

"Thought you'd notice that sooner. They made you?"

"I practically had to send up skyrockets—but yes, they made me."

"What do you know?" Mitten asked.

"That the Germans are still trying to steal our technology, which isn't a surprise. That the CBI has somehow tumbled to the fact, which shouldn't be much of a surprise, and they think I'm a traitor. And that my cover is so blown in Indian Stream that I don't think I can ever work there again."

"The Continental guy got the compact?"

"The Continental guy is a gal—but other than that, yes."

"Even better," Mitten said; then, without noticeable regret, "This is the part where I have to fire you, you know."

Trudy shrugged. "As long as you don't threaten to jail me, murder me, or both. You'd be the first person I've met in the last day and a half who hasn't."

"Even in this business, sometimes it's good to stand out from the crowd," Mitten said. "I'll see you when this is over. Stay away from the office for a while."

After Mitten had left, Trudy poured herself more gin, added enough tonic so that the words "and tonic" weren't an entire lie, and waited for the sun to set. Once the streets were dark beyond the glow of the sodium vapor lamps, she went out, took an underground streetcar to the Elm Court stop, and walked the last few blocks to her own apartment. When she opened the door, she found that the place had been burgled in her absence. She was surprised by how unsurprised she felt.

Whoever had done the job—the CBI, possibly; Selina Mitten, quite probably, to add verisimilitude to Trudy's current legend; any one of the other state or national agencies, for reasons of their own that she could only guess at; or possibly just a random freelancer—had taken pains to let Trudy know that the modest three-room flat had been tossed. The stash of emergency money she'd hidden inside the bedroom door was gone, so it looked like the actual thief was a pro. Her underwear was gone too, however, so maybe not.

Trudy closed the apartment's outer door carefully, propped a chair under the knob, and went back to her bedroom. One of the bedside lamps had a red bulb in its socket—a hint for the discerning that maybe she was the kind of girl who liked a bit of fun. She unscrewed the bulb, took it into the bathroom, and replaced the plain bulb in the light fixture above the sink with the red one.

From underneath the kitchen cabinet she took out jugs of cleaning supplies. A competent housekeeper would realize they were mislabeled at the first whiff after opening, but Trudy's budget—as she was at pains to make clear to friends and acquaintances alike—didn't extend to hired help. She took pans from the kitchen, too, into the bathroom with the jugs of chemicals. Lastly, she turned off all the lights in the outer apartment, re-entered the bathroom, closed the door, put a rolled-up towel against the crack at the bottom, and switched off the red light just to make sure.

The room was black, even after her eyes adjusted.

She switched the red light back on and poured the various mislabeled chemicals into their waiting pans. Then she took the compact the cab driver had given her and unscrewed its bottom half. Inside was a circle of photographic film. Trudy used the chemical baths to develop it. Writing appeared. She hung the film up to dry, then poured the chemicals down the toilet and flushed repeatedly before going back to the film.

The information and instructions she'd been given were written in very small print. Trudy needed a magnifier in order to read them.

When she'd done so, she opened the door and carried the film circle to the dining room. She lit a candle that she kept there for those intimate dinners she never had but wanted people to think were a possibility, and burned the film. The red light went back into the bedroom lamp.

After that, Trudy dressed from the pile of garments thrown onto the floor of her closet, where the unknown visitor had left them after pulling them off their hangers, and packed a small bag with a couple of changes of clothing. Tomorrow she'd buy whatever else she needed.

Only then did she call the police. An honest citizen would do that, she reasoned, and she was still an honest citizen, more or less. A young policewoman arrived eventually, took her statement, took photos, learned that Trudy had been "out of town for a few days" so didn't know when the burglary had happened, and promised that someone would follow up. Trudy herself didn't have a lot of faith in that—a small time burglary with no injuries or major loss of property wasn't going to be at the top of anybody's to-do list—but it didn't matter. Instead, she called her friend Freddy—about the only person she knew who wasn't part of the Wyoming intelligence community—and said, "I've been burgled. I don't feel safe at home. Can I come stay with you?"

"Sure," he replied.

The electric streetcar took her to Freddy's place out on Lackawana Avenue, where she rang his bell and was buzzed in.

"I didn't know whether to buy wine or condoms," he said, when she knocked on the apartment door and he opened it. "So I got both."

"You won't need either one, unless you're planning to drink alone. I'll take the couch."

"No," Freddy said, "I will. If I can't be gallant to a damsel in distress, when can I be?"

"Listen, I've had a rough day," Trudy said. "I'm tired."

"You said you'd been broken into?"

"Yeah, but I don't want to talk about it. I've also been fired from my job, and I don't want to talk about that, either."

The dark circles under Trudy's eyes spoke to the truth of what she was saying. Aside from her attempted nap in the safe house, she'd been awake for well over twenty four hours, coming up on thirty six.

To answer Freddy's unasked question, she said, "No, I don't need to be tucked in. Bedroom's there?"

"Yeah."

"See you in the morning."

She woke when the sun through the window hit her face. Her watch told her it was close to ten AM.

The apartment had an empty feeling; Freddy had gone to work. He'd left a note on the kitchen counter: "Help yourself to anything here. Back around six."

Anything, Trudy decided, included the telephone. She dialed an out-of-state number, asked for a name, waited long enough for a tap-and-trace, and said, "I've reconsidered your offer."

"You're damaged goods," a woman on the other end said. "Can't fetch as high a price at auction."

"I'll risk it."

Then she made sandwiches with the bread and cheese Freddy had in the pantry, and decided the wine wouldn't be such a bad idea after all. She settled down on the couch with a glass and a paperback novel. After a bit she turned on the radio just to have another human voice in the room. Waiting was what she did worst.

Six PM came. Trudy heard a key grate in the lock and Freddy's voice: "Are you decent?"

"So I'm told."

Freddy entered, accompanied by another man Trudy didn't recognize.

"This is Arthur," Freddy said. "He's a friend, and I thought you two might hit it off. Now, if you'll excuse me, I'm going to go get some take out."

When the door had closed, and Freddy's footsteps had gone down the hall, Arthur spoke.

"We don't have much time," he said. "I know quite a bit about you, but Freddy is in the dark about all that. He said you needed a job?"

"Could be."

"I won't play games, Miss Baker. I represent the nation of Cheyenne."

"Looking at you, I'd have thought you were from Swanee."

"Not everyone flies a flag; my appearance is an asset."

"And if I say no?"

"Then you have an unfortunate accident before Freddy gets back with his pierogies."

"You have my full attention," Trudy said.

"Very good. You don't have many choices, but I can offer you one. You provide a set of genuine Wyoming identity documents, under a name which I will specify, and you will receive in return a new name for yourself, a new location, and quite a good number of Continentals in a numbered account in Indian Stream."

"What makes you think I can supply the documents?"

"We know where you work."

"Didn't Freddy tell you I'd been fired?"

"If I believed that, I wouldn't be here. One name, one full set of documents, and the world becomes much better for Miss Trudy Baker." He paused. "Or, since Freddy knows me and knows that I was here, he can meet with an accident, too."

"When do you need the documents?" she asked.

"Day after tomorrow."

"Do you have the particulars with you?"

"I do."

"Then you have a deal."

By the time Freddy got back with an armload of boxed dinners, Trudy had placed Arthur's file folder in the bedroom under the pillow, and was back in the living room playing a game of checkers with Freddy's friend.

Before she turned out the light that night, Trudy opened the folder and skimmed its contents. The front-and-side passport and license photos were of the woman who had introduced herself as "Louise" two nights before, and whom Trudy had last seen being stuffed into a trunk in Indian Stream.

"Interesting," Trudy said, before making sure the bedroom door was locked and switching off the bedside lamp.

In the morning, Trudy went out; Freddy had given her his spare key. The next phone call she made was from a booth, and not the closest one, either.

"Summertime," she said.

"Easy," was the reply.

She walked then to a movie theater with continuous showings, went in the front, and, just as in Indian Stream, made her way directly to one of the rear exit doors and out into an alley, from which she emerged one block away from the theater marquee. She walked up several blocks to an upscale a department store.

No one seemed to be tailing her as she shopped; she took the bag with her purchases and went around the corner to yet another phone booth, where she called a new number. She proceeded from there to Thomas Campbell Park, where she slid Arthur's file folder into a public waste container, drew a chalk line on a bench twenty feet farther along, and continued on without looking back. The path she took back to Freddy's was less circuitous, and the shopping bag emblazoned with the store's logo would provide any watchers—she was certain that at least one would be in place—with a plausible reason for why she had gone out and where she'd been.

A shower and a nap later, Trudy called Freddy at work and asked him to bring home another bottle of wine.

He didn't sleep on the couch that night.

On the second of the two days Arthur had given her, Trudy went out again, and from yet another phone booth dialed another number, heard a mechanical voice say "The time at the tone will be eight fifty-seven" followed by a three-note lifting chime. She ostentatiously set her watch, and walked on.

At the corner of Center and Washington she boarded a streetcar heading toward the Wyoming Mining Museum. At this hour the streetcar was standing room only. A man got on the streetcar two blocks later and stood beside her. He pressed a leather wallet into her hand; she made it vanish into her bag. Neither looked at the other.

She got out at the museum and wandered idly through the exhibits for an hour. By the time she was done, if she was being followed, then whoever was on that detail would have gained some detailed knowledge of auger mining. Then she made her way back to Freddy's apartment.

Freddy himself opened the door before her key had quite turned in the lock. He had a pistol in his hand, pointed at her head, holding it out as if to distance himself from it.

"I'm sorry, Tru—" he said, before she broke his arm. She shot him twice with his own weapon before kicking the door closed behind her.

"And that," she said aloud, "was why I banged you last night. To buy myself those two seconds today."

She walked to the phone, dialed Arthur's contact number, and said, "I have what you asked for."

"Where are you?"

"Where I saw you last."

"Give me twenty minutes."

Freddy was where she had left him. Trudy removed all but one round from his pistol and wiped it down. Keeping it, still wrapped in her handkerchief, in her right hand, she made sure that the apartment door was unlocked. Twenty minutes later, the downstairs doorbell sounded. Trudy pressed the buzzer to admit the caller.

A knock at the door, and the knob turned. Arthur came in; before he could react to the mess on the carpet Trudy stepped up behind him and shut the door.

"Why'd you do it, Arthur?" Trudy asked. "I thought Freddy was your friend."

She stepped away from him.

"The police will be here in a couple of minutes," Trudy said. The pistol was out and unwavering. "You can make things easy on yourself by telling me who the brunette in the picture really is."

"Freddy was meant to shoot you in the face so no one would recognize you," Arthur said. "She was going to be you."

"Try again. Who is she?"

"A Pennsylvanian operative. One of their internal security people. I never knew her real name. She was in deep inside the CBI and wanted to come out. She needed a corpse so she could vanish. You matched her close enough."

"And Freddy?"

"Local talent with family in Cheyenne. He was supposed to work his way into the Wyoming security apparatus, but you were as close as he got."

"That's the whole truth?"

"Yeah. If you're interested, the offer to come work with us is still good."

She shot him, once, at close range in the side of the head.

Trudy locked the apartment door behind her after wiping down the scene thoroughly for fingerprints and slipping Freddy's room key into Arthur's pocket, Freddy's pistol into Arthur's hand. She took away her overnight bag, and with it all the traces that she'd been there. Neighbors would be alerted by the smell in a few days. The police would find the pistol, the extra key, and a nasty murder/suicide, and draw their own conclusions. No one would be looking for any more answers after that.

She went downstairs to the sidewalk and took a cab directly to the Wyoming government complex. Once inside the office building she went to Selena Mitten's office.

Mitten was sitting at her desk, drinking a mug of tea.

"It's over?" she asked.

"Yes." Trudy collapsed into the other office chair. "I hate this job."

"So do we all. What do you have for me?"

"Broke up a Cheyenne espionage ring—they'll be scrambling and you can watch which way they run. Got a line on a Philadelphia mole in the CBI. You can turn her, maybe, and start feeding disinformation to Pennsylvania." Trudy pushed across the false documents she'd been given on the streetcar. "She's looking for these, thinks they're coming from Cheyenne. Making the touch is your problem."

"Only one more thing to do, then."

Trudy nodded. "Wouldn't want to disappoint our German contact."

"Hand over the bogus documentation, and then you can take a get-well tour. Have a nice vacation somewhere—you've earned it."

Two nights later, back in Happy Corner, Trudy pushed a compact across a table to a man who spoke excellent Canadian English with a hint of a foreign accent.

"It's all here," she said. "The transconductance-resistor information. As much as I could get for you."

"Was it difficult?"

"Not particularly."

PETER DAVID

MOOSE AND SQUIRREL

In the year 1958, when Alaska was being considered for statehood, Texas governor Price Daniel strenuously objected. His reasoning was quite simple: He did not want there to be a state larger than Texas. President Dwight D. Eisenhower became so tired of Daniel's protests that he threatened him. He told Daniel that if he did not shut up, he would divide Alaska in half, and there would be two states larger than Texas.

Daniel refused to stop complaining, not taking Eisenhower seriously.

He should have done so.

Eisenhower did exactly that and on January 3, 1959, North Alaska and South Alaska were officially declared states of the Union.

They did not get on well. There was peace between them, but an uneasy peace, and it was certainly not helped by the fact that the majority of the populace wielded guns. A frontier mentality gripped the separated regions and it slowly devolved over time. Since the two states were so far removed from the continental United States, no one really cared.

And then a new governor made it a lot worse, and it descended into war.

"Are you sure he's dead?" Sarah Palin could scarcely believe it. She could hardly form the words. For so long, the fate of the crazy-haired bastard had hung over her, formed such a huge aspect of her life. Now that she was finally receiving the words that she had been looking forward to, anticipating, for so long, now that the long-waited-for news was being uttered over her cell phone... she was having true difficulty accepting its veracity. "I mean, are you really sure? That he's really not breathing dead? That's very important, the not-breathing part. And the heart. The heart has to have stopped beating too, because he could always fool somebody by holding his breath because, y'know, I read about this man who held his breath for something like ten minutes and everybody was just amazed. But you can't hold your heartbeat. Except someone like James Bond, I heard about that, and Nick Fury, their hearts were so slowed down that nobody could be sure they were, you know, dead, which they weren't, but since they were never real in the first place you can't say whether they were ever alive in the first place..."

"Yes, Governor," came the patient voice of her aide over the phone. *"We didn't see the body, but it did not matter. We had positive intel that he was in the bunker when our planes hit it. There was nothing left. There won't be enough left of him to identify him from DNA testing. He is most definitely dead. Shall we come retrieve you?"*

Palin felt all the energy seeping out of her body. To some degree, it was amazing that she was still upright. She sagged against the wall, letting months' worth of tension drain from her. Her security guards, Carter and Vandenberg, were nearby, seated in the same semi-comfortable chairs they typically sat in. They were like twin brothers, both broad-shouldered with buzz-cut red hair and freckles on their tanned faces. Their guns were tucked in their shoulder holsters but were visible as lumps against their jackets. When they breathed, their breath misted in front of them, as did Palin's, because the damned cabin was so freaking cold.

Carter and Vandenberg had been with her for a number of years and she trusted them implicitly. They had helped her get through several close shaves, particularly in the past year when the battle between North and South Alaska had reached a fever pitch. It had been Carter who had suggested that Palin take refuge in the relative outland area of the Alaskan Peninsula, at a hunting cabin he maintained in the Kodiak Island Borough. Since it was his personal cabin, it was quite well furnished, including such personal perks as bullet proof windows and heavy duty walls and ceilings that could resist most assault weapons. Palin had embraced the idea, feeling that the capital city of Fairbanks was no longer safe for her.

Not after what that bastard did to my family...

She pushed the tremulous thought out of her head and had to remind herself what her aide had just asked her. "Tomorrow," she said after a moment of thought. "Come get me tomorrow. Let the South have some time to mourn his loss before they have to look at my face. Not that there's anything wrong with my face. It's a good face, don't'cha know."

"It is indeed, Governor."

"Darn right it is. You see this face looking out and smiling at you, and it just warms the heart of your cockles or whatever that thing is in your heart that gets warmed."

"As you say, Governor. We'll be in to extract you tomorrow at 9 AM."

"We'll be waiting for you."

She handed the phone over to Vandenberg, no longer wanting to hold it for some reason. She felt the energy leaving her legs and sank into a chair. "You okay, Governor?" asked Vandenberg.

"Hmm? Oh. Fine. Yes, I'm fine."

"May I ask why we're not going back today?" said Carter. "I have no trouble staying, obviously, but. . ."

"I have one more shot at tracking him down," Palin told him. She glanced out the window and saw the dark clouds hovering above. "I think the weather should hold up for a little while longer."

"I very much doubt that, Governor." Carter cast a worried look outside. "There's already snow on the ground. . ."

"Which should make it easier to track him! Because he'd leave tracks! Wouldn't he?"

Carter and Vandenberg exchanged looks and then shrugged together. That struck Palin as typical. They had worked together for so long that they frequently mirrored each other's gestures. But then Carter said in a low voice, "Governor, I feel the need to point out. . ."

"Yes, yes, I know," she said impatiently. "He's a legend. He's a myth. He's this thing that people have just made up to lure gullible hunters out into the middle of nowhere bringing their oh-so-wonderful tourists big bucks. That's the story, that's the 9-1-1, that's what they say."

"Four—" Carter started to correct her.

But she wasn't listening. "But I believe. You bet'cha I believe. And I'm gonna take him down. The great white moose is going down today, Carter. I can feel it. Right here. It's totally felt." She thumped her chest and, to her surprise, moisture began to form in her eyes. "It's what Todd would have wanted. And the kids, and. . ." Her voice trailed off and she reached under her glasses and wiped the tears away before they trickled too far down her cheek.

Vandenberg instinctively reached out and put a hand on her shoulder. She patted it a moment, reaffirming the gesture of concern, and then drew in her breath and let it out slowly. "Let's armor up, boys. Let's get out there and celebrate the end of this idiotic north and south war by taking down Big White. If I can't have the late governor of South Alaska's head on a wall," and she grinned mirthlessly, "then I'll settle for Big White."

Big White was indeed a legendary animal. There was some Inuit who believed that Big White was more than just a huge Alaskan moose with silky white fur. Some opined that he was a god, or the incarnation of a god on Earth. Reports of his existence dated back a hundred years, which was absurd since the average moose lifespan was barely two decades. The notion of a moose existing for a century was preposterous. Indeed, Palin was anticipating perhaps having the creature autopsied when she slew it. The body, that was; the head was going to be all hers.

Minutes later the three of them emerged from the cabin. There were two heavy duty black Jeeps waiting outside for them. Normally Palin rode with either Carter or Vandenberg in one while the remaining agent drove the other, but this time Palin strode for the lead car while waving the men off. "I wanna do this alone," she said. She had a Browning BAR Mark II hunting rifle slung over her shoulder, and she felt comforted by the weight of it. She remembered when Todd had given it to her on her thirtieth birthday...

Todd...oh Jesus...

She forced her mind away from him and clambered into the vehicle, once more gesturing that Vandenburg and Carter should follow in the second jeep. The agents looked nervously at each other for a moment but then shrugged and obeyed instructions. There were about two inches of snow on the ground, and more was drifting down from overhead in a leisurely fashion. It was so light that Palin's vision was completely unobscured as the wipers batted away the few flakes that stuck to the windshield.

As she carefully studied the barren ground in front of her, her thoughts wandered back—despite her best efforts—to her life with Todd and her family. How wonderful their hunting trips had been. How splendid had been their lives together. And now it was all gone, all left far behind.

She should have gone with them. It was all her fault.

To this day, she berated herself over her last moments with Todd. What had they been fighting about, anyway? She couldn't even remember. Political? Personal? In the end, what difference had it made? She had yelled something insulting at him, which she mentally cursed herself over because the kids were all there, and they had heard her. That had never been something she wanted her children to witness, her and their father battling over some stupid, trivial concern. She had stormed out of her house because she hadn't been able to keep looking at Todd, but soon something like thirty seconds had passed and she had managed to calm herself down and even begin to feel mortification over her attitude toward him. She had taken several long, slow breaths to calm her pounding heart and then turned back to the house and prepared to reenter and somehow work things out.

That was all she remembered. She had no recollection of the bomb that had dropped from on high. She did not remember the house exploding in a ball of flame. She was thrown off her feet, propelled about ten feet in the opposite direction, had struck her head on a tree trunk and had been found unconscious and badly injured by her personnel an hour later. For days afterward she refused to accept the reality of what had happened. She kept trying to convince herself that her family had fled destruction, that they were hiding secreted in underground tunnels. The fact that there were no underground tunnels near her house did not deter her for some time from fabricating their non-existent reality.

She did not have to ask who was responsible for the assault, who it was that had destroyed her family, her life. He had announced it on national television. Palin had lain there in her hospital bed, watching the screen with frozen eyes as her rival governor boasted of the latest assault upon her. She hated to admit it, but she had never suspected he would stoop to this level; never believed that he would take the states-wide civil war to such a direct attack. Yes, there had been skirmishes, and terrorist assaults in cities, but the government of South Alaska launching a full-blown attack on the leader of North Alaska? It seemed to defy imagining. Who could possibly have expected that he would descend to such depths?

You should have known, should have suspected. You should have realized what he would do. How could you have let your family down by not preparing?

She still had no clue how she could have prepared, but then realized that she should have done what *he* had done. He had vacated the governor's mansion at the very beginning of hostilities, kept himself mobile, always one step ahead. She had disdained to follow suit. She had wanted stability for her family.

And they had paid for it. God help them, they had paid for it.

She did all that she could to dismiss those thoughts from her mind. Instead she tried to focus her concerns on the hunt. She had studied the area in which they were residing and had managed to track down all the most popular areas that Big White had been rumored to frequent. She was closing in on one of them now and she shifted her attentions once more to the ground in front of her. She wasn't seeing anything. There were rumors that Big White was not of this mortal world; that he could walk across snow without leaving any tracks. She knew that was ridiculous, but part of her started to wonder.

That was when she heard the whirring of chopper blades in the sky above her.

She angled her rear view mirror and tried to see from where the sound was originating. Overhead, obviously, but its presence in this vast, snow-covered wasteland was surprising nonetheless. Briefly she wondered if it was her own people, having ignored her instruction and come to pick her up anyway.

And that was when the clatter of machine gun fire ripped through the air.

Palin let out a shriek as she reflexively hit the brake of her jeep. She unbuckled her belt even as she opened the overhead hatch in the roof. She clambered upward, thrusting her head out of it so she could see what the hell was happening, giving no thought to the fact that she was making herself an easier target in doing so.

She recognized the helicopter instantly. It wasn't exactly a brand new brand; a Sikorsky as near as she could determine, possibly a Comanche model. It was painted, of all things, gold.

And she saw who was seated in the passenger seat, operating the controls of the machine guns that were mounted on either side of the chopper.

"Drumph," she snarled.

She was absolutely correct. It was Governor Donald Drumph, not remotely as dead as he was supposed to be. For a heartbeat she thought that maybe it was some sort of trick. That this was a duplicate, showing up to avenge the death of the real Governor. Even as the thought crossed her mind, she tossed it away. That confident smirk, that hideous hair: it had to be him.

The twin machine guns spattered death from their muzzles, but they were not aimed at her. Instead they were tearing into the jeep that was being driven by her agents. The jeep twisted helplessly beneath the barrage. It was a heavy-duty vehicle, but it did not remotely have the resistance required to stand up to such a horrific pounding. She saw Carter and Vandenberg through the shattered windshield, twisting and writhing as the bullets ripped them apart, blood everywhere, and then seconds later her vision of them was erased as the jeep blew sky high. Flames erupted, licking the air hungrily.

Drumph turned his attention to Palin.

She still remembered vividly the first time that they had met, when Drumph had first moved to South Alaska. What a huge deal that had been. Drumph had been so friendly, even charming. *This guy has something going,* thought Palin. *If he ever puts his mind to it, he could completely moved beyond the whole multi-billionaire thing and become someone who could really make a difference in this country.* Her advisors had been concerned about him and had questioned why he had decided to move so far away from the continental United States that had been his home, but she had not listened to them. She was always someone who followed her instincts, and her instincts had told her that she could trust this man.

What a fool she had been. What a goddamned fool.

He had resided in South Alaska for only a year, just long enough to establish residency, and then had declared himself a candidate for governor.

Palin had laughed. Everyone had laughed. Drumph had no political experience at all. The notion that he would be able to persuade voters to support him seemed utterly preposterous.

Yet he managed to accomplish it.

By turning the Alaskans against the Inuit.

Palin would never have thought it possible. Relationships between Alaskans and Inuit had always been cordial enough, although naturally there were occasional, incredibly stupid dust-ups that would occur from time to time. But Drumph managed to tap into a vein of racism that no one could have suspected existed. He relentlessly painted the Inuit as being responsible for every problem that South Alaska had, from crime to joblessness and everything in between. He cited ancient stories about the Inuit condemning their oldest members to an icy death on floes and turned that into blatant distortions that wound up creating a literal race war. He tapped into prejudices that Palin could never have guessed he would be able to exploit, and he rode that hostility straight into the governorship.

And then he got to work.

He introduced legislation that banned Inuit from entering South Alaska. It wasn't as if there were a ton of them entering even under the best of circumstances, but naturally once you tell someone that they cannot go anywhere, they get offended and want to go there even if they had not initially been planning to.

As for the Inuit who were already living there, their lives became a living hell. They were constantly the targets of hate crimes: threats, physical assaults, and cyber harassment. And on the rare occasions when the Inuit fought back against their assailants and triumphed, the news coverage spun it to make it seem as if they were the aggressors rather than the victims. Many wound up fleeing to North Alaska and they were welcomed with open arms, because the residents of South Alaska were appalled by the actions of their brethren.

Finally Palin had had enough. She demanded a face to face with Drumph so that she could appeal to his humanity and make him understand what it was that he was unleashing in the hearts and minds of the South Alaskans. Drumph readily agreed, but the meeting as it turned out could not possibly have gone worse. He derided her as weak and uncaring of Alaska's security, and ultimately wound up declaring that it was time for North and South Alaska to unite as a single state under his governance. Obviously that did not go over especially well with Palin, and in all subsequent press conferences he declared her to be "Weak Sarah." It was repeated so often by the news that as far as the South Alaskans were concerned, the name stuck. It infuriated the Northerners, and matters became worse when skirmishes began breaking out along the borders between the two states as the Southerners attempted to block Inuit endeavoring to flee to the sanity of the North.

And the skirmishes became all out battles, and then Drumph declared war on the North. Palin knew she would never forget the televised segment of the South senate banging their fists repeatedly on their desks, shouting, "Drumph! Drumph! Drumph!"

It was by no means unanimous. Most of the Democrats and even several Republicans endeavored to stand in the way of the madness, but not only were they shouted down, three of them were beaten up by a mob as they endeavored to get to their cars at the end of the day. And the South Alaskan news broadcast covered it not as a cowardly mugging, but as some sort of patriotic action.

Palin sat there, watching the news coverage, and put her face in her hands. She could no longer recognize the people of South Alaska as her brethren. It was incomprehensible that one man could have utterly transformed the personality of an entire state, but that was precisely what Drumph had accomplished. Then again, it was certainly not without precedent. That Russian, Hitler, had done the same thing.

Wait, was he Russian?

It didn't matter. Hitler was a bad guy and obviously Drumph was cut from the same cloth.

Palin watched as Drumph clearly roared with laughter from the passenger seat. Her blood boiled with fury. Her men had been good, reliable, steadfast, and now they were both dead. And she was clearly next.

She ducked back down into the jeep and threw open the driver's side door. There was no point staying in the jeep; she could be too easily targeted. She clutched her rifle tightly and threw herself out of the vehicle.

"Oh no you don't, Sarah," came Drumph's voice, booming out of a loudspeaker. Wonderful. He could make himself heard over the chopper's blades.

The machine guns lit up and hammered at the car. Sarah rolled away across the snow as the bullets shredded the Jeep. She threw her arms over her head for protection. Her rifle was strapped to her back and rattled around her. Palin kept moving even as she heard her Jeep detonate from the overhead pounding. There was a massive explosion and metal rattled all around her, jets of flame leaping past her head. It was nothing short of a miracle that nothing touched her.

She skidded to a halt nearby a grove of trees and scrambled to her feet. There was so much smoke from the fire that it provided her temporary cover, and she unslung the rifle from her shoulder. The helicopter was surveying the area, trying to catch a glimpse of her, and she realized that just for a moment, she had the advantage. She could see them, but they had lost track of her. Perhaps they hadn't even seen her escape from the car and were hoping or assuming that she was dead.

She peered through the sniper scope that was mounted atop the rifle and tried to catch a view of the chopper. It had been moving quickly, but now it slowed, trying to get a better view of the ground, their vision still blocked by the smoke. Palin kept the gun level, trying to get a target, taking into account that the pounding of the blades might push her bullet off course. She knew she should make some sort of adjustment, but damned if she could figure out what it was. *This is a math thing, isn't it. One of those math boojemawadjers. Darn. If only I had paid more attention in school to figuring out those formula, whattaya call them, things with right angles and cute angles and such. Why? Why does math have to be so hard? I should just start a thing, a whole thing in schools all over North Alaska that would simplify math so kids like me won't find it all so intimating.*

Focus. Focus.

The chopper was starting to pivot and Drumph was squarely in her sights. She took in a breath, let it out and fired several shots in quick succession.

Except Drumph, who had been leaning back, chose that moment to lean forward, a pair of binoculars in his hands as he studied the terrain. As a result the bullets whizzed past his head although Palin was sure that she saw a couple of strands waver in response.

What she saw next almost made her heart stop.

She had missed Drumph, yes, but the bullets found an alternate target: the pilot's head. The back of his skull exploded on impact and he slumped forward, his blood decorating the interior of the chopper. There was panic in Drumph's face as the chopper veered wildly to the right and began to tilt.

"Got him," snarled Palin with fierce joy.

The helicopter was now hanging at a forty-five degree angle and drifting steadily downward. She heard an alarmed cry of fury as Drumph desperately tried to take control, but he was at the wrong angle, plus he probably hadn't the faintest idea of how to keep the thing airborne. Despite all this attempts to keep it in the air, the helicopter continued to head for a very abrupt termination toward the ground below. She prayed that he would wind up landing in the midst of one of the fiery Jeeps and go up in a ball of flame. That would be perfect.

But her wish was not granted. Instead the helicopter drifted past it and hit the ground about fifty feet past where Palin's car was a roaring mass of fire. The chopper did not land cleanly; instead it hit on the starboard side and tipped over completely. The blades struck the ground and snapped clean off, and Palin ducked back as a shard of metal hurtled right at her. The blade slammed into the tree and dug halfway through before it came to a halt and hung there, quivering. Palin stayed behind the tree a few moments more and then headed for the chopper's wreckage, keeping her rifle level.

Unfortunately the helicopter had not burst into flame, which Palin considered an inconvenience. She would have loved to see Drumph trapped within, a being of flames whose last mortal moments was a preview of what awaited him in Hell. On the other hand, if he had survived, it meant that she could shoot him dead. How glorious did that sound?

Slowly she approached the helicopter, peering through her scope, trying to get a bead on her target. Had he died in the crash? That would be convenient, but if his head was still attached to his shoulders, she would put a bullet in it just to be certain.

Or. . .maybe not.

He is the enemy governor, after all. What a valuable prisoner he would make. If I had him hostage, I could do anything with him. I could demand that South Alaska surrender. Start treating the Inuit with decency. Lay down their arms. How wonderful would that be to put an end to all of this?

For a moment her wandering mind caused her to lower the rifle sight and she began to think of how superb a united Alaska would be. That, as it turned out, was a mistake as a bullet slammed into her arm. It went right through her right bicep, in and out, but the shock was enough to cause her to drop her rifle and stagger, clutching her arm and stumbling about as if she were drunk off her ass. She fell to her knees and that saved her life because several more bullets tore through the air right over her head. Her glasses were becoming covered with snow and she tore them off, throwing them aside. She was sure she could see well enough without them.

Out of the mass of smoke all around them strode Drumph. He was holding a pistol level and he came right at her. His face was covered with soot and was seriously banged up, blood trickling from a deep cut across his forehead. "You're done, Weak Sarah!" he shouted at the top of his lungs, advancing on her. The muzzle of his pistol was trembling with excitement. "You're over! It's over! Not going to miss again! Won't do it!"

"You're not gonna take me prisoner?" she said, trying to come up with an angle to buy her some time. "Use me to get what you want?"

"I don't need what I want!"

"What?"

"I don't. . ." He paused, realizing what he had said made no sense, and shook it off. "I can get what I want without you! And that's exactly what I'm gonna do!"

"What the hell *do* you want?!" she cried out in exasperation. "I don't understand you at all! What did the Inuit ever do to you, that you had to vilify and attack them?"

Drumph was five feet away from her and now he stood there and grinned. "That's what you never get, Sarah. People want someone to blame! At the end of the day, when they look at their pathetic, miserable lives, they want to know that whatever is wrong with it, it's not their fault! Throughout history, it's always someone! Jews. Christians. Blacks. Gypsies, Italians, Irish, Arabs. It's always somebody who has to take the fall for why life sucks, and this time it was the Eskimo's turn! They fell, I rose, and everything works out for the best."

"They prefer the term 'Inuit.'"

"Like I care!" Drumph snorted. He aimed the gun squarely at her. "I can't wait to Tweet pictures of your corpse. This is gonna break the Internet."

He leveled the gun at her. Palin did not look away. She wouldn't give him the satisfaction.

He pulled the trigger.

It clicked on the empty chamber.

Drumph snarled in fury and quickly ejected the empty cartridge, but before he could slam a new one into place, Palin charged. She slammed into him shoulder first, into his gut, doubling him over, and her forward motion sent him tumbling to the ground with Palin atop him. Palin whipped her fist around and struck him in the side of the skull, whipping Drumph's head around. *"This is for my family, you murdering son of a gun!"* she howled at him as she continued to wail away at him. Drumph brought his arms up, tried to deflect the pounding, but Sarah continued to pound on him. She heard the satisfying crack of bone from his nose as she broke it, and Drumph let out a startled yell as blood flowed from his nostrils.

The pain seemed to provide additional incentive for him as he viciously shoved against Palin, pushing her back. She fell onto her back and now Drumph was astride her. She tried to sit up but he shoved down on her ribcage, keeping her pinned.

"You really thought you could beat me, Weak Sarah?" he said with a snarl.

"Will you stop it with the nicknames? You sound like a first grader when you do that!"

He was holding a knife. He had probably pulled it out of the top of his boot. He had it poised over her and was ready to bring it slamming down. "That's why everybody loves it. Because everybody was a first grader, and things were great when you were in first grade! School was exciting because you were learning to read. Mom packed you lunch! At the end of the day when you came home, she was waiting there for you and your pet dog, Skippy, would come running up to you and lick your face and everything was wonderful!"

To Palin's shock, there were actually tears starting to trickle from his eyes. "Was that what it was like for you?"

Slowly Drumph shook his head. "No. My parents hired teachers to come to the house. Never went to public school. Never got to do that. My father didn't want me mixing with all the other..."

"Other what?"

"The negroes. And Mexicans. Chinese. Jews. Arabs. All the un-Americans who he thought were going to get into my..." He shook his head as if he could physically dispel the concerns. "Why am I telling you this?"

"Because I can understand what you're going through. Because we're both governors. Because I didn't have the easiest time growing up either. Because..." She paused, held her breath, having trouble believing she was saying the next words as she stroked his arm. "Because I can't stop thinking about you. I never have."

He stared down at her, his eyes narrowing suspiciously. "What are you talking about?"

"From the very first time I saw you, Donald... I was amazed by your manliness. Your strength. Your confidence. Everything about you that made you you. What woman wouldn't be? In my heart, I'm really just a plain old soccer mom who wants a powerful man in her life to run it, tell her what to do. And now I don't have any other man in my life, and you're between wives..."

"Actually I got married six months ago."

"Oh."

He shrugged. "Just a spur of the moment thing. Doesn't mean anything. That is..." He caught himself and gazed at her appraisingly, as if seeing her for the first time. "I mean, you know, you are pretty attractive. You're certainly not a dog. You have a great rack."

"Y'think? I've been doing exercises. Flexes and things like that. Keep 'em firm."

"Well, it's been working."

"You think so?"

Slowly his hands moved toward her breasts. He leaned forward...

And she drove her knee up into his crotch.

Drumph cried out and she swung an upper cut that took Drumph straight in the chin. He fell backwards and Sarah scrambled to her feet. "*Dumb ass*!" she shouted at him and looked around quickly to see where her rifle had fallen. She saw it laying a few feet away and she started toward it, but then she heard a very significant sound: a gun clip being slammed into place. She spun and saw Drumph standing there, aiming his gun right at her.

"Wow, you have really small hands," she said, surprised that—standing at death's door—that was what she had noticed.

"No, I don't! I have perfectly normal hands! Why does everyone say I have little hands! I don't have little hands! Or little feet! Or a little penis! You should see my penis!"

"I'd rather not," she said, and then her eyes widened. She was no longer looking at Drumph, but instead behind and to his right.

Drumph saw her gaze shift, and he smirked. "Oh, right, right, I get it. You pretend that you're looking at something behind me, and I'm supposed to turn around so I can see what has you distracted, and the second I do that, you're going to grab up your gun or pull another one out of hiding and shoot me, because that's how stupid you think I am, don't you, Simple Sarah? Hey, that's an even better nickname for you. Simple Sarah. If you were going to be alive for more than another five seconds, I'd start calling you that. Which is a shame, because that's a way better nickname than the one I gave you, but it doesn't matter, none of it matters, because—"

That was as far as he got before the massive moose horns slammed into him.

Drumph went down, the gun flying from his hand. He twisted around and stared up in shock as Big White advanced upon him. It let out a loud, defiant roar that Palin could have sworn caused the trees to vibrate. Its horns were gigantic and there were prongs on the inside curve, and as Donald Drumph scrambled to his feet, the gigantic white moose bellowed once more, lowered its head, and charged him. Drumph didn't dodge; he was clearly terrified with fear. Palin could see him trying to move his legs but he couldn't budge. Then the moose's right horn slammed into him, the points gouging directly into his throat. Drumph tried to let out a moan but couldn't manage more than a choking gurgle. The moose raised its head and Drumph went with it, his feet dangling off the ground, and then Big White snapped his antlers around and sent Drumph flying several feet. Drumph hit the ground and lay there, bleeding out, soaking the surrounding snow with red.

Palin couldn't believe it. It was over. It was finally over.

"Thank you," she said to the moose.

The moose's gaze swiveled to her, and he grunted once more and then charged again.

The last thing Sarah Palin noticed right before she was trampled to death was that the moose indeed did not leave any tracks in the snow. *I'll be darned,* she thought, and then blackness overwhelmed her.